BLOOD NOIR

An Anita Blake, Vampire Hunter Novel

LAURELL K. HAMILTON

www.orbitbooks.net

ORBIT

First published in Great Britain in 2008 by Orbit
This paperback edition published in 2009 by Orbit
Reprinted 2009

A CIP catalogue record for this book
is available from the British Library.

ISBN 978-1-84149-693-1

Typeset in Janson Text by M Rules
Printed and bound in Great Britain by Clays Ltd, St Ives plc

Papers used by Orbit are natural, renewable and recyclable products sourced from well-managed forests and certified in accordance with the rules of the Forest Stewardship Council.

Mixed Sources
Product group from well-managed forests and other controlled sources
www.fsc.org Cert no. SGS-COC-004081
© 1996 Forest Stewardship Council

Orbit
An imprint of
Little, Brown Book Group
100 Victoria Embankment
London EC4Y 0DY

An Hachette UK Company
www.hachette.co.uk

www.orbitbooks.net

To Jonathon,

who loves me when I am at my most dark
and helps me light a candle when it all grows too black to endure.

Acknowledgements

To Darla, who has made herself simply indispensable. Sherry, for organizing a house full of artists. Mary, for bringing order, and someone to call for advice. Charles, for security, research help, shooting range trips, and reminding both Jon and I that this really is cool. Shawn, for research questions answered, and for simply being the only other human being on the planet who understands. Marshal Moriarity, whose input came too late for this book, but we'll fix it next time. Happy retirement.

To the winners of the Jason stage name contest:

Kim Montano, Maitland, FL

R. Malinen, Finland

Sarah Shelton, Arlington, TX

My writing group, The Alternate Historians: Tom Drennan, Rett MacPherson, Marella Sands, Deborah Millitello, Sharon Shinn, and Mark Sumner. Never give in; never give up.

And Lieutenant Robert J. Cooney, Commander of Mobile Reserve, HRT, and K-9 1964–2008.

1

I CAME HOME to find two men sitting at my kitchen table. One of them was my live-in sweetie. The other was one of our best friends. One of them was a wereleopard; the other was a werewolf; both of them were strippers. At least once a month they took off more than just their clothes on stage. They changed shape on stage in front of a live audience. Those nights the club was standing room only. I mean, you can go to other clubs to see men take their clothes off, but their entire skin and body . . . well, that was unique.

Nathaniel came to greet me with a kiss and a hug. I let my hands play in the long, thick auburn hair that trailed down his broad shoulders, the curve of his waist, the tightness of his ass, and the long muscular legs. He was five-seven now, an inch taller than when I'd met him. In my three-inch heels I was still an inch shorter than him. At twenty-one he was finally growing into the promise of those shoulders. His face was less soft than it had been, and more masculine. He would always be beautiful rather than handsome, but the bone structure had changed minutely so he just suddenly looked his age, instead of like jailbait.

He blinked down at me with the soft lilac of his eyes. On his driver's license it said his eyes were blue, because they wouldn't let him put lavender, or purple. His eyes were different shades of color, depending on his mood, or what he wore, but blue was never the color of his eyes.

His hands slid underneath the jacket of my suit, and a little lower to trace the top of my skirt. His hands hesitated a little at the Browning BDM in its shoulder holster. Guns do get in the way of cuddling.

I wrapped my arms around the bareness of his upper body, breathed in the scent of his skin. He was wearing what he usually wore in his off time in the summer, little bitty jogging shorts. Most of the wereanimals would go around nude if you let them. I wasn't quite comfy with that, so he wore the shorts to save my delicate sensibilities. There were some who thought I didn't have any of those left, but they would be wrong, and they would be jealous.

Holding him, breathing in the warmth and sweet vanilla of his skin, I understood the jealousy. Though frankly, not all of it was about sex or even having found love at last. It was about power and them wanting it, and me and mine having it. It was about me being the human servant of Jean-Claude, the Master Vampire of St. Louis. It was about body count, and me having the highest kill count among the vampire executioners in the good ol' U. S. of A.

"I would give a less favored body part to have a woman greet me at the end of the day like that," Jason's voice said.

I had to peer around Nathaniel's body to see Jason. He was still at the kitchen table nursing a coffee mug. It even smelled like coffee, but he huddled over it, as if it were something harder and more intoxicating.

Jason was two years older than Nathaniel, which made him twenty-three now. Strangely, I'd met them both when they were nineteen. Jason was my height, give or take a half inch or so. His hair was that shade of yellow blond that movie stars are fond of, but his was real, and didn't have to come from a good salon. His hair was cut businessman short. I liked long hair, but I had to admit that Jason's face looked cleaner, better, more handsome even, without the hair to distract. He was wearing a blue T-shirt that made his eyes even bluer than they were. The color not of spring, but of summer skies, before the heat has gotten too hot, but you know it's not May anymore.

The clothes hid what I knew, that he looked even better out of them. It wasn't for lack of cuteness and desirability that Jason wasn't my sweetie. He was my friend, and I was his.

"What about Perdita, Perdy? You and she are going steady, right?"

He grinned at me. "Going steady, you're so cute."

I frowned at him. "What else do you call it?"

Nathaniel kissed me on the forehead. "You really are cute."

I moved away from him and scowled at them both. "I'm serious, what else do you call it? You aren't just fuck buddies. She isn't a one-night stand. She's a serious girlfriend. If it's not going steady, what do you call it?"

"You make it sound like I gave her my class ring, Anita. Perdy and I were lovers, and she wanted it to be exclusive."

"I thought you were exclusive."

"Except for you, I was."

"Wait, you're talking past tense. Are you saying you and Perdy broke up?"

"She gave him an ultimatum," Nathaniel said. He trailed

his hand down my arm as he moved away. "I'll get you coffee."

I went to the table and took the seat that Nathaniel had started in. "What kind of ultimatum?" I asked.

Jason stared into his coffee cup while he answered. "She wanted me to stop having sex with Jean-Claude and Asher, and you."

"Wait, you aren't having sex with Jean-Claude and Asher, unless there's something I don't know."

He smiled at me. "The look on your face, man." He raised his fingers in the Boy Scout salute. "I am not now, nor have I ever been having sex with Jean-Claude or Asher."

Nathaniel set fresh coffee down in front of me and took a chair across the table on the other side of Jason, so we'd both be able to look at him. It also meant we wouldn't be able to do more than hold hands, which was probably good; we tended to distract each other.

"But she didn't believe you," I said.

"Nope, she didn't." He took a sip of coffee.

"Why wouldn't she believe you?" I asked.

"I'm not sure."

"If my feeding the *ardeur* off you through sex bugged your steady girl, you should have said something."

"I am Jean-Claude's *pomme de sang*, his apple of blood. I am his blood donor, and I go where my master tells me to go. The *ardeur* is your version of a blood feed and you're his human servant. Jean-Claude shares me with Asher, his second-in-command, for blood and you for sex, and it's his right to share me. I am his. I belong to him. Perdy knows that. She got kicked out of Cape Cod because she wanted to be more than just a blood donor to the master vampire there."

"Samuel didn't say anything about that. In fact, his son,

BLOOD NOIR

By Laurell K. Hamilton

GUILTY PLEASURES
THE LAUGHING CORPSE
CIRCUS OF THE DAMNED
THE LUNATIC CAFÉ
BLOODY BONES
THE KILLING DANCE
BURNT OFFERINGS
BLUE MOON
OBSIDIAN BUTTERFLY
NARCISSUS IN CHAINS
CERULEAN SINS
INCUBUS DREAMS
DANSE MACABRE
THE HARLEQUIN
BLOOD NOIR

ANITA BLAKE, VAMPIRE HUNTER OMNIBUS
MICAH AND STRANGE CANDY

Sampson, said that Perdy was here to spy on him for his mother."

"Yeah, but Sampson went home, and Perdy didn't."

Sampson had gone home because St. Louis got invaded by some of the scariest vampires in the world. Jean-Claude had thought it was a bad idea to risk getting the eldest son of his friend and ally killed. Besides, Sampson was a merman, and they aren't big on offensive abilities, at least not this far inland. Perdy was a mermaid, too. Though I'd never seen either of them turn all fishy. They just looked like people to me.

"Perdy stayed for you," Nathaniel said.

Jason nodded. "She wanted me to be hers. She's very jealous, very possessive. I'm just not into that."

"So you have a woman who greets you like Anita greets me, but the rest doesn't work."

"No, Nathaniel. She used to greet me sort of like that, but for weeks now it's been, *Where have you been? Who have you been with? You fucked the master again, didn't you? You fucked Asher, didn't you? You were with Anita again, weren't you?*"

"I've put you on the back burner for feeding me," I said. "I got the impression Perdy didn't want to share you that much, but I had no idea she thought you were doing more than just donating blood to the vampires."

"She's like crazy jealous, and she won't believe me when I tell her I haven't been with anyone else. It's why I asked Jean-Claude to take me out of your feeding schedule for a while. I thought if I stopped having sex with the only other person I was really having sex with that Perdy would calm down."

Nathaniel and I exchanged glances across the table. He shrugged. I asked the question. "Did it work?"

"No," he said. He took another drink of coffee, and it must have finished the cup because he got up and went for the

French press beside the sink. He took the coffee cozy off it, then put it back on without filling his cup. He set the cup in the sink.

"I don't want more coffee."

"You can never have too much coffee," I said.

He turned and smiled at me. "You think so, but the rest of us get a little OD'ed on your level of caffeine."

"What happened, Jason?" I asked.

The smile slipped a little more. He was solemn when he turned to us. He leaned his back against the cabinets, crossed his arms across his chest, and again didn't quite meet our eyes.

"She wanted me to marry her. Till death do us part and all that. She's a mermaid, which means she'll outlive me. She can live for hundreds of years, not immortal like a vampire, but close."

"You didn't want to marry her," I said, softly.

He shook his head. "She's obsessed with me. She says she loves me, but it doesn't feel like love. It feels like I'm smothering."

"She's not the right one, then."

He grinned, and it almost reached his eyes. "Look who's talking about the right one. You can't pick just one either."

"That's different."

"Why, because you're a living vampire who feeds off sex, so you have to have a bevy of lovers? The *ardeur* is like the perfect excuse to never have to say you're sorry."

"I'd change it if I could, you know that."

He came to me then, put his arms around my shoulders, and rested his cheek on the top of my head. "I didn't mean to make you sad, Anita. God knows I didn't. Please, don't tell me you'd change it if you could. You love Nathaniel, and Micah. They love you. You love Jean-Claude and Asher, and they love you. You're still a little confused about what to do with Damian, but you'll get there."

I shook my head and stood up, moving away from him. "Don't forget Requiem, and London, and sometimes Richard. Oh, wait, and the swan king pops in now and then, no pun intended." It sounded angry and bitter, and I was glad.

"I didn't mean to say the wrong thing. I didn't mean to make you feel bad, or to have another woman mad at me tonight. Please, Anita, please, don't be mad. I'm upset. You have no idea how upset. Please, please, I'm a bastard, but don't be mad."

He held his hand out to me. His face pleaded along with his words. I'd never seen his eyes full of quite this kind of pain. The look in his eyes was more than just losing a girlfriend he didn't want anymore.

I held out my hand, but made him take the step to close our fingers around each other. His eyes glittered in the overhead lights.

I took his hand, held it. His breath came in a soft gasp, and I thought for a second he was going to cry, but he just looked at me. His eyes that had glistened a moment before were almost dead, as if whatever he was feeling he'd locked away somewhere. In a way, to me, that was worse. I went to him, and he wrapped his arms around me as if he were at the edge of a cliff and I were his only handhold. That quiet holding on was so . . . male. A woman would have cried, or talked more, but for a man, after a certain point this is their pain.

I held him back, tried to tell him it would be all right. I whispered it into his hair, against his cheek. "It's all right, Jason. It's all right."

Nathaniel came up behind him and wrapped his arms around us both. He pressed his cheek against his friend's hair and said, "We're here, Jason. We're here for you."

Jason just held on wordless, motionless, the strength in his arms, shoulders, pressing against me, but it wasn't about sex. I'd never been pressed so close to any man and thought only, *God, what's wrong?* Either he had loved Perdy and now he was regretting letting her go, or the other shoe hadn't dropped. What else could be wrong?

We ended up on the floor of the kitchen, simply sitting in a row with our backs to the kitchen island. He still hadn't said what else was wrong, or that he was desperately in love with Perdy and how could he fix it? I kept waiting for him to share. If he'd been a girl friend I'd have asked by now, but guy friends are different. Sometimes you have to sneak up on them like some sort of wild animal, no wereanimal pun intended; all men are leery of their emotions, spook them and they'll shut down. If you're careful, quiet, not too eager, sometimes you'll learn more. Of course, sometimes you have to club men over the head with some question to get any sense out of them, but they prefer to speak from a quiet place.

Jason had his head against Nathaniel's shoulder, and a hand on my leg. At least he, like most of the men in my life, was cuddlier than most. I appreciated that.

Jason's voice came flat, empty, as if he were afraid to let his voice feel anything. "My father's dying of cancer. My mom called last night just after Perdy and I broke up."

I exchanged a glance with Nathaniel. His wide eyes let me know that it was news to him, too.

"Jesus, Jason, I'm sorry," I said.

"We hate each other, of course, and now the cold bastard's dying and I won't have time to forgive him before he dies."

"What can we do?" Nathaniel asked, softly.

He smiled, a little weak, a little watered down, but he

managed it. I thought it was a good sign. I hoped it was. "You really want to know?"

"Name it," I said.

He smiled again, but his eyes flinched, as if I'd hit him instead of told him I'd do anything he wanted if it would take the pain away.

"Perdy isn't here to tell me don't, or to tell you don't. I'm a free man again." He tried for a laugh, but it was a sound more like a sob.

"I get it," Nathaniel said.

I frowned at him. "Then explain it to me, because I don't."

"He wants to have sex with you again."

"What?" I said.

"Perdy can't tell him, or you, *no* anymore. You can be lovers again."

"You mean now, like in right now?"

Nathaniel gave a half-shrug. Jason moved his head off the other man's shoulder. He dropped his hand away from my leg.

"It's okay, Anita, I've fucked this up. I know this isn't the way to approach you. But my head is so ugly tonight; I just can't seem to think clearly."

He pushed to his feet and started for the doorway.

I opened my mouth to say *don't go*, and *yes*. I closed it without saying any of it out loud, and looked at Nathaniel. I frowned at him. He was more than just my sweetie. The *ardeur* made me a sort of living vampire who fed off sex, but with the downsides came some interesting upsides. Nathaniel was my animal to call, which meant he was like my familiar. We shared emotions, power, and sometimes thoughts. "You're projecting inside my head, aren't you?"

"You can shut me out if you want," he said.

Jason hesitated just short of the doorway. He frowned at us both. "I'm missing something."

I looked into the face of a man that I loved. "Is this really what you want?"

"He's my friend."

"You know, most guys don't want their girlfriends to sleep with their friends."

"If you'd never slept with Jason, that would be different, but you have. Why is it wrong to sleep with him tonight?"

I opened my mouth to say something reasonable, then closed it, because for the life of me, I couldn't come up with a clearheaded answer. Why was it wrong to sleep with Jason tonight? Because I hadn't planned on it? Because it felt slutty? Were any of those reasons good reasons?

Jason stopped in the doorway, caught between the light of the kitchen and the darkness of the living room beyond. "I've made you feel sorry for me. I'm not sure I want that to be your motivation for taking me to bed."

"Once upon a time, you wouldn't have cared why you got to sleep with me."

"I was a slut, I know."

"I didn't mean that, Jason."

"Stay here tonight," Nathaniel said.

He half-turned so he could see us, but his face was still mostly in shadow. "Why? Why do you want me to stay?"

I shrugged at Nathaniel, with a this-was-your-idea expression.

"Because you're our friend. Because we care about you."

"And you, Anita, what's your motivation?"

I looked up at him. There was something defiant about the set of his shoulders, as if he expected me to hurt him. I tried very hard not to do that. "It just seems wrong for you to walk out the door right now. Stay, if the sex is an issue, then just stay for a big puppy pile. We can actually just sleep."

He shook his head. "You never want to make me just sleep, Anita."

That made me uncomfortable. "I don't know what to say to that, Jason."

"Say you want me."

I started to say something, but Nathaniel touched my hand. "He needs the truth, Anita."

"And what is the truth?" I asked, taking my hand away from his.

"Tell him how you feel, really feel about him."

I took a deep breath and thought about the truth; what was the truth? "You are one of the best friends I have, Jason, and you shouldn't be alone tonight."

"Jean-Claude would let me sleep with him."

"But you wouldn't let him hold you while you feel miserable."

"How do you know I wouldn't?"

"Call it a hunch."

He stood frozen in the doorway as if he couldn't decide, or as if part of him wanted to and part of him didn't. I'd made him come to me to hold his hand. Now I went to him.

I wrapped my arms around him. He stayed stiff and unyielding. I pressed my head to his shoulder. "Stay with us tonight, Jason, please."

He whispered against my hair, "Why?"

"Because you want to."

"Not good enough," he whispered.

"Because I can feel how much it would hurt Nathaniel to see you leave tonight, and know that you didn't have anyone to hold you while you slept."

"It's not sleep I want, Anita. I'm afraid to sleep. I'm afraid I'll dream. Last night was . . . bad."

I lifted my face up to look at him. "You found all this out last night?"

He nodded.

"Bad dreams?" I made it a question.

"The worst; something about the news about my dad just raked a lot of shit up."

Nathaniel's need pushed at me, almost staggering in his desire to have Jason stay. I tried to shield against him, but realized that one of the reasons I couldn't shield was that I agreed with him. A large part of me felt Jason should stay. Nathaniel was right; Jason was already on my list of lovers. Why was it wrong for me to admit that it was fun to sleep with Jason? Why was it always wrong for me to admit that I simply wanted to be with someone? Not because I had no choice, but because for once, I did?

He kissed my forehead. "I'll go home."

I hugged him tighter, kept him in the doorway. "It would be lovely if you stayed."

He looked startled. "You sound like you mean that."

I nodded. "I do."

He smiled, and it was a shadow of his usual one. "Somewhere in there did you actually say *please*?"

I smiled at him. "I think I did."

"I've never heard you ask a man to please stay with you."

"I don't usually have to."

"Stay with us tonight," Nathaniel said.

I nodded. "Stay."

"The bed will be a little crowded when Micah gets home."

"He's out of town," I said.

"A new wereleopard wanted to join our pard. He's off interviewing," Nathaniel said.

Jason nodded. "I like Micah, you know that."

"But he's not your best friend like Nathaniel is, and he's not a girl," I said.

Jason nodded again. "Tonight, I don't really want an audience."

"Damian is even sleeping over with his latest vampire lover," Nathaniel said. "We have the house to ourselves."

Some tension I hadn't been aware of slid away from Jason. "I love everybody, but sometimes the group thing gets a little old. It was one of the things I liked about Perdy, at first."

"You don't want a group orgy every night, but you don't want to be monogamous either," Nathaniel said.

Jason nodded. "I am so fucked."

"Not yet," I said, hugging him, "but we can fix that."

He grinned at me, and it reached his eyes. "Bedroom, bathroom, living room, or kitchen?"

"The kitchen floor is hard and the tile is cold. Why not just go to the nice soft bed?" I asked.

Jason looked at Nathaniel.

Nathaniel answered the question. "Jason has made love in a bed and only a bed since he started being with Perdy."

I frowned, then looked at Jason, still in a loose hug with me. "I understand no shower or bath sex. Mermaids have trouble retaining human form in water, but nothing but the bed?"

He shook his head.

"Standard positions, too?" I made it a question.

He nodded.

My eyes widened. "Oh, Jason, I'm sorry, I didn't know." I hugged him tighter.

He moved back so he could see my face. "With all the bad news I've had today, and you look that stricken that my girlfriend would only do standard bed sex?"

I tried to put into words what I was thinking, not always my best thing. "You love sex. You're good at it."

"Why, gee, thanks." He grinned.

I gave him a look, but kept talking. I was going to finish this thought, damn it. "Sex is one of the most personal things we do as people. To have someone who says she loves you limit how you express yourself in the bedroom is like a small death. It kills the soul."

The grin left his face, then his eyes. He stared at me, and there Jason was, that part of him that he hid from most people. Heck, that he hid most of the time. He let me see that there was a good mind and a deep thinker inside those usually smiling blue eyes. It made him look sad, and older, but I valued that look. I valued that he let me see him all the way down.

"How did you get to be so smart?" he said, softly.

"I have smart friends who give me good advice sometimes." I smiled. "Sometimes I even take it."

He smiled back and ran his hands down my back. "So, you'd really let me pick where we make love?"

I nodded.

"Just because I haven't had a choice in a while."

"Yes."

"What if I want something too freaky?"

"Then I'll say no, and you can back it down a little."

His eyes had that solemn look again. He searched my face. "You mean it?"

I put my hands on either side of his face and nodded. "I try not to say things I don't mean, Jason." I put a soft kiss at the end of the sentence.

He moved his hand lower on my back to press us closer together. Close enough that I could feel that his body was already happier than when we hugged last.

He closed his eyes and took a breath. He looked at Nathaniel. “Do you have a preference?”

“You’re the guest.”

Jason lifted me off the floor with a hug. We were both short enough that I was in no danger of hitting the doorjamb. “I love you guys; you make me feel less weird about myself.”

“Why, because we’re weirder?” I asked.

“No,” he said, laughing up at me, “because your relationship works. It just flat works for you guys. You make me feel that out there somewhere is someone weird enough to make me happy.”

“I’d rather not do the bathroom,” Nathaniel said, “it takes forever to dry my hair.”

Jason let me down, so I was standing on the floor again. “I’m leaning toward the living room.”

“There are chairs, and the couch has a back and arms,” Nathaniel said.

“How sturdy is the coffee table?”

“Not that sturdy,” Nathaniel said.

I’d caught on. “No, not sturdy enough to have sex on.”

“Start in the living room, move to the bedroom?” Jason said, making it a question.

I looked at Nathaniel. He nodded, and gave a little shrug.

“Deal,” I said.

2

THEY HAD A disagreement on whether I should leave my heels on or take them off. Nathaniel voted for on; Jason wanted off. Jason's point was, "I want to go down on her, and the heels will hurt."

Nathaniel's point was, "Yeah, the heels hurt, what's your point?"

I settled the argument this way. "Whoever is doing the oral sex on me gets his preference on the shoes."

"Lose the shoes," Jason said, and there was a look in his face that tightened things low in my body without him touching me at all.

I lost the shoes. They lay on their side in the dimness of the living room. The only light was what spilled in from the kitchen doorway. I stood in front of the couch, while they moved the coffee table far to one side of the room.

Jason came back and dropped to his knees in front of me. He gazed up at me with one half of his face lit, the other in darkness. The look in the one eye I could clearly see made me shiver.

Nathaniel came to the end of the couch and took his shorts off in one smooth motion. My pulse was in my throat at the sight of him nude in the darkened room. He let the shorts fall to the floor.

Jason's hands slid up my legs, underneath my skirt, and I was back to staring down at him. His hands caressed the hose up to my thighs, went up, oh, so gently, until he found the lace tops of the thigh highs. He traced the very top of the lace, trailing fingertips over the rise and fall of the fabric. He rolled fingers back and forth where the hose elastic had rolled down in back. No matter how careful you were, if you had any thighs at all, the hose always did that. But he treated it like what it was, not an imperfection, but something different to play with.

His fingers slid around that edge, brushing the very upper edges of my thighs. He rubbed his thumbs on that warm inside hollow that frames a woman's groin. He massaged my thighs, but it was the pressure of his thumbs that helped draw my legs farther apart. So he could reach what he wanted, and what I wanted him to reach.

Nathaniel came in behind me. Without the coffee table there was room enough between me and the couch. His arms wrapped around me, pinning my arms against my upper body. The feel of his nakedness pressed against the back of my skirt was amazing. Then he let me feel the strength in his body, as he held me, held me so tight. It sped my pulse faster, caught my breath in my throat.

"So strong," I whispered.

"So trapped," he breathed against my face. He squeezed harder, just this side of bruising my arms against me. But I didn't tell him to stop. I loved knowing that I was trapped. If he had meant me harm, I couldn't have stopped him. My gun was trapped under my arm, digging into my body. All it would take was Jason to grab my legs and I was trapped.

I hadn't much liked that I enjoyed things like this. In fact, I'd hated it. But lately, thanks in part to sharing emotions with Nathaniel, who loved bondage and submission, I was acknowledging that fantasy was okay. That I didn't need to analyze why in real life being trapped made me fight like hell and do all in my power to destroy the ones trapping me, but in sexual fantasy I liked being trapped, a little. In a safe place, with people I trusted, it was more than just exciting.

"What are you doing up there to make her react like that?" Jason asked. His hands had gone still against my thighs.

"Holding her, very, very, tightly," Nathaniel said in a voice that showed the strain of holding me tight.

Jason's fingers suddenly dug into my flesh, from gentle to bruising in an instant.

I whispered, "Yes."

"Is that the game we want to play?" he asked, and his voice had changed, too, deeper, darker, for lack of a better word.

"I do," Nathaniel said.

Jason's fingers pressed harder into my thighs, so that I cried out, and told him, "Enough, enough."

"That's her safe word," Nathaniel said.

"I've already stopped," Jason said.

"But I haven't stopped, have I?" Nathaniel whispered.

"No," I said, voice breathy. He was holding tight enough to be trapped, but not quite tight enough to hurt. It was a fine edge to walk, but Nathaniel knew how to walk it.

"Do I rip the panties off, or take them off?" Jason asked.

"Rip," Nathaniel said, and it was almost a growl.

I said, "Please."

"Please what?" Jason asked.

"Off," I whispered.

He ripped the satin panties in one harsh move that jerked my body. Nathaniel tightened his grip on me, until it was hard to breathe.

I whispered, "Ease up."

He eased until he was back where he'd been. Tight, but not too tight. Trapped, but not hurt. Of all forms of sex that I'd found, BDSM took the most trust, the most communication.

Jason pushed my skirt up until he bared me to the light from the kitchen. "How rough can I be?" There was no sex in the tone of his voice; he was truly asking.

"Start easy," Nathaniel said, "she'll let you know."

I realized that Jason had never given me oral sex before. I'd gone down on him, but he'd never had a chance to return the favor. He used his hands to spread my thighs wider. He let me feel the strength in his hands, but not as hard as he'd been when I told him to ease up. The sensation of being bound by the sheer strength of him was amazing. There was no need of ropes or chains when you could feel how terribly strong they both were.

Jason's hands were harsh, but he leaned in toward me as if he were going to give the gentlest of kisses. The juxtaposition of the harsh and the gentle left my mind not knowing how to react. Then his tongue slid across me, and there was no conflict, there was only sensation.

He dug his fingers into that space inside my thighs, so harsh, I cried out. He forced my legs farther apart. Nathaniel lifted me. I could feel his shoulders and chest flex until I was suddenly off the ground. It allowed Jason to spread my legs more, use the strength of his fingers to force me wider.

Jason plunged his tongue inside me, sudden and abrupt.

I cried out for him, and he leaned back enough to gaze up the line of my body.

It was as if I could feel the weight of his gaze, because it made me look down at the same time he looked up.

"God," he said, "that look."

"What look?" I managed to say before Nathaniel squeezed harder and I had no breath to talk.

"That look," Jason whispered, and lowered his mouth to my body. He kissed there as he had kissed my mouth, maybe a dozen times before. Most men don't kiss between your legs the same way they kiss your mouth, but Jason did. He kissed me just as thoroughly, as completely, as expertly. Then he began to do things that you couldn't do when you kiss a mouth. He licked and explored, trying different things, judging his progress by the sounds I made, and how much I writhed.

He didn't just find the spot and stay on it like it was a button; he explored every inch of me, biting the inside of my thighs between attentions.

Nathaniel held me through it all, sometimes so tight I couldn't breathe, sometimes just tight enough to let me feel his strength, and then he squeezed hard enough that my gun cut into me, and it felt as if he were trying to crush me. I cried out while I had breath, then all I could do was writhe.

Jason drew back enough to ask, "Am I doing that, or you?"

"Me," Nathaniel said, and eased up so my breath came in a ragged gasp.

I managed to say, "So strong."

"I need to try harder," Jason said. He pulled down my hose and bit me, not a love bite, but bit me on the thigh.

I screamed for him.

He plunged his mouth between my legs, rougher this time.

I writhed and cried out. He pressed teeth into the most intimate part of me. When I didn't tell him to stop, he worried at me with his mouth, his teeth, pulling and biting and licking. The pleasure began to build between my legs, like heat and pressure and the beginning flickers of orgasm like previews of the pleasure to come.

Nathaniel tightened his grip just as Jason pushed me over that last edge. The orgasm was one of those that came in waves, one after another as if as long as he kept sucking I would keep going. I shuddered and danced in their hands, cried out when Nathaniel let me, or gasped in breathless silence when he held me too tight for words.

Jason finished with a lick from front to back that made me cry out all over again. Still on his knees he said, "That was fun."

Nathaniel braced, changing positions just a little. "Fuck her."

Jason, still on his knees, said, "While you hold her?"

"Yes," Nathaniel said, and it held an edge of bass growl that wasn't his normal voice.

Jason looked at me, the light from the kitchen glistening on his chin and mouth. Seeing him wet from me tightened things low in my body that had just had their fun, so it started a new wave of writhing.

Jason held my thighs while Nathaniel held the rest of me. When my body quieted, Jason laughed, that sound that is all male. "Anita, are you okay with this?"

"Do it," I said, "please, please . . ."

"No," Nathaniel said, "I'm topping her tonight, it's my permission you need."

Jason hesitated as if waiting for me to protest. There was a time when I would have, but I'd been working at understanding

Nathaniel's idea of sex. I'd found that some of the bondage and submission worked just dandy for me.

Jason said, "You top us both?"

"We top Anita."

Jason smiled, but his eyes held something more serious than a smile. "I always thought it would take at least two of us. Tell me what you want me to do."

Nathaniel said, "Get a condom."

3

JASON PRESSED HIS fingers into the backs of my thighs, spreading my legs wider. Nathaniel squeezed me tight at the same time, as if he'd crush my arms against my body. I made small, helpless noises for him. Jason lifted me minutely, getting the angle he wanted, then shoved himself inside me. There was nothing gentle about it, and I was wet enough I didn't need gentle.

The feel of him shoving himself into me, as hard and fast as he could, drove a sound from my mouth, but not the sound he wanted. He said, in a low, breathy voice, "I can't get the angle I want."

"What do you need?" Nathaniel asked, from behind me. His voice wasn't breathy, but just deep.

Jason had stopped moving inside me, so I could think again. "A new position," I said, my voice breathy, too.

"Oh," Jason said, "I am not doing my job if you can still talk." He put action to word and started moving, slowly, in and out of me.

It felt wonderful, but Jason was right, he needed a different angle to push me over that edge. I looked him in the eyes and said, in a clear voice, "You're right, this position isn't going to do it."

Jason laughed. He kissed me, and if he hadn't still been wet with my juices, I might have called it a friendly kiss. "Some men would be insulted."

"You aren't some men. You like feedback," I said.

Nathaniel had stopped squeezing me, and was more just holding me. That helped me think, too. "Do you want a new position?" and he wasn't asking me.

"Yes," Jason said.

"I want to do one thing before we change," Nathaniel said.

"What do you want me to do?" Jason asked.

"What you were doing," Nathaniel said.

Jason looked at him a moment, but he went back to going in and out of me. He wasn't as hard as he'd started, too much talking, too much hesitating, but he was still hard enough to do what Nathaniel asked. For me, I was simply content to let Nathaniel be in charge. Content to revel in this blossoming strength, as he owned his sexuality in a way that he never had before. I'd been working with Asher to help meet Nathaniel's needs in the BDSM, and it had brought out a deep, inner happiness in him that I hadn't known was there.

While Jason pushed between my legs, Nathaniel raised my skirt the last few inches to bare my ass, so that I could feel his nakedness against me. The sensation of his hardness pressing into my ass, and Jason inside me at the same time, threw my head back, closed my eyes, made me cry out.

"What are you doing back there?" Jason asked.

"Rubbing. What position do you want?" he asked.

"Her, on her back on the couch." This time he didn't ask

me. I think he knew what Nathaniel would say, and there was no bad choice here. It was just a matter of how good it was going to be.

Nathaniel pressed himself harder against me, and it made me writhe again. Asher and Nathaniel had taught me that neither of them had to be inside me to make me react like this. There was just something about being pressed between two men, feeling them rubbing against me, that simply did it for me.

Jason was harder, more securely inside me now. He liked the writhing, but then most men did. It was an involuntary response on my part, but I liked the effect it had on most men, and the effect that their liking it had on me. My body encouraged them with every movement, every spasm, and their bodies responded to that encouragement. Go, team.

4

WE ENDED WITH me on the couch, my arms above my head over the arm of the couch. Nathaniel held my wrists against the arm, but it wasn't like he was holding me down. It was more the way you hold hands when one of you has thrown your body into the sky, and you reach out to catch the hands that you know will be there. The hands keep you from falling. The hands that keep you airborne. Jason found his angle on top of me, his body slamming into mine as hard and as fast as he could. Since he was stronger than your average human, that was very hard and very fast.

He rose above me so that most of his body was held away with his hands on the couch, his lower body the only thing that was touching me. It gave me an unobstructed view of his body pounding into mine. Just the sight of it was enough to throw my head back and make me scream my pleasure. I fought against Nathaniel's hands, fought to touch Jason's body, to carve my nails down that smooth flesh, but

Nathaniel held me tight; his strength held me tighter than any chains.

I felt Jason's body give one last hard push, and I opened my eyes. I watched his body spasm over mine, watched him fight his body to keep his hands on the couch, his body held above mine. He kept his position for one last shudder that made me writhe underneath him. Then he collapsed on top of me, as if someone had cut his strings. He collapsed on top of me, his breathing ragged, heart pounding so hard I could feel it through my shirt.

Nathaniel said, "My turn."

Jason laughed, then said, still on top of me, "Can't move yet."

"Move enough for me to move, Anita," Nathaniel said. He made it sound quite orderish. So unlike Nathaniel only a few weeks ago.

Jason rolled himself off the couch to half-collapse onto the floor. Nathaniel grabbed me under the arms and pulled me over the arm of the couch. He didn't try to get me to walk; he knew better. He scooped me up in his arms and carried me to the bedroom. He tossed me down on the bed, pulled my jacket over my shoulders, and threw it on the floor. The look on his face was so intense, so eager, a controlled franticness. He had to undo my belt so he could get both the skirt and my shoulder holster off. I tried to help, but he slapped my hands away. I was playing bottom tonight, which meant he wanted me either passive or obedient. Obedient wasn't my gig, and he knew that, so passive it was.

When he had me nude, he put his hands on my waist and half-lifted, half-pushed me toward the head of the bed. His voice was breathy, eager, and full of all that newfound force, when he said, "I want you in the cuffs."

He was the dominant in that moment, but he still asked, rather than ordered. Why? Because I'd never worn the cuffs. They were sport cuffs attached permanently, of late, to the headboard. But they were soft nylon and fastened with Velcro. I flat refused to use handcuffs, or anything that I couldn't get out of if I had to. The sport cuffs were perfect. You could be tied up for real, and still know that you could get away if you wanted to. Me, trust issues, nah.

Nathaniel had used the sport cuffs on our bed more than once. Even Micah had done it, though I think he did it more to humor us than because of desire. But never me.

I stared up into his face. His desire, his bravery at asking, was all there in his face. I'd been tied down with Asher and Nathaniel, and if I admitted it to myself, I'd had a good time. Why not this, then? Issues—mine.

I looked up into the face of the man I loved, and I said, "Okay."

The smile he gave me made it worth a yes. He fastened the Velcro around my wrists, nice and snug. I pulled on the chains because I could never not pull. I could never not test the limits.

Nathaniel leaned down, his body kneeling between my legs but not touching. His hair spilled out around us like some sort of warm, living tent. On another man I would have said it fanned out by happy accident, but Nathaniel used his hair in his act, as a sort of extra body part to caress and tease. He knew how to spill his hair around a woman so that it framed and billowed. He leaned down with all that hair framing his face, our bodies, the edges of the thickness of it caressing the sides of my body. He kissed me, soft, gentle, his lips caressing mine.

It wasn't the kiss I was expecting. It must have shown on my face, because he smiled and said, "I am going to fuck you, but

I wanted you to know how much I love you before I fuck your brains out." He grinned at the last.

I had to smile back. "I want you inside me, Nathaniel, please." Tied up, I knew he'd like the *please* even more than normal. I was learning the rules of being on bottom as well as on top.

He gave me a look that made me shiver. A look so dark, so full of potential that I pulled on the cuffs at my wrist. I couldn't help it. There was something . . . dangerous in that look. It was one of the highs of BDSM, that possibility of disaster and pain. Not the pain you wanted, but that this time your partner could go too far. We had our safe words, and I trusted Nathaniel implicitly, or I would never have let him tie me up, but still . . . part of the game was that you looked into your lover's eyes and let him see, that you saw the darkness in them. That you saw the potential for . . . evil, but you trusted that he wouldn't do it. You trusted him enough to be helpless. It was a lot of trust to have. More than I'd ever had in my life for anyone, I think. This odd trust.

He swirled his hair over one shoulder the way you'd sweep a cape to one side. He bared the line of his body and lowered himself toward me. He didn't put on a condom. I was on the pill, but I still made most of the men in bed use condoms. Micah was fixed, so there was no need. But lately, with Nathaniel, we'd just stopped using them. I'd had sex on just the pill for years with no problems, but still . . . But I could feel the difference between condom and no condom, and I knew that Nathaniel could.

There was something about being tied down while he slipped inside me with no protection that added to the illusion. BDSM was like stripping. Stripping was about the illusion that the customer could have the dancers for real sex. BDSM was about the illusion that you would truly hurt the person, that you would truly do exactly what the game pretended.

He plunged himself as deep inside me as he could get, then he hesitated. I caught movement from the corner of my eye. Jason was leaning in the doorway. The condom was gone, so he'd cleaned up.

Nathaniel started to do what he'd said, he started fucking me. Almost immediately, small sounds of pleasure fell from my lips. But I managed to gasp out, "You waited for Jason?"

"Yes," he said, and drove himself in and out of me. He knew where the spot was inside me, from almost every position we'd tried. Tonight was no different. He drove himself over that spot close to the entrance, but he also hit that spot deep inside me, because he knew I'd go from both.

The orgasm from the G-spot grew, a slow, powerful build, but the orgasm from the cervix being hit didn't grow, it was just suddenly there. One minute I was riding the rhythm of his body, the next I was screaming, pulling at the chains hard enough to rattle them. I wanted to touch his skin, wanted to mark my pleasure down his body.

When my body quieted, Nathaniel drew back, so that he no longer hit deep inside me. He played himself over and over in shallow strokes on that other spot. He was in a position similar to the one Jason had taken, but with even less of him touching me, not much more than the tip of him caressing over and over on that sweet spot.

Jason was beside the bed now, leaning on the lower bedpost. He watched us, and I caught Nathaniel looking at him. Nathaniel liked an audience.

He turned his attention back to me, and I watched him fight his body, to keep that shallow rhythm. I watched down the line of his body, watched his stomach, his groin, his hips, all working in that athletic line, that muscular control. And all the while, the orgasm grew like some pressing weight, some building energy between my legs. Then between one stroke and the next, the orgasm spilled up, over, through, and I shrieked my pleasure to the ceiling. Head back, eyes closed, back arching, and screaming.

I pulled on the restraints at my wrist and they added to the pleasure, they made me scream louder. I don't know why, I couldn't have explained it, but I liked being held down. I just did. Sex isn't about logic; it's about what feels right.

Nathaniel waited until my body had quieted before he plunged back inside me as far and as hard as he could. He fucked me until he brought me one last time, and then, and only then, did he let himself go. He shuddered above me, inside me, and I felt his release, and that made me cry out all over again.

He leaned over me, a dew of sweat decorating his chest, a smile spread across his face. He said in a breathless voice, "I love you, Anita."

"Nathaniel, I love you, too."

Jason leaned on the bedpost, staring at us with serious blue eyes. He'd enjoyed the show—that showed in his face, and his body—but there was something a little lost around the edges of his eyes. We were his friends, maybe his best friends, but it wasn't the same thing. Even with sex added, it wasn't the same thing.

5

WHEN WE COULD walk, we cleaned up. Then all three of us went back to lie on the bed and recover a little. I ended up in the middle, as I did most of the time. Jason said, "You are so uncomfortable with sex, Anita, but once you decide to do it, you give yourself over so completely. It's amazing."

"You're pretty good at it yourself," I said, and my voice still sounded breathy.

He laughed, and that one sound made it all worth it. Even if the sex hadn't been incredible, hearing him sound like himself again made it even better.

"My dad thinks I'm gay."

Nathaniel and I looked at him. "Why?" I finally asked.

"My friends in high school were mostly girls, and my best guy friend was, and is, gay. I also didn't want to play sports. I stayed in dance from elementary school to senior year."

"The lone guy in a room full of girls," I said.

He nodded, grinning. "I was the only one who could do the lifts, and tote and fetch the girls. It was fun. I was the male lead in most of the musicals in school."

"I didn't know you could sing."

He laughed. "I dance better than I sing, but I can act, and I can sing, and I can dance. The combination is sort of rare in a small private high school, especially among the guys."

This was a side of Jason I hadn't known anything about. "I thought you were going to college for a business degree when I met you, not theatre."

"My parents wouldn't pay for a theatre degree. They would pay for a business degree."

"If you didn't have to pay for college, why get a job as a stripper?"

"Bugging the hell out of my parents was some of the charm. But it was a way of performing that I could do on the weekends, which meant I could go to college full time."

"Does the rest of your family think you're gay?" I asked.

"My oldest sister does. I don't know about the rest. Probably. I'm a stripper and I live with Jean-Claude."

"They think you're doing him just like Perdy did," Nathaniel said.

"Yeah," Jason said.

I stroked my hand along Jason's stomach—not sexual, just trying to be comforting. "Her issues must have reminded you of your family."

"Yeah, bad fucking timing, huh?"

Nathaniel went up on his elbow, his hand resting on my hip. "What can you do?"

"Short of getting the kind of job that my dad thinks is a manly job, getting married, and starting a family, not a damn thing." He cuddled down in the pillows, putting his arm across my stomach, his face against my shoulder. "You'll never believe what my mother wanted me to do."

"What?" Nathaniel and I asked at the same time.

I felt Jason smile against my shoulder. "She wanted me to bring my girlfriend home to prove to my dad I'm straight. So he can die in peace."

"Bad timing for you and Perdy to break up," I said.

"I couldn't have taken her home, Anita. You have no idea how bad the jealousy had gotten. She'd flip out when the first old girlfriend said hi on the street."

"Like crazy jealous," I said.

He nodded, snuggling closer, as if I were his life-size teddy bear. "I told her that Perdy and I broke up. She said, 'Pick a friend, I know you have other friends. Bring a girl home and make your father happy.' "

"What did she mean about the 'I know you have other friends' comment?" I asked.

"I was a slut in high school and college. I slept with any girl that would have me. The entire town thought my best friend and I were a couple. At best, they thought I was bisexual, and to most people there ain't no such thing."

"You're either gay or straight," Nathaniel said, and something in the way he said it made me look at him.

"You have trouble with people thinking otherwise?" I asked.

Nathaniel shrugged. "I did; now I know what and who I am, and I'm okay with it. But when you're young, it's harder."

"You're twenty-one, that's not exactly ancient."

He smiled and kissed me. "I had a long, hard childhood; it makes me older."

He'd been out on the streets before he was ten. He'd been a child prostitute not long after. By thirteen he'd been addicted to drugs. He'd been clean since he was seventeen, but saying Nathaniel had had a hard childhood always sounded like calling the *Titanic* a boating accident.

I touched his face, drew him down for a more thorough kiss. He drew back, laughing. "Even I need more recoup time than this, Anita."

I blushed, I couldn't help it. "I didn't mean that."

Jason looked up with his body still tight against mine. "Blushing, that's so cute."

"Stop it, both of you."

"Sorry," Jason said.

Nathaniel just smiled at me. "Do you want to take a girl home to meet your dad?"

Jason frowned at him. "I'd love to rub my dad's face in the fact that I like girls. I wouldn't mind if I were gay, but having him not believe me is just . . ." He laid his head facedown on the pillow.

"Frustrating," Nathaniel said.

"Infuriating," I said.

Jason rose up enough to say, "Both, more. We never got along, him and me. I'm his only son after two daughters. I was his only chance for someone to be a chip off the ol' block. He went through college on a football scholarship."

"I take it he's taller than you are," I said.

"He's over six feet. I'm closer to my mother's height."

"Bad luck," I said.

"I don't mind being short, but my dad hated it. If he hadn't pushed so much I might have tried harder at sports, but it really wasn't my thing."

"Why don't you take Anita?" Nathaniel said.

"Take Anita where?" Jason asked.

"Home to meet your dad."

We both stared at him. We stared long enough and hard enough for him to look uncomfortable. "What?" he asked.

"What do you mean, what?" I asked.

"I'm with Anita on this one, Nathaniel. I mean that would be too sitcom. Taking home a girl who happens to be a friend, but isn't my girlfriend, to prove to my dad I'm not gay. That's just too sweeps week."

Nathaniel sat up, the sheet pooling in his lap, barely covering. "You and Anita are friends, right?"

Jason and I looked at each other. "Yeah," I said.

"Yes," Jason said.

"You and she are lovers, right?"

We both said a slow yes.

"You hang out with us. We watch movie marathons, and go out to eat. You aren't with us the way Micah is, but you spend a lot of time with us, right?"

"Yeah, but . . . ," Jason said.

"Why *but*?" Nathaniel said. "She's your friend, she's a girl, you really are lovers. It's not a lie."

Jason and I looked at each other. He shrugged. I turned back to Nathaniel. "I don't think a fuck buddy is what his mom had in mind, Nathaniel."

"You're more than fuck buddies, Anita, even I know that."

I didn't know what to say to that. I was speechless, not out of distraction, but because I just couldn't think my way past it all. I knew there was a reason not to do this, a good one; I'd think of it in a second.

"I can't take Anita home to meet my family; it would imply things that aren't true," Jason said.

There, he'd said it. "Yeah," I said.

"But you aren't going to say you're engaged or anything. Your mom wants you to bring home a girlfriend, so bring one home. If you don't care what your dad thinks, then screw it, but if it matters to you, then why not take Anita with you?"

Jason looked at me, and I did not like the look on his face. "Oh, no," I said.

"You don't have to do this, Anita; it's too big a favor to ask of anyone."

"You really think taking me home would help ease your father's passing?" I tried not to sound sarcastic or too harsh, but probably failed.

"He's a cruel bastard. He wouldn't even let my mom tell me he was sick. He said if I didn't care enough to see him when he was well, he didn't want pity."

"But . . . ," I said.

"But the doctors say he has only weeks. He won't make another Christmas."

"How long has it been since you've seen him?"

"Three years."

I looked at Nathaniel. "I can't feed the *ardeur* off just Jason for long."

"You know you have more control over it now. Jean-Claude can divide the *ardeur* up among us. I know last time it worked because you'd fed off the crowd at Guilty Pleasures—but we can try to feed you for a few days, just like we do when you're in the middle of a police investigation."

Jason looked at me. "You're not seriously thinking about saying yes to this, are you?"

"Are you seriously thinking it's a good idea?"

He grinned. "Probably a really bad one, but watching you and my father go head-to-head might be worth it."

"He's dying, I would think you'd want me to be nice to him."

"Be nice to him if he's nice to you, but don't let him push you around. He's a bully."

"You really don't like him, do you?"

Jason shook his head. "No."

"Did he abuse you physically?" Nathaniel asked.

Jason looked at him, with a strange, almost empty expression on his face. "He was always hurting me 'by accident,' trying to toughen me up. He'd try to teach me a sport and I'd come home bruised and bloody. He broke my arm finally trying to teach me football, and Mom wouldn't let him take me out by ourselves again. He was always careful that it wasn't abuse. Nothing you could call him on, but he was always too rough, too harsh for my age, my size. I started therapy in my teens because the school counselor encouraged it. Therapy taught me that my dad was abusing me. He wanted to hurt me."

I touched his face. "Jason, I'm sorry."

His face was very solemn. "Me, too."

"You don't want to go home by yourself, do you?" Nathaniel asked.

"No. I'd ask you to go with me, but if I show up with you it'll just confirm what my dad and most of the town thinks." He grinned suddenly. "Well, anyone who didn't have a teenage girl about my age. The fathers hated me."

"I would think that your being promiscuous with the girls would make your dad happy," I said.

"You'd think, but he seemed to hate me for that, too."

"If someone wants to hate you, you can't stop them," Nathaniel said.

Jason nodded. "Yeah, my dad has hated me for as long as I can remember."

"You're my best friend; if you want me to go with you for moral support, I'll go," Nathaniel said.

Jason smiled, then shook his head. "Nothing personal, Nathaniel, but you are not going to help me convince my dad I'm straight."

"Nathaniel's straight," I said.

"But he doesn't look like my dad's idea of a straight guy. And it's all about appearances with him."

I took a deep breath, let it out. "How long would you need to be there?"

"I don't know, a couple of days at least."

"I can't believe I'm saying this, but I'll go, if you want me to."

Jason looked at me, startled. "You're joking, right?"

"Do I look like I'm joking?"

"No," he said, and he sat up, kneeling in the bed. The sheet was behind him, so he was very not clothed. Even though we'd just finished having sex, I found myself fighting to give him eye contact. Sometimes my hang-ups puzzle even me. "This is like the biggest favor ever."

"You would owe me for the rest of your life, that's true."

A look passed over his face that I couldn't read. He looked down at me with so much emotion in his eyes that it was uncomfortable to see. I fought to look into those eyes.

"You'd really do this for me? Something this stupid and this sitcom? You'd really do it?"

I finally had to look away from the intensity of his eyes. "Yes, Jason, I'd really do it."

"You realize we'll have to fly."

"Shit," I said, "you will like owe me extra for getting me on a plane."

"But you'll still do it, even though you're terrified of flying?"

I crossed my arms underneath my breasts and sulked, but said, "I said I'd do it, didn't I? How long is the flight?"

He bounced down beside me, and the look of joy on his face made it all seem far less stupid. "I know you don't love me the way you love Nathaniel or anyone else. But you really do care for me, don't you?"

I looked into that face. A face that had been my friend for years and more than just a friend for about a year. I said the only thing I could say: "Yes."

6

WE CALLED JEAN-CLAUDE while it was still night, so we could tell him what his *pomme de sang*, Jason, and his human servant, me, had planned. I thought he might tell me it was a stupid thing to do, and tell us no. He was Jason's boss and master, and technically he was my master. Though honestly, I didn't let him pull the master card on me very often.

Jason told him, then handed the bedside phone to me. "He wants to talk to you."

Jason got up and padded toward the bathroom. Nathaniel stayed where he was beside me. "Hey, Jean-Claude."

"*Ma petite*, I am surprised that you would agree to this."

"Me, too."

He laughed, that wonderful, touchable laugh. It made me shiver and not from fear. Nathaniel cuddled closer to me, as if he'd gotten a taste of it.

"Thank you for taking care of Jason in a way that I could not."

"So you're not going to talk us out of it?"

"Do you wish me to?"

I realized that yes, I did. Now that I'd said yes, I was feeling awkward about it, and even more foolish. "It's going to be sort of awkward."

"It will be difficult for you. You will be his only emotional support in a very traumatic situation."

"You sound like therapy-speak, Jean-Claude."

"What would you have me say?"

"What you're actually thinking?"

He gave that laugh again, and my shields dropped enough so that I knew he was sitting in his bed wearing nothing but the silk sheets. I got a glimpse of that curling black hair over the perfect white of shoulders. I closed the shields down before I could literally see the midnight blue of his eyes.

I took a deep breath in, and let it out slow and counted as I did it. If I wasn't careful the tie between him and me could distract me, a lot.

"What are you thinking about, *ma petite*?"

"You, and trying not to. Where is Asher?"

"He is running late, but he will be here."

"Jason wants to leave in the morning. Who will you feed on while we're both gone?"

"There are always willing blood donors, *ma petite*."

I didn't like the way he said that. A small spurt of jealousy came and I clubbed it to death before it could sound in my voice. "Don't eat anything that disagrees with you."

"Are you jealous, *ma petite*?"

"Maybe."

"I, too."

"What do you mean?"

"You will be going home to meet Jason's family. You will be doing something very ordinary, very human, that will forever be denied me."

"I don't understand."

"My family died long before you were born, *ma petite*. I cannot introduce my mother to you, or my sister. I cannot give you the very normal experience of seeing where I came from, and who my people are."

"I've met the head of your bloodline, Jean-Claude. I figure that Belle Morte is your people."

"*Non, ma petite*, she is my master, or was, but she was never family. She was lover and goddess, if you will, but that is not the same."

"You're jealous that Jason has living family to take me home to."

"*Oui.*"

I lay there with the phone to my ear, and just thought about that. "I never thought that would be important to you."

"I do not regret what I am, *ma petite*, but I do regret some of what I do not have. I would give a great deal to have you meet my mother, and my sister."

"No father," I said.

"He died when I was very young. I don't have many memories of him."

Again, something I hadn't known. Tonight was just chock-full of new discoveries about people I thought I knew intimately.

"Are you upset that I haven't taken you home to meet my family?"

He made a small sound. "No, I . . ." He laughed, but it

wasn't sexy, more laughing at himself. "I think I may be. Maybe I feel you do not think me good enough."

"I think my Grandmother Blake would chase you out of the house with a crucifix and holy water, is what I think."

"She is a devout woman?"

"Fanatical. I've been informed she's praying for my soul because of you."

"Have I estranged you from your family, *ma petite*?"

"No, I was already estranged, if that's how you want to put it. Let's say Grandma Blake was praying for me about the whole raising-zombies-from-the-grave thing. My sleeping with the undead is just another symptom of my damnation."

"I am sorry, *ma petite*, I did not know."

I shrugged, knew he couldn't see it, and said, "It's okay."

"So you will go with our Jason and meet his family, be his girlfriend."

"You are jealous."

"My voice was empty of emotion," he said.

"Yeah, and when your voice is at its most empty, you're hiding something. You know you don't have to be jealous of Jason."

"I am not jealous in the way you mean."

"Then explain."

Nathaniel had gone very still beside me, listening.

"You are not yet thirty and he is twenty-three. You are both so very young, *ma petite*. You will go away to his hometown and be very young together. It is something I cannot be with you. I cannot be young and naïve and uncertain."

"You wouldn't be you if you were any of those things. I love you the way you are, Jean-Claude."

"Did I sound like I needed to hear that, *ma petite*?"

"Yes," I said.

He laughed again, and made me shiver down closer to Nathaniel. "I find myself strangely conflicted. Jason is my *pomme de sang*, and is precious to me. That my human servant is taking care of him in such a caring way is a lovely thing. It will make other vampires think me a very kind master, but I know that you do it because you care for him. He is young and handsome and charming."

"You cannot be insecure."

"Why can I not be?"

"Because you are beautiful and amazing in bed, and I love you."

"But Jason can be one thing for you that I cannot, *ma petite*."

"What's that?"

"Mortal. He can involve you in the youth of his life. He can offer you the mess of his family. He can show you where he grew up, introduce you to people who knew him as a child. All those to whom I can introduce you knew me as a vampire, never as a mortal."

"I think this is your issue, Jean-Claude, not mine. I'm not actually looking forward to traveling down memory lane with Jason and his abusive dad."

"I feel that you mean that, but I find myself strangely envious. I had not missed my family in a very long time."

"You sound homesick."

"I suppose that is as good a word as any." He sounded sad.

"Do you need us to come there tonight?"

"To what purpose? You would arrive not long before dawn, and you would leave before I awoke for the day."

"I feel like you need a good-bye kiss, I guess."

"Thank you for the sentiment, *ma petite*, but I will work on, how do you say, my issues. You, I think, will have your hands full working on Jason's."

What could I say to that? "Yeah," I said.

"Je t'aime, ma petite."

"I love you, too," I said.

I guess in the end, what else is there to say?

7

I HAD ONE other phone call to make before I flew off into the sunset with Jason. I dialed Micah's cell phone, because when he did the out-of-town trips it was the best way to get him.

"Hey," he said, and that one word was full of affection, happiness, contentment.

"Hey, yourself," I said, and my voice had the same tone. I'd felt that way about Micah almost from the moment I met him. Weird, especially for me, the poster child for panic when I was attracted to a man. We'd learned only in the last few months that it had been the *ardeur*, my very own version of vampire powers, that had taken away my reluctance. In a way, I'd rolled Micah and myself. But neither of us regretted it; maybe that was vampire powers, too.

I asked him how the trip was going. He told me he liked the new leopard, and so did his bodyguards, Mel and Noah. Good to know.

"But you didn't call to ask about the new wereleopard," he said.

"Couldn't I call just to chat?"

He laughed, and I could picture his face. He was back to having his summer tan, which made him dark enough to pass for something other than Caucasian. But his features were entirely too Northern European, to really pass for anything else. His face was delicate, and so was he, at my height exactly. His eyes were chartreuse leopard eyes, from where a truly evil man had forced him into animal form long enough so his eyes never changed back. I'd killed the evil man, and Micah had moved in. We'd been a couple ever since.

I told him the *Reader's Digest* version of what was happening with Jason. "I'm sorry to hear about his father."

"Me, too."

"How did you get volunteered for this trip?"

"You don't think I'd come up with it myself?"

"No," he said, and there was no doubt in his voice.

"Nathaniel."

"Hmm," he said.

"You sound upset."

"That you're going off with another man to meet his family? Hmm, let me think, why would that upset me?"

"Are you telling me not to go?"

"I would never do that."

"But . . . ," I said.

"But nothing, telling you what to do isn't the kind of relationship we have. But I'm allowed to be a little jealous that you're getting to go home with Jason."

"Jean-Claude said the same thing, sort of, but his family is centuries dead. It's not possible for him. You never talk about your family."

"When Chimera was alive, he used people's families against them. He tortured them, or made them into wereanimals so he could control them. To keep my family safe, I had to pretend I hated them. I did a good job of it, Anita. I doubt they'd want to see me again."

I heard such regret in his voice. "You never know until you try, Micah."

"We'll see."

"If it works out, I'd love to meet your family."

"Really, you don't seem much interested in your own."

"I'm allowed issues with my own family; that doesn't make me hate everyone's family."

"Okay," but he sounded cautious.

"Really, Micah, Chimera's dead, he can't hurt you or your family anymore."

"I know that, you killed him for me."

"You wanted me to kill him."

"Yes, I did." And there was that note in his voice, that tone, that said he was all right with the violence that I did. He'd watched me kill Chimera, and he'd been just peachy with it. There were so many reasons that Micah and I worked as a couple. One of those reasons was a certain ruthless practicality in both of us.

"I would go home to see your folks, Micah."

"Would we bring Nathaniel, too?"

That stopped me. We all three lived together, but . . . "I don't know. I guess that would be your call."

"I'll think about it, all of it, the family, and whether I have the guts to show up after all these years with you and Nathaniel." Put that way, I could sort of see his problem. It was sort of similar to Jason's problem, actually. Perception is all.

"I'm sorry if my going off with Jason bothers you."

"I'm sorry it bothers me, too. I need to work on that."

"Micah, I love you."

"I know, and I love you, too. Give my love to Nathaniel. You better start packing."

"Micah, I . . ."

"No, it's all right, Anita, really. Do what you need to do for Jason. But I guess I really would like to introduce you to my mom and dad, my brother and sister. I just never thought it was possible."

"A lot of things are possible, Micah."

"I guess. I've got to go. I love you, Anita."

"I love you, too."

"Give my love to Nathaniel."

"I will."

He hung up, and left me not sure how to feel. Guilty that it bothered him, yes, but more puzzled. He'd almost never mentioned his family. How was I supposed to know that he even wanted to see them? Sometimes the hardest part of dating this many men was juggling everyone's emotions. People talked about the sex, because sex was easy; hearts were hard.

8

JASON HAD SAID he lived in a small city. I hadn't understood what that might mean for the flight. What it meant was that we would have been on a freaking prop plane. The only thing that will get me on shit like that is life or death, as in a police investigation, where if I don't go more people will die.

Maybe the panic showed on my face, because Jason made a second call to Jean-Claude. I keep forgetting that he owns a private jet. I don't know why I keep forgetting, but I do. I think I'm just a little uncomfortable that I'm dating someone who owns one. It just seems a little too idle rich for me. Of course, Jean-Claude is about as idle as I am, which means he's always working. He manages his little growing empire of preternatural businesses, and is good at it. I raise the dead and slay bad vampires. Busy, busy, busy.

But it meant that I didn't have to brave a puddle jumper to do the favor for Jason. If I'd had to get on a tiny prop plane, well, I couldn't think of a sexual act deviant enough to make up for the phobia abuse. Luckily for both of us, the private jet, though small by commercial standards, wasn't horrible. If I hadn't been both claustrophobic and afraid to fly, it might even have been comfortable.

The last time we'd been on the plane Jason had been jumping all over the place, teasing me about my phobia. This time he stayed in the swivel seat beside me, staring out the window. Of course, last time he'd been wearing a T-shirt and jeans. Now he was wearing one of the Italian-cut designer suits that Jean-Claude had had made for him. The suit showed the broadness of his shoulders, the narrowness of waist, the sheer athleticism of him.

He was wearing the navy blue pinstripe. Other than the cut it was a conservative suit. A blue shirt made his eyes even bluer than they actually were, with a darker blue tie, complete with gold tie bar. I knew the tie was silk. I knew that the shoes that gleamed on his feet cost a hell of a lot more than my high heels. I refused to pay hundreds of dollars for yet another pair of uncomfortable high heels. They were good shoes, but not as good as what Jason was wearing.

He'd dressed carefully. He might hate coming home, but he wanted to impress them. He and Nathaniel had chosen my clothes, too. I didn't care. If it was in my closet I was usually okay with it, or it wouldn't be there. There was a section of stuff that Jean-Claude had bought me that was more club or fetish wear, but other than that my closet was fine.

I was wearing a royal blue skirt suit, with a silk shell that actually matched. The only thing I'd added to the skirt to sort of ruin the feminine look was a wide black belt. It matched my shoes. The belt also held a Browning BDM at the small of my back at an angle, not up and down. I didn't often carry guns at the small of my back. I usually favored a shoulder holster, but I didn't go anywhere unarmed, and I'd worn the gun this way before when my boss thought being armed was a little too scary for clients. If they had a metal detector at the hospital I'd flash my federal marshal badge.

I had more guns and holsters in the luggage, but I figured for the hospital visit I'd try to be low-key about my job and the whole violence thing.

Frankly, I never thought about going home to meet anyone's folks, let alone Jason's. But I'd play by the rules. Rule one had to be not to scare the prospective in-laws. Yeah, Jason and I both knew that we had no plans for marriage, but I was the first girl he'd brought home, to my knowledge. People would assume a lot, and I wasn't sure how much Jason wanted them to assume. My only goal was not to lie outright to anyone; beyond that it was all game.

Jason let me keep a death grip on his hand, and complained only once that he was losing feeling in his fingers. He was too worried to tease, which made me worry about him. Jason teased the way he breathed. Solemn wasn't his thing.

I tried to comfort him. He finally turned to me with a smile so sad it made my throat tight. "It's okay, Anita. I appreciate the effort, but I can't think of anything you can say that will make me feel better."

He raised my tense hand to his face and rubbed his cheek against my knuckles. The horrible tightness inside me eased just a touch.

He smiled, and it was almost his old smile. His eyes sparkled with it. I knew that look. He was about to say something I wouldn't like.

"A little more touch made you feel better, too."

I nodded.

The smile was pure Jason when he said, "We could do the whole mile-high club; that might make me feel better."

"Mile-high club?" I made it a question.

He kissed my knuckles, soft, a little more open mouth than would be polite in public. "Sex on a plane."

I shook my head and laughed. It was almost a normal laugh. Points for me. "Now I'm not so worried," I said.

"Worried about what?"

"You, if you can flirt and tease, you'll be all right."

He pressed my hand to his face, and his eyes went from teasing to too serious. "Who says I'm teasing?"

I gave him the look the suggestion deserved. "I could not possibly have sex on a plane. I can barely keep myself from running up and down the plane screaming."

The lascivious look changed instantly to that sparkling, teasing look. "Might take both our minds off our problems."

I tugged at my hand.

He smiled, and kissed my hand, the way it was supposed to be done. A bare touch of lips, not open mouth, no tongue, chaste. "I'll behave if you insist."

"I insist."

"The extra touching made you feel better, too, Anita. I could sense it in the way your hand felt, the way your body smelled less like prey. Seriously, why not have sex? Why not feel better?"

I frowned at him, because I realized he really was serious. "One, the pilot might walk in on us. Two, we're on a plane, Jason, I couldn't possibly. I'm too freaked."

"Can we have sex when we land?"

I frowned harder. "You mean when we touch down?"

"No, hotel, I guess."

I wasn't offended anymore, I was too puzzled. He wasn't

teasing. He was dead serious. It wasn't like him. "Won't you want to go to the hospital or your old house before we get all messy?"

He smiled, but it left his eyes worried. "I don't want to go to the hospital. I don't want to go to the house. I don't *want* to do any of it."

I held his hand tight, not because of my fear, but because of the pain in his voice. Strangely, worrying about him helped me be less afraid about where we were. Who knew therapy for someone else was the answer all along to my own fears?

"I don't think having sex is going to make this visit easier."

He smiled then, and a look ran through his eyes so quick I almost didn't catch it. But it was similar to a look that Nathaniel had, so I knew it, all too well. It was a look that said I was naïve. Jason was years younger than me, and he hadn't had all the bad experiences that Nathaniel had had, but he'd had his share.

"I am not being naïve," I said.

"You read me that fast?"

"Nathaniel has a look pretty close to it," I said.

"Of course, it couldn't just be me you knew that well." He sounded bitter.

I began to worry that I was in a much different problem than I thought with this favor. "What's that supposed to mean?" I asked.

"I want someone to want me the way you want Nathaniel. I want someone to love me the way you love the men in your life."

"Perdy loved you that way," I said. Was it mean to say that, or just true?

He gave me an unfriendly look. "Are you trying to be mean?"

I took a deep breath, let it out slow, and tried to be honest, but not mean. "I am on a plane, which means I am not at my best. Let me try this: you've told me before that you want to be consumed by romance, by love. You want to burn with it. Since I spent years fighting against anyone who wanted to love me like that, I don't quite get why that is your goal, but you say it is, so it is."

"What am I supposed to say now, Anita? That I threw away someone who wanted to consume me with her love? I guess I did."

I shook my head and tried one more time. "No, I don't mean that. I mean Perdy's idea of love and your idea of love aren't the same. You want to be consumed, not smothered. A fire needs air to burn bright. She took your air away, and the fire died."

He studied my face. "That was actually smart."

"Gee, Jason, thanks, you sound surprised."

He smiled. "I don't mean that. I mean, that makes sense, that makes me feel less stupid about not wanting Perdy to love me. I do this big thing about wanting someone to be obsessed with me. I get it and I don't want it. I thought I was being fickle."

"Obsession isn't love, Jason. It's possession."

"I want to belong to someone, Anita."

"But you want closer to what Nathaniel has, than a traditional marriage."

"You mean I want to belong but not be monogamous."

I shrugged. "Technically, Nathaniel is monogamous. He doesn't have sex with anyone but me."

Jason grinned, blue eyes shining. "He *so* has sexual contact with other people."

"He's a stripper. Sexualized contact with other people is part of the job description."

"I didn't say *sexualized.* I said *sexual.* At our jobs we cut it pretty fine, but actual sex is illegal."

I closed my eyes, but that made the purr of the engines seem louder. I opened my eyes wide and tried to think of what I'd been saying. "What do you mean then?"

He gave me another of those looks that said I was being either naïve or obtuse. Since I wasn't being either on purpose, I didn't know what he meant.

"Don't give me that look, Jason. I honestly don't know what you mean."

It was his turn to frown. "You don't, do you?"

"No, I don't." I couldn't help but sound grumpy.

"What do you consider sexual contact, Anita?"

"I don't know, sex."

"Anita, I've seen Asher feed on Nathaniel. Hell, I've had him feed on me. You'd have to be a hell of a lot more homophobic than either Nathaniel or me not to understand that when Asher feeds, it's sexual."

One of Asher's abilities was to make his bite orgasmic. It wasn't just mind tricks either. It was like a special ability. When he'd been a bad little vampire he'd used that ability to get money, land, protection from his victims. People had begged him for one more night, even when they knew it would kill them.

"I know what Asher can do, better than you do, Jason."

"Oh, geez, I'm an idiot. How could I forget that?" He hugged me. "I'm sorry, Anita, I'm so sorry."

Asher and I had had sex and blood alone for the first and only time. He'd nearly killed me with pleasure, because I asked him to. Begged him to. We weren't allowed to be alone anymore, because I'd admitted to Jean-Claude that I still craved what we'd done. Of all of Jean-Claude's vampires, Asher was the one I feared the most. Because he was the one who made me want him to do deadly things to me.

Jason hugged me and said, "I'm scared and that's making me stupid. I'm sorry."

The pilot's voice came over the speakers. It made me jump and make that girl *eep*. Jason kissed my forehead.

"We're about to land, Ms. Blake, Mr. Schuyler. If you could take your seats, that'd be good."

"I'm okay, Jason, neither of us is at our best."

"Forgive me."

"Nothing to forgive," I said.

Jason nodded, but not like he believed it. I wasn't used to him being like this, emotional, forgetful. His father was dying. His mother was blackmailing him, emotionally. I guess he was entitled to be a little off his game.

I tightened my grip on the seat and his hand. I'd be better when we landed. It would all be better when we landed. I tried to believe that, but part of me knew if Jason was already having problems, it was only going to get worse.

How did I end up holding his hand for this? Oh, right, Nathaniel volunteered me. I was so going to make him pay for this. The plane bounced a little on the runway, and I gasped a little. But we were on the ground. Things were looking up, at least for me.

9

I SAT IN my swivel seat for a second relearning how to breathe and fighting down the nausea. I told my stomach to stop being such a baby. We were on the ground, for God's sake. I could always insist on renting a car for the ride home—though I knew I wouldn't. I'd never be able to live with myself if I let my fear get that much of an upper hand. Fear was like cancer in remission. If you gave in to it, even by an inch, it would flare up again and eat you alive.

Jason stopped at the open door and looked back at me. "You are coming, right?"

I nodded. The nausea was past. I could breathe again. It was cool. Okay, that was a lie, but it was the best I could do.

Jason came back to stand and look down at me. I couldn't quite read his expression. "It really scared the shit out of you to do this, didn't it?"

I shook my head, then shrugged. I finally said in a voice that was way too breathy for comfort, "The runway is kinda small, don't you think?"

He bent down and kissed my forehead again.

I looked up at him. "What was that for?"

"Being brave," he said, and he looked serious when he said it. He offered me his hand.

There was a time when I wouldn't have taken it, when I would have seen it as a sign of weakness, but I'd grown up a little since then.

I took his hand. He squeezed it and gave me a smile. This smile was one of the reasons I was on the damn plane—the smile that said he understood how much it had cost me, and that he understood me in a way that a lot of people didn't. We would never be real boyfriend and girlfriend. We'd never be each other's sweetie, but Jason got me in a way that some of the men I was dating didn't. And I tried my best to understand him.

I realized as he led me down the narrow aisle hand in hand that it wasn't just Nathaniel who considered Jason one of his best friends.

Jason went first down the little folding steps, bent sort of backward, to help me. That was a little more help than I probably needed, but then I was wearing heels.

A man met us at the bottom of the steps. He was average height, more bald than hair, in a nice suit. Not as nice as the one Jason was wearing, but it wasn't a bad suit.

"Mr. Summerland, I didn't expect you until tomorrow." He was smiling until Jason helped me down the little stairs in my heels.

"I'm not one of the Summerlands," Jason said. He said it as if the confusion wasn't unexpected.

The man looked at Jason, then at me, as Jason helped me

down from the plane. The man winked at him. "Of course not, you're Mr. . . . Smith?"

I was finally on solid tarmac, yea! "Why don't you make it Mr. Allbright, it's more original," I said. I thought I was making a joke.

The man began to scribble down *Allbright* on his clipboard. "Of course, Mr. Allbright, we're glad to have you with us."

Jason sighed. "She was making a joke. The name is Schuyler, Jason Schuyler."

The man crossed out *Allbright* and wrote in the right name. "Whatever you say, Mr. Schuyler."

"Crap," Jason said under his breath.

"What's going on?" I asked.

"If I was a Summerland, why was I coming in tomorrow?"

The man looked puzzled, but he played along in whatever game he thought we were playing. "Your bachelor party, of course. You're getting married at the end of the week. Your brother arrived yesterday with his fiancée."

"Look, I am a distant cousin of the Summerlands. I got mistaken for the twins all through school. My name really is Jason Schuyler. This is my friend Anita Blake. I'm here to visit my family."

"Of course you are." It was clear he didn't believe Jason, but at the same time very clear that he would repeat whatever lie Jason spouted, and swear to it in court afterward.

"I take it the Summerlands are big shots around here?" I said.

"The biggest," Jason said.

The man with the clipboard looked from one to the other of us. "The bride-to-be is already in town. Her bachelorette party is tonight."

"You invited?" I said.

He looked flustered. "Of course not."

"Then how do you know so much?"

"I've been helping get the guests settled," he said, and sounded indignant.

"Fine, but we are not guests."

"Of course not, and if asked, I haven't seen Keith Summerland. He will arrive tomorrow as planned." The man seemed pleased with himself as if he'd said a smart thing. Then he walked away with another wink.

I looked at Jason. "We are speaking English, right? I mean he does understand what we're saying, doesn't he?"

"You have to know Keith to understand the man's problem. It would be like him to come in a day early with another woman. He'd probably bring the stripper in personally."

"A wild child?" I asked.

"He thought he was. I just thought he was a dick."

"Do you really look that much like him?"

"Yes." He said it flat and unhappy. "I look enough like them both to make this visit even harder. The media will be all over this wedding."

"But they're like local celebrities, not national, right? I mean, it won't be that bad."

"Do you know who Governor Summerland is?"

I stared at him. "You're joking."

"I wish."

"The governor that they're thinking about running for president is this Summerland?"

"Yep," Jason said.

"I don't watch TV or read newspapers much, but even I know who he is."

"If his eldest son is getting married this week, the media are going to be everywhere, and I look like his twin. We were always getting confused for each other in high school."

"You can't look that much alike."

"He pretended to be me on a date with my girlfriend. She caught on, eventually. He took a beating for me once from some of the guys at school. I'd smarted off, and they found him first. He was hitting on a girlfriend of mine again. Pretending to be me."

"And he got beat up for it?" I said.

"He did."

"Very karmic," I said.

Jason nodded, actually looking happy. We had our bags on the tarmac and the pilot was asking for a return schedule when we were joined by a man who, though well dressed in a nice conservative suit, had *thug* tattooed across his forehead. Metaphorically speaking.

The suit was tailored well enough that if I hadn't been looking for it I might have missed the bulge on his hip. But I was looking, and I knew a gun when I saw it ruin the line of a suit. The Browning did not ruin the line of my suit jacket. For such a big gun it was strangely invisible under my little jacket in its new sideways holster.

I actually moved in front of Jason. Just automatic. After all, I was packing a gun, and he wasn't. The conservative thug didn't even look at me. He had attention only for Jason.

"The girl gets back on the plane."

"The girl has a name," I said.

"What I don't know, I can't lie about. Please, Keith, don't do this."

"I am not Keith Summerland. Do I have to prove it?"

"Keith, stuff like this isn't funny anymore."

"Do you want to see my driver's license?"

The man finally looked puzzled. "What?"

"Call up the governor, or his wife, or even Kelsey, tell them that Jason Schuyler is just trying to visit his family, and you won't let us leave the airport."

The muscleman looked at Jason. "Keith, I thought this kind of shit was over."

Jason got out his wallet and flashed his ID. "I got confused with them both in high school, too."

The man looked at the ID, like he was really studying it. He looked at Jason, then got a small flip phone out of his outer jacket pocket. "This is Chuck, I'd swear it's Keith, but I'm looking at an ID for a Jason Schuyler." He said *uh-huh* a lot, then closed the phone and handed Jason his ID back. "I'm sorry about this, Mr. Schuyler. The governor says he's very sorry about your father's illness."

"Yeah, my father is dying of cancer, and instead of being able to see him in peace, I'm going to get stopped by every piece of media from here to the hospital. Jesus, if I'd known about the wedding I might have held off a week."

I touched his arm. "You couldn't have done that."

"I know," Jason said, "what if he died this week?" I think he tried to make it a joke, but it fell flat and bitter.

"I am truly sorry about the misunderstanding, Mr. Schuyler. We have limos waiting for the guests to arrive; if we can drop you anywhere to make up for the difficulties, just say the word. The limos have dark glass, and we've had lots of the bride's friends arriving. The media has stopped hounding the limos, because the interviews all sound the same."

"And if I take a taxi they'll wonder why Keith is with a brunette that isn't his fiancée, and why he's not in a limo," Jason said.

Chuck shrugged massive shoulders. "That did occur to the governor."

"Fine, drop us at the hotel."

"But won't us getting out of a Summerland limo sort of add to the confusion?" I asked.

Chuck looked perplexed, as if I was forcing him to think about things that weren't usually his business. He'd been perfectly comfortable shoving me back on the plane. Forcing Keith to be a good boy. But figuring out what to do with an identical cousin who wasn't close enough to be included in the wedding, that was beyond him.

"We'll take the limo, and get a taxi to the hospital. I don't know what else to do," Jason said.

"I'll call the press secretary from the limo," Chuck said. "You guys look enough alike that it could be a real problem. If the media think you're Keith and are cheating with this *chiquita* here, it'll get ugly."

"You've called me *girl*, now *chiquita*. Chuck, you are not winning brownie points with me."

He gave me a look that clearly said he didn't give a damn, and who was I to complain?

"This is Anita Blake; she's my very close friend, Chuck."

"Girlfriend?" He made it a question.

Jason nodded. "I'm bringing her home to see my dad before he dies, that put it in perspective?" Jason squeezed my hand as if to say, *Just agree with me.* I wasn't sure I disagreed, or agreed, so I just stood there and let Jason handle it. It was his crisis, not mine.

Chuck nodded and gave me a much more respectful look. "I'm sorry, Miss Black."

"It's *Ms.* and it's *Blake*," I corrected.

He blinked at me, then said, "All right, Ms. Blake. I didn't understand that you were more than a . . . girlfriend. I'm sorry, I didn't mean any disrespect."

"Yeah, you did, but my ego doesn't bruise that easy, Chuck." I admit to making his name sound a little choppy at the end.

He frowned at me.

Jason squeezed my hand again. "Let's just get us to the hotel as quietly as possible. I want to go to the hospital today, just in case."

Chuck's face managed to look truly sympathetic. "Your dad that bad?"

"They gave him weeks to live, but I'd hate to be in town and miss him by a day."

"Then let's get you in the limo, Mr. Schuyler, Ms. Blake." He put a little irony in that last part, and when he bowed to match, he flashed the gun on his hip. I realized he'd unbuttoned the jacket so I'd see it. Like a vampire that wanted you to see the fangs. Wanted your fear.

I smiled sweetly at him. "Your hands are a little big for a thirty-two, aren't they, Chuck?"

His own smile wilted around the edges. "It gets the job done." But he sounded uncertain, as if my reply didn't match the box he'd put me in. Fine with me. I liked it when muscle underestimated me. Made it easier later if later got bad.

Jason didn't push me into the back of the limo, but he made sure I didn't linger trading clever repartee with Chuck.

The big man asked, "What hotel?"

Jason named it.

Chuck said, leaning in the doorway of the limo, "Damn, that's the same hotel the wedding guests are staying at."

"It's the best hotel in town," Jason said.

Chuck nodded. "Yeah." He gave me a look as he closed the door. It was the first look from him that didn't think *piece of ass.*

Which meant he was brighter than he looked. I'd have to be careful not to underestimate ol' Chuck.

Why was I worried about him? Answer: he was a thug. I'd been working with the police too long not to know one when I met one. What was a presidential hopeful doing with someone like that?

"Don't tease him, Anita," Jason said as the limo started. We rode out of the hangar and down a separate drive, a little distance from the rest of the main airport.

"Sorry," I said, "I'm not sure I can help myself."

"Try, for me." He patted my hand, but was already looking out the window. It was worth a look. There were wooded mountains rolling out, and out, like layers of soft dragon spines curled everywhere.

For a few minutes I forgot about thugs and politicians and just looked at the mountains.

"It's beautiful," I said.

"Yeah," Jason said, "I guess it is."

"You guess?" I motioned at the mountains. There were hotels and fast-food places tucked in near the road, but it wasn't close enough to ruin the view. A river cut along the left-hand side of the road, all silver shallows and sparkling rapids, set in all that green, all those trees. "This is prettier than the Smokies in Tennessee."

"Well, it's the Blue Ridge Mountains," he said matter-of-factly.

I had a smart thought. "You grew up here, so it's not spectacular to you, it's just normal."

"Yeah, and have you ever noticed where it's beautiful, there's a lot of pretty, but not a lot of jobs. Unless you worked for the university."

"University?" I made it a question.

"University of North Carolina at Asheville." Jason didn't seem to want to talk about the scenery. Okay, I could stay on track.

"You don't seem surprised that the Summerlands have someone like Chuck working for them."

"They've always had someone like him working for them."

"Why?" I asked.

He looked at me. "Don't do this, Anita."

"Don't do what?"

"Don't play cop. Just let it be."

"You know something."

"Let me see my father, Anita. Let me see some old friends. Let me just try and keep out of the Summerland family mess. I don't want any part of them. Okay?"

"Tell me why they have muscle and I'll let it go."

"What did Chuck think he was doing at the airport?" he asked.

I frowned at Jason. "He thought he was keeping this Keith from bringing in another woman just days before his wedding."

"Exactly."

I frowned harder, and then the light dawned. "He's their cleanup man."

Jason nodded.

"Why does their cleanup man need to be armed?"

"Why are *you* armed?"

"I don't go out of the house unarmed," I said.

Jason gave me a look. "Maybe Chuck is as paranoid as you are."

"I don't . . ."

Jason knelt on the floorboard of the limo at my feet. He took my hands in his and gazed up at my face with a look of pure begging. "Please, please, God, let this go, Anita. I will do anything, you name it, if you will just not poke at the Summerlands. Because of the wedding and the family resemblance we are going to have enough trouble."

He laid his head in my lap, and said, "Please don't make more trouble, please, don't make this harder for me. Please."

I said the only thing I could say. "Okay, Jason."

He raised his face up and flashed me that infamous smile. It wasn't his real smile. This was the smile I'd seen him use on customers at Guilty Pleasures when he was trying to part them from their cash. Jason didn't want cash from me, he wanted peace. I'd have rather shoved a twenty down his pants then let go of the niggling feeling that there was something wrong with the Summerlands. Something that needed an armed cleanup man. Something beyond a womanizing son. But I did for Jason what I wouldn't have done for almost anyone else. I let it go.

If Chuck of the too-small gun would leave me alone, I'd leave him alone. I wasn't here as a marshal. I was here to help Jason say good-bye to his dad. I'd just keep repeating that over and over, no matter how many clues I tripped over. The question was, clues to what?

None of my business. I'd promised Jason, and it really was none of my business. Unless the Summerlands turned out to be evil vampires, it would never be my business.

I went back to looking at the amazing scenery on either side of the road. There was no bad view. Jason was back to looking out the window, too, but he didn't seem to be seeing anything special. I thought the drive into Asheville, North Carolina, was one of the prettiest drives I've ever been on, but then I hadn't grown up looking at it all. I guess you get jaded about anything you see every day. Was I jaded about zombies and vampires? Maybe. But the mountains were pretty.

10

THE SCENERY STAYED all mountains and hills and green with more evergreens than we have at home until we turned off the Highway and onto Charlotte Street.

Then we were in small-town America. No building too tall, nothing too built up, a lot of houses and small businesses among the trees.

The limo had dark glass so no one could see in, but we could see out just fine. One of the interesting things you find out if you ride in limos. Jason was more interested in the scenery now. I guess he was just a city boy at heart.

"There's the dance studio," he said in an excited voice. There was a sign with a silhouette of a ballet dancer outside one of the larger homes. Two little girls in leotards were being led inside by a laughing woman.

"I wish we could stop. I'd like to see my old teachers again."

If it had been our limo, or rather Jean-Claude's, I would

have said *stop*, but we were borrowing. It would be the height of rudeness to ask.

"We can come back," I said.

He nodded and pointed at a small mom-and-pop grocery sitting just doors down from the studio. "I would have thought Siglier's would have gone out of business. I got my first cigarettes there."

"You don't smoke," I said.

He turned and gave me a grin that filled his eyes with laughter. "I don't smoke, but everybody tries them at least once."

Something on my face must have shown, because he scooted closer to me. "You never tried to smoke, not once?"

I shrugged, and moved a little in my seat to try to keep the gun in a comfortable spot. I was beginning to remember why I seldom wore a gun there. It made sitting down harder. "I had a couple of cousins who were bad influences."

"So you did smoke."

"I tried cigarettes, not the same thing as smoking."

"So you weren't completely pure when Jean-Claude met you?"

I frowned at him. "I'd tried cigarettes, Jason; that didn't really prepare me for Jean-Claude."

Jason was suddenly solemn again. "No, I guess it didn't. It's hard for me to believe that you'd only had sex with one other guy before Jean-Claude."

"Why?" I asked, not sure I really wanted to know the answer.

"I told you, I slept with just about anyone who would have me. I can't imagine turning down all the guys who must have asked."

"Trust me, Jason, there weren't that many."

He looked at me like I was joking. "Come on, Anita, I have eyes. You are sooo hot."

I squirmed in my seat, which ground the gun into my back, which made me cranky, and the conversation had already made me cranky.

"I won't debate that with you. You know that sometimes I can see it, and sometimes I can't. There were guys attracted to the packaging, but they didn't want what was inside."

"I don't understand," he said.

"I had at least three guys in college say something along the lines of, *If only your inside matched your outside*. Or one of my favorite first dates, who told me I was perfect until I opened my mouth."

Jason stared at me. "I know you're serious, but damn, how stupid were these guys?"

I smiled and patted his hand on the seat. "That's sweet, but I've always spoken my mind. I've always been independent. That is not the trait that draws men to pretty, petite, delicate-looking women. They want to protect and coddle, and do stupid shit like that."

"You intimidated them," he said.

I nodded. "I know that now."

"I like strong women," he said.

I smiled at him. "I've noticed."

He flashed me the real version of the smile that parted women from their money at the club. If they thought the fake version was something, they should have had the full weight of the real deal. It was enough to turn a girl's head. Or make them blush, damn it.

"You're blushing," he damn near chortled. He bounced in the seat. "I love that you do that."

I covered my face with my hands. "I don't."

His hands on my wrists were the first clue I had that he was so close beside me again. I let him draw my hands away so he could look into my eyes.

"I love that I'm one of the men you react to, Anita. I was like invisible to you. I mean, I'm not in Jean-Claude's league, but there are women who would do a lot to be with me, and have," he said, with a look to the side that tried for humble and almost made it.

"I've seen the fans at the club, and the women going in and out of the Circus."

He took my hands in both of his and rested his chin on our joined hands. He wasn't exactly looking at me. More at the memory in his head.

"But you never saw me like that. I was a responsibility first. Someone else you felt you needed to keep safe, and then I was your friend." He looked at me with that mischievous grin. "You'd seen me buck naked and you didn't react to my body. That was a real ego bruiser, let me tell you."

I blushed again and looked away from his face. "You were my friend, Jason, you don't look at friends that way."

"You don't, but I did. I thought I wasn't up to your standards."

"The homes are really nice here," I said. They were. The more narrow road was surrounded by lovely, older, expensive homes.

"You're changing the subject," Jason said.

"Trying to, yes."

"I don't want to change the subject."

I pulled at my hands. This conversation was too intimate for me. I'd forgotten one thing Jason did that made me the most uncomfortable. He had a penchant for in-depth soul-searching talks. When I needed one, it was great, if sometimes painful. But I could not spend the next two days being analyzed; it would drive me mad. I kept staring out at the beautiful houses nestled into their green yards and trees. It was still pretty, but no amount of pretty was going to make up for being analyzed for days.

He kissed my hands gently, then let me pull away. “You know that wasn’t it, Jason.”

“I know you were trying to hold on to what virtue you felt you had left.”

I nodded, still not looking at him. “Can I ask you a favor, Jason?”

“Sure.”

“I’m not up to you analyzing me on this trip, okay?”

“I wasn’t—”

I held up a hand. “Just don’t poke at my wounds too hard. I’m supposed to be here to support you; if you make me face my demons too head-on, I won’t be as good for you here. Do you understand?” I looked at him at the last.

He was solemn again, but he nodded. “I have trouble when I realize something about someone, some secret thing I didn’t know before. I want to know why, or what the other person was thinking, feeling.” His face went from solemn to pained. “I’ve always been that way.”

Something about the way he said it made me wonder what truth he’d pushed for as a child that he hadn’t wanted to know. If our roles had been reversed he would have asked me, but it was me, and I was already out of my depth.

Alone with Jason for a few days, I’d thought the sex and his problems with his family would be the awkward bits. What I was realizing now, far too late, was that Jason himself was the danger. It was too intimate, this visit. I had trouble keeping my emotional boundaries up once sex was involved. What the hell had I been thinking?

11

THE NARROW, TWISTING road was edged by evergreens, and other trees, but mostly evergreens. There were still a few nice older houses, and some newer expensive houses dotted along the road, but mostly trees. We were climbing, though. Climbing out of the valley that most of Asheville sat in. The rich always seem to live up.

The first hint we had that the hotel was ahead was the cluster of news vans blocking the road.

The curving drive that led between the trees and the vans was being kept clear by men in uniform. Not police uniforms, but really nice valet uniforms. They kept the photographers, reporters, and cameramen at bay long enough for the limo to slip by.

The gently curving driveway spilled out among yet more trees, and suddenly we could see the Grove Park Inn.

The setting in the hills was lovely, but the building helped make it lovely. It was all stone and sort of pseudo-Bavarian, as if men in eighteenth-century clothing should come striding into view with dogs and servants. It should have looked overdone, or silly, but it didn't.

The inn looked like it had sprung up from the rocks and trees around it, perfect in its setting, organic and right.

"I've loved this place since my parents brought us here for Mother's Day when I was seven."

"I see why you want to stay here," I said, and I did.

The window between the driver and Chuck and us whirred down. Chuck turned and said, "You saw the media out front. There is no way they will let you explain, or believe, who you really are. If you go in there, it will be all over the news that Keith Summerland is cheating on his fiancée days before the wedding."

"What did the publicist want us to do about that?" I said, and my voice wasn't friendly when I said it.

Chuck's eyes flicked to me, then back to Jason. "If you would change hotels, we'd pay for your stay as long as you are in town."

"I can pay for my own hotel," Jason said.

"I can see that, but you see the problem from our end, right?"

Jason sighed, and settled back in the seat.

"Look," I said, "we need to check into the hotel and get to the hospital today."

"How about if we drive you to the hospital? We'll wait outside. You visit with your dad, and we'll drive you back to the airport. That way there's no confusion with the media."

The limo had stopped a little short of the front of the building, where more well-dressed valets waited. We idled at the side of the parking lot.

I stared at him. "Are you telling us to get out of town?"

"No," Chuck said, but his eyes were all on Jason.

"I'm not sure one hospital visit will do the job, Chuck," I said, getting angry and not caring that it showed.

"Mr. Schuyler," Chuck said, voice soft, almost deferential.

Jason shook his head. "No, I'm sorry; tell the governor that I don't want to be a problem. But I haven't seen my dad in three years. We're estranged, that's why he wouldn't let them tell me sooner. Now he has weeks to live and I've got to try and make up with him. He's a bastard, and always has been, and I've got a few days to try to get that Hallmark moment." He looked at Chuck. "Tell the governor I'm sorry, but one hospital visit won't get the job done."

"Will you change hotels then?" Chuck asked.

"No," Jason said, "I've earned the right to be here. Not because my daddy paid for it, but because I earned it. I'm not going to slink away because Keith Summerland is a dick. Talk to your publicist, try to figure out a way to do damage control that doesn't include me being hidden away at some cheap motel."

"You could stay with your family," Chuck said.

"No," Jason said, "I couldn't."

Chuck's eyes hardened. Just a flash of a look, but it was one I'd seen before. He had just put Jason in the problem box. A box that men like Chuck usually took care of in unpleasant ways. Maybe I was overreacting, but he just made my bad-guy radar go off too loud to ignore.

I had to repeat Chuck's name twice to get him to look at me. Even then it was a dismissive look. He, like most of the guys in college, was looking at the physical package and making assumptions.

"Chuck, let's be very clear with each other. We will do our best to stay out of your hair, and the wedding, but Jason needs to see his dad. It's bad timing that it happened on the same week as this wedding, but that is not our bad."

"You are going to give them fodder to trash Governor Summerland's family in the media."

"We'll do our best not to, but if it happens, then Summerland is paying people to do damage control. Let them do their jobs."

"She always this pushy?" Chuck asked.

I hated it when men did that. Asked the men I was with why I was such a pushy broad.

Jason laughed. "If you think this is pushy, Chuck, you have been hanging around with some weak-ass women."

The driver asked, "Do I drop them off in front of the inn or in the parking garage?"

"You won't change hotels?" Chuck asked.

"No," Jason said, "we won't." He sounded so serious, so unlike himself, that I touched his shoulder. Almost as if I was reassuring myself it was still him. He could be firm, and strong, but he usually chose not to be. I'd always known that it was a choice on Jason's part, but for the first time I was seeing just how much strength of will he hid behind that charming smile.

"Drop them off in the parking garage; it'll slow down the feeding frenzy."

The limo passed the front entrance and glided into the dimness of the parking garage. There were armed security guards making sure that no one got back there who wasn't supposed to be there. I'd never seen uniformed security at a hotel before. I wondered who was paying for it.

The driver got my door, and Chuck got Jason's side. I ignored the driver and slid out with Jason. A show of solidarity, yeah, but also that creepy feeling I had. I'd have flashed my badge at Chuck if I'd been certain seeing a federal marshal would have spooked him more. Some professional bad guys react really badly to badges of any kind.

I'd hold the whole badge thing in reserve. This was Jason's gig, not mine. My flashing my badge when I didn't need to might undermine his . . . whatever the hell he was doing.

The driver got the bags out of the trunk. Chuck said, "Can you at least not be too intimate in public so they don't get pictures of you doing the brunette?"

"She has a name," Jason said.

"I'm sorry; can you please not be up close and personal with Ms. Blake in public while you're in town?"

One of the uniformed security came close and whispered something to Chuck. "Shit," he said.

"What's wrong?" I asked.

"They've spotted a photographer hiding among the cars. I thought we were paying you guys to make sure this didn't happen."

Jason looked around, and I followed his gaze. There was a figure crouched between two midsized cars. He had a camera with a huge lens on it.

Chuck grabbed a suitcase and tried to get us moving. I was willing, but Jason took my hand. He drew me in against him. I knew what he was going to do before he did it. I said, "Are you sure this is a good idea?"

"No, it's a terrible idea." He said it just before he kissed me. He kissed me, not like he meant it. He kissed me not because he wanted to kiss me, but because it would cause trouble. I didn't like it, but I knew if I struggled that it would both smear my lipstick and maybe make him try for more of a kiss. He was in such a strange mood that I just wasn't sure how to handle him.

Chuck came and shielded us from the camera with his

broad back. To the unfamiliar guards, he said, "Get that camera." To Jason, he said, "Why?"

Jason broke from the kiss and gave the taller man a look I'd never seen before. It was a *look*: part anger, part stubbornness, part just strength and ill will. It was a look more at home on my face than Jason's.

"I don't like being told what to do, Chuck."

"Now you *do* sound like Keith."

"You have no idea how much like Keith I can be."

"I don't need the two of you fucking this week up, Schuyler."

"I am not one of the Summerlands, Chuck. You don't get paid to boss me around, so don't try."

Jason reached for my hand. I made sure he got the left one. I wanted my gun hand free just in case. Because if looks could have killed, Jason would have been a greasy spot on the pavement.

Teasing large armed men was not a healthy hobby, and I'd be talking to Jason about that when we weren't in public.

The big man's hands were flexing slowly at his sides, while I think he counted to twenty. If a camera hadn't been aimed at us, I was pretty sure we'd have seen more of Chuck's temper than just a little flexing.

The photographer was running toward the sunlight with the guards in pursuit. He was taking pictures over his shoulder the way you'd shoot a gun to slow down your attackers, but not really sure you'd hit anything. But he was aiming at Jason and me, not the guards.

"Carry your own damn bags then." Chuck said it through gritted teeth.

"Happy to," Jason said, and his voice was angry. His eyes were very blue, a rich, deep color. I realized it was the color of his eyes when he was angry.

The photographer was out of sight now, and the guards had vanished with him. Jason picked up both suitcases, got the balance of them, and headed for the door. I took the overnight case with all the guns in it and followed him. I kept an eye on Chuck as we moved up the back entrance.

He was right about one thing: Jason had deliberately put a rumor into that camera. It would hit the news before anyone thought to ask if it was some distant relative. They'd all believe it was Keith Summerland with a lover going into a hotel just five days before his wedding to someone else.

Shit.

12

WE GOT TO the room after Jason had proved with his ID that he was not a Summerland. They kept trying to check us into Keith's room. Jason got overly familiar looks from several of the female staff. One even tried to give him a note while I was holding his hand in the elevator.

We finally got to the room, tipped the bellperson, shut the door, locked it, and were alone. Jason leaned against the door.

The room was big, with two different conversation areas complete with couches and chairs. Large windows let in sunshine and a view of the mountains. There was even a four-seat table near one set of windows so you could eat and look out at the view. Big, roomy, but the décor stopped me in my tracks. The couches and chairs were all deep purple and red, but their shapes were vaguely organic. The drapes were heavy as if the sunlight were fighting to get through, and there were paintings everywhere on the walls. Most of them were modern art, which is okay, I own some, but modern art isn't meant to be plastered on like wallpaper. It was all very artsy and sort of claustrophobic.

"They call it 'the Gallery,' " Jason said. I looked at him. "Hey, it was either this or the 'Swinging '60s.' It's painted completely in pink."

"Pink?"

"Pink."

"The room's lovely," I said.

"Thank you," he said.

The bed was around the corner. There was a fainting couch near it. I sat down on the edge of the bed and took off the high heels. Maybe if I concentrated on the problem at hand, I wouldn't keep trying to figure out how many noses the picture in front of me had. "What the hell was that all about? You begged me to leave the Summerlands alone, especially Chuck, and then you tweak his tail badly."

"I know," Jason said. "It was really stupid, and petty."

"Why did you do it?"

He loosened his tie and flung himself onto his back on the bed hard enough for me to bounce a little where I was sitting. "I don't know."

"Liar," I said.

He turned his head to look at me. "What's that supposed to mean?"

"It means you have some kind of history with these people."

"They moved away when he became governor. I didn't know they'd come back here for the wedding. It must be a local girl. God, I pity her."

"Yeah, I saw how the women on staff were looking at you, like as soon as I turn my back they'll pounce."

"Keith looks like me, and I clean up well, but he's rich, and his dad's rich. There always seem to be women who want to be close to rich men."

"And now his dad is governor and about to make a run for president. I think that's adding to the Summerland appeal," I said.

Jason nodded, then sat up. He leaned his elbows on his knees and held his head. "I should not have posed for the cameras like that. That was childish, but the twins were the bane of my childhood. We were always getting mistaken for each other, by teachers, girls, guys, strangers. Keith would deliberately do shit and get me blamed. He did the same thing to his brother, too, so I wasn't so special there."

"Kelsey, right, the brother?"

"Yeah."

"Is the brother any nicer?"

"Kelsey was in some of the plays with me. He was quieter, a little shy. As awkward with the girls as Keith was smooth."

"Sounds like you like Kelsey."

"I would have, if he hadn't been a Summerland and Keith's brother. You couldn't be friends with Kelsey unless Keith allowed it, and he hated me."

"Why?"

"I got a few girls who had turned him down. I mean they turned him down, then slept with me, Anita. Think about that."

I did. "They turned him down not because he wasn't cute, but because he personally was an asshole."

"Yeah, and all his daddy's money couldn't buy him the girls who knew what he really was."

Jason got up and went to the mirror, started straightening his tie. "I went to college in St. Louis, and he stayed near the state capital. But I heard rumors that he had a couple of date-rape charges. Dropped, never saw court, but I'd believe date rape for Keith. He never took *no* very well."

"And his father is making a run to be president on a family conservative ticket," I said.

"That's probably why they're in such a rush to get him married off."

"Marriage doesn't cure you of being a bastard," I said.

He grinned at me. "Nothing cures you of being a bastard." He came to me and held his hand out. I took it and let him get me on my feet. "Let's go to the hospital."

"I thought we might eat first."

He shook his head. "If we start taking off more clothes for comfort I'm going to want sex, and as you pointed out we'll get all messy. I desperately don't want to go to see him. So that means go now, get it over with."

"I thought I was the jerk-the-bandage-off type, not you."

"Maybe years of watching you be brave is rubbing off on me."

I was sort of embarrassed. "I'm not that brave. I nearly threw up on the plane."

"Before I knew you, I thought brave was not being afraid. You've taught me that bravery is being terrified and doing it anyway." He drew me closer into his arms, and because of the nearly identical height it had that intimacy that Micah could do. When you aren't looking *up*, really, but *at* a man.

I studied his face, tried to see the fear he was talking about. "I see more anger in you than fear, Jason."

"You're going to ignore the compliment and go straight to the business, aren't you?"

I shrugged, a little awkwardly, with my arms around his waist and his around me.

He closed the almost invisible distance we'd been keeping

between our bodies, so we touched from chest to groin and thigh. The closeness made me both uncomfortable and more comfortable. It felt good, and bothered me that it felt good. I never said I wasn't conflicted about my sexuality. What helped it not be that sexual was Jason's attitude. He'd gotten closer to comfort himself, not to start foreplay.

Jason gave a smile that was more a baring of teeth. "Yeah, I'm pissed. I'm pissed that the Summerlands ruined my childhood and now are going to ruin my last visit with my dad. I'm pissed at my dad. Pissed that he wouldn't let my mom call me sooner. Hell, I'm pissed at my mom for not calling me sooner, or my sisters. They could have called me, but they all sat around waiting for the big bully to give them permission."

"Is he really a bully, or are you just pissed?"

Jason hugged me, burying his face in my hair, as if to breathe me in. "You'll meet him in a little bit. Judge for yourself. I've hated him and tried to love him for so many years I can't see him clearly."

I hugged him back, then said, "Let me put the heels back on. Do we call a cab?"

"Yeah," he said, and reached for the phone.

13

THE TAXI COULDN'T get out of the drive in front of the hotel unless the driver was willing to run over members of the press. That would probably qualify as some sort of First Amendment violation, and I'm all about defending the Constitution. Besides, manslaughter sucks, too.

The driver turned around. "I can't get through, Mr. Summerland, I'm sorry."

"My name is—oh hell!" Jason stared at the crowd that had descended from the road to surround us. Where were the valets who had been at the road earlier? Cameras were exploding everywhere. Reporters shouting questions. "Who is she? Did you break up with Lisa? Is the wedding off?"

"Shit," he said softly, but with feeling.

The windows were covered by people and cameras. It was suddenly hard to breathe. I forced myself to breathe slow and even, but the press of people around the cab was claustrophobic. Fuck.

Finally uniformed security and the spiffily dressed valets appeared in the crowd of press. They began to push them back, an inch at a time. The cab tried to ease forward, but even with the guards and valets we were stopped.

The cabbie turned around and looked at us. "You want to just give up?"

"I think we're going to have to," Jason said.

I looked out in time to see a guard and a photographer get into a pushing match.

"I can't get through this," the cabbie said.

Jason looked at me. "If I hadn't done the kiss in the alley I'd say fuck them, but it's my fault."

I just looked at him. I mean, what was I supposed to say? He'd wanted to cause a scandal, and he'd succeeded.

A uniformed security person knocked on the window. Jason opened it a crack. The man said, "I think you should come back inside, Mr. Summerland. We need more people to guarantee your safety, and they're going to follow you wherever you go. It's not safe."

"What do you want us to do?"

Another guard pushed in against the window; he stumbled as if he was being shoved from behind. "We can't clear the road enough for the taxi to move, unless we start busting heads."

"We don't have permission for that," the first guard said. That seemed to imply that with permission they would have happily waded into the press. What kind of guards were they?

"We're going to force them back, and then you get out of the taxi. There's enough of us to form a circle around you both. Stay in the center and it'll be fine." His mouth was saying *fine*, but his eyes weren't as certain.

I leaned around Jason. "We'll be stampeded."

"No, ma'am, we'll protect you. It's our job."

"He'll keep us safe," Jason said, "because otherwise the governor will be very, very unhappy with him. With all of them. Isn't that right?"

The uniformed guard licked his lips. His eyes actually showed too much white. He was well and truly scared. Either his nerve was weak, or Governor Summerland was scarier than your average politician. Or maybe it was the whole lose-your-job thing; yeah, that might do it.

"Yes, sir," he said.

He turned and started shouting orders to the other uniforms.

"You spooked him on purpose," I said.

"I did."

"Why?"

He motioned at the mob they were pushing back. "The guard was right; unless we're willing to get rough, we could get hurt. I don't want to take another beating for Keith."

They pushed them back, like a weird version of a football scrimmage line, except with cameras and microphones. The reporters were shouting at us, at the guards, at each other, so that it was noise like a storm, so all the sounds combined into one roar of unintelligible noise.

When there was room, the nervous guard opened the door for Jason. I wasn't sure it was a good idea, but I didn't have a better one. He got out and helped me out of the cab.

I thought we would go blind from the flashes before we'd moved two feet. I clung to Jason's hand, trying to shield my vision and wondering what the hell I'd done with my sunglasses. If I'd ever needed them, it was now.

There were cries of "Keith, Keith!"

Jason waited for a little lull in the murmurous noise. He spoke loud and clear, "My name is Jason Schuyler."

They didn't believe him. They said so. They also pressed in on the circle of men protecting us. We came to a standstill on the sloping driveway. The guards and valets kept them back but couldn't move forward.

Jason shouted this time, "My name is Jason Schuyler. Who wants proof?" He got out his wallet. "Who wants to put my driver's license on camera?"

There was a lot of jostling for that, and while they argued over who got it, I whispered, "Cover your number and address."

He nodded, and changed his hands around so only his picture and state were visible. The lucky winner got to come forward with a camera and a crew, and filmed the license. The guards actually let them through, but the rest were more patient now, waiting their turn or hoping for blood. The talking head who came with the camera shoved a mic in Jason's face.

"If you really are this Jason Schuyler, then why do you look so much like the Summerland boys?"

"We were always getting confused by people in school. You can see why."

"You could be triplets," she said.

He nodded, sort of grimly. "I'm home to visit my family, which has nothing to do with the Summerland wedding. I just need everyone to let me have some room to visit my folks."

"What brings you home?"

He looked at me. I shrugged. "My father is dying of cancer. He doesn't have long. I'd ask that everyone give us some space to say good-bye."

"And who is your father?"

"If I tell you, are you guys going to bug him in the hospital?"

"We'd love your family's take on having a son who looks so much like the famous Summerland twins."

"My dad is dying. He has weeks. Please, I'm begging you, don't torment him. Please."

Someone yelled from the crowd, "Who's the brunette?"

Jason stepped back and I was suddenly on mic. "I'm Anita Blake."

"Who are you to the Summerlands?"

"No one to them; other than knowing of Governor Summerland I'd never heard of his family until today. I'm Jason Schuyler's . . . good friend." There, the first awkward pause. I was betting it wouldn't be the last one.

Jason put his hands on my shoulders from where he stood beside me. The flashes intensified.

Another voice yelled out, "Hey, you're Jean-Claude's Anita Blake, aren't you?"

Jean-Claude's Anita Blake; not federal marshal Anita Blake, not the vampire executioner Anita Blake; no, I was just Jean-Claude's girlfriend. Great.

"Yes," I said. Who was I to quibble?

"Oh, my God, you're Ripley!" A woman's voice from the crowd. Ripley was the name Jason stripped under. Yes, he had chosen his stage name because of the movie *Alien*. When I'd asked him why, he'd replied, "Sigourney Weaver is so hot." His more ardent fans called him Rip for short. He had a fan among the press. That was going to be either good, or really bad.

Other voices asked the reporter, "Who's Ripley?"

Jason leaned over my shoulders to say, loud enough for other mics to pick it up, "Ripley is the name I strip under at Jean-Claude's club in St. Louis, Guilty Pleasures."

A shiver went through the collected press, almost as if they were one beast with a single skin that had just been touched by a giant hand.

The press let the woman who seemed to know who we were come to the forefront; she had better questions. "Anita, you are Jean-Claude's girlfriend, right?"

"Yeah," I said, again, not really happy that all my own accomplishments had been boiled down to being someone's—anyone's—girlfriend.

"Then what are you doing here with Ripley, I mean Jason?"

"Jason told you that his father is gravely ill, that's true. He's coming home to say good-bye, and I'm with him for moral support."

"Oh, my God," she said, "you've come home to meet his family. You've left Jean-Claude for one of his strippers."

Holy shit. "No," I said, "I mean, it's not what you think, it's . . ."

But it was too late. Another kind of feeding frenzy had begun. It was simply out of our control, like some force of nature.

The reporters started yelling answers to each other's questions, as if they were questions for us, but the answers they were giving were actually drowning out ours. It was one of the most bizarre experiences. It was a hurricane of rumors, and there was no stopping it.

Chuck appeared with the plainclothes guards, and I was happy to see all of them, even Chuck. They got us out of the press, down the driveway, and inside the hotel. I couldn't even argue. The taxi wasn't going anywhere.

14

WE ENDED UP in a spacious room just off the main lobby that was filled with chairs and had a podium. I think this was the place where the tamer press events happened.

There was a woman in one of the chairs. She wasn't that tall, but she managed to be leggy in spike heels and a killer designer suit. Her auburn hair was in a tight bun that left her perfect makeup and overly dramatic eyes suitably noticeable.

"No more talking to the press unless you clear it through me," she said.

"I am not one of the Summerlands," Jason said, and he sounded tired. I didn't blame him.

"He fell on his sword out there for us, Dubois," one of the other suits said. This one was older, his gray suit only a little darker than his hair. His face was lined, but it was a good face. If he'd dyed the hair he wouldn't have looked his age. A different suit would have helped, too. Gray wasn't his color.

She gave one abrupt nod. "He did give them something else

to chew on, I'll grant that. But the little kiss in the alley was childish."

"I know that," Jason said, "but Chuck here had bossed me around, and I'm not Keith. I don't need the babysitting."

"After that kiss and the impromptu press conference, the hell you don't," she said.

"Are all press agents this pleasant?" I asked.

She gave me an angry look. "And you"—pointing a long painted nail at me—"are not helping."

"I'm a federal marshal and a vampire executioner. I also raise the dead for a living. But all the press cared about was my boyfriends. But I didn't argue with the reporters. I let them ask sex questions and didn't get mad on camera. I think I behaved myself admirably."

Jason hugged me one-armed. "You really did control your temper. I'm very proud of you."

I gave him a look that made Ms. Dubois's look seem tame. He winced, but he didn't mean it.

"Frankly," I said, "I was too surprised to know what to do. I've done some press with Jean-Claude, but nothing like this."

Dubois seemed to have gotten over her snit, because she offered me her hand. Me, not Jason. It earned her a brownie point or two. "I'm Phyllis Dubois, press secretary on site for the wedding week."

I took her hand. She had a good firm shake for a woman, but then so did I. "I'm Anita Blake, and I guess all I am today is Jason's girlfriend."

"Jean-Claude is that sexy master vampire of St. Louis, right?" she said.

I nodded.

"Did you leave him for Jason?"

I gave her an unfriendly look. "Don't you start."

She smiled and it made her face younger, more in tune with the nearly club makeup. "Sorry, but if it were true it might help us deflect some of the heat from our boys."

"You'd blow the story up even more so they'd feed on us," I said.

She shrugged narrow but elegant shoulders. "My job."

"How do I get to the hospital to see my dad?" Jason asked.

"We'll put you in a limo, and if we have to we'll get you a police escort," Dubois said.

"Why?" Jason said, unusually suspicious for him.

I answered it, "Because a limo with a police escort will draw off part of the press that is hanging around for the bachelorette party tonight."

"You really do think I'm going to throw you to the wolves, don't you?"

"Oh, I like wolves," I said, "it's the reporters that scare me."

Gray Suit said, "I don't think there's any way to get you quietly to the hospital. In fact, we should send people ahead to warn the hospital so the reporters don't get into Mr. Schuyler's room."

"Good thinking, Peterson, as always. Call our liaison at the hospital."

Peterson, aka Gray Suit, took out a cell phone and went toward one side of the room. Apparently for some privacy for the call.

Another phone sounded. Dubois got a slim one out of her pocket and started talking into it.

Chuck said, "You're a federal marshal, for real?"

"For real," I said.

He looked me up and down, not like a man will, but like he was sizing me up for other things. Things that had nothing to do with sex.

"You've got a gun at the small of your back. It's lying sideways, not up and down, so it's almost invisible."

I nodded. "And you missed it completely when we first met."

"My bad," he said.

"Sloppy," I said.

"It won't happen again."

"What won't happen again?"

"Me thinking you're just a . . . girlfriend."

"You always hesitate before you say *girlfriend*, Chuck; what do you actually start to say?"

"You won't like it."

"I'm betting I already know the phrase that's on the tip of your tongue, Chuck."

Jason was watching us, the way he did sometimes when people were doing something that interested him or puzzled him. He'd watch, file it away, and talk to me about it later. Sometimes much later.

Chuck glanced around, and when he realized that both Dubois and Peterson weren't in earshot, he said low, "Piece of ass, I won't make the mistake of thinking you're just a piece of ass."

I nodded. "Yeah, that's what I thought you were thinking."

15

WE ARRIVED AT the hospital in a style that even Jean-Claude couldn't have managed. The city wouldn't have given him a police escort unless he was being arrested. But we got one to St. Joseph's Hospital, with its nearly brand-new trauma unit. The trauma unit was in the Summerland wing of the hospital. I smelled an amazingly large donation.

It took us awhile to get past the upper brass of the hospital, who had spilled out to the sound of sirens and the limo. Hell, we had some of the suits with us. Peterson was in charge instead of Chuck, which was a step up, but it was still an understandable mistake on the hospital administration's part. If someone had given me enough money to put a wing on my hospital I'd be nice to them, too.

In the lobby, while we were trying to explain that Jason was neither of the Summerland twins, I saw a portrait. It was an old-fashioned painting of a man in a black cloth suit, white shirt, stiff collar, and dark yellow mustache.

But underneath the strange clothes and facial hair, it was Jason's face.

I actually walked toward the portrait without meaning to. Jason's blue eyes stared down at me from this stern-faced stranger.

Jason came to stand beside me. I looked from him to the painting. "Creepy, isn't it?" he said.

"It could be you in a few years, if you did the mustache."

"Meet Jedediah Summerland. He was the head of the religious community that came here to get away from the worldly temptations. He was a very self-righteous guy, but strangely a lot of families that trace their ancestors back to when he was alive have a lot of kids that look eerily like him."

"A lot of cult leaders seem to have a weakness for women," I said.

He nodded, then smiled, though it left his eyes empty. "Jedediah was actually killed by vampires. Apparently he tried to convert them to the Lord, and they didn't like it. Frankly, I think he tried to seduce the wrong undead lady and paid the price."

He turned to me, not with a smile, but with something in his eyes that I couldn't quite read.

"What?" I asked.

"I guess getting hooked up with vampires runs in the family." He turned away, keeping his face to himself so that whatever he was thinking, I couldn't see it.

I looked at the face on the wall. It was Jason's face, but if the artist had captured Jedediah correctly, then there was no humor in the eyes, no smile always tugging at the corner of that mouth. Same face, but a very different person.

Peterson came up beside us. He gazed up at the portrait,

too. "The family resemblance is almost disturbing, if you don't mind my saying so."

"I don't mind," Jason said.

"I've cleared the way for you to see your father, Mr. Schuyler. I'll accompany you up with a second man. The hospital staff have already caught two reporters trying to sneak upstairs. I've asked them to treat your father's privacy as they would the governor's. I think that should keep the press away."

"Thank you," Jason said. He was still looking at the painting when he said it. He turned and gave Peterson a grin. It filled his eyes with laughter, and changed the face to . . . Jason's face.

Peterson looked almost startled, then smiled back. Jason had that effect on people.

Jason reached for my hand, and I helped him find it. The smile faded around the edges, and his eyes looked almost as stern as the ones in the portrait. "Let's get this over with."

We went for the elevator, but there was already a suit holding the door, and the admin for the hospital. Apparently, she was going to ride up with us. The rich and powerful really are different, or at least they're treated better.

Jason's hand was a little warm to the touch, not sweat, just nerves. He was a lycanthrope, which meant that nerves could bring on the change. He had control, really good control, but his body temperature was rising with his anxiety. That wasn't good.

For the first time I wondered what would happen if Jason shifted in front of his family. Surely they knew he was a werewolf. Didn't they?

The media would know once they checked the website for Guilty Pleasures. It listed not just the usual stats for strippers but if they were vampires, or wereanimals, and what animal you could watch them shift into. If the media stayed interested enough in the story, they'd out him.

The nice admin was talking to Jason, who was making small noises at her and not hearing a thing. I actually looked across him to her and said, "It's very nice of you to help his father like this."

"Any friend of the governor's is a very special guest of ours," she said, smiling.

Jason said in a voice bitter enough to hurt, "My father isn't a friend of the governor's."

The woman looked at me, then at Peterson. "I thought . . ."

"The governor felt that since Mr. Schuyler's resemblance to his own sons was the problem with the media, the least we could do was make certain his father's last days weren't hounded by the press."

"The resemblance is uncanny," she said. "Even standing this close to you I'd swear you were one of the governor's sons."

"Jedediah was a busy boy," Jason said, softly.

"Excuse me?" she said.

Jason shook his head. "Nothing."

I tried small talk, never my best thing. How long could the elevator ride be? "Jason didn't know the twins would be in town, so the press caught us off guard. With the wedding and everything, it got wild. I don't envy the real Summerlands if this is typical for the way they're treated by the press."

"It's gotten worse since the presidential bid," the other, younger suit said.

Peterson gave him a look. The look said clearly, *Don't talk*. The younger suit stopped talking and did his best to both stand very straight and ready and vanish into the corner. Not easy to do at the same time, but he tried.

"Of course, of course," the admin said.

The doors opened, and we got to step out into a hospital corridor. No matter how nice the hospital, it is still a hospital. They'd chosen nice paint, a color that was actually cheerful, but the smells hit you—that antiseptic smell they use to try to hide the smell of sickness, the smell of death. The only corridors that don't smell like this are maternity wards. It's almost as if death truly has a smell, and so does life. You can't fool the difference with cleaning solution. The nose knows, and so does the part of the brain that doesn't understand elevators and presidential bids. That part of the brain that's been hopping around with us humans since we weren't sure walking upright wasn't just another fad.

Jason stopped dead in the hallway. His hand clenched around mine. I realized if I could smell that, it would be a hundred times stronger to his nose. Even in human form the wereanimals could smell things humans couldn't.

The admin stopped and turned. "Your father's room is just down this way." She actually motioned as if she were directing us to anywhere. I guess she worked here every day. Maybe you don't smell it after awhile, or feel it.

Jason squeezed my hand again, gave me a watered-down version of his smile, and nodded. We moved, we followed, we went where she pointed. Jason's hand was hot against my skin.

16

A WOMAN APPEARED in the corridor just ahead of the admin. The woman wore a soft pink suit and had short blond hair. She was about our height. She turned toward us, and the moment I saw her face I knew she had to be Jason's mom. The same eyes and hair; the face was different, thinner; a little more pointed chin, but the eyes were like looking into Jason's eyes. But just like the painting downstairs had filled those eyes with disapproval, her eyes were filled with worry.

She saw Jason, and her face lightened for a moment. Her eyes flicked to me, there was a moment of doubt in her face, and then she came toward us smiling, arms out, but her eyes never quite lost the thought, the clear thought, *Is this a good idea?* I hoped his mother never played poker, because she would have sucked at it.

He let go of my hand long enough to hug her. She wrapped her arms around him, her hand patting the back of his hair as she broke away from him. She tugged at his suit, putting it back in place as if she'd mussed him.

"You look good," she said.

Jason nodded, and reached back for me. I came to his hand. "This is Anita Blake. Anita, this is my mom, Iris."

I shook Iris Schuyler's hand. It was about the same size as mine. Her handshake was a bare touch, then away, as if she didn't shake hands much.

"I'm being silly," she said, and she hugged me. I fought not to be stiff in the embrace. I don't like being touched by strangers. I also wondered if she'd find the gun, but luckily she hugged like she shook hands: barely. It was a nice awkward hug on both sides. I did my best, and found the suit loose on her frame, as if she'd lost a lot of weight recently.

"It's nice to meet you, Mrs. Schuyler," I said, as I got to go back to Jason. Unlike his mom, I could lie with the best of them.

"Iris, please, call me Iris."

"Then you have to call me Anita," I said.

"Anita," she said, and she touched me again, on the arm.

I managed to keep my smile, but it was a little strained. God, was his family one of those touchy families? Richard's family was like that. I'd made peace with the fact that Richard's mother would hug me, and touch me, but I never liked it. The men behaved better because of the whole sexual taboo thing. But Richard's mother and his sister were both touchers. Eeeh.

Jason put his arm around my waist and drew me tight in against him. Either he'd picked up my discomfort or his own had gotten worse. Either way, I was okay with it. Jason had permission to touch me.

Jason's mother took his free hand and led us toward the

room she'd come out of. I didn't like her leading him by the hand like a child. But I let it go; one, I wasn't really his girlfriend-girlfriend, and two, her husband was dying, so maybe she'd earned the right to hold her son's hand.

A woman whose hair was almost as black as my own came out of the room. She was tall and broad-shouldered, but still gave the impression of delicacy of bone. She wore jeans and a T-shirt with some sort of slogan on it. She saw us and gave a glad cry of "Jason!"

The next thing I knew, she and Jason were hugging. She damn near smothered him in a nice chest. The height difference was considerable, with her on the tall end.

Jason drew back enough to say, "Anita, this is my sister Julia."

Sister? No one in my family hugged their brother like that. Then I got a Julia hug, and realized it wasn't the least bit sexual. She was just one of those enthusiastic huggers. I was the same height as Jason, so I had more proof than I wanted that she was about as well-endowed as I was. Dear God, even Richard's family wasn't this touchy-feely.

Jason laughed and rescued me. "Let her breathe, sis."

Julia backed off, but kept an arm around my shoulders. "It's just so good to see you, little brother. And I don't think you'd have brought a girl home if it wasn't serious." She hugged me again, a little less furiously, but still I was really wondering how to get away from her.

Her shirt said *Browning and Schuyler Gardening Center* with a few plants done in line art. The shirt was a shade of yellow that most people couldn't have worn, but it looked fine with her coloring, and great with her summer tan. It looked like she'd tan almost as dark as Richard's family, and they had American Indian in their background.

I wondered if Julia was a half-sister.

"You run the gardening center?" I asked, hoping to distract her from the hugging.

"Me and my hubby, Brian. He's minding the store so I could come visit Dad." The sunshine faded a little from her big brown eyes. It was like watching a flower sag from lack of water; you just knew if some good news came soon she'd perk back up.

"Let—Anita—go—sis." Jason said it laughing. He took my hand and drew me away from his sister.

She flashed him a grin. I knew that grin. It was a totally different face, but the grin, that was Jason's.

I slid an arm around Jason's familiar waist with a sense of relief. Strangers hugging me. Aah.

"Hello, Jason." A woman who looked too much like Julia not to be another sister stood in the doorway. She was wearing a navy business skirt suit with a white shell. Sort of a more conservative version of what I was wearing. I was betting she wasn't wearing a gun under hers, though.

"Roberta, hi. This is Anita." He led me forward, and she moved to meet us. I tensed for another hug, but she offered a hand instead.

She had a firm, but not too firm handshake. It felt like she shook hands a lot. I gave her a smile, grateful she hadn't touched me more.

Conservative but nice makeup brought out the brown eyes that dominated her face. It was her best feature. Where Julia had a delicacy to her height, Roberta was tall. The bones of her face were too square for beauty. She'd done well with the makeup to sort of carve out the face she wanted you to see. She was attractive, but it was an almost masculine beauty, for lack of a better word.

Where Julia's hair had been carelessly cut just above her shoulders, Roberta's was carefully styled past her shoulders.

"Are you really his girlfriend?" she asked me.

I let myself look startled. "Why would you ask that?"

Iris came up, touching Roberta's arm. "You're being rude."

"No, I don't want Dad upset." She turned those eyes back to me. "Are you really Jason's girlfriend, or just someone he brought here because Mom panicked?"

I looked at Jason. I was trying to figure out how to answer this question and not lie. I guess I simply hadn't expected anyone to be this bold about it. "You in the habit of bringing girls home who aren't your girlfriend?"

"I brought home a few fuck buddies, but other than that, no."

"Jason," his mother said, in that tone that mothers have that lets you know you've been naughty.

"Why are you being mean, Bobbi?" Julia asked.

"My name is Roberta," she said, as if she had to say it a lot, "and I'm not being mean. I just want to be clear. Dad will know if you're lying, Jason, and that will bother him more than the truth."

The admin shook some hands and made herself scarce, going for the elevator. Peterson and the suit took up posts in the hallway. The young suit looked like he'd rather have taken the elevator with the admin. Peterson gave great blank face; all in a day's work.

Roberta's dark eyes glanced at the men, then back to Jason. "You finally have your own guards, just like the rest of the Summerlands."

"Roberta." Iris said it like she meant it. That one word cracked into the sudden silence with more force than I thought

Mrs. Schuyler had in her. Under that delicate exterior there were tougher bits. Good to know.

Roberta gave her mother a look almost as angry as the one she was flashing at Jason. I was beginning to think Roberta just wanted to be pissed at someone, anyone. Sometimes grief will do that to you, make you attack random targets.

"Tell Dad the truth, Jason," she said in a softer, but still tight voice.

"And what is the truth, Roberta?" he asked, and his voice was flat and unfriendly. I don't know if I'd ever heard him sound quite like that. No love lost between him and this sister.

"You're gay, Jason."

He laughed, but not like it was funny. "You and Dad have believed that since high school. I don't know why, but you have. Mom says come home; bring a girlfriend if you've got one, so your father can die in peace. Can't let him die thinking his only son is a faggot, can we?"

"He'd rather you just admit it."

I raised a hand. "Can I say something here?"

Jason said, "Yes." She said, "No."

"Yes," Jason said more vehemently.

"I'm his very good friend, Roberta. Your mother called him yesterday. I dropped everything to get on a plane and come out here with Jason. I wouldn't do that if he wasn't important to me."

She gave me a look of damn near rage. I had no idea where this anger was coming from. "He always had a lot of fag-hag girlfriends."

Iris and Julia both said, "Roberta!"

I stared at her openmouthed for a second.

"Thanks, Bobbi, love you as much as you love me," Jason said.

She turned that rage-filled gaze to Jason. "I know you slept with girls in high school, but you slept with boys, too. That makes you gay, Jason."

"Technically, that would make me bisexual, Bobbi. Would you or Dad tell me why you are convinced I slept with guys in high school?"

"I saw you."

"One night, you think you saw me, and you told Dad, who always thought I was gay anyway. I told you then and I'll tell you now, I wasn't there. I don't know what or who you think you saw, but I was with someone else."

"Who? Just tell me who, and maybe I'll believe you."

"I promised her no one would ever know, and I keep my word."

"Isn't that convenient. I know what I saw."

Jason's hand started rubbing back and forth on my hip, gently. He was doing it to comfort himself, like all the lycanthropes do. The Browning at the small of my back forced him to put his hand low enough to touch my hip. My waist was used up with the hardware.

"Touch her all you want in public, it doesn't change the truth."

"Look," I said, "I don't know what family problem I've walked into, but Jason and I are lovers."

"And how many men are you sharing him with?"

"None," I said.

She gave Jason a withering look. "You've got her fooled."

Julia got between them at that point. "Bobbi, stop it. I know you're hurt about Dad, but hurting Jason won't save him."

Roberta looked away from us. She shook her head. "I've got to get out of here." She went, not for the elevator, but down the hallway. We watched her walk around the corner out of sight.

"I am so sorry, Anita," Iris said.

Julia hugged Jason. "I believe she's your girlfriend."

"Thanks, but I'm betting that Dad will agree with Bobbi."

Julia hugged him a little tighter, but her face showed the same thought. Julia, like her mother, I'd have played poker with any day of the week. Roberta, I wasn't sure about yet.

A deep voice came from the open door. "If you're going to fight, do it where I can see it."

Jason sighed and leaned in against me. He put his face against my neck. He breathed in the scent of my skin, the way you get a last breath of oxygen before diving into the depths.

Iris went ahead of us, saying, "Frank, be nice."

I was betting that Bobbi took after her father. Fun, fun, fun.

17

FRANK SCHUYLER TOOK up most of the bed, so that his feet were sort of stranded over the edge of it, as if they hadn't been able to find anything big enough to fit him. Even lying down he was obviously over six feet. But the cancer had left him almost nothing but the height. The strong bones of his face that had shown in Roberta's face were prominent in the way that skeletons are. His eyes were deep sunken brown caves. He still had a head full of black hair and a mustache just as dark. Apparently, either he'd refused chemo or they hadn't found the cancer in time for it to be worthwhile.

He was hooked up to tubes in his arms and nose. The smell of death was heavy, but not worse than the corridor. Whatever was killing him hadn't taken all his dignity with it, not yet at least.

"Jason's come to visit, and he brought his girlfriend, isn't that nice?" Iris tried for happy, but it came out strained.

"Hi, Dad," Jason said in a flat voice.

"Why did you come?" his father asked.

Jason took a stronger grip on my hand. "Mom asked me to come." His voice was still careful.

"You don't have to hold the girl so tight," the man in the bed said, in a voice that was so deep it was almost painful to hear. "You don't have to pretend for me, Jason." His voice was a lot less hostile than his eyes. Maybe he just couldn't help the eyes.

Jason let go of my hand and put his arm around my waist, one hand on my hip below the gun. I played my hand back and forth on his side underneath his jacket, trying to give what comfort I could.

"I'll hold Anita any way I like."

"Roberta's right, boy, you can touch the girl all you want in public. It's what you do in private that matters."

"What do you think I'll be doing in private that I don't do in public . . . Dad?" Jason asked, softly.

"Your mother told you to bring a girl home so I could die happy thinking my only son wasn't a—" He stopped as if he wasn't sure what word to end the sentence with.

"A what?" Jason said, still soft, but with an edge of anger to it. His otherworldly energy was beginning to creep along my skin where I touched him. Not good.

"A fruit," Frank said.

"A fruit," I said, and fought not to laugh. It was just one of those moments when the tension gets too high and you want to laugh.

He looked at me as if I'd just appeared. "Sorry," I said.

"You think it's funny that my wife told him to bring you and lie to me. To lie to me on my deathbed, you think that's funny?"

I bumped my head against Jason. "What do you want me to do?"

"Be yourself."

I moved away enough to look at him. "You sure?"

He smiled. "Positive."

I shrugged, still with my arm around him. I looked back to the man in the bed. I tried to think of a polite way to begin. "I think it's funny that you think Jason is gay."

"You hanging all over him doesn't change that he's a homo."

"Fruit, homo, can't you even say *homosexual*?"

"You like that word better, girlie, fine. He's a homosexual."

His mother had moved closer to the bed, but not to it. She was hovering somewhere between her husband and her son. I got the feeling that she'd spent a lot of Jason's life caught like that.

"I think I'm in a better position to know what Jason's sexual preferences are than you are, Mr. Schuyler." There, that had been polite.

"Dad," Julia said from near the door, "Jason brought Anita here to meet you, doesn't that say something?"

"It says she'll lie for him."

Jason moved away enough to just have my hand. He drew me toward the door. "Let's go, Anita."

"No," Iris said, grabbing his other hand.

"Dad," Julia said, "he came all this way. Both of them left work and everything to come here. Be nice."

"I'm dying, Julia, I don't have time to be nice. I want my son to be a man, and he's not going to be."

Jason's shoulders rounded as if he'd been struck a blow. That was it, the last straw. This camel wasn't taking any more crap from anyone, not even the dying.

I kept Jason's hand, but turned toward the bed. "Jason is a better man than you are, Mr. Schuyler."

Those cavernous eyes glared at me. "What's that supposed to mean?"

"It means that a man is courteous. A real man is kind. A real man loves his family and treats them like human beings."

"I'm dying, I've earned the right to be a son of a bitch."

"I bet you've always been a cruel bastard."

A look I couldn't read came over his face. "*I'm* not the bastard."

"Oh, I think you are. So you're dying, so fucking what? We're all dying, Mr. Schuyler, you just know the checkout time and how much the bill will be."

"Get your little chippie friend out of here. Putting a cross around her neck doesn't change what she is," he said.

Jason's hand tensed on mine, drawing me back a little. I must have moved toward the bed without realizing it. I'd been told wearing my cross was wrong because I raised the dead, but never because I was a whore. It was a new insult. I didn't like it much.

"You should not have said that," Jason said.

"Does *chippie* mean what I think it means?" I asked.

"Yeah, he called you a whore," Jason said. I couldn't read his tone, but it wasn't angry exactly, more shocked, as if even for his father it had been too much.

Julia and Iris were standing openmouthed, as if they too were too shocked to know what to say.

"Franklin," Mrs. Schuyler said, finally, in a breathy, uncertain voice.

"Stripper is just one step up from whore," he said, totally unrepentant.

"So now I'm a homo and a whore," Jason said. He didn't sound angry, more like tired.

"If the shoe fits," his father said.

"Franklin, don't do this."

"You told him to lie to me, Iris. You told him to bring his little stripper friend, so I'd die in peace. He's a fucking fairy and fucking coffin bait to boot."

Jason turned away; the otherworldly energy just stopped, as if he'd put up some big shield that cut off everything. The furry energy, the emotion, all of it. He shut down.

I held his hand, kept him in the room. "If you walk out of this room, that's going to be it."

"I know," he said softly.

"If it's over, can we go out with a bang instead of a whimper?"

He looked at me, studying my face. Then he nodded. "Why not?"

I smiled at him, and knew it was *that* smile, most unpleasant. The one that used to scare me in the mirror, but I'd gotten used to it. I knew it was in there now. I turned it on the bed and the man in it.

"Some of my best friends are strippers, Mr. Schuyler, people I love, even. So that's not the insult you want it to be. I'm Federal Marshal Anita Blake." I let go of Jason's hand so I could get my badge out of my pocket with my left hand. I moved close enough to the bed for him to see it.

"I don't believe it."

I put the badge back and slipped off the left sleeve of my jacket so I could show him the worst of my scars from my job. "The scar tissue at the bend is where a vampire gnawed at me. The doctors thought I might lose the use of my arm. The cross-shaped burn is from some human servants who thought it would be funny for a vampire hunter to have a scar like a vampire. The claw marks were from a shapeshifted witch."

"So you're one of the federal marshals who hunt vampires."

"Yeah, I am."

"You know he's fucking the master vampire of St. Louis."

"Actually, I know he isn't. Jean-Claude gets a lot of people thinking he's sleeping with anyone who's seen with him in public. One of the downsides of being a beautiful man, I guess."

Those deep brown caves of eyes stared up at me. "You telling me he doesn't give him blood?"

"I thought we were talking about sex."

"Same thing."

"If you think taking blood is the same thing as sex, Mr. Schuyler, then you're the pervert, not either of us."

Iris said, "Anita!" as if she were my mom and that tone had ever worked on me.

He said, "No, no, don't stop her, I started it." He gazed up at me. "But you'll finish it, won't you?"

"You damn bet I will," I said.

He smiled, just a little one. "You're really my boy's girlfriend?"

"What do I have to do to prove to you and his other sister that we're dating? We're lovers and we're friends, so I guess that makes me his girlfriend. The word just sounds a little too junior high, don't you think?"

He smiled again. "I guess it does." He reached out as if to touch the scars, then hesitated. He wasn't the first to want to touch them. I moved closer so he could.

His fingertips were very rough, as if his day job had been something with his hands. There was a gasp behind me. I turned and found Mrs. Schuyler with her hand to her mouth and her eyes a little surprised.

Jason moved up to lift my jacket into place. "She saw the gun."

"Gun?" Julia asked.

Jason helped me on with my jacket, and the scars were invisible again. Well, except for the one in the palm of my right hand. It's a smaller cross-shaped burn scar. That one I got because a very big and bad vampire was trying to possess me and someone shoved a cross into my hand. The vampire hadn't given up until the cross had sunk into my flesh.

"I don't go anywhere unarmed," I said quietly.

Jason kissed my cheek, and I moved back to stand with him. "I'll take Anita back to the hotel. We'll leave in the morning."

"Stay a day, or two." His father said it, flat, almost no emotion. But the two other women in the room all tensed, as if that one small statement meant more than you'd think.

Jason put his face next to my neck and breathed in the scent of my skin again, as if he needed another hit. I felt him use that touch and scent to help his voice be calm when he said, "We won't leave tomorrow, but beyond that I'll have to see. We both have jobs."

"I'll see you tomorrow," his father said.

Jason nodded. "I guess you will."

We went for the door. His father said, "Glad to see you cut your hair."

Jason looked back, and it was not a friendly look. "If I'd known I'd be coming home, I'd have started growing it out again."

"Because you know I like it short."

"No, because you think when it's long I look too pretty to be a boy. Anita likes long hair."

"Then why did you cut it?" his father asked.

"For a change. I'll see you tomorrow, Dad."

"I'll be here."

His mother started to follow us out, but his father said,

"Iris," in a tone that called her back. She waved at us, and called, "Bye . . . I love you." Jason didn't reply.

Julia followed us out and hugged us both very thoroughly. Jason hugged her back; I did my best.

Peterson and the suit fell into line around us. Jason put my left arm through his so he could touch my hand and arm with his hands. He was icily calm in the elevator going down and in the lobby, and perfectly calm as we slipped into the limo.

Peterson closed the door. We were alone. Jason held on until the motor started, and then his shoulders started to shake. He put his hands in front of his face and cried. He cried with his whole body, shaking, shivering.

I touched his shoulder, and he flinched. I tried one more time and he fell sideways into my lap, so that I held him while he wept. I held him while he cried in huge racking spasms, but he wasn't loud. His body felt like it was being torn apart with grief, but he didn't shout with it. He cried like someone who'd been taught not to attract too much attention with his grief. Too much noise and they come find you, to find out why the tears.

Call it a hunch, but I was betting that Franklin Schuyler had thought boys weren't supposed to cry, especially his very small, very pretty, very-unlike-him son.

18

THE TEARS BEGAN to slow, and finally he just lay in my lap, very still, as if the tears had emptied him of everything. I stroked his hair; I made the noises you make when you know that the pain is so vast that nothing you can do will fix it. The soft *It's all right*, when you know that it isn't all right, and never will be again, and perhaps never had been.

Peterson opened the door for us. Jason wiped at his face and sat up. If he'd been a woman he would have asked if it looked like he'd been crying, but he was a man, and he didn't ask. We got out, hand in hand again. They'd taken us around to the parking garage again. I hadn't even noticed. The world had narrowed down to the man in my lap and his grief.

Peterson led us up the back stairs, which meant there was probably some real Summerland newsworthy event in the lobby. Fine with me; I'd had enough circus for a while. I was ready for some bread.

Peterson and the suit waited for me to open the door with

the little key card. They waited until we were inside the room. I half-expected them to check that the room was safe, but they resisted the urge. Bully for them.

"Thanks," I said.

Peterson handed me a business card. "If you have anymore incidents with the press, call. It's going to be a mess here this week. It's very unfortunate that your friend and his father are going to be caught up in it. The governor is very serious about helping keep you out of the limelight."

"I appreciate the effort, Mr. Peterson."

"My job, Ms. Blake."

I nodded. "Good night."

"Good night."

I closed the door, locked it, and put on the flip-bar door lock at the top. I always locked up tight. Yeah, most of the things I hunted could bust through a door without a problem, but you never knew, some bad guys were only human.

I didn't expect bad guys tonight, but then I hadn't expected to need the gun today either. I'd brought it anyway.

Jason had gone for the bathroom and closed the door. I heard water running. I almost left him alone, but I was starving. I knocked on the door.

The water stopped. "Yes."

"I want to order some room service, what do you want?"

"I'm not hungry."

"You have to eat, Jason." It wasn't just normal *have to eat*. Wereanimals all had better control of their beast if their bellies were full. One hunger feeds the other, and one emptiness calls another.

"Nothing is going to sound good to me, Anita."

"I know." I leaned my forehead against the door. "I'm sorry, Jason."

I heard him at the door, and moved away enough for him to open it without bumping me. "What are you sorry about?"

"That your dad was so awful, I guess."

He gave a smile that was so bitter it hurt my heart to see it. "He's been awful to me my whole life. I guess I thought, he's dying, we'll have that Hallmark moment, but it's not going to happen, is it?"

I didn't know what to say, except, "I don't think so."

"He liked you, though. That surprised me."

"Why?"

"He likes Mom all soft and *yes, dear*. He likes Roberta best of the girls because she always agrees with him. But he liked that you stood up to him."

I shrugged. "My peculiar charm, I guess."

He smiled at me. "Is that what they're calling it these days?" He walked past me into the room.

I frowned at his back. "What's that supposed to mean?"

"It means he touched your scars."

"A lot of people are fascinated by them."

"No, they aren't. They ignore them and pretend they aren't there. Or they stare, but don't want to. Your scars embarrass people, make them uncomfortable."

"I try to ignore it all," I said.

"Yeah, but they're your scars, so it bothers you. I get to just watch people's reactions." He took off his tie and threw it on the floor.

I shrugged. "I didn't know you were that interested in how people reacted to my scars."

He smiled at me as he took off his jacket. "I like people-watching, you know that."

"All wereanimals do; I've always thought it was the same

way a lion watches a herd of gazelles. You know, looking for the weakest link."

He shook his head and started unbuttoning his shirt. "I've always liked watching people, but then once I thought I'd be an actor. We collect mannerisms the way other people collect stamps."

I thought about it. "I guess that makes sense."

"You took your high heels off the moment we came through the door last time. Get comfortable."

It seemed like days ago that we'd first been in the room. I was drained from all the family shit that I'd witnessed. Jason seemed okay, as if the crying in the car hadn't happened at all. He was a little hollow around the eyes, but other than that he seemed back to his usual self. I knew it was a lie, it had to be. Which made me wonder how often Jason hid his emotional turmoil back in St. Louis. If he was this good at it, he could be hiding how he truly felt all the time.

"What?" he asked. His shirt was open down the front, with only the French cuffs with their gold cuff links left to unfasten.

"I'm just wondering how often you do this in St. Louis."

"Do what?" he asked.

"Pretend everything is fine when inside it's not."

His blue eyes hardened, and some of the strain showed in his face, but only for an instant. Then he smiled at me, and it filled his face up all the way to his eyes.

"I'll eat if you make me." He moved close to me. And just like that, I wanted to move back from him. He hadn't done a thing, really. His expression was still pleasant. But there was a promise in the way he just stood there that made me uncomfortable.

"I'll eat because you're right," he said. "I don't need to be hungry when I'm under this much"—he touched my face—"stress."

That one play of fingertips made me shiver. I closed my eyes, not sure whether I was closing them to keep the sensation closer, or so I couldn't see his face. His eyes weren't smiling now. They held something too grown-up, too real, too . . . uncomfortable.

His hand slid along the curve of my jaw, to cradle my face. He kissed me, and with me in the heels I was a little taller. It felt different enough that it made me open my eyes. I was suddenly staring into his eyes from inches away.

"You look startled," he said, voice soft.

I had to swallow before I could say in a voice that was oddly breathy, "I guess I am."

"Why? We've kissed before."

I stared down into his face. I couldn't put it into words, but . . . I licked my suddenly dry lips and whispered, "I don't know."

"You look almost . . . scared," he said, and he was almost whispering, too.

I stepped away from him, far enough that he couldn't touch me. That was better.

He put his head to one side and looked at me. "You're nervous," he said, and he sounded surprised.

I walked to the little sitting area to the side of the room, with its chair and ottoman. I sat down and didn't look at him as I took off my shoes and set them beside the chair.

"Talk to me, Anita," he said.

"Let's order food," I said.

He came and knelt in front of me. His shirt was still held in place by only the French cuffs. The shirt spread around the smooth expanse of his chest, the muscles of his stomach bunching as he knelt.

I looked away again and started to get up. He put his hand on my wrist. My pulse sped under his touch. I stood up and was caught between Jason and the ottoman. I started to fall backward. He moved in one of those incredible too-fast-to-see moves. He was just suddenly standing, holding my wrists, pulling me forward. I ended up falling into his body, and he caught me around the waist. We were the same height again without the heels.

I was left staring into his face; the eye contact was so intimate, too intimate. I pushed at him, almost fought to get away.

He let me go, but said, "What's wrong?"

I opened my mouth, shut it, took a deep shaking breath, another, and finally said, "I'm not sure."

"Liar," he said.

I frowned at him. "I'm not lying."

"Normally, I can't tell when you're lying. You don't even smell like you're lying, but your pulse sped, and your eyes showed it. What's wrong, Anita, please, talk to me."

"Let's order food first, and then while we wait I'll try to explain."

"You want the time to organize your thoughts." He made it a statement.

"Yeah," I said.

He nodded. "Okay, let's find the room service menu." His face was careful, closed down. He did not need me to go all weird on him now. I was supposed to be his refuge while we were here, and I was blowing it.

He went to the desk at the side of the room and found the menu on top of it. He opened it without looking at me again. But he was too good a friend for me not to see how he was holding his shoulders. The line of his body told me he was unhappy. Shit.

I knew what was wrong—my own weird internal argument with myself about sex. Nathaniel helped ease me through it, as did Micah, and Jean-Claude. Even Jason himself had helped me deal with some of my issues about Nathaniel when I was still trying not to be his lover. But though Jason could help talk me through issues with other men in my life, Jason had never tried to talk me through issues about him. I hadn't known I had any issues about Jason. But I had one.

I loved Jason. In that friend way, yes, but he lived on that emotional edge for me. That edge that felt familiar. The edge that Nathaniel had lived on for a while. That edge that Asher had lived on. I had other men who were more frequently in my bed, but none of them were as close to that emotional moment. Love, whether it's friendship or more, is like a cup. It fills up drop by drop, until one last drop and the cup is full. The liquid hangs there almost above the rim, hangs there on the surface tension alone, and you can feel that one more drop and it will spill over. Once, I hadn't been aware of the process, but I'd had it happen too many times now. I couldn't afford another spill. I couldn't afford another man in my life, not like that.

Could I just not tell the difference? Was that it? Was I so confused about sex and love that without Nathaniel or someone else I couldn't tell the difference between wanting a man for lust, and wanting him for love? Maybe, maybe. God help me, I didn't know.

"I know what I'm getting," Jason said. He offered me the menu. I took it, trying not to look at him. Trying not to let him read whatever was in my eyes.

He knew what he wanted. I wish to hell I did.

19

JASON CALLED THE food orders down: grilled chicken Caesar for him and grilled chicken sandwich for me. He had to argue with them to make sure they didn't put some weird cheese or sauce on my sandwich. Who the hell puts blue cheese on chicken? He sat down on the bed, finally undoing the cuff links and taking off his shirt. He followed with his socks and walked around barefoot for a few moments before he bounced down on the bed and said, "Now, talk to me."

I got up, walked to the closet, and put my jacket on a hanger, while I tried to figure out how to start. "I've never had sex with you when we were alone, except when I had to feed the *ardeur*."

"Okay, I guess that's true."

I turned and looked at him. He was lounging on the bed, propped up on one elbow. I admitted to myself he looked pretty cute lying there. I didn't want to admit it.

Get a grip, Anita, I thought. I made myself walk to the bed and sit on the corner so I could undo the stockings. I had to lift the skirt to get to them, and that, too, felt too intimate. My fingers felt clumsy as I tried to undo the garters.

"Leave the hose," he said.

I looked at him, and I don't know what look was on my face, but whatever it was it made him slip off the bed and come to me on his knees. "Anita, what's wrong? God, you look like I'm going to attack you or something. You can't be afraid of me. It's Jason, just Jason."

I stopped fiddling with the garters, and tried for truth. It had always been truth between Jason and me. It was one of the reasons we were friends.

"I'm afraid of how I feel about you."

He gave me a look I couldn't read, and leaned back on his knees again, with them too wide, so his stomach muscles bunched again. I realized it was a position he used a lot on stage. It was either comfortable, or habit.

"I don't know what you're trying to say, Anita. Normally, I'd be the first one not to push, but I'm a little stressed tonight. Just talk to me."

"I'm embarrassed that I want you, just want you. Not because of the *ardeur*, or any metaphysical thing, but just because you are Jason. I like you."

"I like you, too," he said. He looked at me, sort of perplexed. "But you feel bad that you want me, not because of the *ardeur*, but just because."

I nodded.

He smiled and took my hand, gently, in his. "That you could still feel this nervous around me is sweet, Anita. Really, it is." He took my hands in both of his. "But I need you to work through whatever issue this is. We'll eat, but then I need closeness. I need you to help me drown out this day. Do you understand?"

I did, actually. "Sex is almost the only time that I relax completely. Nathaniel jokes that it's my only hobby."

Jason grinned, and raised my hands up to kiss them. "It's one of my favorite things to do, too."

I started to blush and tried to catch it, knowing I couldn't. "I don't mean it like that."

He kissed me on the nose. "You are so cute."

I pushed him away and stood up. "I am not cute."

He lay on the bed on his stomach, gazing up at me, still grinning. "You are cute, beautiful, but cute when you get like this."

"Get like what?"

"Try to complicate your life."

"What's that supposed to mean?"

"You're feeling all squidgy about wanting to have sex with me, right?"

"Something like that."

"You have permission from every man in your life to be here with me. They all knew we'd be fucking like bunnies if I had anything to do with it. So you can't be feeling guilty because you're cheating. Cheating implies lack of knowledge. Heck, one of your live-in sweeties volunteered you for this trip."

I crossed my arms under my breasts, and knew I was pouting but couldn't stop it. "That's sort of bugging me now, too."

"Why?"

I shrugged, arms still crossed. "It's not just the sex."

"What is it then? Tell me."

"I'm afraid that the way I feel for you will change."

"That you won't like me anymore?"

"No, that I'll like you too much."

He rolled off the bed and stood in front of me. "Anita, are you saying that you're afraid you'll fall in love with me?"

I shrugged, and didn't meet his eyes.

He touched my arms, peered under my gaze, so I had to look up and into his face. His face was a little surprised, and almost a little sad. It wasn't the look I expected. "If I really thought that was possible, I'd be the happiest guy in town, but you are doing what you always do. You want me for sex, and as a friend, but you want sex and I'm here. But that makes you feel guilty for some reason, so you're starting to try to convince yourself that it's more than just friendship."

"How can you be so sure?"

"Because you do not watch me in a room the way you watch Jean-Claude, or Asher, or Nathaniel, or Micah, or Richard. I'm a little ahead of Requiem and London, and Damian, but I'm not ahead of the others. You see me now, your body reacts to me, and that is wonderful. I can't tell you how I hated being the invisible boy around you."

"I saw you," I said.

"You saw me, but you didn't *see* me."

I started to move away, but his hands tightened on my arms. "Jason, I'm not sure I know the difference between loving someone and just lusting after him."

"A lot of people get that one confused, but honestly, Anita. If Nathaniel were here and it were a choice, you'd drop me in a hot second, wouldn't you?"

"I wouldn't have to, he likes sharing."

Jason grinned. "He does that, but if Micah were here you'd choose him over me. My ego hates it, but it's true."

"Micah shares pretty well, too."

"He shares you with Nathaniel, and Jean-Claude, and sometimes Asher, but he doesn't share you with me."

I thought about that. "I guess it's never come up."

"Micah shares you, but he doesn't enjoy sharing you the

way Nathaniel does. My best friend likes watching you with other men. I don't think the same is entirely true of Micah."

I thought about it, and said, "I'm not sure what Micah thinks about the sharing. He's cool with it, but you're probably right. He doesn't prefer it."

"Nathaniel almost does," Jason said. "Sharing you appeals to a lot of his kicks."

"I guess so."

Jason hugged me, and laughed. "Don't talk us into a problem we don't have, Anita. Please, please, I need you to just have uncomplicated sex with me after the food, okay? I need you to be a friend with benefits; don't make it more or less than it is, okay?"

I nodded. Most of me even agreed with him. There was just that tiny voice in my head that said, *Be careful.* Maybe I was borrowing trouble, or maybe Jason didn't understand that he had charms of his own.

20

THERE WAS A knock on the door. I thought it was food, but Jason said, "I don't smell food."

I took the Browning out of my holster and went to the door in my stocking feet. I used the peephole and found that it wasn't room service. It was Chuck.

I kept the flip-bar on and opened the door just that much. I kept my gun out of sight, but in my hand against the door. "What do you want, Chuck?"

"Now is that any way to greet me? I came to tell you to turn on the television, channel thirteen."

"Why?"

"It's a media shitstorm, but not the one we thought we'd have. You'll want to see it." He looked sort of tired around the edges.

"Wait here," I said.

"I'd like to come in," he said.

"I'd like to be taller, but that ain't happening either." I closed the door, gently.

"He says to turn on channel thirteen."

Jason found the remote and turned on the TV. The woman we'd seen earlier, who had been a fan of Jason's alter ego, Ripley, was on-screen. She was in midsentence: ". . . When asked earlier today if she had left Jean-Claude for one of his own strippers, zombie raiser and vampire hunter Anita Blake had no comment." They showed bits of the press conference and us leaving with the questions still being shouted at us. Jean-Claude's glossy was on-screen now with her voice-over: "The Master Vampire of St. Louis has refused to comment on rumors that the love of his life has left him for Jason Schuyler." The picture from the website for Guilty Pleasures flashed on the screen. Jason looked pretty, well, strippery, in the picture. Cute, but the picture was not going to help squash any rumors.

I said, "Shit," soft, but with feeling.

Jason went to the door and let Chuck in, then came to stand by me. Chuck stayed near the door, but he was watching the TV, too. It was like a car wreck; you couldn't look away, even though you knew you didn't want to see it.

"Rumor has it that they've come back to Schuyler's hometown for a quick marriage so his father, who is dying of cancer, can see his only son married before he passes. It looks like Anita Blake, pinup for the supernatural set, has finally picked one of her men to settle down with, and it is a surprise to everyone, except those closest to the situation. We have a live interview from St. Louis."

A man appeared; he was standing in front of Jean-Claude's dance club, Danse Macabre. "We have one of Jean-Claude's master-level vampires here in an exclusive." The camera pulled back to show Gretchen.

"Shit!" I said.

She was still the blond, blue-eyed baker's daughter whom Jean-Claude had seduced centuries ago. Her name had been Greta then. She was pretty, but not breathtaking in that way of most of the vamps of Belle Morte's line. But I guess Gretchen would say the same of me, if not worse. She had an almost pathological jealousy about Jean-Claude, and a hatred of me. She saw me as the only thing preventing him from being her lover once more. Even if I vanished tomorrow, he wouldn't go to Gretchen. But it was easier for her to blame the other woman than accept that the man for whom she'd given up her mortality and her family inheritance didn't love her, and probably never had.

Jean-Claude had landed in this country pretty much penniless. His first few "seductions" had all been about financial or physical security.

She was dressed in modest club wear, because she was one of the vampires who roamed the dance floor at Danse Macabre. One of the selling points of the club was that you could dance with a real "live" vampire. Gretchen was the vampy equivalent of an old-time taxi dancer. You could even get tips, depending on how good a dancer you were, or how friendly you were. Gretchen wasn't making many tips. There was only one man she wanted to dance with, and he was the boss.

The reporter held the mic near her pretty face and asked, "Are you surprised that Anita Blake has run off with one of Jean-Claude's strippers?"

"No," she said in an oh-so-reasonable voice. She could sound so sane if you didn't let her talk long enough. "She's been sleeping with Jason for months."

"Isn't he Jean-Claude's *pomme de sang*, his blood donor?"

"Yes. He donates blood to Jean-Claude and sex to Anita."

"Did Jean-Claude know that they were lovers?"

"I don't know."

"Liar," I said, softly.

"What do you think Jean-Claude will do when he learns that Anita and Jason have eloped?"

"What would any man do if his honor and his heart were so betrayed?" she asked.

"None of the other vampires would speak on camera with us; why did you decide to come forward?"

"Here it comes," Jason said.

"Jean-Claude deserves a woman who will honor him above all other men like a true wife would. Anita will never be faithful to him, never."

"But she's willing to marry Jason Schuyler."

"She'll cheat on him, too. She is incapable of being true to only one man." Her carefully made-up eyes were a little wider, her breathing faster. "She is a whore, and whores know no loyalty."

"Isn't that a bit harsh?" the reporter asked, but he moved closer to her, as if encouraging what his words were discouraging.

"She has a string of lovers. Eleven that I know about. There are probably more."

There was movement behind them, and vampire bouncers came out of the club. They went for the reporters and for Gretchen. The reporters backed up, but kept filming. They filmed as the vampires took Gretchen by the arms and started escorting her into the club. She screamed back over her shoulder, "I love Jean-Claude. I've always loved him. Anita doesn't love him. She doesn't love anyone but herself. She's a whore, a . . ." Then they started having to bleep out what she was saying. The camera crew beat a hasty retreat, with the male reporter saying, "And that's the scene here in St. Louis where the vampire community is shocked that their Master of the City has been dumped by his girl. Back to you, Candice."

Jason hit the remote and made the TV go dead. I sat down on the bed with him. My gun was still in my hand, but it couldn't help us against this. "Mother of God," I said, "what the hell just happened?"

"Phyllis Dubois helped the rumors along a little, but she didn't know that she should have helped you get a lower profile, Mr. Schuyler. I wanted to come and assure you that the governor had nothing to do with this, and did not approve this."

Jason nodded. "I know he didn't. He would never want me in the spotlight at the same time as his sons. I know that."

I looked from one to the other of them, with that feeling that I was missing something.

Chuck looked at me; his eyes glanced at the gun in my hand. "You always answer the door with a gun in your hand?"

"Most of the time, yeah," I said.

He almost smiled. "The governor sent me to tell you that anything you need to help with this mess, you have it."

"Can we just deny it?" I asked.

They both gave me a withering look, as if I'd said something incredibly stupid. "We can," Jason said, "but how? How do we deny it, and make it stick?" He looked at Chuck. "What did the press agent do to get things this bad, this fast?"

"She mentioned the surprise marriage thing."

"Why did she do it?" Jason asked.

Chuck looked uncomfortable. "I'm not at liberty to tell you."

Jason stood up. "Not at liberty to tell me? You have no idea what you have just done. Jean-Claude isn't just my boss, he's my master. I'm his blood whore. He is not going to be happy about this."

In my head I thought, *He's going to have to punish Gretchen for what she said.* The last time they put her in a cross-wrapped coffin, she'd come out crazier. If she went much crazier she wouldn't be safe out in public. In the old days before vamps were legal citizens he would simply have killed her, probably. A lot of masters would have anyway, but if she vanished now the police would ask questions. Shit.

"What can we do?" I asked everyone and no one.

"You need to leave now, Chuck," Jason said. "Anita and I need to talk."

"The governor wants to offer his help."

"Just go, give us your cell phone if you want, but we need to talk in private."

He looked at Jason, then at me. I was no help to him. I said, "You heard the man, get out."

"If you want to wait in the hall you can, but we need some privacy," Jason said.

Chuck scribbled a number on the back of a business card. "I'll go to the hotel bar; call when you're done discussing it."

Jason took the card without really looking at it. I motioned at the door with the gun. "Get out, Chuck."

He went. Jason locked the door behind him. He came to stand by me at the foot of the bed. "We've got to help Jean-Claude clean this up."

"What do you mean, help Jean-Claude? Isn't it you and me that are in the mess?"

"This story is going to cause Jean-Claude to lose serious face among the other Masters of the City," Jason said.

"When we come back not married, they'll know it was all lies."

"If you were a normal human servant you would have a lot less freedom, Anita. Some of the masters see your freedom as Jean-Claude being sort of pussy-whipped."

"What the hell are you talking about?"

Jason held his hands out, as if to say, *Don't shoot the messenger.* "Remember, most of the masters are men and most of them come from an age when women knew their place, so there's that problem, but most of them also see human servants as very much servants."

"Are you saying that I'm making Jean-Claude look bad in front of the other masters?"

"Remember when Jean-Claude invited all the main Masters of the City that he sort of trusted to the big party?"

"I remember."

"They were supposed to meet you that night. They had brought *pomme de sang* candidates for you to taste."

The entire thought of it all had made me so uncomfortable that I'd dreaded the night. The idea was that I could simply dance with each candidate, turn them down as not my cup of tea, and be done with it. That way I didn't have to be alone with any candidate, and I could politely refuse them all. It had seemed like a good plan until my version of the *ardeur* had shown itself so unpredictable.

"We decided I was too dangerous to 'taste' the candidates. I would have been introduced to everyone, but that would have been it."

"But you never even got to be introduced, did you?"

"You know I didn't." I sounded sullen even to myself.

Jason went down on his knees in front of me. "Don't be mad, but don't you see how it made things look for Jean-Claude? He had commanded his servant to do something and she didn't. You didn't even bother to make the grand entrance with him."

"I was a little busy," I said.

"I know you and Asher were confronting some very bad vampires—the leaders of the vampire dance troupe that had damn near rolled every Master of the City in that audience. Jean-Claude and you, and Auggie, saved the day, kept them from eating us all." He put his hands over mine.

"Asher and I were negotiating with the leaders."

"Yes, and the other masters were okay with that. Jean-Claude did it deliberately to show how much he trusted Asher's powers."

I widened my eyes at him.

"Asher is seen as weak, Anita. A very weak second-in-command, there only by the grace of love and centuries of friendship."

My hands were still under his. He was touching me, but I wasn't touching him back. I didn't like this conversation and I really didn't like that Jason was beating around the bush. He was leading up to something. The more careful he was, the more I was certain I wouldn't like it.

"Asher proved himself when Jean-Claude nearly died in December."

Jason nodded and squeezed my hands; when I still didn't respond he dropped his hands away from me, and just stayed kneeling. "He was ruthless and effective, and he surprised a lot of people."

"Not me," I said. "I knew he was tougher than everyone thought."

"So tough he nearly killed you."

I stood up and walked a little distance away from him. "Jean-Claude told me to feed and go meet the other masters."

"Asher was food, I know that. But food doesn't usually bite back."

"You're creeping up on some idea here, Jason. It's not like you to play twenty questions so gently. You usually go straight for the meat of the problem."

He stood up. "Okay, if you don't like the gentle approach, we can skip to the point."

"I wish you would."

He gave me a look. "Liar."

"All right, I don't want to hear your point, because I think I won't like it, but I'd rather just hear it and get it over with than have this long lead-up."

Jason made his point, holding up a finger for each part of it. "You have more freedom than any human servant is ever allowed. You dissed the other masters when you didn't appear for the party, especially when they knew you were having sex with Asher. You bailed on your master to fuck one of his underlings."

"It wasn't like that," I said, but felt myself beginning to blush anyway.

"I'm telling you how it seemed to them."

"Jean-Claude never mentioned that he was having a problem with the other masters because of it."

"And if he had, it wouldn't have made any difference. You are who you are, he accepts that." Jason sat on the edge of the bed closest to me. "He loves you, Anita. Hell, in his own way, he loves us both, but he cannot let this story stand, Anita. He cannot be perceived as so weak that he can't even control his woman, and his food."

"But it's not true, Jason. We haven't run off together. We aren't getting married."

"But it's a really good rumor, Anita. Everyone loves a good rumor, even master vampires."

"Has Jean-Claude been having trouble with rumors like this before?" I asked. I got up and moved to the middle of the room toward the door. I was pretty sure Jason wasn't done with his revelations, and being closer to the door made me feel better. I always feel better when I know where the exit is.

"Anita, some of it isn't rumors, it's fact."

"What do you mean?"

"He does let you sleep with men other than him, while he isn't allowed the same privilege with other women."

I stared at him. "So if I let Jean-Claude sleep around, his reputation would be better among the other masters?"

"Maybe."

I shook my head. "If you have a point, you'd best be getting to it."

"If you and Jean-Claude were simply not monogamous, then the other vampires could understand it. You have no idea the world-class talent Jean-Claude has turned down lately."

"I don't know what you're talking about."

"The other masters keep trying to send him gifts."

"What kind of gifts?"

"You know what kind."

"I haven't noticed a bevy of strange women at the Circus lately."

"They start with pictures on the computer or home movies. They've decided that if he could see them in action and pick the ones he likes best, he might take some of them into his group."

"He never mentioned any of this to me."

"Why should he? He knows you would never share him with another woman. He waits a polite amount of time, then turns them down."

"Does he watch the . . . stuff?"

"Sometimes, enough so he can answer questions when they call and ask him how he liked what she did in this or that scene."

"Scene?"

"Vampire porn is a growing business, Anita."

I shivered. "I wasn't aware of that."

"Auggie's been branching out into it, as a legitimate business."

"Legitimate." I made it sound like I felt.

"Legal, then." Jason seemed tired.

I had a thought, and I let it go all the way through. "Does Jean-Claude *want* to sleep with other women?"

"He's never mentioned it to me," Jason said.

"Then why are *you* mentioning it to me?"

"Because this story is going to need some punishment."

"What, the lies about us?"

Jason nodded.

"What do you mean, punishment?"

"Jean-Claude is going to have to be seen as regaining control of you and me, Anita."

"That's insane. We aren't out of control."

"Aren't we? You're here alone with me. We are lovers. You're meeting my family. Most people will consider all that pretty serious."

"Are you saying that Jean-Claude will have to appear to punish us for something we haven't done?"

Jason nodded, and he was way too serious about it.

"That's crazy. Jean-Claude won't punish us for something we haven't done."

"No, he won't," Jason said, voice soft.

I came to stand in front of him, arms crossed over my chest, then had to shift my arms. Standing like that works so much better without breasts. "Then what the hell are you talking about?"

"I'm saying that we need to come up with punishments for him to use on us."

I shook my head. "You are making no sense at all."

"I'm making a lot of sense. You have no idea how badly your behavior at the party affected your master's standing among the rest of the vampires."

"I didn't mean for—"

"You didn't mean to have sex with Asher?"

"No, I mean, yes." I sat down on the bed beside him. "I don't know what I mean. Neither Asher nor I meant for things to go so wrong. It got out of hand."

"Which is why you and he aren't allowed to be alone together anymore. The other masters saw that as fitting punishment, but expected more severe punishment for Asher. That made Jean-Claude look weak, too."

"How serious is this, Jason?"

"Jean-Claude has to be seen as bringing his house back to order. He must do things that make him look strong to the others."

"Are you seriously saying that some other master might challenge Jean-Claude for his territory, just because of this rumor?"

"Remember, Anita, most of these guys come from a time when if a man couldn't control his wife, he was seen as less than a man. There are vampires out there who are beginning to think that it's not his power, but yours that makes him strong."

"I'm his human servant, Jason."

"Yes, a human servant with her own vampire servant, and her own animal to call. An animal to call that is a different animal from her master's."

"It gives Jean-Claude a hold on the leopards, too."

"No, it doesn't. Micah and his leopards answer to Jean-Claude out of courtesy and Micah knowing a good thing when he sees it, but he is not drawn to Jean-Claude. He's drawn to you, just like all the other big cats. That's your energy, not Jean-Claude's."

"But I'm drawn to the wolves."

"You're metaphysically tied to Richard, our Ulfric, our wolf king, too. So who's to say that it's your tie to Jean-Claude that gives you wolf or your tie to Richard?"

"I'm still missing something, aren't I?"

"Jean-Claude heard a whisper, not even a rumor yet, that some of the masters are speculating that if you were their human servant they could be as powerful as Jean-Claude, but they would be strong enough to keep you in line."

"They would, would they?" I said.

"This isn't funny, Anita."

It wasn't like Jason to discourage any attempt at humor on my part. Things were bad, maybe much worse than I knew. "I'm sorry, Jason."

He smiled at me. "It's okay, you can't know what you aren't told."

"Why would Jean-Claude not tell me?"

"Because you aren't going to change. He doesn't even want you to change, really, but we have to find a way to change the perceptions of what is happening in St. Louis."

"How?"

"Stop discouraging the rumors that have Jean-Claude making love to all your men. If you shared them with him, then it would explain his patience."

"But it's not true."

He gave me a look.

"A master vamp can smell a lie on me, if they're powerful enough. I can control my face, my eyes, my body, my voice, but Jason, I don't know how to control the scent of my skin, or the speed of my pulse. I'm not that good at lying."

"Almost no one is," he said.

"Then how do we lie to a bunch of Masters of the City?"

"Don't lie," Jason said.

"What does that mean?"

"Let Jean-Claude share the men, or let him sleep with others."

I stared at him, openmouthed, and finally recovered enough to say, "You volunteering?"

He laughed then, and let himself fall back on the bed with his legs dangling off it. "I've told you before, Anita, I asked and he turned me down. He turned me down because he thought you wouldn't approve."

"But you don't like men," I said.

"Not generally, but Jean-Claude just gets past all the exceptions for me. Maybe it's being his *pomme de sang*, but you'd have to be a lot more purely heterosexual than I am not to think about it."

I remembered Jason telling me this, but I had put it in that box with all the other thoughts I didn't want to think.

"I thought you told me you experimented with some other guy, and it wasn't your cup of tea."

"Let's just say I like giving more than receiving."

I must have looked puzzled, because he sat up and kissed me on the forehead. "You are terribly cute for someone who is the first living succubus in recorded history."

"I am not cute."

"You are, you just don't like that you are."

I don't know what I would have said to that, because there

was another knock on the door. This time it was food. I wasn't sure I was really hungry anymore, but I was grateful for anything that stopped this conversation. I'd had about as much honesty for one day as I could handle. I hoped Jason felt the same, but doubted it. When Jason got an idea into his head, he saw it through. Even if you didn't want to hear it.

21

WE LET THE waiter, if that's the term for room service, put the food on the dining table. I'd never been in a hotel room that had a full-size table for eating before. Since the room was in his name, Jason signed the check and figured out the tip. I just sat there and let them do it. I was thinking, or trying not to think.

The chicken sandwich wasn't bad. The French fries that came with it were excellent. Jason seemed to be enjoying his Caesar and chicken. Once I would have let the conversation stay dead, but I'd grown up a little since then. Though I couldn't help thinking that the last time I'd gone out of town with one of my guys it had been Micah, and we had had an uncomfortable and revealing conversation, too. What was it about being alone in hotel rooms with them? Maybe it was that whole alone thing. Maybe.

"Some of the other guys in St. Louis have suggested that everyone who is a regular in my bed grows in power."

Jason looked at me, a bite halfway to his mouth. He put the fork down and looked surprised. "I was going to drop the conversation, and let you think about what I'd said."

I shook my head. "If there is even a whisper that some of the other masters are thinking if they took me over, they'd be more powerful than Jean-Claude, we need to nip that idea in the bud. I've had vampire marks forced on me before and I didn't like it. I've had a Master of the City do it, a couple of times. It's pretty horrible. I *so* do not want to go through that, ever again."

He took a bite of his chicken and looked at me. Those spring-sky eyes showed every bit of shrewd intelligence, all the deep thinking that he normally hid behind the flirting and the smiles. "You're right, but I thought it would take you a few days of thinking it through before you realized how bad it could get."

I shrugged. "Maybe I'm growing up, finally."

He grinned at me. "You are one of the most grown-up people I know."

"What's that supposed to mean?"

"You have a lot of trouble letting yourself enjoy yourself. You don't play well."

"I think a lot of the guys in St. Louis would say I play very well."

He actually almost looked embarrassed, but fought it off. "You are an amazing bed partner, Anita, but you don't have any hobbies. You don't do anything to relax except sex."

"I like going to the firing range."

He *tsk*ed and wagged his fork at me. "That's work, and you know it. You're not a gun nut like Edward and his friend Otto, or Olaf, or whatever secret identity he's using."

I couldn't argue that, so I didn't try. I went back to concentrating on my food.

"So that's it, you make one comment and it's no more talk," he said.

"Hey, I put the ball in play, you can pick it up, or you can let it sit there. I've been brave, I restarted a conversation that I don't want to have; now it's your turn."

He smiled, and put his silverware beside his plate. His salad was mostly gone. He, like most men in his age group and younger, could eat damn fast when they wanted to, or weren't forcing themselves to slow down.

I still had most of my sandwich left. Of course, the French fries were crisp and yummy, which was also distracting me from the chicken. Was I concentrating on the food so I wouldn't concentrate on the conversation? Maybe, but not on purpose.

"Okay," Jason said, "we have to help Jean-Claude appear as powerful as he is, or more so."

"How do we do that?" I asked. I ate French fries while we talked. Jason had left some of his chicken and a lot of his grilled veggies.

"I'm not sure, but first we have to put a stop to this new rumor about us."

"How do we do that?"

"I think we need a reporter who gets an exclusive that we can trust."

"No one I saw here today is trustworthy."

"I was thinking of a fellow werewolf and St. Louisian."

I stopped eating and blinked at him. "Irving had to back off on all the exclusives I was giving him, because people started asking questions."

Jason nodded. "I know you almost outed Irving as a werewolf by accident."

"Yeah, the idea is that I wouldn't be sharing secrets with a human being." Did that last sound bitter?

Jason reached across the table and patted my hand. Apparently, it had sounded bitter. "It's hard to be painted as a monster when you're still human."

I shook my head, and moved my hand away from his. "I haven't been straight human since I was a child, Jason. Remember, I saw my first ghost in elementary school, and called my first zombie by accident in junior high. That isn't human by most people's standards."

"People can be pretty cruel," he said. His face had gone all serious. Somehow I didn't think he was thinking about my childhood. Shit.

I stood up and came around the table to him. He gazed up at me. I kissed him on the forehead.

"What was that for?" he asked, but he smiled when he did it.

I smiled back. "So you'd smile."

He pulled me into his lap, and our arms were just suddenly around each other. "I can think of other things that would make me do more than smile."

"I give you a sisterly kiss on the forehead and all you can think about is sex."

He gave me that smile, the real version of the smile that helped separate customers from their money at the club. He could look like everyone's favorite brother, or the best friend you had in college or high school; he was everyone's buddy, until he got that look. The look that stripped him of the pretense of innocence. The look that let you know behind the boy-next-door charm was someone wicked who would help you be wicked, too.

The look brought my breath out in a sigh and made me lean in, not quite close enough for a kiss. "Is there a reason you left food uneaten on your plate?"

The lascivious look faltered. "You never do or say exactly what I expect you to."

"You aren't the first man who's noticed that," I said, still not quite close enough to kiss.

He acknowledged that with a small nod. "A too-full stomach impedes good sex."

"Only if you plan to be vigorous," I said, leaning in just a little closer, so that I was staring into those blue eyes so close, so very close.

He grinned, and then that look filled his face. "Oh, I plan to be vigorous, eventually."

"Eventually," I said, and closed those last inches, so that his lips touched mine as he said, "Oh, yes."

22

JASON MIGHT HAVE planned on being vigorous, but he started out slow. When I got carried away and wanted to move things along, he finally turned me on my stomach and made me touch the headboard.

"Slow, Anita, we have all night. I've never had all night with you, and I want to enjoy it." He said that with his nude body kneeling beside me.

"Why is it that all of you remind me that you never get me to yourself?"

"Because it's true."

I went up on my elbows and gazed down my body to find him at my feet with his body stretched out so that his feet were closer to me than anything else. "Are all of you tired of sharing me?"

"Not tired, but every man likes to think a woman likes him just for himself, not because he's an extra pair of hands, an extra mouth, a spare dick."

I must have looked as shocked as I felt, because he crawled back up the bed and hugged me. "I'm sorry, Anita, I shouldn't have said that, I really shouldn't have."

"Is that how you all feel?"

He shook his head. "No, I swear to you, no. Nathaniel enjoys sharing. Jean-Claude loves that you let him share you with other men, especially Asher. I don't know about Micah, he doesn't talk to me like that. Richard, well, our Ulfric doesn't like sharing anything lately."

"But it's how *you* feel, isn't it?"

"Truthfully, me and most of the men who only get a little of your attention. Come on, be honest, we are just extra men in the bed."

"That's not true."

"If it's not true for me, then why don't you ever approach me when the *ardeur* isn't in emergency mode?"

"I'm with you now."

"Yeah, but it's a different kind of emergency. I know this is sort of mercy sex."

"I don't do mercy sex." I sat up.

"Oh, God, I am not in the right mindset for this."

"Then maybe we should stop," I said, moving so that I was sitting against the headboard.

He hid his face in a pillow and made a muffled scream of frustration. He came up for air, and said, "Maybe you're right. We should probably call Irving first and give him the real story about this trip."

"You agree we shouldn't have sex right now?" I made it a question.

"Yeah, and maybe we should call Jean-Claude and get his approval on our plan. I guess the other masters are right. Your word is enough to get things done. I'm as bad as anyone else.

We don't always check with Jean-Claude or anyone else. You say *jump*, we jump. Richard really hates that about the wolves, by the way."

"Does Jean-Claude hate it?"

"He hasn't said so."

I pulled a pillow into my lap and hugged it. "I'll call Jean-Claude; you call Irving and tell him that the story doesn't run unless Jean-Claude approves it."

Jason nodded. "Good plan." He used the landline, and I used my cell phone. I got Jean-Claude on the line while Jason was still trying to find Irving.

Jean-Claude's voice was as neutral as I'd ever heard, empty. I knew that if I'd been standing beside him he would have held that stillness that the really old vampires could do, as if, if you looked away they would be invisible. "I wondered if you would call, *ma petite*."

"I should have called earlier, but the reporters sort of threw us."

"It was unexpected," he said, still in that empty voice.

"Jean-Claude, Jason is trying to find Irving Griswold to give him the truth about why we're down here. Do you think an exclusive will help?"

"You do not usually ask my opinion when you are far away, *ma petite*."

"I guess I deserved that, but Jason explained some things to me, and I'm sorry."

"What are you sorry about, *ma petite*?"

"I'm sorry that my freedom has made you look bad in front of the other Masters of the City. I'm sorry that Asher and I having our little problem made you look weak in front of our guests. I'm sorry that I haven't included you more in decisions that affect you."

His voice held a hint of surprise. "*Ma petite*, is this truly you?"

"Fine, fine, make fun of me."

He laughed then, that touchable, glide-down-your-skin laugh. "I am sorry, *ma petite*, but you have surprised me. Give me a moment to recover."

"Am I really that big a pain in the ass? No wait, don't answer that. I know the answer."

He laughed again, and it made my body shiver. "Stop doing that, if you want Jason and me to concentrate on the problem at hand."

"You have not had sex with our young werewolf yet?" He again let me hear surprise in his voice.

"We thought about it, but we thought we'd try to be good little servants before we got distracted."

"I do not treat you as my servant," he said.

"No, you don't, and maybe I need to reward that by acting in public a little more like one."

"What do you mean, *ma petite*?" His voice had gone cautious.

"First, can Jason give Irving the truth, and will it help?"

"He can, and it will, but won't it ruin your cover story with his father?"

"I guess it will, but what else can we do? Jason says that this rumor is going to make you look weak to the other Masters of the City. We have to let them know it's not true."

"Yes, but what can Jason say to our reporter friend that will kill the rumor, but not spoil the reason you are both there?"

I glanced at Jason. He seemed to have Irving on the phone at last. "Hang on a minute," I said to Jean-Claude. I got Jason's attention.

He said, "Hang on a second, Irving." He put his hand over the phone.

"Jean-Claude is curious what we can say to Irving that will fix the rumor but won't ruin things with your folks?"

"You've met my folks now, Anita. I can't please my father, not really, not in the time he's got left anyway. My sister Roberta isn't going to be won over either. It was a good try, Anita, but we've got to tell the truth. It's more important that Jean-Claude be safe than that my family believe some lie."

"It's not a lie," I said.

He shrugged. "What isn't? We aren't getting married. We aren't leaving Jean-Claude. We didn't run away, and do some stupid *Romeo and Juliet* thing. It is all lies."

I touched his arm. "We are lovers. You do like girls better than boys."

"Yeah, but there are a handful of guys that I wouldn't mind getting up close and personal with, and bisexual is just 'gay lite' as far as my family is concerned." He shrugged again. "We'll have one more visit at the hospital tomorrow and then we'll go home to St. Louis."

I wanted to say something, but didn't know what to say. Jason turned back to the phone and started talking to Irving.

I went back to my cell phone, which I hadn't bothered to cover. "Did you hear all that?"

"I did," Jean-Claude said.

"I feel like I've screwed up."

"You could not have foreseen these events."

"I guess not, but I should have thought how the other master vamps might think you were, well, that I wasn't behaving like a very good human servant."

"You are who and what you are, *ma petite*. I love you as you are."

I smiled, though he couldn't see it. "I know that, but Jason said we need to come up with punishments for us. That you have to be seen as getting your house in order, that you can't be seen as losing control of your woman and your food."

Jean-Claude was very quiet on the other end of the phone. Sometimes it was unnerving talking to vampires on the phone. They didn't have to breathe, and the old ones had no sense of movement. I finally said, "Jean-Claude, breathe or something to let me know you're still there."

"The other masters see my allowing you access to my *pomme de sang* on a romantic trip as a weakness; if they only understood what a strength it was."

"Which means that Jason is right. We need to be perceived as being punished for this, even though it's not true. You need to be seen as bringing your house in order, so they don't keep thinking you're weak."

"I would never have suggested it, *ma petite*, you know that."

"I do, but now that Jason has let the cat out of the bag?"

"It would be helpful to my standing among the other masters."

"Would you have just waited until someone made a move on you before you explained that it was my fault you appeared that weak?"

"That would have given me the opportunity to bring the subject up, yes."

"Jesus, Jean-Claude, you've got to stop keeping this much from me."

"I do not know what magic our Jason has over you, but it seems that he is one of the few people who can tell you hard truths and you accept them. You are not even angry."

I thought about it. "I guess I'm not. I think I'm too worried to be angry. Jason told me there's a hint that some of the masters think if they could take me as their human servant, they could be as powerful as you, but control me better. That kind of talk could go really badly since I travel all over the country doing my job. I needed to know that, Jean-Claude."

"I thought you would see it as manipulation either to curtail your travel or to force you into a more servile role."

"My ego is secure, Jean-Claude, but my safety and yours might not be if the other masters keep talking shit behind your back."

"What are you willing to do to help stop this *merde*, this shit talk?"

"I haven't thought that far, but I'm sure you have, so either tell me now, or wait and we'll have this talk when we get home."

"I have put some thought into things that might satisfy the perceptions of others, but not harm us in our own eyes," he said, again his voice very careful.

"Is it anything we can do right this minute?"

"Non."

"Then save it, let me digest all the news tonight. We'll talk tomorrow."

"And you will do what is necessary to repair my reputation?"

"Some of it, but if Jason was right, and he usually is, he suggested that if you were truly having sex with some of the other men, it would help repair your reputation."

The silence on the other side of the phone was thunderous.

"Well, shit," I said.

His oh-so-neutral voice said, "Why the exclamation, *ma petite*? I have said nothing."

"Sometimes silence with you is louder than words," I said.

"I do not understand."

"Let's say that I know the quality of your silences, and that last silence means Jason is right. So I'll say this: I have no idea how the other men would feel about it, and I sure as hell don't know how I feel about it. Though Asher would probably turn cartwheels."

"That is unfair; he has been very patient."

"I know that." I struggled to keep the impatience and near anger out of my own voice.

"Now you are angry."

"It's a lot of stuff to digest, Jean-Claude, and the reporters going berserk today was a little weird. And what's up with Gretchen?"

"She is being punished."

"The last time you put her in a cross-wrapped coffin, she came out even crazier than she went in; I don't think she can survive another round of it."

"I am open to suggestions, *ma petite*."

"You can't kill her, because it was too public, there'd be too many questions."

"If it had not been so very public?"

"It's not just me and the men that make you look weak to the other masters, Jean-Claude. Most of them would have killed Gretchen and Meng Die, already."

"I could kill Meng Die; she has not made a public display."

"I don't mean kill her, but they have both behaved badly and most master vamps wouldn't tolerate it. I love that you feel guilty about taking their humanity away. I love that you feel guilty that you never loved them, but only seduced them. I love that you are that . . . human. But the other vamps see it as weakness, don't they?"

"They see me as weak for the very reasons you love me."

"Well, most of them are men, they can't help being a little . . . male."

He laughed, and it slithered across my skin as if he'd trailed a feather across my body. "Oh, God, Jean-Claude, don't do that again. We're being good over here."

"You are being very, very good." He made the *very, very* sound utterly suggestible.

"Stop that," I said.

He laughed again, and I clung to the pillow like a lifeline. I said, "Do you want to raise the *ardeur* in me and force Jason and me to have sex?"

"You will have sex either way, *ma petite*, I know you and our Jason. Sex for the two of you is only a matter of when, not if."

"Well, thank you very much."

"Why should a healthy appetite for carnal knowledge be a bad thing, *ma petite*? It is good to know what you want and need, and to have those needs met."

"Have I been keeping you from meeting some of your needs?"

"We have spoken enough of difficult things. When you have finished giving the truth to Mr. Griswold, then enjoy yourselves."

"We were planning to, but I don't like that you seem to be rooting for it."

"Would you enjoy it more if I did not give my permission?"

"No, I would never cheat on you."

He was quiet for a moment then he said, "*Je t'aime, ma petite.*"

"*Je t'aime*, Jean-Claude."

He hung up, and I did the same. He always had an excellent sense of when a conversation was over. I, on the other hand, was always trying to beat a dead horse. He'd learned long ago to just leave the conversational mazes with me. Conversational mazes only worked when you had someone to talk to, but wait, Jason was still here. I could always talk the two of us into a corner after we stopped spilling our guts to Irving. Yeah, the night was young; there were all sorts of unpleasant topics we could cover.

23

I HADN'T TALKED to Irving Griswold in months, ever since he told me that my "exclusives" to him, and him alone, were beginning to make people question his humanity. He was a werewolf and a member of our local pack, but he was deep in the closet. His choice, but when he told me to back off, I did.

I could picture him on his end of the phone: short, a little round, built sort of like a square, not fat, but just that body build that if he'd been taller would have made him a great linebacker. He had curly hair and a bald spot starting, but apparently that had begun before he became a werewolf, and being a werewolf meant it would never go further. I'd seen him in wolf form and the animal didn't have a bald spot on its head. Interesting.

"Anita, I know I told you to leave me alone about the exclusives, but I didn't expect you to vanish off the planet for me."

I had expected a lot of things from Irving, but not hurt

feelings. "Are you really upset I stopped talking to you, or did you just miss what the exclusives were doing to your career?"

"That is cold, Anita, very cold."

"Just a question, Irving."

He laughed then, and his laugh was so nicely ordinary after the magic of Jean-Claude's that it made me smile. "Couldn't I miss both you and the career opportunities?"

"I suppose. Jason filled you in on the problem."

"That's you, Blake, all business."

"We're in deep shit, Irving, so yeah."

He sighed, and his voice was serious when he said, "Yes, Jason explained the problem. Though someone here at the paper made sure I saw the segment about you. They said my old girlfriend was on the news."

"Girlfriend?" I made it a question.

"Apparently, no man can be seen too often with you without it ruining his reputation."

"I didn't know that," I said.

"You didn't need to know."

"So it wasn't just about your career, was it?"

"No, I'm dating someone here at the paper pretty seriously. She was a good sport, but the office gossip was pretty virulent."

"*Virulent*, huh, that's a big word, and a serious one."

"Heh, they won't let me trot my vocabulary out in my articles; I've got to prove I've got that college education somehow."

I smiled again. I'd missed Irving more than I thought. "Can we fix this mess?"

"Articles by me can help minimize the damage, but a good rumor is really hard to kill once it hits the major media."

"What can we do?"

"I was thinking a series of articles about what it's like to be part of Jean-Claude's life. You know, talk to Jason about what it's like to be his *pomme de sang*. What it's like for you to be his girlfriend. We'll start with a denial of the rumor, but maybe our Master of the City is overdue for some good press."

"Press that makes him seem in control of his city."

"Yeah, Jason hit the highlights that I'm not allowed to write about. If I weren't afraid of being outed, this would be such a better story."

"Being outed would be the least of your worries if you wrote everything you know, Irving."

"Is that a threat?" he asked.

I thought about it. "No, not consciously, but I am still Bolverk for your pack, the evildoer."

He lowered his voice. "Yeah, you punish the bad little werewolves, I know."

"But no, it wasn't a threat, just an observation. I think Richard would get to you long before I could."

"Yeah, our Ulfric seems to have acquired a temper."

"Sorry about that."

"Is it true he's inherited part of your temper?" Irving asked.

"Seems so."

"Then my compliments for your self-control all these years."

I wasn't sure what to make of the compliment, so I ignored it. "Thanks, now what do you need from me?"

"We'll run the first article about Jason's dad and the cancer, and how his master couldn't travel on such short notice so you came with him for moral support. It'll play very sentimental."

"Won't that make Jean-Claude look weak in the eyes of the other masters?"

"Anita, there are only so many ways to explain this rumor away. Showing Jean-Claude as generous to his people may make the other masters think him weak, but trust me, us underlings will read it and go, *Wow, he'd be a great master to work for. I wonder how I get to move to St. Louis.* Revolutions start from the bottom up, Anita, rarely top down."

"Are we starting a revolution?"

"The way Jean-Claude runs his territory is revolutionary, Anita. I'm not the only reporter who's in deep cover. There are a couple of us who sit around and bemoan the great stories we could write if we weren't pretending to be normal."

I leaned back against the headboard, the pillow still in my lap. "I guess I thought you were the only reporter in that deep a cover."

"No, there's one swanmane, and another werewolf, and even a weretiger."

"And you've all managed to hide what you are?"

"Yep."

"Must be hard," I said.

"It's hard to hide, but you're seeing how hard it is not to hide."

I sighed. "You got that right."

"Though you being his human servant isn't going to be part of the articles, just the dating."

"I've looked it up, and me being his human servant isn't legal grounds for my dismissal as a federal marshal, or even an ordinary cop, if I were one."

"You saying I can use it?"

"No, but I'm saying it's not legalities, but perceptions that I'm hiding from."

"Okay, I'll write up the article saying how misguided my fellow reporters are, and then we'll start with Jason's article. Then yours, and then we'll see who else wants to talk; my editor is going to love it."

"How about your girlfriend?"

"I'll talk to her when I get off the phone. She'll be okay. She's in the business."

"Okay."

"You sound tired," he said.

I leaned my head against the wall behind the headboard. "Maybe."

"I'll go hunt up my editor and get this started. You guys be careful."

"I'm always careful, Irving."

He laughed then. "If this is your version of careful, then be reckless; it's gotta work better."

We hung up, both laughing. I put the phone in its cradle and went back to leaning against the wall. I even closed my eyes. I was tired. I couldn't even decide why I was this tired.

I felt the bed move and opened my eyes to find Jason kneeling in front of me. His eyes were very close to mine. He was also still nude, because other than the pillow in my lap, neither of us had thought to get robes.

"We've done the best we can, Anita," he said.

I gave him a smile to match how I felt, which wasn't all that much of a smile. "Sometimes it would be nice not to have to do my best. Sometimes it would just be nice not to have a crisis to deal with."

He grinned. "I know what you mean." The grin went from his normal to his I've-thought-of-something-naughty-to-do grin.

"What?" I said, and the one word held a wealth of suspicion.

He laughed, and it made his face look even younger than he was, like a glimpse into a Jason I had never met. Jason before Raina nearly killed him, making him a werewolf. Jason before he became

Jean-Claude's morning snack. Jason before life rubbed all his edges away.

The laughter leaked away and his eyes were serious as he gazed down at me. "The look on your face, what are you thinking?"

I shook my head. A dozen thoughts ran through my mind; that I was tired, that he'd given a story to the media that would spoil our cover story with his family, that he was being very brave, that I knew he must be hurting, that he was my good friend and I wanted him to know that. What I finally said was, "Kiss me."

He had a moment of looking startled, and then he smiled, and the smile was worth the careful choice of words. That smile that said I had asked first; without the *ardeur* loose, I had asked for a kiss from him.

24

THE KISS GREW until he pressed me back to the bed, and his body grew eager against the front of me. Eager enough that I wrapped my legs around him, and the most intimate part of him was suddenly pressed tight against the most intimate part of me. He drew back with a shaky laugh.

"We need a condom."

I closed my eyes and had a moment of embarrassment. "Of course, we do, I'm sorry I got carried away."

He leaned down and kissed me quick and hard, and let me see the delight on his face that I had forgotten myself that much with him. "Jean-Claude gave me very few restrictions, but this was one. No unprotected sex." He kissed me again, then slid off the bed to hunt for condoms in the luggage.

I lay there thinking about the fact that I might have forgotten enough to have unprotected sex with Jason. I was on the pill, so technically, it wasn't exactly unprotected. I'd been so careful since the pregnancy scare a few months back. How could I have been so careless? Irving's words came back to me, about how my caution hadn't worked, so maybe it was time to be reckless. Was that it? Was I just tired of my best efforts going so wrong, so why try? No, no, just carried away with a handsome man in my bed. Jesus, that didn't sound any better.

Jason came back with a little string of unopened condoms in his hand. I counted at least four. "Aren't we being ambitious."

He glanced down at the condoms, then laughed again. "In case one gets put on inside out, or has a hole. I don't want to leave the bed to look for another one."

I had to smile at him, and that was one of the best things about being with Jason. He always made me smile. No strings, no love on the line, just good friends who had managed to be lovers and still be friends. It was good.

He put the condoms on the bedside table, then climbed onto the bed, still smiling. The smile changed as he moved closer—his eyes growing more serious, the smile sliding away to leave his face almost empty of expression except for the intensity of his eyes. His eyes were all blue skies, spring skies, but as he leaned in toward me the blue had deepened, so that his eyes were the color of summer, and nothing as soft as spring.

He hesitated, then half-leaned in for a kiss, his body still to the side of mine. "The look on your face, Anita," he breathed.

"What look?" I asked.

He smiled, but it left his eyes that serious, deeper blue. He leaned in and answered with his mouth just above mine. "That look."

He kissed me. Gentle at first, then it grew, and as the kiss grew, he let his body fall against the side of mine, so that the nude front of him was pressed against the long, bare line of my side. The sensation of his groin against my thigh made me thrust into the kiss with hands and arms and mouth. Either he understood, or his body simply responded, because he grew harder, and pushed against my thigh, while he thrust deep into my mouth and I thrust back. The kiss became another way of fucking, gaining its own rhythm as if we both knew what we were mimicking. Our bodies grew with the kiss, so that he began to thrust against my thigh in time to our mouths.

He drew back, laughing breathlessly, pulling his body inches away so that he was no longer touching my thigh. "If we don't stop, I'm going to go like this."

I had to try twice to find enough air to say, "Then we have to stop, because that's not how I want you to go."

He propped himself up on one elbow, his other hand playing lightly over my bare stomach. If I'd been just a little less metaphysically powerful I'd have had some really serious scars for him to play with, but the weretiger that had tried to gut me hadn't left any mark at all.

"You've gone all serious on me," Jason said.

"I was just thinking that if I were a little less powerful, there'd be scars for you to play with on my stomach."

He touched my face. "Don't think about what we've lost, Anita. Think about what we have."

I smiled at him, because he wanted me to. "You mean don't think about the fight that would have gotten me the scars, and don't think about who died to save me."

His face went soft, serious, tender. "Now you've done it."

I opened my mouth, and he touched a finger to my lips. He shook his head. "If you keep this up, you're going to have to help me get back in the mood."

I smiled with his finger still against my mouth. He moved, so I could say, "You still look in the mood to me."

"Girls have such an unfair advantage," he said, "you just look down and there we are."

"I like that about boys," I said.

He gave a soft laugh. "I've noticed."

He leaned into me again, showing that he was still erect, but not quite so hard. "My mood's gone a little soft, so no serious thinking. I want you thinking only about now, about me."

I searched his face. His body was happy, but his mood was more serious than normal. I guess I should have expected that, but Jason was my cheerful lay. The sex, at least, was uncomplicated. The pillow talk afterward could get downright therapy-deep, but the sex, never.

"That's a serious face again," he chided.

"I was doing what you asked, thinking about you."

"Why so serious then?" he asked, frowning a little.

I slid my hand through the short silk of his hair, just at the base of his neck, ran my hands up through the utter softness of it, and drew him down toward me at the same time. "You have the softest hair of anyone I've ever touched."

"Softer than Nathaniel's?"

"Yes," I said. I tried to bring him down for a kiss.

"Fibber," he said, and pushed against my hand so he didn't come closer.

"Fibber?" I said.

"I've had sex with the two of you, remember. His hair is like fur on the skin."

"Yeah, but it's not as purely soft. It's a different texture than yours."

"Jean-Claude's hair is soft."

I frowned at him. "Yes, but not as soft as yours. Curly hair is never as soft as straight hair can be."

"Asher's hair is like foam."

I frowned harder, and took back my hand, so I was just looking up at him. "I give you one compliment and you have to pick at it?"

"I'm sorry, but I just suddenly didn't believe you."

"I don't lie during sex, Jason. I don't say things I don't mean, and I don't fake anything."

He lowered his face, so I had only his profile. It was a nice profile. "I'm sorry, Anita, this isn't your issue, it's mine." He looked at me, and his eyes had begun to fade back to his normal, paler blue.

"What issue?" I asked.

"You've met my folks now. I've spent my life not being the person anyone wanted in their life. My dad wanted a different son, Anita. Do you know what it feels like to know that your dad is always wanting some other kind of son?"

"Not the son part," I said.

His eyes intensified, getting that look of interest he got. "Did your dad want you to be a boy, or something?"

I smiled. "No, he was happy with me. I was still his hunting buddy, and we did all sorts of the guy stuff together."

"Your stepmother, Judith," he said.

"You are a little too smart sometimes."

"Sorry."

"They married when I was ten, and from the moment she came I was not good enough. Not blond enough, not girly enough, not nice enough, not cooperative enough, not the daughter she wanted."

"She's got a girl your age, right?"

"Yeah, Adriana. She's the perfect daughter for Judith."

"What's she do?"

"She's a lawyer, engaged to another lawyer."

"Wow, a lawyer, and engaged to be married before thirty. Hard to compete with that," Jason said.

"I figured out somewhere in my midteens that I couldn't compete, so I stopped trying. You acted out your way, I had my own version."

"Like what?" He lay down on his stomach, with his arms cradling his head, his face alive with attention. He wanted the sex, yes, but he wanted to learn more.

"I became the ultimate tomboy. I refused to wear a dress. I refused to play the game with Judith."

"Did you do the whole black T-shirt and gloom?"

"Was I Goth?"

He nodded, head still cradled on his arms.

"Yeah, I guess so, but not really because it pleased me, more because it didn't please her. I found the most offensive T-shirts I could get away with, and most of them came in black. But my friends in high school were the nice girls, not the death poetry writing crowd. I found them . . . tiresome."

"Why?"

"Because I'd had real death in my life, and I thought most of them were pretenders."

"You don't have much patience with pretending, do you?"

"No."

"But you could always tell yourself that Judith is the wicked stepmother."

"Yeah, but Grandma Blake, who raised me for the two years before my father found Judith, well, that's a different problem."

"What sort of problem?"

"Remember, I saw ghosts in elementary school; by my early teens I'd accidentally started raising roadkill. I raised my dead spaniel from the grave at fourteen. My dad took me to see my mother's mother, Grandma Flores, so I could learn to control it. But Grandma Blake didn't want me to learn to control it.

She was convinced that if we prayed hard enough, the evil would just go away."

Jason looked at me, eyes a little wide. "She really believes that, even now?"

"I think so. I know she prays for my soul. I know she believes that raising the dead is evil. I know she believes that sleeping with vampires is a mortal sin."

"How does she feel about shapeshifters?"

"Oh, you're damned, too."

"Does she know you're living with two of them?"

"Nope."

He grinned at me. "Saving the news for a moment when it will bother her the most?"

"No, I plan to never tell my family."

He looked at me. "You're never going home for the holidays and taking anyone with you?"

I sighed. "Who would I take?"

He seemed to think about that. "The vampires are out, I guess."

I nodded.

"Wait, you don't want to go back home for the holidays, so living with two shapeshifters means you don't have to go back, because your family would never understand."

I thought about what he'd said for a few seconds. "Maybe, but Nathaniel and Micah aren't an excuse to not visit my family. I love them, and I've finally got a domestic arrangement that suits me."

He nodded. "I've known you longer than either of them, and I've never seen you this relaxed, or this happy."

I smiled. "All right, now that we've analyzed me, is it your turn?"

He actually looked a little embarrassed. "I'm sorry."

"If I didn't want to talk about it, I'd have just said no."

"True, why did you confess so much?"

"Because I've seen your family, and I thought you'd earned the right to know a little more about mine."

"You did it to try to make me feel better," he said.

"Maybe. Did it work?"

I watched the thoughts trace over his face, and then he nodded. "Yes, it did. I guess I needed to know that I'm not the only one who's the stranger at every holiday meal."

"Yeah," I said, "that sums it up. Everyone else goes home for nostalgia, and happy memories. I end up feeling like I never fit in with the family as a child, and being older hasn't changed that. When I was little I thought I'd been left by gypsies, or switched at the hospital, except I had my mother's pictures to look at. I look too much like her not to be her daughter."

"She was from Mexico, right?"

"Her family was, she was first-generation American."

"You don't look very Hispanic."

I smiled. "The skin color is my father's, but the hair, eyes and bone structure are more my mom's. My father's cheekbones have given me less of that nice high, ethnic line, but I am the ghost at the banquet, Jason. The older I got, the more I reminded Dad of the wife he lost, and Judith of the woman she replaced."

"Is that your issue, or theirs?"

"A little of both, I think. Remember, my mother was Dad's first love, maybe his first lover, I don't know, but a lot of firsts. That's a lot of baggage to overcome. Then you have that whole dying-young-and-tragically thing, it tends to put a romantic haze around everything."

"Hard for Judith to compete with a dead saint?" he said.

"Something like that."

"Are you projecting, or do you know for certain that wicked stepmom felt this way?"

"I don't know, Jason. I know that's how I feel, and how they seemed to feel, but I was a kid, and now I can't see them clearly. There's too much baggage in the way."

"I hear that," he said, and his face was back to being all serious, and unhappy. "I wanted to drown in the sex and not think, but here we are doing the whole therapy thing that you hate."

I touched his shoulder. "You've earned some talk."

"Why, because my father's a bastard and dying?"

"Yeah, and you're my friend, and I'm supposed to be here to give you what you need. If you need talk more than sex, then we can do that."

"You need to feed the *ardeur*," he said.

"Yeah, but if worse comes to worst, I can just release the *ardeur* and it will take away all our doubts."

"The *ardeur* is great, and it can take the place of a lot of foreplay, but it's not what I want right now."

"What do you want, then?" I asked.

He looked at me, and his face was that serious, almost a stranger's face, as if the things he'd seen today had changed him. Or maybe the things that had happened today had allowed him to show me a part of himself he'd kept hidden. Or maybe the stroll down my own tortured memory lane was just making everything seem more serious. I couldn't tell anymore, and I didn't have Nathaniel or Micah here to help me work it out. The only other man who could usually help me see through the maze of confusion was lying beside me on the bed, lost in his own problems.

"I want you," he said, simply.

I frowned at him.

He gave a gentle smile that left his eyes untouched. "To that question in your eyes, I'll clarify."

"You know me that well?"

"In bed, yes. You stop trying to control your face once the clothes come off. Dressed, you're almost as hard to read as Jean-Claude sometimes."

I thought about that for a second. "I guess I feel like I don't get naked with people I don't trust."

He smiled. "Yeah."

I settled back against the pillows and said, "So, clarify."

"I can find women to sleep with, or fuck. I'm a stripper. They're always trying to give me their numbers, persuade me to go beyond what's legal. I'm Jean-Claude's *pomme de sang*; a lot of women want to sleep with me just for that. To get close to the vampires. The whole werewolf thing gets you a different type of groupie." Then he flashed me that grin that filled his eyes with sparkle for a moment. It made me smile to see it. "And, I get my share of women who don't know any of that, and probably could be persuaded."

I waited for him to continue, but had to watch the shine fade from his eyes, and the grin fade. His face was caught between his usual charm and this new, serious side.

"But . . . ," I finally prompted him.

He took a breath and said, "But only you will tell me the truth. Only you will tell me exactly what you want, or don't want. You said it yourself, you don't fake anything here. You don't protect my ego. Either I'm good, or I'm not. You don't want to trap me into anything. You don't have an agenda beyond the pleasure. You aren't worried about what we're going to do afterward, or what we did a moment before. You are completely and utterly into the sex, almost from the moment you touch a man. It's relaxing, you don't know how relaxing."

"Doesn't everyone do it that way?"

He smiled and shook his head. "No, no, they don't. Most people let their day get in their head and in the way of the sex. A lot of women just can't turn off their heads long enough to relax to even begin to enjoy themselves."

"I've known some men that way, too," I said.

He smiled, again. "Me being one of them."

"Not usually, but sometimes. You usually save the analyzing for after the sex, as if the sex clears the way for you to have the big heart-to-heart."

He grinned. "That's not it. I want the sex more than I want the talking."

"But not tonight," I said, softly.

His eyes held onto the humor a little longer, but his face began to slide toward that more serious, older version that I realized was probably going to start peeking through more and more as the years went by. Maybe we were all growing up, even Jason.

"No, not tonight. But I'm done with the talk. I want to touch you, and I want you to touch me. I want to drown in the scent of your skin, the taste of your body. Sex has been my addiction since I was a kid, and it's still my escape of choice."

"Actually addicted to sex?" I asked.

"Therapy-speak again?" he said.

I had to smile. "You know, Nathaniel is in therapy."

"I know that he is diagnosed as a sex addict, or was, if that's what you mean?"

"Then you know how bad it got for him?"

"I know," Jason said, "and no, if you're really going to make me give a definition, then no, I'm not a sex addict. I was close in high school, and really close in college. But Raina nearly killing me during sex sort of cured me of the risky behavior, better than any therapy could have."

Through a metaphysical accident I'd shared that memory with him once. It had been horrible, because I'd been in Raina's head, and I knew for a fact that the ex-lupa of our werewolf pack hadn't given a damn whether Jason lived or died. He'd agreed to be tied up and have her change on top of him, and have that as his way of being brought over to the pack. What he hadn't understood was that she would slice him up with no care. It had been about violence more than sex for her, true serial killer mentality. I think the only thing that had kept her from having a higher body count was that the lycanthropy saved her victims' lives. Though, in honesty, I couldn't find anyone else she'd brought over as violently as Jason. I pushed the thought away. I was still able to channel her, sometimes, and this was not the time.

"So, because you could stop the behavior through a shock, you weren't a true addict?"

"Something like that, though it depends on what therapist you're talking to, I guess."

We were left looking at each other, both too serious for being in bed naked. Both of us thinking too hard for what we were supposed to be doing. I wondered how to get us past this and into something else, or whether it was time to put the clothes back on.

"I love watching you think," he said.

I frowned. "What does that mean?"

"It means that even in the middle of sex, sometimes something will happen and I'll watch you think. Not about your day, or about something extraneous, but about the sex, about the man you're with, about what you're doing."

"How can you be sure that's what I was thinking?"

"Fine, what are you thinking?"

I tried not to smile, and failed. "Wondering how to get you from this to sex."

"See?"

"What are you thinking, right now, Mr. Serious-Face?"

He smiled. "That I want to watch your face while you stare up at me while we make love."

"So you get to be on top?" I asked, and tried to make a joke of it. The joke fell flat in the face of his serious eyes.

"Eventually."

"Eventually, huh."

He leaned in toward me, and that smile crossed his face, the one that if the customers at Guilty Pleasures could see it, they'd empty their bank accounts. "Yes."

I started to ask what he wanted to do first, but he kissed me, his hands slid over my body, and I didn't have to ask what he wanted to do first. He showed me.

25

JASON SHOWED ME with his hand between my legs, his mouth on mine. He showed me that he was done with his doubts, done with everything but my body and his.

I'd never been with him alone when the *ardeur* was not riding me. I'd never been with him when we could pay attention only to each other, without anyone, or anything, else to distract us, to distract him. He was all hands, and mouth, and teeth, and need. He brought me with his fingers between my legs, then slid his fingers inside me and found that sweet spot. He brought me again, and again, with a flick of fingers and flex of hand. Brought me until I shivered, twitched, and writhed, and damn near convulsed on the bed, while he knelt between my legs so he could find just the right angle for his hand.

I managed to gasp, "God, Jason, God!" Then he stole my words with the pleasure of his hand inside me. He left me with my eyes rolled back into my head, so I was blind to everything but the sensations of my body. Only then did I feel him above me. Feel the press of his body, the weight of him settling on top of me, making me cry out again. I struggled to open my eyes, to see his face hovering over me. The look in his face was everything you want to see in that moment. There was no uncertainty, only the knowledge that he had done this, that his body, his touch, his expertise had brought me to this moment, when the innocent lay of his weight above me could make me cry with pleasure.

He whispered, "Now I'm going to fuck you."

I whispered back the only word I could think of. "Yes."

He smiled, and I would have tried to decide what kind of pleased smile it was, but he chose that moment to work his hips between my legs and push himself inside me. I was so wet, so ready from everything he'd done that he slid inside me in one strong movement.

It rolled my eyes back into my head again and tore a sound from my throat as my neck bowed backward, and my spine bowed underneath us both.

His voice came from beside my ear, against my hair. "So wet, so tight, so ready." He shoved himself as deep inside me as he could, made me cry out again, and writhe. Then he kissed me, kissed me with our bodies buried as close as they could get. He kissed me, as if the kiss were all, and he weren't beginning to move himself in and out of my body. He kissed me, explored me, fucked my mouth as he fucked my body. He'd done his foreplay right; it seemed only minutes and I was screaming my orgasm into his mouth, squeezing it around his groin, clawing it into his back and shoulders. My hands slid in the glisten of sweat on his back. I screamed for him, and he fought to keep his mouth on mine, his body's rhythm inside me. The only thing he changed was that he fucked me harder, pounding himself inside me harder and faster. I screamed and shrieked, and clung to his body with nails and hands and arms, as if the pleasure would tear me apart, or I would tear him apart.

He finally rose up enough to pin my wrists to the bed. It meant he couldn't kiss me anymore, but he could still fuck me, and he did. I could watch his body work in and out of mine now, and the sight alone brought me again. Without his mouth to stop me, the screams were long and ragged.

His voice came breathy, strained with effort, as his body kept working in and out of mine. "Feed, Anita, feed."

It took me moments to fight back from the waves of pleasure, to hear the words, to even try to understand them. I managed, "What?"

"Feed the *ardeur*, Anita. Feed before I go."

I blinked up at him, and it must have shown on my face, because he laughed, a wonderful masculine laugh, so happy, so Jason, but more. "You forgot, you forgot about the *ardeur*."

I managed to nod.

"I do good work," he gasped, "but feed now, I'm almost . . ." His body convulsed above mine, eyes closing, his body beginning to lose its rhythm.

"Feed, now!"

I almost didn't have enough concentration left to find that metaphysical piece inside me and let it go. But at the last moment, with his body almost gone above mine, and the effort showing on his face, in his shoulders, his arms, his chest, I found the *ardeur*, and let go. It rose from me like a nearly visible force. Jason's body reacted to it, like a blow. He cried out above me, his body shoved inside me one last time, and I felt him let go, too. Let go of his control, let go of his effort, and give himself over to the *ardeur*, give himself over to that piece of me that fed on pleasure. It fed on the feel of his body buried deep inside mine, it fed on the strength of his hands holding me down, it fed on the salt taste of his skin as my mouth rose and licked at his chest. I fed, as his body convulsed inside mine, not once, but twice, three times. I brought him with my body squeezed around him, pulsing for every last drop. I brought him with my mouth on his skin, his chest, licking the last salty bit off the hardness of his nipple.

He paused above me, head hanging down, the ends of his hair plastered to his face with his efforts. His shoulders began to collapse, so that he finally lay down on top of me. He kept his hands loosely on my wrists as his face lay beside mine on the pillow. He was still inside me, but we were both done. We lay there, not for more sex, but to catch our breaths, and let our bodies be able to move again.

He kissed my cheek, and I turned, with effort, so he could kiss my lips. It was a gentle, breathless kiss, and I swear I could taste his pulse in his mouth.

"I like you," he said, and managed a smile as he said it.

It made me laugh, and that made him wince, rather than writhe. "No more, God, please."

He'd reached that point where he was too sensitive to do more. Cool. I kissed him back and said, "I like you, too."

When *love* isn't on the menu, *like* isn't a bad thing to be able to say, and mean it.

26

THE SEX HAD been good enough that it wasn't a matter of deciding how long to cuddle afterward, it was simply we both fell asleep. We fell into that deep, exhausted, damn near unconscious rest that comes after the sex has been long, and hard, and sweaty, and amazing, and the day has been too long, too hard, and you can finally let it all go. You can finally rest, against the skin and touch and weight of your lover.

I woke with Jason and I wrapped around each other; legs and arms intertwined, bodies almost melded together with sweat, and fluids, and sleep.

He made a small, soft sound that was almost a laugh, but not. The sound was one of those utterly contented noises that have no spelling, no place in a dictionary, but they are often the sounds that say more than any full word just how happy we are.

He turned his head enough to see me, and gave me the

smile and the look that went with that soft almost-laugh. I moved my head toward him, still on the pillow, and he moved, too, so that our lips met in the middle of the pillow, our bodies still intertwined.

Jason drew back just enough to look at my face, our faces still pressed to the same pillow. "That—was—amazing."

I smiled. "Yes, it was." I focused a little past his face and saw marks on his shoulders. I lifted my head enough to see better, and found nail marks on his back. "Jesus, Jason, I'm sorry."

"It's a compliment," he said, giving that lazy smile.

I laid my head back down on the pillow, because it still seemed too much effort to move much. "That's why you pinned my wrists."

"Yeah," he said, grinning, "I love that you lose control with me like that, but I wasn't really in the mood to bleed too much tonight."

I rose up again, to see the marks more clearly, bending from the shoulders this time and not just the neck. There weren't many marks, but what there were had dried blood in them. I made a face. "Sorry."

He shook his head and cuddled closer to me on the pillow, so that our faces touched when my shoulders relaxed. "Never apologize for enjoying being with me, Anita. I love that you enjoy me."

I kissed his forehead because it was closest. "I know a lot of women enjoy you."

"They have," he admitted, "but not lately."

I stroked my hand down his shoulder. "She really screwed with your head, didn't she?"

"You mean, Perdy?" he asked. He'd gone very still beside me.

"Yeah."

"She said she loved me, but she told me what I wanted to do with her was wrong, perverted."

"Did she actually say *perverted*?" I asked, and put another kiss on his forehead.

"No," he said.

"See, you're projecting."

"She said *evil*."

That made me go still beside him, with my lips against his face. "Evil?" I made it a question.

"Yep."

"What the hell could you have asked for that she would have called *evil*?"

He tensed beside me and looked toward the door. "There are people at our door. One of them has been drinking, a lot."

"You can smell it," I said.

He nodded, still looking at the door. I didn't immediately go for my gun on the bedside table. I mean, they could just be a bunch of partiers going to their own room.

Then someone pounded on our door, and a woman's voice said, "Keith, I know you're in there, you bastard! Open this door, you cheating bastard!"

Jason looked at me. "Don't look at me," I said, "this is so not my kind of problem."

"So you don't know what to do either?"

"Not a clue," I said.

"Great," he said, "me either."

She hit the door so hard it shook. Where she was hitting the door said she wasn't that tall, but she was giving it all she had, and drunk she was using more strength than she would have used sober. She'd be bruised in the morning, and probably not remember why.

Jason went for one of the thick robes that were always in the nicer hotel rooms. He tossed me the second robe.

"We're not going to open the door, are we?" I asked, and let my voice sound suitably horrified.

"She's not going away."

"She's also drunk enough that one look at us in this room like this is going to convince her she's right."

"I can't help that I look that much like him."

"Keith, you son of a bitch, open this door!"

"Mr. Summerland, do you really want the eleven o'clock news to show you leaving your fiancée outside your door while you have sex with another woman?"

I sat up, suddenly very serious about the robe. "Oh my God, there are reporters with her."

He started looking for Chuck's business card. "You call Chuck, tell him what's happening." I didn't argue, I just took the card and started punching buttons.

Jason went to the door but didn't open it. He yelled through it, "My name is Jason Schuyler, I am not Keith Summerland."

"You tried that in high school, Keith, pretending to be Jason when you were screwing Nan Brandweiss."

I had Chuck on the phone. "This is Chuck."

"Anita Blake. We have reporters outside our door with Keith Summerland's very drunk fiancée, demanding to know why he's cheating on her."

"Oh, shit." He said it with real feeling.

"My sentiments exactly. What do we do?"

"I thought you weren't going to call, I'm not at the hotel. I'll be there as soon as I can. I'll alert some of the other guards. Hell, they should be with her now. Do not open the door."

"Do you want the eleven o'clock news to show Keith's

fiancée banging on the door, but not having it open? That's what the reporters are threatening. She's crying and she's drunk."

"Damn it, I'll be there. Just, oh hell, this is going to go to shit."

"Going, Chuck? I think it's already gone."

Jason called through the door, "Lisa Bromwell, is that you?"

"Keith, this isn't funny, don't humiliate me like this, don't make me beg."

Jason started to unlock the door.

"Gotta go, Chuck, Jason is unlocking the door."

"Can't you control him better than that?"

"About as much as you can control Keith and his fiancée," I said.

"Then we're screwed," Chuck said. He hung up. I hung up. And I couldn't have agreed more.

27

I GOT MY gun from the bedside table and put it in my robe pocket. Not because I thought I needed my gun handy, but because it was my gun and it was my job to control it. A very drunk woman scorned was about to come through the door. I did not want to give her any ideas. A loaded gun unattended could be a real disaster. The robe hung funny on that side, but it was better than the alternative.

Jason opened the door and a short blond woman spilled through, pounding fists on his chest. She was screaming at him. A reporter, complete with camera and lights, pushed in behind her. Perfect.

Jason was trying to out-yell her. "It's Jason. Lisa, look at me, it's Jason!"

Lisa's eyes were squeezed tight as she pounded at him and screamed. She had wanted in the room, but she didn't want to see.

I stood there without a clue as to what I could do that might help. I could have forced the reporter and cameraman out; I was armed. But somehow I thought that might play badly in the press. To the hysterical Lisa I was the other woman, so trying to touch her would be bad. I had no freaking idea what to do. Fuck.

The camera was getting it all: me standing in the robe, the mussed bed, the string of condoms in their wrapper on the floor where Jason had dropped them. There were even a few pieces of clothing draped on the room's chair. Again, perfect.

The reporter shoved a microphone into Jason's face. "Keith, is this the new woman? Is the wedding off? Lisa deserves the truth, Keith."

Jason spoke into the mic. "My name is Jason Schuyler. I went to school with Lisa and Keith and Keith's brother Kelsey."

Maybe they would have listened, maybe not, but struggling with Lisa had finally loosened his robe so that it spilled apart enough for the camera to try to get the whole show. If it was network they wouldn't be able to show it, but how often do you get a chance to get film of a presidential hopeful's son nude? The cameraman wasn't missing his opportunity.

Lisa's hands were on Jason's stomach, and she'd stopped screaming. She was blinking down at him, not up at his face. She muttered, "Jason?" as Jason managed to get his robe a little more closed.

The fact that seeing him nude had made her believe it was him made me wonder, just how close a friend had Lisa Bromwell been to Jason in high school?

Voices from the hallway, mostly men, yelling. Peterson was the first one in the doorway, but he had other suits with him, and some of the uniformed guards we'd seen earlier. They were what we needed. Someone to be bad guys to the press and rescue us at the same time. I didn't usually wait to be rescued, but this level of press attention had thrown me. How do you handle people this rude that you can't belt in the nose?

Peterson and his men got the press out. They tried to get Lisa Bromwell out, too, but she was now clinging to Jason and blinking up at him blearily. A second woman from the hallway was trying to help Peterson persuade Lisa to let go of Jason. The new woman was tall in heels that made her at least six feet, with sleek brunette hair that had been styled straight, but was thick enough I was betting it curled when left to its own devices. She was beautiful in that perfect-makeup, I-read-*Cosmo* sort of way. You know, beautiful enough to make other women jealous and men stare, but she didn't seem quite real. Women like that almost never make me feel insecure. I don't understand them enough to be jealous.

Peterson got the reporters outside the room with the help of the uniformed guards. Two of the younger suits stayed on our side of the door and took up positions against it, as if the press might try to break down the door. Surely not, but I was beginning to realize that we'd passed into a sort of press *Twilight Zone*, where the normal rules did not seem to apply.

The brunette offered me her hand. "I'm Trish, friend of the bride's, and I'm sorry that I couldn't stop her in time." She had a good handshake, though her hand was big enough, and her nails long enough, that it felt almost dangerous, as if she'd cut me if she shook too hard.

"How did she find our room?"

"The reporter knew your room number. He told her they'd seen Keith check in with a brunette. They had pictures of the two of you in the hotel obviously going to a room."

"The bachelorette party must be in full swing for her to be this drunk," I said.

Trish shook her head. "It hasn't really started yet. She was this drunk when we got to the room for the party."

I looked over at the small blond woman, inches shorter than Jason and me. She swayed against him, clinging to his robe as if without it and his hands on her slender frame she'd have hit the floor. It must have shown on my face because Trish said, "Apparently she got drunk alone in her room. Her bridesmaids found her this way, clutching a handful of pictures of Keith with you."

"Not Keith," I said.

Trish nodded. "Apparently not, but the resemblance is eerie."

I couldn't argue with the eerie part. Now that Lisa wasn't screaming or crying hysterically or trying to claw Jason's eyes out, I realized that she and he looked alike. In fact, Lisa Bromwell looked more like Jason's sister than either of his actual sisters.

"You are the first woman I've gotten to talk to who isn't from this town. Is it just me or do they look alike, too?" Trish said.

"It's not just you," I said.

"Have you seen many of the descendants of old Jedediah and the original families from his little town in the hills?"

"Not yet," I said.

"They all look like that, like they're related."

"Jason said that Jedediah Summerland helped populate most of the town in his day."

"When you see the wedding party, you'll believe it."

I gave her a look.

She nodded, eyes a little wide. "Just wait, you'll see, it's very *Twilight Zone*."

"We just had a reporter with camera and lights burst into our hotel room, I already feel like I'm in the *Twilight Zone*."

"I'd like to say it'll get better, Anita, I can call you Anita, right?"

"Sure."

"I've been friends with them since they announced the wedding, and the closer it gets the weirder the press get. One of the reasons that they were so sure of you and—Jason, right?"

I nodded.

"—of Jason being Keith is that there is a rumor going around that he has a brunette on the side. It may even be true."

Jason had sat Lisa down in the chair. He rubbed her shoulders as he talked softly to her.

"If it's true, then why is she marrying him?" I asked.

Trish gave me a look.

"What?"

"He's rich, he's handsome, he's fun as hell when he's not being a bastard. His father is governor of the state and about to run for president. He may even make it all the way to the Oval Office."

She stopped talking, as if that explained why a woman would put up with a man who would cheat on her days before her wedding. I finally said, "You haven't said anything that would get me down the aisle with someone who would cheat on me days before my wedding."

"How about it's one of the biggest weddings of the year in this country, and backing out now would be more humiliating than going through with it?"

I shook my head. "That doesn't work for me either."

Trish studied my face, as if she were trying to decide if I was serious or not. "You really would just dump his ass, wouldn't you?"

"In a hot minute." It was my turn to study her. "Wouldn't you?"

She gave a laugh, a nervous laugh. "I've married for worse reasons than money and politics, Anita."

"And divorced, I take it."

She shrugged. "Yeah, but the alimony was the kicker."

In that moment I knew I might like Trish eventually, but I would never understand her, nor she me. We were both women, but our girl culture was too different. She was a girl-girl, and I was just a woman. She married for money and politics and potential alimony. I couldn't think of anything that would get me down a church aisle, but love would have been higher on the list than anything the woman beside me had listed. Who the hell married already planning how much alimony she'd get? That wasn't a marriage, that was a business transaction with rings exchanged.

How much trouble would we get into if I managed to talk Lisa Bromwell into dumping Keith Summerland's ass days before their wedding? It had possibilities, and not all of them were bad.

28

I GOT INTRODUCED to the bride-to-be eventually. There'd been a point in my life when I wouldn't have wanted to meet strangers dressed in nothing but a robe, in a hotel room, with a man who I wasn't married to, who was also in a robe. Strangely, this was so mild in comparison to my life lately that I didn't even flinch.

She blinked pale blue eyes at me. What makeup she'd started the night with had surrendered to tears and the damp rag that Jason had fetched for her. She blinked up at me, stray wisps of yellow hair clinging to her face where they'd been wetted down, other bits of her hair just all around her face. Without the makeup she looked about twelve, though I knew she had to be Jason's age. Twenty-two or twenty-three; she did not look it.

I said automatically, "Nice to meet you, Lisa."

She blushed a nice pink color and looked down. "I am so embarrassed."

Jason knelt in front of her, making sure his robe covered him. "It's okay, Lisa, you didn't know I was back in town, and the reporters lied to you."

"And I was drunk," she said, softly.

I thought, *That, too*, but out loud I said, "Did the reporters lie, or could they really not tell the difference between you and this Summerland guy?"

Lisa and Jason looked up at me together, and the mirror effect was startling. They really did look alike.

"They do look that much alike," Lisa said.

Trish came up beside us, towering over all of us in her heels. "Wait until you see Keith, you'll freak at how much alike they look. I swear it's like the Summerlands had triplets instead of twins."

Jason stood up. "Yeah, everyone intermarried a little too much in Promise."

"Promise?" I made it a question.

"It was the name that Summerland gave to his little religious community in the hills above Asheville. Promise to God was the full name, actually."

"You mean like those Puritan names, Pass-through-the-valley-of-death Smith?"

He smiled and nodded. "Yeah, like that, but it got shortened to Promise."

"The school is still called Promise School," Lisa said, as if she were trying to focus and making some headway.

"You can still get free tuition if you prove your ancestors came in with Jedediah," Jason said.

"I take it your mom's side of the family came in with ol' Jedediah," I said.

"Mine, and Lisa's, and others."

In my head, I thought, *So does that make Keith and Lisa some sort of kissing cousins?* But it wasn't any of my business; once you leave first cousins behind, most states don't care. I decided to concentrate on something that interested me more than ancestors and religious zealots who got eaten by vampires.

"Lisa figured out that it was Jason, though, even drunk," I said. Okay, I was trying to be subtle, because what I wanted to ask was, *Why did seeing him nude convince you he wasn't Keith?* I just couldn't figure out a polite way to ask it.

Jason grinned at me, eyes not quite sparkling, but it was his grin.

I gave him a look that I'd once thought would squash that grin, but now I did it out of habit; nothing I could do would ever take the spark out of that smile.

Lisa blushed again, and was very flustered. "I . . . Keith isn't . . . I . . ." She stood up, abruptly, swayed.

Jason and I both caught her arm.

"May I use your bathroom, please?"

"I'll take her," Trish said. The taller woman eased Lisa out of our arms and toward the open bathroom door. Uncharitably I hoped she wouldn't throw up in our room anywhere, but I was glad for the privacy. Though, looking at the two suited guards at the door, I guess *privacy* was stretching it.

We waited until the door closed behind the women, and then I looked at him. "I take it you and Lisa dated in high school."

He nodded. "We did." He was going to make me ask. Fine.

"She recognized you once you were nude, Jason. What clued her in? You and the Summerland boys not quite identical when the clothes come off?"

"You're mad I made you work for it," he said, grinning.

"Not mad, just tired of being embarrassed about stupid things. Answer the question."

"I shave."

"I assume so does Keith."

"I wasn't talking about my face."

Oh. "You mean you shaved totally smooth in high school, too?"

"No, but I did shave enough so that no body hair showed in the costumes for dance recitals. I didn't start shaving completely until after I started stripping. I got enough grief from the other guys about what I did shave, I can't imagine what they would have said if I'd showed up smooth as I am now." He shook his head. "I liked parts of high school, but other parts sucked."

"Amen to that," I said.

There was a knock on the door. One of the suits turned and spoke quietly to the door. He started to take the flip-bar off.

I called, "Stop."

He glanced at me, hand still on the flip-bar. He had brown eyes and hair to match. His eyes tried for hard and empty, but he was too fresh out of the package to carry it off.

"Our room, so we get to say who comes and who goes."

Brown Hair looked at his partner, who was also young, with hair cut so short I could see his skin through the hair. He wore small silver-framed glasses over pale eyes. The haircut made me think ex-military. I'd have to wait and see if the haircut matched anything else before making the final call.

Military Cut gave a tiny shrug.

Brown Hair said, "It's Peterson and the governor's man."

"The governor's man, you mean, Chuck?" I asked.

Another exchange of looks between them, and then they both nodded as if they'd timed it.

I exchanged a look with Jason. Did he think their referring

to Chuck as "the governor's man" was as strange as I thought it was?

Jason shrugged. "I think we have to let them in; we did call them for help."

He was right, darn it. I nodded at the suits by the door. "Let them in."

The two suits exchanged another look. It was Military Cut who said, "You do know we don't take orders from you."

"All right, guys, first, what are your names?"

They looked at each other again. Did they do that before they answered any question, or was it just because I was confusing them?

"I'm Shadwell," Military Cut said.

"I'm Rowe," Brown Hair said.

"You're Shadwell and Rowe?" I made it a question, because I knew if they hung around I would never be able to resist calling them Shad and Rowe, it would just be too fun.

Jason proved he knew me well, because he touched my arm and said, "Be nice."

I grinned at him for a change—but controlled myself out loud. I could always be irritating later; I was good at it. "Okay, guys, here's the deal: you say you don't take orders from me; well, we don't take them from you, either. We'll need to figure out a way to cooperate or it's going to be a very unpleasant few days."

There was a sharper knock on the door, and I was pretty sure it was Chuck's voice saying, "Open the door."

Rowe said, "Can I open the door now?" in a tone of voice that said he was unimpressed with anything I'd said.

"Sure," I said. Because he could be unimpressed, as long as he did what I wanted him to do.

29

PETERSON AND CHUCK were having a fight, sort of. They weren't yelling or throwing punches, nothing so uncivilized, but they were pissed at each other. It was there in the way they spoke to each other, the set of their body language, the way their eyes worked when they had to look at each other. The point of contention seemed to be something to do with us, or maybe Lisa. Trish had helped her out of the bathroom; she looked pale, but better. She'd even brushed her hair and put it back in a neat ponytail.

"I'll take Lisa back to the party," Trish said.

Everyone agreed that was a good idea.

Lisa grabbed Jason's arm. "You have to come to the party"—she looked at me—"both of you. Please, most of my bridal party are girls from school. They'll want to see you, Jason, and they'll want to meet your new girlfriend."

I soooo did not want to go to Lisa's bachelorette party. But I was pretty sure what Jason was going to say, and he did not disappoint me. "We'd need to get dressed first."

"Of course, of course," Lisa said, and then she turned that fragile face to him, "but you'll come, right?"

He nodded, and I did not like the look he gave her. It was way too intimate a look from a man to another man's fiancée. I'd wanted to throw a monkey wrench into the wedding plans, but not like this, no, this was a bad idea.

As if he'd read my mind, Chuck said, "This is a bad idea, Lisa."

She looked at him, and the one look told me two things. One, she didn't particularly like Chuck; two, there was more force of will inside her than I'd seen yet. It blazed to life in those blue eyes, gave some color to her face that wasn't embarrassment.

"I say who comes to my party, not you, not my future in-laws, me."

He took a breath as if he'd argue.

Trish said, "Let's not fight."

Chuck frowned at her.

Lisa said, "I'm not fighting; Chuck is an employee, you don't fight with employees." She said it cold and hard. Point for her, but the look on Chuck's face made me want to touch my gun in its robe pocket. Chuck didn't like Lisa any better than she liked him. Interesting.

"Fine," Trish said, "fine, but let's get you back to your party. The other girls are going to wonder what happened to us." Her tone of voice alone said that she'd been doing a lot of managing in the last few days. I wondered if Lisa had a drinking problem. That would be bad.

Lisa wouldn't let go of Jason's arm. She gave him all the eye contact she had in those blue eyes. "You will come to my party, right? Promise me that you and—Anita, right?—promise me you'll come. The other girls are going to flip."

"Who's all there?" he asked.

"All the Jennifers," and she grinned. It wasn't quite his smile, but it was still close.

He grinned back. "All of them?" he asked.

"All of them: Jen, Jenna, and J. J." She grabbed his arm with both hands. "And Ashley, and Kris. Oh, they'll kill me if you don't at least come say hi."

He nodded, as I'd feared he would. "We'll get dressed and I'm sure someone here will be happy to take us to your bachelorette party." That last was almost mean for Jason, because he knew damned well that none of the men wanted him at that party. Hell, *I* didn't want him at that party, though not for the same reasons. I just didn't want to go.

She let go of his arm with one hand and grabbed my hand. "Please, Anita, I know I've been horrible. I guess it's wedding nerves, but please let Jason come. Please, come with him. Give me a chance to prove to you that I'm not some crazy woman, please."

I looked down into her face. She had to be under five feet tall. I didn't get to look down at many people. But it wasn't the height that made it hard to say no. It was the look in her eyes. But I could have withstood that, too. It was the look in Jason's eyes. He wanted to go. He wanted to talk to his old friends. Well, I'd already met his family, what were a few old girlfriends compared to that? I tried to believe that as I agreed that we'd get dressed and join them at the party.

30

THE FIRST THING we did after we got the crowd out was shower. The sex had been good enough that you needed a shower the way you do after a good workout. We tried to get Shadwell and Rowe to step out of the room while we cleaned up, but they wouldn't do it. So two strange, armed men whom I'd just met got to sit out in the room while Jason and I took turns in the shower. Why turns? Because I didn't want two strange, armed men whom I'd just met alone in our hotel room. Paranoid, who, me?

What do you wear to a bachelorette party for the future daughter-in-law of one of the richest men in a given state, who is also a presidential hopeful? I'd brought nice businessy clothes and comfortable clothes, and a lot of weapons. The choices were limited in everything except armament.

They were Jason's friends, so I let him choose. I know, if the girl union ever hears that I asked my straight male friend to dress me for a party I'll get my union card yanked, but hey, left to my own devices I'd have grabbed jeans, a T-shirt, my jogging shoes, and an extra gun. Maybe a couple of knives for added comfort.

Jason didn't think the bachelorette party would get that out of hand, but I remembered the last bachelorette party I'd gone to. It had been my friend Catherine's, and it had gotten so out of hand that what started that night almost got me killed.

Jason had said, "There won't be vampire strippers at this party, Anita. I think you and I together can handle the normal humans."

He had a point, but . . . we compromised. I switched the Browning from its more hidden location at the small of my back to its normal shoulder holster rig. I put a nice black suit jacket over a perfectly red T-shirt and nice blue jeans. My badge went in the jacket pocket. The Nikes gave way to a pair of short boots. I added knife sheaths in two wrist sheaths under the jacket.

Jason had protested, but I'd told him the truth. "I won't be able to take off the jacket or I'll flash the gun, so I might as well have my knives."

"You're not wearing the big-ass knife that sits at your spine, are you?"

"No," I said, "I left it at home, thank you. I didn't think your family was that dangerous."

We'd tried again to get Shadwell and Rowe to step out of the room, but they had said they couldn't disobey a direct order, and if they left their posts, they would lose their jobs. Fine, they had watched the negotiations. It had strained their professional bodyguard blankness to its limit, I think. At least Rowe had given me wide eyes a few times. Jason and I had to take turns changing clothes in the bathroom.

I was finally dressed, and armed, and sitting in one of the room's many purple chairs waiting for Jason to finish changing. I'd gotten my cross out of the bedside table, and it was pretty visible against the shirt. What wasn't visible was the charm under my shirt. I wore it almost all the time, too. But the cross was a religious symbol and protection against bad vampires. The ancient charm was protection against only one vampire—the Mother of All Vampires, who'd taken an unhealthy interest in me a few months ago. The charm was made of metal so ancient it bent if I pressed against a hard surface. It bore magical symbols so old that I had found no human able to read it. But there were vampires who could, because that was who had given it to me. They'd given it to me to keep Marmee Noir from using my necromancy to wake herself up and become their queen again.

Shad and Rowe tried not to look at me. It was sort of a very mild version of what the guards do outside Buckingham Palace. Duty first and foremost, nothing else exists. Once I would have left them alone, but first, I was a girl, and that meant I felt damn near compelled to talk to anyone in a silent room, and second, I just wanted to yank their chain. Maybe I'd been hanging around with Jason too long.

"How long have you been out of the military, Shadwell?"

His body reacted, but not his face, a stiffening of the shoulders, the spine. "Haircut?" he said.

"That and you just don't taste like a civilian."

He turned those pale eyes to me behind their wire frames. It was not a friendly look, or an unfriendly one, more neutral. "Two years."

Rowe looked at me.

I fought not to smile. God, he was still so bright and shiny. "I can't peg you, Rowe. You don't taste like military, or cop, but you taste like something that isn't civvie."

He grinned at me, eyes sparkling with pleasure. "Yeah, I kicked ass at undercover."

"So cop, or fed?"

"Wouldn't you like to know?" he said.

Shad gave him a look, and a brief, "Don't."

Rowe stopped smiling, but his eyes still gleamed with some inner happiness. So Shadwell was senior man.

"Don't what?" I asked.

"We are supposed to guard you, not fraternize."

"Fraternize," I said, and laughed. "Fraternize, haven't heard that word in a while."

Shadwell frowned at me. "It's an accurate word."

I nodded, and fought to look more serious. It didn't help when I caught Rowe's gaze. His eyes were practically shining with suppressed mirth. The edge of his mouth twitched and I had to look away, or I'd have lost it.

Shadwell seemed to sense it, because he gave Rowe a hard look. Rowe had to have a coughing fit to cover the laughter that was almost spilling over.

"What got you off undercover work, Rowe?" I asked.

Still recovering from his "coughing fit," he said, "My sense of humor."

I looked at him, tried to see if he was serious. He was implying that he'd been fired, or at least reassigned, because his sense of humor had gotten him in trouble.

"Rowe," Shadwell said, "she does not need to know your background."

"Yes, sir." Rowe went back to attention by the door, but his eyes and a certain set to the mouth said he didn't really mean it. I was beginning to see how Rowe might have gotten in trouble with his superiors.

Shadwell gave us both a hard look, and it was a good look,

a real look. Bad guys must have flinched under his gaze, but I wasn't a bad guy. I was just someone wondering why the guards were on our side of the door. It seemed a little excessive.

"Fine, Shadwell, are you and Rowe here going to stand inside our room all night?"

"No."

"Then why are you standing here now?"

"Because we were told to," he said.

Rowe's mouth twitched again. Someone with a sense of humor had partnered them with each other.

"Isn't it kind of weird to be on this side of the door? I mean the danger is out there, not in here."

Shadwell frowned, then smoothed it out. "I'm following orders, Ms. Blake."

"Marshal Blake," I said, because it just seemed good to remind rule-and-order Shadwell that I wasn't really a civvie either.

His eyes flickered to me, then back to staring into space. "If you're a federal marshal, then you'll appreciate that I'm following orders."

That made me laugh. "Nicely done, Shadwell. *If* I'm a federal marshal. I assure you I am, badge and all, but I'm not really real, am I? I mean I got grandfathered in, and didn't go through the training, so I'm not really a marshal, right?"

"I did not say that."

"You implied it," I said, and my voice was no longer pleasant.

"Are you trying to pick a fight with Shadwell?" Rowe asked, his face curious.

I shrugged, slumping back in the chair as much as the shoulder rig would comfortably let me. "Maybe, and if I am,

I'm sorry. I'm just a little bored, a little tense, and I really, really, don't want to go to this party."

"It's a bad idea," Shadwell said.

"The worst," I said.

He looked at me. "Then why are you going?"

"Because Jason is going, and he wants me with him."

Shadwell nodded. "My wife's the social one. I hate parties, too."

I tried to pretend that Shadwell hadn't just done exactly what he'd yelled at Rowe for, which was overshare. "Yeah, but I bet your wife doesn't drag you to parties where strange men will be taking off their clothes."

"You don't think your friend in there will want to stay for that part of the party?" Shadwell asked.

I shrugged, and sat up straighter. "He may."

The two men exchanged glances. Even Rowe didn't seem to think it was funny. Then Rowe grinned as if he couldn't help it. "The last time I saw male strippers I was getting a lap dance."

We both looked at him. He shrugged, and actually blushed, which you don't see in an ex-cop much. "We'd had a rash of gay bashing that turned into serial murder. All the vics had frequented this one club." Then he grinned again. "I was the only one on the undercover unit who was secure enough in my manhood to do the job."

With that revelation the door to the bathroom opened. Jason came out in a blue T-shirt that matched his eyes to perfection, so that his eyes were incredibly blue. The T-shirt also fit very well, so that all that muscle work showed. The blue jeans were date jeans, which meant they were tight and fit well. He'd added his own short boots and had a black suit jacket to throw over it all, so it looked somewhere between semiprofessional and club wear. But he looked good, and he knew it. He'd dressed to be yummy. He might not be planning to date anyone at the party, but he wanted them to see him. Sigh. He was so going to flirt his ass off.

31

I HAD LEFT the big-ass knife at home and the special leather rig that let me carry it along with a handgun. But one of the reasons I had an entire carry-on of weapons was that I had to bring my vampire hunting kit. Why? Because the regulations for the preternatural branch of the federal marshal program had changed. Now, if we traveled, even on personal business, we had to have all our gear with us so that if an emergency call came up near us, and we were the closest body, we could take it. This new regulation had come up when one of my colleagues had been on a family vacation that turned into a vampire hunt for the local cops. The hunt had gone badly, and the report that he'd had to submit had listed the major problem as that his kit was at home. He needed his stuff. Didn't we all.

So that meant I had some really dangerous stuff with me. Stuff that if I'd had to get on a commercial airline, they'd have never let me get on the plane. Not even with a badge. I had the usual: extra guns, extra ammo, stakes, holy water, holy wafers, extra crosses. I'd even thrown in some holy items from other faiths because I'd had occasion to work with local law enforcement that were not Christian, and having everybody armed with a holy item was a good thing. If you got a few atheists, pray that they are well armed, but don't tell them you're praying for them. Some of them have about as much a sense of humor as the right-wingers.

What would have gotten me kicked off the plane, or in an interrogation room with Homeland Defense, was the Heckler and Koch MP5 and the phosphorous grenades. I'd never actually used the grenades, but my friend Edward, alias Ted Forrester, also a federal marshal for the preternatural branch, had said they worked wonders. Frankly, all grenades scared me, but something that burned even in water would be truly bad news to the undead of any kind. It would even work on zombies and ghouls, which are both so much harder to kill than vamps. The government said I needed all my toys, so I brought them—well, not all of them. I have resisted Edward's desire to teach me how to use a flamethrower. They scare me.

All this to say that we had to make a stop at the main desk with my little carry-on. Shad and Rowe had not liked that I had to do this, but when they realized I was dead serious, they ordered up enough uniformed guards to form a phalanx around us and escorted us to the lobby. I thought it was excessive until we caught the full barrage of the cameras in the lobby. I actually slipped my sunglasses on to keep the glare down. No wonder movie stars wear them.

The guards formed a wall around us so I could flash my badge to the nice lady behind the desk and explain that I had some sensitive items in this case and didn't want to leave it in the room unattended. Before everything got weird, I might have, but I had this horrible image of reporters breaking into our room when we weren't there. If I didn't want the uninitiated playing with my guns, I sure as hell didn't want them playing with phosphorous grenades.

The lady, whose name tag read *Bethann*, was more than happy to help us. She even let Jason and me walk the case back to this huge-ass safe. The fact that she never blinked or asked a single question showed that I wasn't the only guest with "sensitive" materials. Though I was willing to bet I was the only one with this much firepower in one little case.

When the case was secure and we'd shaken hands with Bethann, we all turned around and went for the elevators. The reporters were screaming at us, "What did you put in the safe?" We had some of them shouting "Keith," but some were actually shouting the right name. "Jason, Jason, have you talked to Jean-Claude?" "Anita, is he better in bed than the vampires?" We ignored all questions. The earlier disastrous impromptu news conference had taught us our lesson. The press was a danger neither of us knew how to handle, not at this level. It was like being really good at peewee football and suddenly realizing you were up against pros. We were out of our league, and now we knew it.

Most of the uniformed guards stayed in the lobby, probably to wrangle the press so that other guests had a chance of walking through the lobby without being brained by a boom mic.

Shad and Rowe took up posts near the door, with us behind them. I looked at the line of their suits and knew where everyone's gun was, and that Shad was carrying something extra in his pocket, and Rowe had something on his ankle. I was betting the ankle was a small gun, but the pocket could have been a lot of things, just not a gun. *Not a gun* opened up a wealth of possibilities.

Jason leaned over and whispered, "I would accuse you of checking them out, but you're looking for weapons, aren't you?"

I just nodded.

He hugged me one-armed and gave an excited sound, almost a laugh, but not. His eyes were bright with anticipation.

I whispered, "How many of these girls are old girlfriends?"

"All of them."

"How many are old lovers?"

He grinned. "Most of them."

"Great."

He hugged me tighter. "I'll be good, I promise."

"You're always good, Jason," I said out loud, "but will you behave?"

He gave me a look, and the look was enough. He'd try, but no, the honest answer was no. I sighed and settled back against the wall as the elevator came to a stop. We had, of course, gone all the way to the top. The rich and powerful always seem to prefer the tops of buildings. Hasn't anyone ever explained to them that higher just means you have farther to fall?

32

SHADWELL STEPPED OFF the elevator first. Rowe stayed with us. I'd had enough bodyguards of my own not to argue. When Shadwell was certain it was safe, he'd let us know. He stepped to one side with a nod and Rowe motioned us forward.

That was the most serious bodyguarding they'd done, and it made me nervous. Were there threats on Keith Summerland's life? If so, Jason and he looked enough alike that it could be a serious problem. Maybe there was more than one reason that we suddenly had guards. Shit.

One of the doors in the hallway had Peterson standing sort of at attention by it. Chuck was talking low and urgently to him. So this was where the two of them had vanished to.

Chuck turned, and gave Jason a look. It was neither friendly nor unfriendly, but it wasn't a good look. It was more as if he were trying to see Jason, see what he was made of, and what it meant. I didn't like the look. It meant Chuck was thinking too hard about Jason. We were leaving this town in a day. That look was too serious for *in twenty-four hours we're gone*.

Chuck smoothed his suit jacket where it had bunched over his gun, and as he moved past us for the elevator said, over his shoulder, "It's your ball until I get back, Peterson."

"You aren't technically my superior, Ralston."

So Chuck did have a last name after all. Peterson didn't sound very happy with him by any name.

Chuck walked past us like we weren't there. The uniformed guard was holding the doors of the elevator open as if he'd been ordered to. "If you don't like it, Peterson, call the governor, see who he thinks is in charge tonight."

Peterson's face closed down, fighting for blankness, but his hands flexed, and I knew pissed when I saw it. What had been happening between the two of them while we'd been in Shadwell and Rowe's tender care? Something was up; question was, what? It was none of my business; I kept repeating that in my head like a mantra. Jason had gotten me to promise that I would not mess with Chuck, but God, he made it hard not to yank his chain.

I was good. I let Chuck get on the elevator. Let the doors close, and said not a word.

Jason squeezed my hand and kissed my cheek.

"What was that for?" I asked.

"For being good. I don't know why, but Chuck seems to make you want to pick at him."

"You, too, Mr. Kiss-Me-in-the-Parking-Garage."

Jason actually looked embarrassed, which I didn't get to see often. I treasured it for the rare gift it was, and we were left facing Peterson. Him I didn't want to mess with; he seemed sort of harassed. Or maybe he'd been nice at the hospital and it cut him more slack than Chuck.

Shadwell and Rowe were still with us like good bodyguards. Until Shadwell had gone all serious getting out of the elevator, I'd begun to suspect they were guarding us to make sure we didn't do anything embarrassing to the Summerlands as much as they were guarding us from the press. But the exit from the elevator had been too real. I could leave Chuck alone, but I needed to know what was up from someone.

"You have about a half hour until the . . . entertainment arrives." He said *entertainment* like it hurt.

"Are you kicking us out then?" I asked.

He shook his head. "I just assumed that Mr. Schuyler would be more comfortable leaving then, but no, I don't have any orders for when you leave the party, or if." Again, his voice said he didn't like it.

Jason said, "I'm sorry if our coming to the party is a problem."

Peterson looked surprised, but recovered himself. "I think you mean that. You may look like Keith, but you don't sound like him."

Shadwell and Rowe stiffened beside me, as if they weren't used to Peterson being quite that honest.

Jason gave him a bright smile. "That's one of the nicest things anyone's ever said to me."

Not true and I knew it, but it made Peterson smile, and I think that was what Jason wanted. Jason liked everyone to be happy if he could manage it.

The door opened behind us, and a flock of blond women who all looked like Jason's sisters should have looked swarmed over him, squealing happy cries of "Jason, Jason!" They pulled him into the room, and he went, laughing.

I was left in the hallway with the bodyguards. Peterson looked at me. It was a wondering-what-I'd-do look. Was he worried I'd be jealous? Was that part of why he hadn't wanted us here?

Rowe stifled a laugh that he tried to turn into a cough.

Shadwell said, in a dry voice, "You really should get something for that cough."

I smiled at them all. "It's okay, guys. I'm not going to go all jealous because Jason is flirting and they're flirting back. I'm cool."

"No woman is that cool," Shadwell said.

I smiled and shook my head. "Jason flirts like he breathes. Both will stop only when he's dead."

Shadwell said, "You are not his girlfriend, or this would bother you."

I gave him full eye contact as I said, "He'll flirt with them, Shadwell, but he'll be fucking *me* later."

His pale eyes flinched, and his face went sort of grim. "You trying to shock me?"

"No, Shadwell, I'm trying to make you understand that if there's a problem tonight it won't be me."

Peterson said, "Enough. I don't know what is happening with the two of you, but I do not need it tonight. Is that clear, Shadwell?"

Shadwell gave one clear nod.

"Good." Peterson looked at me. "Ms. . . . Marshal Blake, do you have an objection to Shadwell and Rowe being inside the room with you for at least the beginning of the party?"

"Okay, that's it, the civvies are inside the room, with more guards, I assume?"

Peterson just nodded.

"Shadwell and Rowe stayed on our side of the hotel room door. They did a serious exit from the elevator up here. They had a shitload of uniforms downstairs when I insisted on putting my carry-on in the hotel safe. I thought that was to keep the press at bay, but something's happened. What is it?"

"You may not be a civilian, Marshal Blake, but you aren't one of us. We can't—"

"Is the threat against all the Summerlands, just the kids, or is it Keith specifically?"

Rowe and Shadwell exchanged glances. Peterson fought not to look at them, and to keep my eye contact. He had to work at it.

"We are not at liberty to discuss—"

"Don't give me that bullshit, Peterson. You were at the hospital today. I do not want to go to his family and say we got their only son killed because he was mistaken for a Summerland boy. Not to mention that I would"—I waved my hand in the air, trying to think how to say it—"it would leave this big hole in my life to lose Jason. So we aren't going to lose him, are we?" I glared at all three of them.

"We are doing our best," Peterson said.

"What has changed in just the last few hours?"

"I cannot share the information, you don't have clearance."

"How much danger is Jason in?" I asked.

"You know it's not him."

"But he could be hurt by accident," I said.

Peterson made an exasperated sound low in his throat. "Yes, he looks enough like both the boys to be in danger."

"In danger of death, or kidnapping, or what?" I asked.

This time they exchanged a flurry of looks, including Peterson. Shadwell said, "She isn't cleared for this."

"I will have to clear it with my superiors, but I'll try to get permission to fill you in on some of it," Peterson said. "Go to the party, enjoy yourselves, stay longer than thirty minutes; maybe by the time the party is over I can tell you more."

"They'll never go for that," Shadwell said.

"Until they give you *my* job, Shadwell, *I* will run this operation the way *I* see fit. Is that clear?"

"Very, sir," Shadwell said, and managed that great neutral military voice, where you can say *Yes, sir* all day long while inside you're thinking *You motherfucker*.

"Then do your job. Ralston will be back to check on things later."

"Ralston, sir?" Shadwell said.

Peterson nodded. "Yes, Ralston."

"Why is Chuck in charge of the party?" I asked.

"Ask the governor," Peterson said. He leaned back and opened the door for me. He was going to see me safely inside the room before he left, apparently. I didn't argue, just let Rowe go into the room first, then me, then Shadwell. Shouldn't they have done that for Jason? Oh, wait, he'd been safe behind the wall of beautiful blond women. Now that's body armor.

33

THE ROOM WAS almost identical to ours except for the décor. It was all white and golden-tan, much cleaner lines, less fuss than our room. It was much airier and through the windows, which were still open to the night, I saw a balcony railing. The two groups of sofas and chairs were empty. There were presents on the glass dining table still in their sparkling wrappers. Apparently it was a combination bachelorette party and bridal shower. Either that or they'd changed the rules for bachelorette parties and now you got presents.

Where were Jason and the girls? Then I heard a giggle. It came from around the corner where, if it had been our room, the bedroom lay. Of course, it did.

Shad stopped me with a hand motion. I hadn't even realized I'd made a movement forward. He called out, "Price, Sanchez?"

A man came around the corner. He was the first non-WASP that I'd seen in this town. Well, unless you counted

Jason's dad and his sisters. They, at least, weren't blond. But Sanchez was nicely dark; other than skin tone he looked like all the other guards. They all had this stamped-out-of-the-same-mill feel to them. Rowe was the closest to his own person, but everyone else smelled of a system that trained large groups of men to fight other large groups of men. They came out of the military straight into another kind of unit, which had not helped them lose their cohesiveness.

He talked as he moved in front of the minibar to stand beside us. "They wanted to show the man the wedding dresses," Sanchez said.

I looked at Shad. "May I?"

He nodded.

I stepped forward and offered a hand to Sanchez. He looked a little startled, but he gave me a good handshake. He had small hands for his size, or at least for the shoulders that were straining his suit. It looked like he'd hit the gym a lot recently and hadn't bought the next size up suit. It made his gun show very stark at his hip under the jacket.

Rowe said, "Sanchez, you gotta get a bigger jacket, man. Your gun shows bad."

Sanchez shrugged the big shoulders, though he was only about five foot six, the shortest guard I'd seen among Peterson's people. Maybe that's why he'd hit the gym so hard; compensation.

His eyes were so brown they were almost black, darker even than my own. He flicked the eyes to Rowe with a frown, then said, "Not in front of—"

"The mark," I said, "the job, what do you call the people you babysit?"

He gave me a speculative look out of those very dark eyes. "You're from out of town." He made it a statement.

I smiled. "You have no idea."

He actually grinned, before Shadwell said, "If they're changing clothes you and Price can stay outside the room."

Sanchez shook his head, frowning again. "They aren't changing, but our orders were explicit. Until further notice we do not lose sight of our"—he glanced at me, then finished with—"charges." He said the last softly, as if it wasn't quite the word he would have used if one of the "charges" hadn't been standing in front of him.

I smiled at him, and something about the smile made him shift, or maybe the gun was digging into his side.

"Your jacket fits nice, but it's harder to hide a shoulder holster," he said.

Oh, he'd noticed the gun. It was my turn to shrug. "I got used to wearing it."

Shadwell said, "She's a federal marshal, and the girlfriend of the man."

Sanchez's eyes went a little wide. "He don't act like he has a girlfriend."

I smiled, and this time it was a happy one. "Are his clothes still on?" I asked.

Sanchez tried not to look startled, but failed a little around the edges. "Last I checked."

I smiled wider. "Then Jason hasn't gotten too carried away yet."

"He take his clothes off in front of groups of women a lot?" Sanchez asked.

I nodded. "All the time," I said. I didn't explain what Jason's job was; I was enjoying Sanchez's reaction too much. It was helping me delay going into the next room, which was pretty much my goal.

"He's a stripper," Shadwell said, a little disgusted.

I gave him a dirty look. "I'll thank you to keep a civil tone about my boyfriend's job, thanks."

Shadwell's eyes flashed at me from behind his glasses, showing that there was a little blue to all that gray in his eyes. "No offense."

"Sure," I said.

"He the entertainment?" Sanchez asked.

"No," Shadwell said, and he didn't explain either.

Great, we were just going to play need-to-know until we were all confused.

It was Rowe who moved around so he could look me in the face. His eyes had seemed very brown, until I had Sanchez's to look into; now they seemed pale.

"You're delaying so you don't have to go into the other room."

I gave him an unfriendly look. "You don't know me well enough to make that guess."

"It's not a guess," he said.

I turned the look into a glare.

He laughed, and raised his hands ceilingward. "Hey, don't give me that look just because I'm right."

I shrugged, and tried not to be childish about it. I settled for sounding a little sulky, but I couldn't help that part. "You're smarter than you look, Rowe."

"Now you're just being mean," he said.

"Accurate," Sanchez said, with a smile.

"You said if we had a problem tonight it wouldn't be you," Shadwell said.

I turned the remnants of the unfriendly look on him. But explaining might keep me in this room until they stopped looking at the wedding clothes. "I am an unmarried woman who is dating a man seriously enough to drop everything and come home to meet his folks. We have no plans to marry, but if I go into the other room with the wedding dresses being *ooh*ed and *aah*ed over, the women are going to ask about our plans. Jason and I don't have any plans, and that will bug the women. I don't want to mess with it."

"Why would you come home to meet someone's family if you have no plans to marry?" Shadwell asked.

"I'll answer your question if you'll answer one of mine first."

He looked suspicious, but I think they weren't much more eager to go into the next room than I was. The sound of giggling was being punctuated by Jason's laugh. "You can ask."

"What caused the order to come down that you aren't to let your charges out of your sight?"

Shadwell shook his head. "If Peterson gives us permission I'll be happy to tell you, but until then, I can't."

"Orders," I said.

"Chain of command," he said.

I nodded. "What happens when Chuck comes back? Is he higher in the chain of command than you are?"

They all exchanged glances. Shadwell actually rolled his lower lip under, which was the most nerves I'd seen him show.

"You don't know where he stands in the chain of command, do you?"

"That's none of your business," Shadwell said.

"Whatever you say. Shall we go see if everyone's still got all their clothes on?"

"We could just keep talking out here," Rowe said.

"We could, but I've delayed as long as my self-respect will allow. Time to brave the giggling horde."

"All women giggle," Rowe said.

"I don't," I said.

He gave me a look that was neither professional nor okay from a strange man. "I bet I could make you giggle."

"Rowe," Shadwell said, in a serious voice.

"You just lost points in my book, Rowe, serious points."

He held up his hands in a push-away gesture. "Sorry, that was out of line."

"Yeah," I said, "it was, and if you expect to be in the room with us while we sleep tonight, you are so very wrong."

Shadwell actually stepped between us to break the eye contact. "We hope the orders will change by then."

"I'm sorry," Rowe said again, "it's just nice to talk to a woman that doesn't have that look in her eyes."

"What look?" I asked.

"That how-fast-can-I-get-you-down-the-aisle look."

I laughed. "I think that's your nerves projecting, Rowe."

"This from the woman who didn't want to go into the next room because she's afraid they'll press you to marry your boyfriend."

"You can tell how happy a couple is by how hard the women try to fix up their single friends," I said.

"Some men do that, too," Sanchez said.

There was a loud thump from the next room, and near-hysterical laughter.

"Shit," I said, and started for the room.

"I thought you didn't want to go in there," Rowe called.

"I don't, but I just realized I'm actually nervous about it, which means I've got to go in."

"That makes no sense," Rowe said. "You're going to do it because you know you're afraid to do it?"

I didn't correct his *afraid* to my *nervous*, because my pulse was up, my muscles tense. I was just meeting some of Jason's old girlfriends, for God's sake. He and I weren't even really an item.

"She's got to do it now," Shadwell said.

"Why?" Rowe asked.

"That you gotta ask that question is why you had to leave the cops early."

"What the hell does that mean?" Rowe asked.

Shadwell had hurried his step to catch up with me, then slowed down because his stride was about twice mine. We didn't have to look at each other to understand. If something scares you, no matter how small, you gotta face it, because if you start failing on the small stuff, you'll eventually fail on the big stuff. Shadwell got that; Rowe didn't. Shadwell and I didn't necessarily like each other, but he'd go through into the bedroom with me. Sanchez was right behind us. Rowe trailed behind.

I could see a metal folding screen that hid most of the bedroom from view. Shadwell went past the screen first, and suddenly we could see in. There was a storm of giggling, and deep blue crinoline was everywhere. A pale blue dress came flying through the air to land at our feet. It was raining blue bridesmaid dresses.

34

I ACTUALLY HAD to stop beside the fainting couch just inside the room, because it looked like someone had planned the image. The bed was covered in blue dresses. In among the dresses were Jason and the women. They were all blond, blue-eyed, delicate, and looked like cousins or closer. They were all out of breath, and lying or sitting like they'd just finished doing something strenuous. The blue dresses near their faces made their eyes incredibly blue.

Trish stood to the side of the little party like she'd fled the bed when the fun started. She stood behind a man in a suit who had to be Price, Sanchez's other half.

"What did you guys do," I asked, "have a dress fight?"

Lisa pushed back a puffy blue slip and said, "Yes. We are going to be in such trouble when the wedding coordinator sees the wrinkles, but it felt so good."

Trish bent over and picked up a dress that had fallen to the floor. "If we hang them up now, they won't wrinkle."

Most of the women on the bed started picking things up and searching for hangers. But one of the women slid off the bed and came to me. She was taller than the others, taller than me by several inches, at least five foot eight, but still had that delicacy of bone that seemed par for the course.

She was wearing either a sheath dress or a slip with the thinnest of spaghetti straps that clung to her body to show every muscle, every curve. She didn't have enough body fat to really have curves. Her breasts were small and tight to her body. But she moved well, and the muscles that showed in her bare arms and the body of the dress were more than the muscles you get from working out to keep in shape. There was a physical potential to her that you didn't see in many women.

Jason bounced off the bed, literally, and caught her hand before she got to me. "Anita, this is J. J.; she and I were in dance together all through school."

J. J. gave me an appraising look that I couldn't quite figure out. It wasn't just an old girlfriend looking at a new one, but that was in there. I couldn't read the look, and that bothered me a little.

I took her hand, carefully manicured but with nails short enough for function. She had a good grip. "I take it you're still dancing."

She gave me a smile that was shy, eyes turned down, looking under her long lashes at me. The lashes were golden and very long, and the color had to be natural because mascara would have ruined it. "Does it show that much?"

"The workout does," I said, and realized she seemed to have no intention of breaking the handshake. I had to draw my hand away from her. Her fingertips lingered on my wrist, and down my hand.

She was flirting with me. Great. I had no idea why, or what

to do about it. Women always confused me when they hit on me. I kept forgetting that they could do that, or would want to. If it stayed this subtle I could ignore it, but for J. J. to be even this bold right out of the box made me pretty sure that it wouldn't stay subtle.

I gave Jason a look, as if to say, *What have you told her about me?*

He gave me a look back that said, *Not my fault.* I didn't believe the look. He moved between us and hugged me tight. He breathed against my ear, more than whispered, "I did not tell her that you would be interested."

If he said it outright, I believed him, but . . . I still didn't know what to do about it. I did what I always did when someone confused me: I tried to ignore her. The other women helped, by wanting to be introduced to Jason's girlfriend. First Jean-Claude's girlfriend, now Jason's. Sigh. You get a career, work your ass off for a reputation, and you still end up being introduced as someone's girlfriend. Peachy.

35

JENNA WAS A real estate developer, or worked for one. Jen was a stay-at-home mom married to her high school boyfriend. They had two kids. Kris was about to graduate with her degree in architecture. She'd done most of the set design for the plays at school. Ashley was finishing up her student teaching; she was hoping to teach drama somewhere along with English classes. They talked about the time she'd directed *Pygmalion*, which was the nonmusical version of *My Fair Lady*, and what an amazing job she'd done. So glad you stayed in the business. J. J. was performing with a professional dance company in New York City. Lisa had come home to work in her dad's law office as a paralegal. He was the local lawyer for the Summerlands. It's where Keith met her again. No one said it out loud, but it was strongly implied that her father wished fervently that he'd sent his daughter on that European trip she'd wanted instead of insisting she get a job right away.

They talked about plays they'd worked on, dreams they'd had, dreams they'd followed, dreams they'd lost. Only Jason, Ashley, and J. J. had stayed with the dance outside school all the way through college—though Jen was taking an adult ballet class, trying to get back into shape after having two kids in less than three years. She wasn't out of shape, but the weight made her look older than the other women. Or maybe, just the lack of sleep of having two kids still in diapers. It'd age anybody.

Trish and I were the odd girls out. We had no old times to remember, so we drifted back to the edge of the group, finding a spot in the far conversational grouping. There was only a white sectional sofa with its back to the bedroom, because the dining table took up the room near the windows. We sat on the sofa, a discreet distance from each other, both of us a little uncomfortable. I never warmed up instantly to strangers, and I think Trish was waiting for me to be mad at Jason, or the other women.

They were on the sectional nearest the door with its back to the windows. There were chairs there, but none of the women were using them. They were all cuddled on the sectional, very Roman, as in ancient; very decadent, as in any century. The happy group was beginning to drink a little, except for Jason. He wouldn't drink for the same reason that most lycanthropes didn't drink. It lowered your inhibitions, and that meant it was harder to control the inner beast. No, drinking and drugs did not go with being a good little wereanimal.

"Doesn't it bother you that Jason is flirting like that?" Trish asked, sipping her drink.

I glanced over at the group on the couch. At the moment, Lisa was draped in his lap, almost prone, while he stroked her hair. Kris was behind him, cuddled so close she was in danger of spilling her drink over him and Lisa. They'd all had their turns of hanging all over him.

I shrugged, and sipped my Coke. I never did drink, and almost for the same reason Jason couldn't drink, neither could I.

"One, it's Jason, he flirts like he breathes. Two, he's a stripper, which has sort of encouraged his natural tendencies in this area. Third, he wants them to see him as attractive. He wants to flirt with his old girlfriends."

"Wow," Trish said, "that is like way more secure than I would be right now."

I smiled, and tried to think if I'd feel the same if it were Nathaniel, or Micah, or Jean-Claude. I really tried to think about it. Micah almost never flirted. But Nathaniel did for many of the same reasons that Jason did, and Jean-Claude flirted when he wished to, to perfection. Would I have been more jealous of them than I was being of Jason? Maybe. Probably. I just didn't know.

But it was more than the fact that Jason wasn't my main squeeze. My version of the *ardeur* gave me the ability to see people's desires, sometimes—if the *ardeur* was very active, or the people's desires were that strong.

Jean-Claude had worked with me so that I could sense things with the *ardeur* but not have it rise for feeding. I was getting better. Tonight let me know how much better. I could feel that most of the women hanging all over him didn't mean it. They were flirting, but not with intent. The flirting and the physical contact was an end in itself for most of them. The exception was the bride-to-be.

Lisa was desperate. It was the only word I had for her energy. She was desparate to fuck someone. It didn't have to be Jason. Her need was the strongest of any over there, and it had an edge of panic to it.

I had not reached out with the *ardeur* on purpose, but the energies from the couch were strong enough that they leaked around me, like whiffs of perfume. The bodyguards were the biggest problem for sheer lust. Not all of them, and I tried not to pay attention to which ones were basically thinking thoughts that would have gotten them slapped if the women had known. I didn't read minds, especially of strangers, but I caught touches of their desires. Not feelings exactly, because the *ardeur* didn't work on emotions except those that had to do with desire, love, and the associated stuff.

Marianne, my metaphysical tutor, psychic, and witch, said that I was like an empath, someone who could read emotions, but only a very limited list of emotions. Fine with me; I had enough trouble with the short list. The long list that Marianne waded through was beyond me.

Strangely, the one person who wasn't projecting anything at me was Jason. He was like a blank. I might have risked sending the *ardeur* into his psyche on purpose, but I wasn't feeling confident enough to risk it. I might accidentally touch his inner beast, too, and that might bring on mine. That would be bad.

Jason caught my eye, and I toasted him with my Coke. He extracted himself from the other women and came to sit on the arm of my chair. He put his arm across my shoulders. "You okay over here?"

I put my arm around his waist because it seemed like the thing to do. He snuggled into the hug. "You mean am I getting pissed that you've been flirting your ass off for the last hour and completely ignoring me?"

He laughed, then kissed me on the cheek. "Yes, that's what I mean."

I smiled up at him. "You've done about what I thought you'd do, except for not checking on me sooner."

He let himself slip down into the chair so that he just ended up on my lap. He took my Coke out of my hand with a practiced move of his hand. Probably something he did at the club to keep customers from spilling their drinks on him. He took a sip of the Coke without asking, and leaned in close enough to kiss me as he murmured, "I'm sorry."

I pushed him back enough to see his face clearly. "I admit the flirting has been a little more than I thought it would be, but it's okay. You flirt, you just do. It took me a long time to realize that flirting for you and Nathaniel, and even Jean-Claude, doesn't always mean a damn thing."

He nuzzled my cheek. "But when you flirt, you mean it."

"Most of the time," I said.

He nibbled his lips along the side of my neck. It made me shiver. "Stop that, it tickles."

He did it some more, making me wiggle again. "It's supposed to tickle."

I put a hand against his shoulder and pushed him away enough to look up in his face. Whatever he saw there didn't make him happy. I saw that in his own face.

"You're mad," he said, softly.

Trish said, "My cue to leave. Have fun." She got up and walked away in her spike heels to join the other ladies.

I thought about what Jason had said, then shook my head. "You know how you said that you hated being invisible to me as a guy, and loved me reacting to you now?"

"Yes."

"I think I just realized that you react to all women the way you react to me. You complain that you're not special enough to me in comparison to the other men in my life, but Jason . . . what do you do different with me that you don't do with other women?"

He frowned, clearly puzzled.

I tried again. "What did you do with Perdy that was different, special?"

He frowned harder. "She restricted the sex to a point that made it not fun anymore. Her idea of straight was too straight for me."

I nodded. "But what I mean is, that you react, or interact, with all women the same. Watching you with them, I can't tell the difference between the early foreplay with them and what you do with me. It's not flattering to realize that you don't differentiate."

He sat in my lap, my Coke still in his hand, thinking at me. He was thinking so loud I could almost hear it. I actually watched the light dawn in his eyes.

"Nathaniel acts differently around you than the women at the club. Jean-Claude, too." He seemed to think about it a little more, then nodded. "Even some of the men who aren't in love with you treat you differently. They want different things from you than from anyone else, like Requiem and Asher."

I nodded. "Exactly."

He leaned in to whisper, "I thought one of my charms was that I didn't want to be anything more than fuck buddies."

I had to smile. "Elegantly put, Jason, but watching you with the women just now, I realized that I like to be special. I don't tolerate being part of a crowd. If you want to tell them that I'm just a front to please your family, then do it, tell them the truth. They seem close enough friends. But if you are going to tell them that I am your girlfriend, a good enough girlfriend to bring home to the family, then you can't cuckold me with them."

He smiled. "Cuckold?"

I frowned at him. "Pick a different word, but you know what I mean."

"If it was Nathaniel, or Jean-Claude, you wouldn't have sat here for an hour and watched, would you?"

"They wouldn't have made me."

He set my Coke on the table the lamp was sitting on. It forced him to turn his body awkwardly, but he made it look vaguely promising, as if to say, *Look how flexible I am*. But I had Nathaniel's flexibility to compare with, so I was less impressed than I might have been.

Jason turned back to me and gave me very serious eyes. "I've hurt your feelings."

"Yes, but more than that I came here under cover for you, in a role that is not comfortable for me, and you just made all your old friends think that I would allow any boyfriend of mine to ignore me for an hour as he was pawed by old lovers. I wouldn't. The only thing that kept me in the chair was that I couldn't decide what to do. If we are just good friends and nothing more, then have at it, Jason. But if I'm still supposed to be this serious girlfriend, you can't do shit like this."

"Even if it's only pretend that you're my serious girlfriend?" he asked.

I nodded. "Tell them the truth, and crawl all over them, have at it. But if you don't tell them the truth, then you cannot humiliate me like this, not if you want to maintain that I am in any way a serious girlfriend to you."

I watched him think some more. He opened his mouth, closed it, and glanced at the crowd of people behind us, all trying to pretend they weren't there. He got off my lap and took my hand with him, drawing me to my feet.

He led me toward the bedroom. Rowe and Shadwell peeled away from the section of the wall they were holding up and tried to follow. Jason stopped them at the opening. "No, and I'm going to move the screen so we have some privacy."

"Our orders . . . ," began Shadwell.

"I'm wearing more weapons than you are, Shadwell. I think we'll be all right."

He and Rowe exchanged glances, and then finally Shadwell nodded. "If you're in there too long I'm coming in, no matter what kind of sounds I hear. Just so you'll know."

"I think we can behave ourselves," I said.

Jason pulled me into the room and let go of my hand to move the metal screen over so it hid us from view, if we were on the bed. It was the best we could do without a door. Jason sat on the end of the bed and held his hand out to me.

I went to him, let him pull me to sit on the edge of the bed with him. "I'm sorry," he said.

"Me, too, but you need to decide."

"If I tell them the truth, what will you do?"

"What I want to do is go home, but I won't leave until I know what has the bodyguards all freaked. I think there's been some kind of threat against Keith Summerland, and I'd never forgive myself if you got hurt by mistake."

His hand came up and cupped the side of my face, ever so gently. "You care for me, and I return the favor by making you feel bad about yourself. I'm sorry, Anita, really, I wasn't thinking."

"Oh, you were thinking, just with the little head instead of the big one. As much as I enjoy both, I like you to make decisions with the top end."

He gave a small laugh, and moved our faces so he could kiss me. The kiss started to get out of hand, but I drew back, so that it didn't; drew back enough to look him in the eyes, his hand still against my face.

"That look," he said, "I know that look, that look of iron

resolve. I don't know what it means in this instant, but it makes me a little nervous."

I smiled. "Iron resolve, huh. It's just this, Jason: I don't share. Unfair or not, if you want to break our cover story, then you are free to try to sleep with whoever you want. You're a big boy, but don't come dragging yourself from some stranger's bed into mine."

"You have to feed the *ardeur* at least one more time before we can go home," he said.

I nodded. "I'll figure something out. Jean-Claude can help me feed from a distance, maybe. I've been catching little bits of emotion from the women and the bodyguards and it hasn't raised the *ardeur*. I'm getting more control."

"You haven't perfected the technique, Anita. Not of feeding from a distance, or control."

"It's time we did. Maybe it will all work out for the best. If I could feed the *ardeur* through Jean-Claude, then I could take more out-of-town jobs without having to bring along lunch."

He grinned at me. "Lunch, huh?"

I nodded, and smiled at him in spite of myself. I was never sure why he could make me smile when I wanted to strangle him, but he could. It was one of the reasons we were still friends.

"What am I going to do with you?" I asked.

He spilled himself back against the bed, giving me that lecherous grin. "I can think of something."

I stared down at him framed against the bedspread. I knew that I could have touched him and done nearly anything I wanted. He'd let me. The knowledge made things low in my body react, but . . . I was beginning to realize that maybe that was true of most of the women in this room tonight. Somehow that took some of the shine off it for me. "I bet you can, but if it's one of the blonds you're wanting tonight, you need to 'fess up to them."

"The last time I had sex with any of them was high school, Anita. It was fun, and a few times were very fun, but I have no idea how good they are at anything. The only person who'd do nonstandard for sure would be J. J., and that would be complicated. I mean, recapturing the glory days usually goes badly."

I nodded. "Yep."

"But you'd let me go out there and confess and flirt with intent."

I smiled. "Flirt with intent, I was thinking exactly that earlier, but yeah, tell them the truth and you can have all the intent you want."

"But if I don't tell them, then I have to behave myself better?"

I nodded. "I'm afraid so. I feel sort of guilty asking that of you, but I can't bear it. I can't let them think that any man I might marry would be allowed to diss me this badly." I added, "It sets a bad example to the other women, Jason. I mean, if even one woman seems to put up with shit like this, then it makes the other women more likely to put up with it for real. I just can't endorse it."

He clasped his hands across his stomach, looking serious. Only Jason could manage to look this serious and winsome on a bed at the same time. It was a gift.

"I guess I understand that."

"They think I'm like almost your fiancée and they are all over you like white on rice, right in front of me. Jason, that is lack of respect, from you *and* them."

He sighed, very heavy. "You're right, you're right."

"Tell them the truth, and you can go back to what you were doing with them."

He sat up slowly like it was some sort of stomach exercise, making the T-shirt demonstrate just how tight it was. "I love that," he said.

I blinked and looked from his stomach to his face. "What?" I asked.

"That you watch me like that, that you notice me. I don't want to go back to being invisible to you, Anita."

I shrugged. "I don't think you'll ever be invisible to me, Jason."

"But if I hurt your feelings this badly, reject you, then you'll make sure you never act on it again."

"You can't reject me if we're just fuck buddies."

"That's what I thought, but I realize that we're more than fuck buddies. A fuck buddy does not call in to work at a moment's notice and say *I've got to fly out of town with a friend.* A fuck buddy doesn't drop everything to come play some stupid charade. Someone who is just a fuck buddy doesn't come hold your hand when you see your father in the hospital and smell death on him. Fuck buddies are just about sex, Anita. I'm the closest thing you'll probably ever have to one, but the idea of a fuck buddy is that they are casual. Once I asked you to fly out here with me, that wasn't a casual request. I could only have asked that of someone who was my very close friend." He leaned in toward me, as if for a kiss.

I drew back a little. "Kissing won't answer my question, Jason. Do we walk out of here as a couple, or just friends? I need to know what role I'm playing for you here."

"How about both? I'll tell them the truth, but I won't sleep around on you while we're down here. That way, if any of what they seem to feel for me is real, it leaves it open for them to hunt me up afterward. But if it's just old times and wedding nerves, then no harm done."

"Actually, the *ardeur* sort of checked them out. For most of them the flirting is an end in itself. Most of them seem pretty levelheaded. Lisa would fuck you in a heartbeat, but her desire has an edge of panic to it."

"She's about to marry someone. I think she's scared."

I nodded. "I can understand that, but I've always thought if you were that nervous about the wedding, then you're marrying the wrong person."

He smiled. "You *would* think that, but then you are one of the least commitment-phobic people I know."

I stared down at him. "I know some people who might argue that with you."

He grinned. "They think because you haven't chosen one man above all the others that you don't know how to commit, when actually, I think your problem is that you commit too easily, and once you commit to someone you stick."

"One woman cannot be committed to this many men."

"Maybe, but you treat your lovers better than a lot of women treat their boyfriends."

"Sorry to hear that," I said.

He looked wistful for a moment. "I shielded as hard as I could so I didn't hit the radar for either the *ardeur* or your beasts."

I smiled. "You did an excellent job; you were a blank."

He smiled again. "Good, I'm really wishing we hadn't come at all. For me, it's great, but not for you. I didn't think it through. It's a bachelorette party; there is going to be a lot of sexual tension tonight. It's going to really challenge your *ardeur*."

"Hard to have a quickie with Shadwell and Rowe in the room," I said.

"What's with them not leaving us alone?"

"I told you, I don't know yet, but I'll find out."

He sighed. "I think I'll tell the girls, but only them. We'll pretend for everyone else but my friends."

"Friends you haven't seen since college may not be as good a friend as you remember."

"I know, but when Irving's article comes out tomorrow, our cover is blown anyway."

"True. So tell them the truth, but keep your options open?"

He nodded, and then a smile began to creep around the edges. "Though with J. J. we could do both. Had my first ménage à trois with her and a friend."

I shook my head. "A ménage à trois in high school?"

"No, I came back for winter break from college and so did J. J."

"Trust you to have the two-girl fantasy come true before you were legal to drink."

He grinned full-out. "I've always been precocious."

"I'll just bet you have."

He stood up and offered me his hand. "I'll try to be as good a friend to you as you are to me, Anita."

I took his hand. "Deal."

I tried to make it a handshake, but he raised my hand to his lips and kissed me. I guess either way, we had our compromise. Now we just had to see how the blonds in the next room took the news.

36

WHILE WE'D BEEN having our heart-to-heart, so had the women. Lisa was crying on the couch with all the women hovering around her. J. J. left the group and came to us.

"We're so sorry, Anita," she said. "We behaved badly."

Lisa sobbed and talked at the same time. "Please, don't be mad, Anita, please . . ." She came to us, a little unsteady on her feet. Trish stayed at her side like a spotter. Lisa clutched at my arm, swaying gently on her high heels. The little black dress and heels that she was wearing made her look pale now that all the makeup had vanished from crying.

I tensed my arm under her hands to give her something more solid to hold on to, because without it she'd have fallen.

She tried to focus on my face, and looked like it was hard work. "I'm so sorry, Anita. I was so awful to you."

"It's okay, Lisa," I said. She had that feel to her of one of those depressed drunks who might dissolve into tears or hysterics if I didn't just forgive her. Frankly, I blamed Jason more than anyone, so I wasn't mad at her. He hadn't set the rules, nor had I. If the couple doesn't set the boundaries, then you can't blame strangers for not knowing what those boundaries are.

She staggered toward me, I think to see my face better. I was beginning to wonder if it was more than drink. Did she need glasses and wasn't wearing them? She leaned into my face, peering close enough that it was too intimate in the suddenly silent room. She studied my eyes from inches away, clinging to my arm. She was nearsighted, I'd have bet money on it, because closer, she seemed to see me better. If I could use her guilt for two things, I would. Try to sober her up, and have someone find her damn glasses.

She overbalanced on her heels and fell into me. I let go of Jason's hand and grabbed her. I found out two things about Lisa Bromwell. One, she was drunk enough she couldn't right herself; in fact her knees started to go. Two, she wasn't wearing a damn thing under the little black dress. How'd I find out that last bit? I grabbed her at the lower waist and inadvertently raised the short skirt enough to bare most of her ass to the room. If I hadn't been worried about flashing the room, I could have just picked her up. She weighed maybe a hundred pounds. But I couldn't figure out how to lift her and not let the men in the room see the entire show. One of those moments when you just go, *Huh, no idea what to do.*

Jason and J. J. saved me. They both came in and took an arm apiece, which let me shift her dress back down. I watched her eyes roll back into her head. J. J. had time to say, "Lisa—"

I moved to catch her. I didn't mean to move faster than human-normal, but I suddenly found one arm across her back and one arm under her thighs. Jason saw the movement and let go of the arm he was holding. J. J. was left clinging to one of

Lisa's arms, eyes a little wide. I stood there holding Lisa and being looked at very seriously by everyone in the room. The women were just surprised; the bodyguards had that look—that if-things-go-bad-we-shoot-her-first look.

Shit. I wasn't used to being faster than a speeding bullet. Okay, not that fast, but I was almost as quick as a real lycanthrope. My reaction times had become bloody spectacular. I had spent most of my life struggling with the best I could offer being barely good enough physically, and now . . . now just catching one drunk woman had startled a room full of armed men. Crap.

Jason kissed me on the cheek, softly. "It's okay," he whispered.

J. J. let go of Lisa's arm and gave me full wide eyes. "That was like magic. One second she was falling, and then you just had her in your arms. Are you that fast, or did you fuck with my mind?"

"Yes," Shadwell said, from where he was standing away from the wall, hand a little hovery over his weapon, "which is it, Marshal? Speed, or did you mind-fuck the entire room like some kind of vampire?"

"It's speed," Jason said.

"Are you a shapeshifter?" Shadwell asked.

I shook my head. "No, not exactly."

"What does *not exactly* mean?" he asked.

I gave him an unfriendly look and said, "You like your secrets; you tell me what I want to know, and I'll share. Until then, you aren't cleared for this information." I admit, that last part was said in a voice with an edge to it. Was I teasing him, or just pissed at the situation in general? Both.

Trish recovered first and came over with a light jacket that someone had taken off. She draped it across Lisa's lower body.

I guess she was right. The dress was short enough that nothing I could do holding her in my arms would keep her from flashing the room. That's what underwear is for, girls, so if an emergency happens you only show your cookies to the people you love.

"Let's put Lisa on the couch," Trish said.

I started walking toward the couch with the woman in my arms. Trish said, "Isn't she heavy?"

"No," I said, and she wouldn't have been even before I got stronger than the average human, but then I could still bench-press my own body weight, and I weighed more than Lisa did. Which was why I could carry her across the room and lay her on the couch. There was plenty of room to lay her down because the women had scattered like pigeons when a child runs through them. None of them seemed to want to meet my eyes, or be too close to me. Prejudiced bitches.

I laid her gently down and made sure the jacket stayed over her. "Is she out for the night?" I asked no one in particular.

Jason said, "Guys, I told you that I was a werewolf, and you were okay with cuddling on the couch. Now you're treating Anita like she's scary just because she kept Lisa from hitting the floor."

J. J. said, "Jason's right. We're being stupid." She offered me her hand again, but this time there was no flirting, just a very direct look from those blue eyes.

I took the hand.

She said, "Thank you for catching my friend. I'm sorry it startled us." She gave an unfriendly look to all the others around the couch. "We are going to behave ourselves better than this toward our friend's girlfriend, aren't we, girls?" It was phrased as a question, but it was said as an order.

Some of the other women glanced at each other, but it was

Jen who walked over and offered me her hand. The mother of two was dressed in the only pantsuit of the bunch. It was a nice pantsuit, though, and showed off the new baby curves to advantage. Her shoulder-length hair formed a yellow frame to all that pale skin and blue eyes. Her makeup was understated, and almost invisible.

She gave me a good solid handshake, and even better eye contact. She'd been one of the few who hadn't hung all over Jason. I guess it was that whole married thing. Monogamy at its best.

"First we disrespected you by climbing all over your steady boyfriend, then we react like schoolkids when you save our friend from a fall. I don't know what you must think of us, Anita—please, give us another chance."

I nodded, and was more nervous or pissed or whatever than I knew, because I said what I was thinking. "You didn't do anything inappropriate with Jason, Jen. So no harm done. And a lot of people are spooked by the preternatural stuff."

"I guess that was aimed at the rest of us," Jenna said. She came forward in her own version of the little black dress. It was heavier material and not quite as short as Lisa's had been, but it was still the proverbial black dress, just the clubbing version. There is a little black dress for business, funerals (those can be the same dress), and parties. The latter are usually shorter and show more cleavage. Jenna's dress was no exception to the rule.

Her hair was almost the same white blond that Lisa's was. She even had her hair back in a ponytail, too. They looked like Barbie clones, or maybe Paris Hilton clones. Eek.

Jenna offered a perfectly manicured hand with nails painted black to match the dress. She was a little unsteady on her heels, but her voice was firm and didn't sound the least bit drunk. "I promise we will do better than this."

I had to smile for some reason. "I believe you," I said.

She smiled back, and the others came up one by one to shake my hand and apologize. Kris, who was a wee bit more drunk than everyone but Lisa, hugged me clumsily. "Pawing your guy right in front of you, I'm so sorry."

I patted her bare back awkwardly. I didn't like strangers hugging me. Why bare back? Because the back of her little white dress was nothing but straps. But most of the group had small enough breasts to carry off a dress where a bra was out of the question.

Kris got a little teary. "I've been a bitch."

I patted her and looked for someone to rescue me from the drunken blond. J. J. took her off my hands and led her away to the end of the couch.

I looked at Jason, waiting for him to tell his friends the truth. That we weren't really that close a couple and he could date them if they wanted. Jason was studying us all, and didn't seem about to raise the topic. I'd be damned if I'd do it.

There was a knock at the door. Shadwell nodded and Sanchez and the silent Price went for the door. Sanchez called back, "It's Chuck and the entertainment." He said both *Chuck* and *entertainment* like they were bad words.

I looked at the women, most of them already a little drunk and overly emotional. I really didn't want to see what the group would do around strippers. I went to Jason and whispered, "Can we go now?"

It was Ashley, who had the most elaborate hairdo of the bunch, like she'd gone to a beauty shop and had help, who said, "Don't go, Anita. Please, you have to stay. We want to be your friends. If you go now, you'll think we're terrible."

Kris raised a tear-streaked face. "Stay, Anita, stay and enjoy the party with us. Please."

I leaned in and whispered to Jason, through gritted teeth. "I am not staying here alone."

He put an arm around my waist and kissed me. "Wouldn't dream of leaving you alone." He gave me that look at the end of the sentence. I realized that if I'd asked him to leave with me, he would have, but I'd in effect asked him to stay with me. Was it too late to do a take-back?

37

CHUCK CAME THROUGH the door, scowling. I wondered who had gotten his panties in a twist. Then I got a glimpse of the man behind him. He was tall, tanned to a nice even brown, with medium-brown hair cut so short on the sides that you got a glimpse of paler skin underneath. His eyes were gray, and looked almost white in the dark of his face. He was around six feet, built slender but with the bulk that a weight room will give you to cover a build that might have been willowy otherwise. He was wearing a white tux that gleamed against his tan and made everything darker and lighter, at the same time.

Two uniformed guards came next, carrying a large trunk between them. Jason tensed beside me, and a second later I felt it, too. A prickle of energy breathed into the room. A second later, the reason for it glided through the door.

He was as tall as the first stripper, but with short curls that fell around his ears, so blond his hair was white. His eyes were blue with an edge of some other color dancing in them. I'd have to be closer to know what that second shade was, and I didn't plan on getting closer. Not if I could help it.

Then I felt another kind of energy. A cooler energy.

A second set of guards came through with another trunk, and the last dancer was the cherry on top of this bad idea. He was the same height as the other two, like they'd been chosen for it as though a matched trio of horses. His brunette hair was almost black, but I had mine and Sanchez's to compare it to, so it was only brunette. It fell in soft waves to his shoulders, framing a face that was more handsome than pretty, but it was a nice face. There was even a dimple in the chin, and another at the corner of his mouth when he smiled at the room. He smiled delicately, so as not to flash fangs.

"No vampire strippers, huh?" I said.

Jason put his arms around my waist and drew me against his body. "My mistake."

Jason breathed against my ear, rather than whispered, trying not to be heard by the other preternaturals who had just strolled into the room. "I've seen his pictures. This is the vampire that pretends to be Jean-Claude in Vegas."

What Jason meant was that this was the lead performer in a vampire strip revue in Las Vegas. The master of their city, Maximillian—Max for short—had petitioned Jean-Claude to allow him to do a Vegas show that was based on some of the acts at Guilty Pleasures. Some negotiations later and we had our first spin-off show.

Since they couldn't have Jean-Claude, they found a vampire that looked like him. To me, it was a superficial resemblance, but from a seat in the audience it might do.

Jason's arms tightened on my waist, and he breathed against my ear, "He calls himself Lucian."

I whispered, "Calls himself?"

He kissed the side of my neck, and whispered, "Stage name."

Ah. Part of me wanted to leave, but part of me was curious. And, at least, the men getting groped by the women wouldn't be any of my sweeties. Which meant I wouldn't have to work at the whole jealousy issue while the show was going on. That'd be almost relaxing.

I settled my back more securely against the front of Jason's body. He snuggled the side of my face and said, "Busman's holiday for me."

I turned so I could see his face. "You want to go?"

He smiled at me. "Just surprised you want to stay."

I shrugged. "I don't want to stay, or not want to stay."

He kissed me from behind, pressing my face backward so it was a good, rough kiss. A good enough kiss that it left me a little breathless. "We go to our room and we can do this for real."

I smiled at him. "You offering me a private dance?"

"The absolute most private I give." He smiled when he said it, and it was a good smile. A smile that left only one answer.

"Let's go."

"Keith," the vampire said, coming over to us, "I didn't know you'd be here, and with another brunette." Lucian glanced behind at the couch and the still-unconscious bride. "Won't her friends tell?"

"He's not Keith," the white-haired dancer said. "He looks like Keith, but he doesn't smell like Keith." The dancer glided over to us and started trying to circle us, but Shadwell and Rowe moved up so the movement was aborted.

The dancer smiled at them, and us, and backed up a little. "You vampires, always relying on your eyes. Can't you feel it? He's one of us, and so is she."

"Weretigers?" Lucian made it a question.

"No," the dancer said, and moved close enough to invade our personal space. He sniffed the air in front of us. "Wolf, and something . . ." He moved a little closer, inches closer. I could feel his energy like heat rising off his skin.

"Back up," I said.

He sniffed just above my face. The energy jump was bigger, harsher, like electric bugs biting along my skin. "I don't know what you are," he whispered.

"She said to back off." Rowe moved in front of me and forced the weretiger back. I was glad of the help. Because there was a stirring of energy inside me in that dark place where my beasts hid. I breathed through it, concentrated. I could do this. I'd been practicing. I could control my beasts, all of them, most of them. Oh, hell, tiger was the newest and new always means a learning curve.

I licked suddenly dry lips and said, "Rowe, Shadwell, escort us to the door."

"My pleasure," Rowe said.

Shadwell moved up to join him. They moved the dancers back.

"Why leave?" the weretiger said. "Stay and play."

"You have plenty of women to play with," I said. "You don't need me."

"But they're not as alive as you are," the weretiger said.

Chuck said, "You're being paid to entertain the bridal party, not . . . our visitors."

They turned and looked at him. The vampire gave blank face. The weretiger gave him a speculative look, as if not quite sure what to do with him. But there was an implication in the eyes that eating him was a possibility. It was a very alien look out of a human face. But it wasn't a cat look. It was what you might get if a cat could think like a human but still have the morals of a cat. It opened up so very many possibilities.

I got a flash of something down deep inside me. A flash of orange and a flash of gold. Oh, shit. One of the reasons I was having problems with the tigers was that I held more than one. One was a strain of lycanthropy that I'd gotten like you normally do by surviving an attack, but the other was a gift, or a warning, from Marmee Noir—the Mother of All Vampires.

Some said she was the oldest vampire in the world, the first of them—but having met one vampire that was an *Australopithecus*, I wasn't sure how that was possible. But whatever she was, she was ancient, and she was powerful, and she scared the hell out of me. She was still mostly asleep in her room in Europe, where she'd been "asleep" for more than a thousand years. In her dreams, she terrified me, the other vampires, and anything she wanted to haunt. But her strain of vampirism was old enough that you could be both a vampire and a lycanthrope, which was not true of modern vampirism. The viruses killed each other off, so whatever you caught first, that's what you were.

She had visited my dreams and put a piece of her animal to call inside me. Why had she done it? Because she could.

"Isn't she part of the wedding party?" the vampire, Lucian, asked. His voice tried for that emptiness of the very old, but didn't make it. He was younger than he was trying to play. A lot of the younger vampires tried to play older. The more they tried to pretend to be older, the younger they were, usually. He also hadn't reacted to my cross being visible. That marked him as very young. Most of the vampires a century or more old reacted to holy objects as if they were always a danger. In truth, if the vampire didn't try to use powers on me, the cross might just sit there.

"No, they aren't part of the wedding party," Chuck said. "The man is an old high school friend of the bride and this is his girlfriend."

I thought it was interesting that he didn't give our names. That, in fact, he introduced us as blandly as possible. That was very interesting.

"Just a friend of the bride's?" Lucian said, and let his voice hold his doubt.

"I'm a distant cousin of the Summerlands," Jason said.

"You look like a close cousin," the weretiger said, and again he tried to move closer to us.

My tiger, tigers, reacted to it. They stalked through the darkness inside me like a glimmer of red-gold, and a swirl of palest yellow-gold. They, more than any of my other beasts, seemed to hide in the depths of that inner place. They used the shadows like trees and foliage to glide in and out of, so one moment there was a striped glimpse, then they were gone. I'm told that real tigers are like that in the jungle. Invisible until they want to be seen.

Jason turned me in his arms so that my face was buried against his shoulder and neck. I breathed in the scent of his skin. He smelled like Jason, but underneath was the musk of wolf. It helped keep those glittering shapes away.

"The scent of tiger comes and goes like a dream of wind in the desert," he said.

"Poetic," Jason said, "but we're out of here." He started moving us across the floor. I turned my head enough to see where I was going. I caught a glimpse of blue eyes, but they weren't human. The color was, but there was something about the shade, or shape, that wasn't human. The sight of those eyes clinched things low in my body, not sexually, but painfully. The tiger flexing its claws, letting me know that it resented being trapped in my human body with no way out.

"My name is Crispin," the weretiger said.

Jason touched my face with the hand that wasn't around my waist. "Don't look," he whispered.

I did what he said. I kept my eyes forward. Rowe and Shadwell moved with us. I felt Crispin moving up behind us without needing to look behind.

Chuck said, "Leave her alone."

I felt someone behind us, and it was Sanchez. "Got your back," he said. I wasn't sure who he was saying it to, but my back, their back, our back, I'd take it.

My stomach felt like there was something more solid in it than food, like the heaviness of a phantom pregnancy. Except it wasn't some ghostly baby inside me. It was something far more solid, and just like a real baby, it wanted out.

38

THEY GOT US out of the door and into the elevator. Sanchez waved us onto the elevator. Shadwell, Rowe, and Chuck got in the box with us.

"What was all that about, Marshal?" Chuck asked.

I shook my head and leaned into Jason. I drew in the scent of his skin, trying to use the scent of wolf to loosen the sensation in my gut that something solid was down there. I breathed through it, slow and even. I could do this. This sort of situation was what I'd been practicing for, so I could travel without an entourage of lycanthropes.

Jason answered for me. "I'm a lycanthrope, and Anita's psychic abilities make her hit the radar as one of us sometimes."

"What does that mean, her psychic abilities?" Chuck asked.

"She raises the dead for a living, and is a vampire executioner. You can't do the first without the talent of necromancy, and there are no vampire executioners without psychic abilities that survive long."

"What kind of abilities?" Chuck persisted.

The tightness in my abdomen was finally loosening. I could breathe without feeling like a weight was pulling at me. I spoke carefully, my face still close to Jason's neck. "I'm good with the dead, Chuck. It's what I do."

"The tiger said you felt more alive than the rest of them."

The doors opened. Rowe stepped into the hallway first, and only when he nodded did Shadwell let us know we could move forward. Chuck didn't check the hallway as well as they did. He was a fixer of problems, not really a bodyguard.

"He was flirting," I said.

"Weird flirting."

"I've seen weirder."

Chuck gave me a look like he didn't believe me. I didn't care if he believed me; all I needed was our room and privacy. I needed Jason to help me push the tiger back and feed the *ardeur*. When that was done we'd worry about what Chuck knew, or thought he knew about us.

"You don't look so good," Rowe said.

"Thanks," I said.

"You know what I mean. Did the were-whatever or vampire do something to you that we mundanes couldn't see?"

That was a good question; a smart question. Too smart a question. Again, Jason saved me from trying to answer.

"For those of us who can sense the energy of the unseen, you have no idea how it can affect you. It can be the biggest rush, or the biggest downer."

"What makes the difference?" Rowe asked.

Shadwell said, "Once we're inside the room you can ask twenty questions, Rowe. We need our eyes and ears for work."

We let Shadwell save us from answering the second question, but his being so serious about the hallway walk to the room made me remember that I had questions. Ones that needed answers. But the metaphysical problem was going to outrank the mystery. I had to get better at this stuff. It was affecting my jobs, and my life, in ways that were not good.

When we reached the door to our room, Shadwell held out his hand. "What?" Jason asked.

"Key card, so I'm first through the door."

"Jesus," I said, "Shadwell, you didn't do that earlier. Did you guys get another message that the threat is even worse?"

Shadwell tried for blank cop eyes, but ended up just looking angry. "Please give me the key card."

Jason looked at me. "He did say *please*."

I started to argue, but something in my stomach contracted so hard that it doubled me over. I thought *What?* and saw the pale gold and white of the weretiger that had nearly killed me. The tiger looked at me for a second; the old and orange eyes were overlaid with an echo of Crispin's from the room above. The thought doubled me over, took my knees out from under me. Jason had to catch me or I would have fallen.

The door got opened by Shadwell while I was still fighting to breathe and remain calm. My fear was part of what allowed the beasts to get the upper hand. But it was so hard not to be afraid. So hard not to anticipate the feel of claws and teeth trying to eat their way out of me. I was tired of the pain; tired of the problem; just plain tired. I had been arrogant. I took a metaphysical ability to feed on lust to a bachelorette party with strippers. Fuck, what had I been thinking?

Shadwell held the door and Jason helped me inside. He picked me up, carried me to the bed. I was staring into the tiger's face, but it wasn't just the pale-gold-and-cream tiger, but like a second tiger was superimposed on top of the first as if my eyes were blurring. What was happening? The phantom cat, or cats, stood eye to eye with me in some sort of waking dream. Except this dream never changed; eyes closed, eyes opened, I saw the tigers staring at me. I'd never had that happen before.

"Everyone out," Jason said.

"Our orders are that no one gets left alone," Shadwell said.

"Then stay outside the door," Jason said.

"Our orders are very clear," Shadwell said.

The tiger moved closer to me, as if it were some huge dog phantom, and wanted to touch my nose with its own. But this was no dog.

I found my voice and spoke carefully, as if afraid that I would spook it. "Jason, something's wrong, different."

"I know."

"Can you see it?" I whispered.

"See what?" Chuck asked.

"No," Jason said, "but I can smell it."

"Smell what?" Chuck asked.

Jason said, "You have to leave now, all of you. If you don't go I'll call down to hotel security."

"They won't help you," Chuck said.

"I'll call the reporters and tell them you tried to molest Anita. How would that play on the network news, Chuck?"

"You wouldn't do that."

There wasn't just one tiger superimposed over the pale gold one now. It was like looking at a triple negative. Colors of stripes, and one that looked like a shadow of the others, so dark, all smeared over the face of the one strain that the doctors had found in my blood. The rainbow of tigers eased closer to my face. I knew one thing for certain: I did not want them to finish the movement. How do you stop something that isn't solid, that isn't even really there? I lay on the bed, but the tiger walked through it, or occupied the same space as it. It moved toward me as if the ghost of its body weren't standing in the middle of a bed. It wasn't real, but I'd learned years ago that just because something isn't real doesn't mean it can't hurt you.

I began to ease back on the bed, pushing with my hands, slowly, as if the tiger were real, and I were trying not to attract its attention. Claws ripped through my body from the inside. I screamed, "Jason!"

He was on the bed beside me, putting his body between me and the phantom tiger. Though the tiger seemed to be able to get through the bed just fine, Jason's body was solid to it. He wrapped his arms around me. I buried my face in his chest and neck, breathing deep of the scent of him.

The sweet musk of wolf was there underneath the cologne, his skin. It was like the truth under all that civilization. He was Jason, but I needed what lay within. I needed the wild truth of him.

A shape moved within that dark part of me that held the animals. My wolf shone in the darkness, the white part of her fur ghostlike in the gloom. She had dark markings on her, but they blended into the darkness, breaking up her outline the way they were supposed to.

Shadwell's voice startled her, made her look up, and begin to retreat into the dark, as if she'd been a real wolf. "I'll call a doctor."

"A doctor won't help," Jason said.

The wolf vanished into the gloom, and suddenly the darkness was alive with tigers. Tigers the color of rainbows, impossible colors, wending their way up through the darkness. It was as if instead of being a dark tunnel, it were some phantom forest of huge black, leafless trees. The tigers were coming, and it was more than just my own beast.

"Jason, there are lots of tigers, different colors that don't occur in nature. What is happening?"

"Are they in the room or inside your head?"

"Inside," I whispered, "for now."

Jason rose up, pressing my face against his chest. "Unless you know a practitioner of the arts, you can't help Anita, but you can hurt her."

"Practitioner of the arts?" Rowe said.

"Witch, he means a witch," Chuck said.

"Yes," Jason said, "the metaphysical shit is about to hit the fan. Guns won't protect us against anything that is about to happen, but you delaying me from doing what I have to do to stop this is hurting her."

I'd thought this was just my tiger trying to get the upper hand because of the weretiger upstairs, but the shapes gliding through the dark and light were not my beast. Oh, maybe she was in there, but this wasn't my body trying to finally pick an animal to turn into. Something else was happening. Something I had no words for, and no metaphysical experience with. That was bad.

"I don't know what's happening, Jason. This is wrong, different."

He held me close. "Get out," he told them.

"We have to tell him," Rowe said.

"We can't—" Shadwell began.

Chuck cut him off. "The threat says that vampires will try to hit the governor and his family. That means the window is an entry point, and not just the door."

"The least of our problems right now is a vampire coming through the window," Jason said.

I smelled rain and jasmine. Oh shit. The charm that rode under my shirt grew warm against my skin. It was supposed to keep Marmee Noir at bay, but it had never glowed before. That couldn't be good.

I rose up away from Jason and jerked the chain out of my shirt. The lines of the carving on the charm glowed red like someone had taken a red pen and traced every character, every faded image in the center. It was usually like an old tombstone. You knew there was a picture carved in the center but it had worn away, soft with age and wear. Now it glowed, and looked fresh-made at the end of the chain.

Jason said, "It's like a cat, a many-headed cat."

"What the hell is that, and why is it glowing?" Chuck asked.

I answered, "It's a charm against the oldest vampire on the planet."

"The vampire's here," Shadwell said, and guns came out.

I didn't bother with a gun. I told them the truth. "She's in Europe somewhere, but her magic isn't." I looked up at them. "You don't get it. A vampire doesn't have to come through the damn window to fuck you over. If they're powerful enough they can do you from a thousand miles away."

"We have to do magic," Jason said, "and you aren't allowed to see it." He told half the truth. We didn't *want* them to see it, but I let the half-truth stand, because I couldn't think of a better way to get rid of them.

"Why, you have to kill us if we see it?" Chuck said, voice derisive.

Jason and I looked at him. I was the one who said it. "We wouldn't *have* to kill you, Chuck. We'd consider it a bonus. Now get out. *Now!*" I screamed the last at them, flinging myself off the bed. I drew the Browning and pointed it at them, screaming for them to leave. Me calm might not have moved them, but me hysterical and armed helped Jason get them out of the room.

I fell to my knees, the gun still naked in my hand. The tigers swirled inside me. I waited for one of them to run up toward me, inside me, and try to tear its way out, but they didn't. They just paced in the not-trees, the almost-shadows. They seemed to be waiting for something.

The smell of jasmine filled the air. My cross flared to life alongside the glowing lines of the charm. Then the smell of rain and flowers faded. It faded, and the cross quieted. The room was suddenly very quiet, quiet enough that I could hear the blood in my own ears pounding.

Jason knelt beside me. I saw his lips move, but could hear no sound. My gun fell from my hand, and I grabbed his arms, tried to say something, anything. Then I felt it. A sound, a call, a smell, a feeling, and yet that wasn't it either. It was all of those things, none of those things. The tigers that I could see in my mind's eye like some sort of waking nightmare stood still. They raised their faces to the air, and roared. The sound of it bowed my spine, sent me to the floor, screaming. It was as if my body were some great bell, and their sound had struck a chord in me. I heard that sound not with my ears, but with my skin, like a silent tuning fork pressed against the spine to vibrate its message along every nerve ending.

Jason's hands were on me. He tried to hold me. I heard his shouts, broken in pieces, as if the ringing call let me hear only snatches of any other sound.

The charm's lines glowed again like metal taken fresh from the fire, cherry red, hot enough to sear flesh. I could feel the warmth of it through my shirt. I waited for it to begin to melt through my shirt the way a cross could do, but if it would keep the vampire's tigers from tearing me apart, I was willing to get one more burn scar.

Jason tried to get up. I held on to his arm. He mouthed

something; I heard, "door." He went to the door and opened it. Someone must have knocked, but I hadn't heard it.

It was Crispin, the white-haired stripper. He must have done his dance already because he was wearing nothing but an iridescent G-string. He knelt beside me, and the moment I looked into those strange blue eyes there was silence inside me. The tigers all looked up that long metaphysical tunnel.

Jason came to kneel on the other side of me. "Is it better?" he asked.

"Yes," I said, my voice a hoarse whisper.

"I heard your call," Crispin said. "I had to answer it."

I wanted to ask, *What call?* or what he had heard, but he touched my arm. It was such an innocent gesture. The white tiger leapt forward from the rest. It charged up that impossible path inside me like a white blur of grace and muscle and death.

Jason tried to give me his arm to smell, but it was too late for distractions. The tiger was coming, and I wasn't sure how to stop it.

39

CRISPIN LAY DOWN beside me so that we could look each other in the eyes. He gave me those human eyes with that tiger color, and just seeing his eyes like that calmed me. Calm usually meant that the beast in question would stop and begin to retreat, but the visual in my head showed the white tiger gaining speed the way they will do when they've committed to the hunt—that last burst of speed, strength, everything thrown on one leap.

Crispin put a hand on the side of my face, and the touch helped, quieted my pulse. He leaned over me and spoke just before he kissed me. "I hear the lady's call and I answer." It sounded more ritualized than anything we did at home, but it was as if he knew exactly what I needed from him.

The tiger hit the surface of my body, bucking me off the floor, slamming me into Crispin's body. It was like being hit by a small car from the inside out. Crispin's hands held my face secure, so the kiss didn't hurt either of us. I had a fleeting thought, that he'd done this before, and then there was no thought, only pain.

The tiger roared through me, poured out of me. It felt as if it had made its own exit, as if it were tearing out through my stomach. I screamed, shrieked, and Crispin screamed with me.

He was up on his arms above me, as if he were trying to get farther away. The charm floated between us. It fucking levitated, and I don't think either of us was doing it. The tiger flowed between us like a rush of white light that you could almost see between his stomach and mine. He should have changed by now. But he stayed human above me. The charm burned bright, and was almost touching his chest.

Crispin put an arm between his body and the charm. It touched his arm, and several things happened at once. The charm stopped glowing, and fell back like any other piece of jewelry. Crispin's body flowed with fur, like white-and-cream water flowing over that tall body. I was drenched with clear fluid as his body remade itself above me, on top of me. But it wasn't his beast that rode him, it was mine. I lay pinned underneath him as muscles and bone moved and popped and reknit themselves. Always before when I gave my beast to a shapeshifter in an emergency it had been more like an explosion. One second human, the next they'd been their beast. So violent that bits of flesh had decorated the room, and I had been drenched in that hot clear liquid that ran from their bodies. But this was different, slower, more controlled, more . . . powerful.

The white tiger wasn't tearing me apart anymore; it was filling up the man on top of me. I could feel his beast, or *a* beast, or a power, something warm and real, and more than just the shifting of forms. I had a flashback to the first time I'd been underneath a lycanthrope when they shifted. It had been

Richard, and he had just won his fight to be Ulfric. He'd offered me the power to be bound to the pack. I could have ridden the power and run with the pack that night, but they were about to feed on human flesh, and I couldn't do it.

Richard had said, "You refused the power." He'd been right.

Crispin stared down at me with a face gone white and fur-covered. His eyes were still in there, but the rest of him was that graceful half-man, half-cat shape. It was similar to the wereleopards, but different. The proportions were different, bigger, a little less human in the head shape, and a little more tiger.

There were brown stripes on the white fur, narrow but there; he wasn't completely white like the tiger in my vision. He stared down at me with the blue eyes that he'd had all along, as if the eyes never changed the way Micah's leopard eyes were always in his face in whatever form he chose.

The only weretiger I'd ever seen in half-form had been female, and pale yellow stripes on white. Again, not like the color of a real tiger. Staring at the white-and-chocolate image above me, I wondered if none of the weretigers shifted into that classic orange-and-black design. Maybe I'd spent too much time with the wereleopards in their half-forms, but I gazed up at Crispin and noticed that his chest, like theirs, was less furred and more like an overly muscled human chest. The half-form was taller, more muscular, and edged by that white and pale-chocolate-striped fur, but the skin revealed was pale and human-looking down the center of his body. The wolves seemed to be furrier in half-form than the cats I'd met, so far. My gaze traveled down his body to find that, like in every half-form, everything was bigger. Noticing made me turn my head, and fight not to blush. I might have told him to get off me, but I saw who'd been watching the show.

Chuck, Shadwell, and Rowe stood staring down at us, guns bare but not pointed at anything. Jason said, "You both screamed like you were being killed. I had to let them in or they would have busted down the door."

I raised a hand and smoothed some of the clear, slightly thick liquid away from my forehead so it wouldn't drip into my eyes. I wasn't covered in it, but there was enough of it that I'd need a shower before I left the room. With as much dignity as I could muster, I said, "As you can see, I'm fine. Now get out."

"What we just saw is a lot of things," Rowe said, "and fine ain't one of 'em."

I think because I hadn't told him to move, or maybe because things hurt, Crispin curled on top of me. He moved his much taller body down so that he wasn't covering my face with his chest. It meant that certain things weren't touching me as intimately as they had been through my jeans, which was fine, but it did mean that he was curled around me like some gigantic stuffed toy. A stuffed toy with a pulse that snuggled against me when I touched its furred back. But Crispin had saved me, saved me in a way that Jason couldn't have—in fact, that no one in town could have done. I owed him, so I didn't tell him to get up in front of the humans. I didn't embarrass him, or react like some . . . mundane. I acted as if this were all just as ordinary as it could be, as if I did this all the damn time.

"I wouldn't expect you to understand; just leave so we can . . ." Several words went through my mind: *talk*, *finish*, *do what we have to do*, none of them sounded right.

Jason finished for me. "There are things we need to do, and they'll weird you out just as much as this. You should see your faces: white, shocked, horrified. You look like you've been to the freak show."

"That's not fair," Shadwell said. "We had no idea what was happening in here."

"Now you do," I said, still on the floor. "Go, just go."

Shadwell licked his lips and glanced at Rowe. Rowe shrugged.

"I think we should give the . . . marshal here some privacy like she asked," Chuck said. I wondered what he'd been about to say before he came up with *marshal*? Better not to know.

I half-expected the other men to argue, to say they didn't take orders from Chuck, but they didn't. I think they wanted out of the room, too. Sometimes the weird factor just goes too far for comfort.

Shadwell nodded, and holstered his gun. Rowe hesitated, giving the weretiger wide eyes, but a hard look from Shadwell made him holster his weapon. He didn't like it, but he did it. Training; it will keep you alive, and out of trouble with your superiors.

"We'll be outside," Shadwell said, "until we're relieved."

Rowe said, "How do we know if there's a problem? I mean the screaming . . . we really thought that was it. That you were being attacked."

"Sorry about that," I said, "I'll try to be quieter."

The weretiger moved against me in a motion that seemed to send a wave down his entire body. His tail rose up, to twitch, and then to curve back over the very human rise of his buttocks.

He turned and gave the men the full look at that half-and-half face. His voice came growling low, "I'll be good."

Rowe swallowed hard and began to lose the little color he'd regained. He just nodded and started for the door. Shadwell followed him, and never looked back. Chuck was the last to leave. He hesitated with his hand on the open door.

"I didn't think you knew our dancers tonight, Marshal Blake."

"I didn't," I said.

He looked at the tiger on top of me. "Do you usually make friends this fast?"

What could I say? "Sometimes."

He nodded. "Sometimes," he repeated, shaking his head. "You go back to making friends, Blake. I'll leave Shadwell and Rowe on the door. Though I think you're right. If the vampire threat is real, I sort of hope he picks your window tonight, Mr. Schuyler. Nothing personal, but I think if he climbs in here, he won't be climbing back out."

Jason and I spoke at the same time. "No." We looked at each other, and then he motioned at me, and I said, "He won't."

Crispin said, "Is there a big bad vampire around?"

"Maybe," I said.

"Oh, goody," the weretiger said, "something to play with."

Chuck shook his head again, and closed the door quietly, but very firmly behind him.

40

THE WERETIGER SIGHED and was suddenly heavier on top of me, as if some tension had left his body. "Always so hard in front of the humans," he said in that growling voice.

"Off," and I added, "please." He had saved us; saved me, but he was still heavy.

He half-rolled, half-fell off me, to collapse on his side beside me. He blinked those strange blue eyes at me.

"I'm sorry if I hurt you," I said.

He smiled; it was a smile full of teeth that could have shredded my throat, but it was a smile. And I'd learned through working with the police on serial killer cases that humans had teeth, too. I had so learned things about my fellow human beings that I did not want to know. It made me calmer around the "monsters," because I knew scratch us deep enough and we were all monsters.

"You fought your tiger. If you had just given it to me, then it wouldn't have hurt either of us."

It must have shown on my face, because his face looked curious, speculative. "You didn't know that," he said.

"I know that if a lycanthrope fights his beast, the change is more violent; I guess I just never made the logic leap."

"You've done this before with someone," Jason said.

"Of course I have. I'm an adult male of my clan. This is how we keep our pregnant females from losing our babies."

Jason and I both looked at him. I said it out loud. "The weretigers do this routinely with their pregnant females?"

"Yes," Crispin said, and then he frowned, though his face made it more of a snarl. "And you should know that." He frowned/snarled harder. "Though your tiger was white, and we're the only white tiger clan in the United States. You should be one of our females, but you're not." He rose up on one elbow, balancing with the other arm flat on the wet carpet as if he were still shaky. His face showed concern, all sympathy. "You survived an attack, but it can't be one of our clan. We would never do that. It's against the law of every clan to bring someone over against their will." He went back to frowning. "And when our master says to attack, it is for killing. We don't leave survivors." He said it easily, as if he knew he could confess all his sins to me.

I felt compelled to say, "I really am a federal marshal, Crispin. Be careful what you say to me."

"Do they know you're one of us?"

I looked at Jason. What could we tell this stranger? What was safe to share? He seemed to understand the look, as he so often did.

"You're one of Max's tigers from Las Vegas, right?" Jason said.

Crispin moved his gaze to the standing man. "Yes."

"Max knows what Anita is, and isn't. If he didn't share that with you, it's probably not something he wants shared with you. Nothing personal, but I think my master would have to talk to yours before we could explain."

"Are you hinting that she's not a weretiger?" Crispin asked.

"The humans say a picture is worth a thousand words. We know a smell is worth a hell of a lot more."

Crispin just nodded.

Jason knelt in the damp carpet on the other side of me from the weretiger.

"The beasts are quiet," I said. "I really don't want you both to go furry on me, literally or figuratively."

"Do you feel well enough to sit up?" he asked.

I thought about it, explored my body not with hands but with thought. I hurt, but not as bad as I'd feared. I started to struggle to sit up, and Jason's arm was there only seconds before Crispin's longer one. They looked at each other over my head, and I had a moment to feel the testosterone rise.

"Don't even think it," I said.

"Among our people a female mates with only one male. It's all about competition."

Jason swallowed a laugh, which puzzled the weretiger and made me frown at him. "Sorry," Jason said, "but I'm just thinking that tiger would so not be Anita's animal."

I frowned harder at him.

"Just think about your wolf, just enough to bring it to smelling depth."

"Smelling depth?" I made it a question.

"Trust me, Anita, just a little thought, and he'll get the idea."

"I don't want to, Jason. I'm tired, and I hurt, and I don't want this to get out of hand again."

He tried to hug me to him, but Crispin's arm was in the way.

Crispin's long, clawlike hand curled around my waist, between my body and Jason's.

I leaned in against Jason's body as much as that furred and muscled arm would let me. Jason cradled my face against his chest, pressed me to the scent of his skin underneath the T-shirt. I got a glimpse of dark gold eyes surrounded by white and dark fur. My body reacted to it, and the wolf simply started trotting up the metaphysical path inside me. I thought, *No. Back.*

She hesitated, the wolf, then looked at me. There was suddenly something in her eyes that said *No* right back at me.

"You smell of wolf now," Crispin said. He leaned in, snuffling along my hair and face. It brought the scent of tiger again. Tiger should have been quiet, but there were still tigers inside me. Still striped faces to move in the dark.

I clung harder to Jason, but the wolf wasn't cooperating either. The wolf gave me that flat look, as if to let me know that she obeyed me because she had to, but she still wanted out. She still wanted freedom.

"She can't be both wolf and tiger," Crispin said.

"You have no idea," Jason said.

Crispin snuffled against my neck, tickling with fur and almost nibbling. It made me shiver, made my body react low and hard. It wasn't a fear reaction. The wolf started trotting harder, and the tigers trailed behind, not too close, but coming. The only thing that made it not an absolute complete clusterfuck was that leopard and lion were still in hiding. But we didn't need them to have it go horribly, horribly wrong.

"You have to feed the *ardeur*, Anita, now. That's part of what's wrong."

"We fed the *ardeur* before the party."

"You're acting like we didn't, like you need to feed again."

I pushed away from both of them, trying to breathe in things that didn't smell like either animal. God, it was like I almost needed someone who wasn't furry to quiet the beasts tonight.

"The *ardeur* was the talk of everyone who came back from St. Louis after the big meeting. That you have to feed off sex like a real succubus. I thought it was just rumor. Are you saying it's true?"

I got up on all fours, debated whether I could stand, thought I could, and tried it. I was a little unsteady but I managed. Away from the two wereanimals the beasts had slowed, but they hadn't gone away. I could still see them behind my eyes like a waking dream.

"If it's true," Crispin said, "I volunteer to help in any way you need."

I shook my head without looking back at them.

Jason said, "I've got it covered, thanks."

"I don't think you do."

A low growl came from behind me, and I didn't think it was Crispin. "Get out," Jason said.

"I think if it comes to a fight, you won't win," Crispin said.

"Let me be clear here, tiger. I'm grateful for the help, but don't threaten Jason. He's my friend, my lover, and my master's *pomme de sang*."

"He wants to kick me out, but I can feel your tiger, Anita. I can feel it. It's not gone. I'm the only weretiger within a hundred miles or more. You need me tonight."

"I need his wolf, too." I finally turned and looked back at them. Jason was standing, but the weretiger was on the floor. He'd rolled away from the wet spot we'd made on the carpet, but he was lounging more catlike than human. If he'd been a cat it wouldn't have been erotic in the least, but he so wasn't a cat. All the fur in the world wouldn't change what he was, and what he was not.

"I smell the wolf, but you can't be both, can you?"

I shook my head, again. "Long story."

"Anita, you need to feed," Jason said.

"I know, but every time I'm close to you, Jason, the wolf seems stronger."

"I'll help," Crispin said.

I gave him a hard look, which didn't seem to faze him in the least. "The tiger reacts to you. I don't know what's wrong tonight."

"I took you to a room that was so thick with sexual tension you could have walked on it," Jason said. "We both know that can make it hard on the *ardeur*, on you. I wanted to see the girls. I wanted to flirt and be flirted with, and I forgot my duties." He shook his head. "You and Jean-Claude trusted me to take care of you and I failed. We have to feed you again. I think once we do that the beasts will calm."

"By the way," Crispin said, "what the hell is with that necklace of yours?"

I glanced down at the charm on its chain. It was back to being dull and almost unreadable. But I had the image burned inside my mind, as if I would never forget it.

Crispin went to all fours and started crawling toward me, in that graceful I-have-muscles-in-places-you-can't-see way that they could do in this form, or even human form. It was just a little more disturbing in this form.

"No closer, Crispin," I said.

Jason stepped between us. "You heard her."

Crispin growled, a sound that made my body react both for sex and for the tigers crowded at the back of my wolf. *No fighting*, I thought, as hard as I could. The beasts could fight inside me, and it hurt like hell. "Stop it; stop it, both of you. I am having real trouble here with both the tiger and the wolf. I don't need you to make it worse."

"Then you should stop calling to me," Crispin said.

"I didn't."

"Yes, you did." He sat back on his haunches, hands hanging down between his knees so that at least he was covered and I could look at him without worrying about staring at his groin. I tried not to stare at strange men's genitalia; just politeness, I guess. Or squeamishness.

"I didn't mean to," I said.

"You call to me like a little queen."

"You don't mean that as a pet name, do you?" Jason said.

He turned those strange blue eyes to the other man. "No, *little queen* is what we call our dominant females who would be powerful enough to eventually break off and form their own clan if our queen would allow it."

"What happens if she doesn't allow it?" I asked.

"She kills the little queen, or has her killed, after she's bred at least once."

I just stared at him. I couldn't read the tiger face quite well enough. Jason said, "I think he's serious."

"I am." He held his arm up, and showing through the white fur was a raw burn mark. "What is this mark on me?"

"Jason," I said, "you look at it. I don't think closer to the tiger is better."

Jason did what I asked, and Crispin raised his arm up obediently. "It's the charm. The symbols in a circle and the many-headed tiger inside it. You've branded him."

"I didn't mean to," I said.

"What is that charm supposed to do?" Crispin asked.

I debated on what to say. It was supposed to keep Marmee

Noir from taking me over from far away in Europe. It was designed so she couldn't be as big and bad a vampire as she truly was, but I was beginning to wonder if the charm could do other things that no one had told me about. Had the werewolf who gave it to me known that it had other magic in it? Was it a trap instead of a treasure? Shit. I needed Jean-Claude. I needed to be home, not out here in some strange city with just Jason. If the metaphysical shit hit the fan, I needed more help.

"Your face," Crispin said. "You're afraid to tell me."

"I can say this, that it's never reacted to anyone like it did tonight."

"Am I the first weretiger you've been around since you got the charm?"

A very logical question. "One other, but she . . . we've been very careful around each other." I didn't add that Christine was an attack survivor. I was beginning to wonder if a "born" tiger—their word for it—was different enough to make the charm react this differently. Maybe. Or maybe Marmee Noir was figuring out ways around its magic. I needed help.

"He is the first male you've been around," Jason said.

I looked at him. "So?"

He gave me a look. "Anita, come on, your magic is based on sex, and girls just don't do it for you. Not that that doesn't disappoint me sometimes."

"Hey, fantasize about your little girl-on-girl ménage à trois on your own time. I've still got wolf and a herd of tigers staring at me in the dark inside my head. I don't know what's wrong, Jason, and I don't know how to fix it."

"You need to feed."

I nodded. "We need some privacy, Crispin. Thanks for the help, and sorry you've got a brand, but I need to feed now."

"You mean you and the wolf are going to have sex."

I closed my eyes and counted slowly to ten, then said, calmly, "Yes, that is what I mean."

"The tiger inside you may not like that."

I looked at Jason. He hung his head. "Honestly, your beasts have been quiet. I would never have brought you with just the two of us, if I thought you needed all your animals with you. I mean, at least it's only the two. This is a small town, Anita. There aren't going to be that many wereanimals."

"Only the two," Crispin said, standing. "What does that mean? Are there more inside you?" He started toward me, and again Jason moved in his way. The tiger gave a low, rumbling sound from that wide chest. He towered over Jason, but he, like me, was used to being towered over. It didn't impress either of us. But we were used to playing these games at home with people we knew, or who knew us. Playing where we had other people to back us. Crispin didn't know us, didn't understand us, and we didn't understand him.

He went from standing there to attacking Jason. One minute fine, the next claws and teeth, and Jason was still in human form. Blood spattered; Crispin hitting him too fast, too much for him to change. Fuck.

The Browning was on the floor on the other side of them, which said more than anything else how messed up I was. I had a choice of wading into a fight with silver blades, or going for the gun. I went for the gun.

I had the gun in my hand, was raising it up to aim at that tall white figure, when he threw Jason at me, literally. I had just enough time to point the gun up so that it didn't accidentally go off into Jason's body, and then I was on the ground with him on top of me, stunned by the force of the blow, and the weight.

His blood spattered my face, and my wolf started running. *No, no!*

There was a white blur above me like an out-of-focus mountain. Clawed hands pinned my gun hand and tried for Jason's throat. Jason put up an arm to block the blow. I tried to move my hand for an angle that would let me fire into the weretiger. Jason's hands fumbled at my sleeve, ripped it. He drew my silver knife and struck out at the tiger. Blood spilled across me in a hot arc. I waited for the tigers to chase my wolf, but they looked into the dark. There was something in the dark that was not my beasts.

I'd told Chuck and the guards that a vampire didn't have to be in the room with you to fuck you over, but I hadn't realized just how true that was about to be.

Marmee Noir had tried to mark me, and failed as a vampire, but she was truly a shapeshifter, an older strain of both that could live in the same host body. The darkness inside my mind wavered and I heard her voice. "Your control is formidable, necromancer. I need it gone."

One moment there was a fight, the next the *ardeur* was free. She tore my shields down. She destroyed me. She made of me something that simply needed. If it had been blood lust she had raised, I would have torn out Jason's throat, anyone's throat. There was nothing but the need. It rose up out of the darkness that she had planted inside me. It hit the cross that shone on my chest, and I tore it off, threw it away. It hit the charm, made it glow, and that, too, went spinning away.

There was no gun, no knife. There was only flesh, and hands, and mouths, and bodies. Then there was only darkness.

41

A SLIVER OF light across my eyes woke me. I blinked up into a lamp. I tried to turn my head away from it and found the pillow stiff and sticky with some fluid. That made me open my eyes wider, and I found that there was a wolfman in bed with me. The long snout, the furred body, all so much taller than Jason in human form.

I had this jumbled memory of sex and him changing in the middle of it. It was a first for us, and I wondered if he'd remember any more of it than I did. Why couldn't I remember?

The bed moved on the other side of me. It made me tense and turn like you do in those horror movies when you hear something and know, suddenly, you aren't alone. The white-haired stripper from the party last night lay on his stomach beside me, nude. I had a confused image of him in tigerman form above me. The memory was definitely sexual. What the hell had happened last night?

I looked down at my own clothes, and it looked like they'd been torn off me. I had bits and pieces of cloth and leather clinging to parts of me, but for the most part I was nude, too.

I tried to think back to the last clear memory, but it made no sense. It was a fight. Crispin, that was the tiger's name, he had attacked Jason. Jason was hurt, and I was trying to shoot the weretiger, but he'd pinned my arm to the floor. Jason had gotten one of my silver knives from my free arm, and cut the weretiger. Blood on my face, so hot. Then . . . then nothing. Nothing. Just bits and pieces.

Sex, and . . . something. But it was as if the harder I tried to think of it, the fuzzier it all got. I remembered feeding the *ardeur*. I remembered sex with Jason and him shifting in the middle of it. I remembered sex with Crispin already in half-man form. The visual of him going in and out of my body was embarrassingly clear. But how we got to the sex was a blur, no, worse than a blur, missing. Shit.

Missing, something was missing, but what was it? I touched my neck and found my hair plastered to my shoulders with that clear gunk that the lycanthropes lose when they shift. The bed was thick with it. Jason had shifted on the bed, I remembered that now.

Had the *ardeur* risen up and stopped the fight? Had it just overpowered us? It had never done that before. Which raised the question, was Crispin our enemy? When he woke, would he try to hurt us again? Where was my gun? Where were my knives? My cross, that was it, I was missing my cross.

I needed off this bed. I needed my cross. I needed weapons. Shit. My weapons were still in the hotel safe, but my gun was here, somewhere, and at least one extra magazine of ammo, and my knives. I needed to be armed, and then I'd worry about the rest.

Jason was still in wereanimal form, which meant he was probably still hours away from waking. Crispin was in human form, which meant he would wake first. I needed to be armed before that happened.

I tried to ease to a sitting position and let out a small pain sound before I could stop it. I ached deep inside my body almost up to my belly button. I knew what the sensation was: really good, but really rough sex with someone well-endowed enough to put the *deep* into deep fucking. Jason was very good, but he wasn't big enough for this. Not in human form anyway.

I glanced at him, but he was lying on his stomach, and I wasn't touching anyone in this bed. I wanted out.

I started easing out from between them and had to bite my lip not to make more noise. I was actually a little raw between my legs. What the hell had we done last night?

I hurt in other places, too, like I'd been in a real fight. My right arm had fresh claw marks covered in dried blood. From the feel of things there were other marks on my back and legs. I fought not to look for what hurt, but just to keep inching closer to the end of the bed. Once I was armed I'd look at all my injuries.

I was at the end of the bed, one leg half off the edge, when I froze, staring at what lay on the floor.

A second weretiger, still in tigerman form, was curled on his side. His fur was red and black stripes. The sight of him brought a flash of memory like a broken picture. I remembered being above him, straddling him, his claws in my back. Not a fight, but sex. For the life of me I couldn't remember him in human form. I couldn't remember how, or when, he joined us. Oh, my God.

Fear ran over my skin in a cold wash. What had I done? What had the *ardeur* done to me? Shit, shit, shit.

Weapons, then call Jean-Claude. Someone had to know what the hell was happening. Didn't they?

I angled to the corner of the bed, where I'd touch Jason's furred legs. I knew enough about lycanthropes to know that being in tiger form meant the red tiger would not be waking anytime soon, but I had the horror-movie image in my head of me stepping off the bed and him grabbing my ankle. I knew better, but still I couldn't make myself step close to his clawed hands. I climbed over Jason's unresisting legs rather than risk that imaginary grab. God, I needed Jason to shift and get closer to waking. I did not want Crispin to wake first and be the only one awake with me.

I was finally on the floor; yea! I hadn't woken either of the weretigers; double yea! I stood there a moment in the hush of the hotel room, only the sounds of the men's breathing deep and even competing with the air conditioning. I enjoyed simply not being on the bed with them. I felt a little less trapped.

Standing, I ached more, as if bruises and cuts had been waiting to tell me they were there. I ignored them as best I could while I scanned the floor for weapons.

The floor looked like a clothing store had put up a fight and lost. I saw the remnants of Jason's blue shirt tangled with a man's white dress shirt. Jeans lay beside dress slacks. A man's suit jacket lay whole and untouched near the doors, as if when the red tiger hit the door he had immediately taken off his jacket. It had to be his, unless another man was hiding in the room somewhere.

I really wished I hadn't thought of that. I pushed the thought away and concentrated. One problem at a time.

Finally, in a tangle of my shirt and jeans I glimpsed my shoulder holster, which meant the Browning couldn't be far behind. I walked toward it, and it hurt to walk, as in I had to fight not to limp or put a hand over my stomach as I moved. Fuck. Something was wrong with my back, too, as if some muscle or other was hurt.

Kneeling was an experience in controlled movement and not reacting to everything that hurt. I knelt on carpet that was stiff with dried fluids, and tried not to think too hard about what some of those fluids might be. I remembered now that this was where I lost most of my clothes. I checked the Browning to make sure it was still loaded as the memories washed over me. Crispin and Jason and I on the floor. There'd been no more fighting. Whatever the fight had been about, they'd shared me just fine. Oh, God.

I remembered sex with the weretiger here and on the bed. Jason had lost human form here during sex, too, but I also remembered sex on the bed with him. Dear, God, what in hell had gone wrong with the *ardeur*?

With the gun in my hand I felt a little better, a little more myself, but I had still woken up in a hotel room with three men, two of them strangers, and apparently we'd had sex. Lots of sex, and I could remember only bits and pieces of it. That had never happened before with the *ardeur*. I was supposed to be gaining control over it. I looked at the wreck of the carpet and finally back at the bed and the men there. This was *so* not gaining control of anything. No, this was definitely losing control.

I was digging through the clothes trying to find my cross when there was a sound from the bed. It froze me; I held my breath like an idiot. All wereanimals could hear a heartbeat, and there was no way to hold that.

The sound wasn't repeated, so I went back to searching and found my cross. The chain had been snapped. Damn. I gripped it in my hand and that was a little better. I felt that prickling energy of lycanthropy, like a wash of electricity across my skin. I turned to the bed, gun pointed. No one moved, but one minute Jason was all movie wolfman and the next his wolf body was melting away and his human body rising up through the receding fur like an island rising from the ocean. The larger wolfman body melted back into the more compact human form. He was still probably a couple of hours or more from waking, but it was progress.

If it had been Micah, or Richard, or a few others, they wouldn't have had to pass out for hours after the change, but Jason and apparently the two tigers weren't powerful enough not to fall into the coma just before the shift and just after. Or . . . I lowered the gun, having thought of another awful possibility.

Had the massive *ardeur* feeding taken too much of their energy? It was possible to drain someone to death with the *ardeur*. Logically, I knew that if they died they would revert to human form. But fears like this have nothing to do with logic. I suddenly went from afraid of the two weretigers to wondering if I'd killed them. No, no I'd seen Crispin and Jason breathing. I'd heard it. But I hadn't really looked that closely at the red tiger. I stared at him now, trying to see the rise and fall of his chest.

I actually held my breath trying to see that wide striped chest move. I thought for a heartbeat he was dead, and then his body moved with his breathing. I let out the breath I'd been holding in a long sigh.

The bed moved as someone shifted position. I knew who it

had to be before Crispin rose up on his arms and blinked blue tiger eyes at me.

I pointed the gun at him, two-handed, and the move was too fast. It pulled on the claw marks on my arm, and hurt like a son of a bitch. I held the pose, but had to fight my body to do it. I told him, "Don't move!"

42

HE DIDN'T MOVE, but he said, "Do you wake all your lovers up at gunpoint?" His voice seemed deeper than it had last night. He coughed to clear his throat. It made me jump, not good when holding a gun. I fought to calm my body. If I shot him, I wanted it to be on purpose, not because I flinched. But I was afraid to take my finger off the trigger, because he was a lycanthrope, and they were just that bloody fast.

"I remember you fighting with Jason and me," I said, gun still pointed at him.

He frowned. "Yeah, but the fight with your wolf was about you, being your mate. There was plenty of you to go around last night."

"Thanks for the phrasing," I said.

He smiled. "Sorry, I didn't mean to offend a woman holding a gun on me. But my point is that there's no reason to fight when you share yourself so well. Besides, I got to go first." The smile filled his eyes with a dark light. Not otherworldly, just a man looking at a naked woman whom he's fucked. That possessive, sure-we'll-get-to-do-it-again look. Crispin hadn't earned that look, not yet.

My wounded arm was beginning to try to twitch. I fought to keep my aim steady. How badly was I hurt?

"If you're not going to shoot me, may I get up and use the bathroom?"

"You don't believe I'll shoot you, do you?"

"I don't remember everything from last night, which means I've been rolled. You rolled my mind just like any other vampire. Not that I'm complaining, the sex was mind-blowing, but you did mind fuck me. Legally, it's rape. You raped me, not the other way around, Anita. I mean, I would have said yes, but a man likes to be asked. I should be the angry one, not you."

I wanted to argue with his logic, but couldn't. I did the one thing I could do: I lowered the gun. My arm was going to make me do it soon anyway.

"Does this mean it's safe to go to the bathroom?" he asked.

"Yes," I said.

"Great." He got up, and it was interesting to see him moving a little stiffly, too. When the sex has been rough enough for the lycanthropes to be sore, us humans are going to be hurt.

There were scratches on his back, and they didn't look like claw marks. Had I done that? And if I had, why hadn't they healed when he shifted back? Only damage by silver or another lycanthrope could survive the shift of forms for the most part. So why would my nail marks still be on his body?

I pushed the thought away. I'd worry about it later. I had way more immediate problems to worry about. What had Crispin said? That I'd mind-fucked him just like any other vampire. Had I done that? Had the *ardeur* done that?

Water started running in the bathroom.

I needed Jean-Claude. I reached out to him down that long metaphysical cord that bound us and found . . . nothing. I could not sense him. It was like some huge, white blankness where he should have been for me.

Fear came back in a rush of near panic. I started shivering and couldn't stop. I fought the urge to scream at Jason to wake up and tell me if he could sense Jean-Claude. Was it just me, or was something wrong with Jean-Claude? I had a cell phone once. Where was it? When metaphysics fails, you can always try technology.

I started digging through the ruined clothes with the one empty hand I had. Where the hell would the cell phone be? Had I had it with me last night? Or was it in the luggage still? I couldn't remember. Damn it, what was wrong with me?

The water stopped running in the bathroom. Crispin opened the door and came out. "Did you lose something?"

Just my mind, I thought. Out loud I said, "My cell phone."

He frowned, thinking. "I remember weapons, but not a phone."

"I thought you didn't remember last night."

"I remember parts, so you're right, maybe there was a phone. I'll help you look for it." He came to kneel by me. It was too close after last night, and we were both too nude for comfort, but I needed the help. Was it silly not to want to be this close to him naked? Silly or not, it made me uncomfortable. Did he really think I'd rolled him on purpose? Did he really think I'd done the equivalent of metaphysical rape? He'd said it, but he didn't seem that upset by it. I'd threatened to kill people for less; hell, I *had* killed people for less.

"You know, you could look more effectively if you had both hands free," Crispin said.

"The gun makes me feel better," I said.

"And the cross in the same hand?" he asked.

"The chain broke."

He stopped rummaging through the clothes to look thoughtful again. "You jerked it off and threw it away."

"I wouldn't do that."

He shrugged, then winced. "You did it." Then he looked at me a little harder. Those strange blue eyes studied me. "You don't remember everything, do you?"

I debated on what to admit, but finally went for the truth. "I remember it breaking, but not who did it."

"You did it, and that charm of yours, too."

"Charm," I said, "what charm?"

He looked at my face like he was trying to see through me, then finally said, "This charm." He held his left arm out to me. At first I didn't understand, and then I saw the burn in his arm. It was a circle with an animal in the middle of it, done a little soft the way brands get most of the time. I peered at it, getting closer to the skin of his arm. I thought at first it was Cerberus, the dog that guarded Hades in Greek myth, but the animal had five heads. Cerberus only had three. Then I saw, or thought I saw, stripes on the animal. It was a tiger, a tiger with five heads.

He'd said it was my charm that had done it. I stared at the mark on his arm and didn't know what he was talking about. I reached out toward the brand, stopping just short of touching it. Something stirred in my mind. Was it a memory? Was he right? Had I done this?

I tried to remember. Tried to bring that nebulous thought to the front of my head, but it was like this darkness. There was nothing there to remember. Crispin was a stranger to me. Was he lying? I needed Jason to wake up. I needed someone I knew and trusted. Shit. Something was wrong with me.

That much I knew. But I didn't know what was wrong, or why I couldn't figure anything out. It was . . . wrong, too. The fact that I couldn't figure out what was wrong. That was a clue. I knew it was, but it was as if my brain wouldn't, or couldn't, make sense of it.

Crispin growled low in his bare chest. "I smell wolves."

A second later I felt the energy of them coming down the hallway, but I knew the taste of this energy. I reached out, and could suddenly smell forest, the rich earth of leaves, and the comfort of pine. I had a tactile moment of paws on the leaves and earth of the forest floor. I smelled the harsh, sweet musk of wolf, so thick that it tightened things low in my body, in a good way. Only one werewolf could make me react like that. But it couldn't be him. He would never have risked coming here with other wolves. He would never have risked this much potential media. He was in deep cover, our Ulfric, and coming here like this was not the way to stay hidden.

But impossibly, I felt him out there in the hall, felt him move closer, and knew that there were at least two other wolves with him. Our wolves, our pack.

Crispin was on his feet, his otherworldly energy swirling off of him like invisible fire. It was way more power than he'd had last night. Had he hidden it? Was I that bad at tiger energy? Shit.

I stood up, a little slower, gun in hand. "It's my Ulfric and my pack."

"What are they doing here?" he growled from human lips. Once I'd thought growling voices from human mouths was strange. Now it was so low on my weird list, I didn't blink.

"I don't know. I think they came for me." I was already going for the door. Did we still have guards out there? What would they do about Richard and his men?

I had a moment to realize I was naked, covered in blood and other things, along with wounds. I might have tried to throw something on, but I heard male voices by our door. "Stop right there."

Shit.

I took a deep breath and went for the door. Maybe I could hide to the side, and not flash the entire hallway. I had a memory of doing this last night. The red tiger had come and the guards had stopped him. I'd opened the door nude and let him in. I'd told the guards that I knew him and had asked him to stop by, or something like that. I could remember his human form now. Tall, short hair the dark red of his own fur, and his eyes. I'd looked into his eyes and been disappointed. They'd been brown, just brown. I'd known that was wrong, very wrong. I had a glimpse of him with human eyes that were dark rich golden yellow, with edges around the iris of orange, red. He'd had to take out his contacts that hid his tiger eyes before I'd let him touch me. Why was that important? Why had that mattered to me? Hell, for that matter, why had I let in a stranger at all?

I heard deep voices, and the guards repeating, "Back off, now."

I was out of time to get clothes. The returning memories had distracted me. I took a deep breath and opened the door.

43

I HID AS much of me behind the door as I could, but with one hand on the doorknob and the other hand still holding a gun; it was a little awkward in so many ways.

The guards were Shadwell and Rowe. That was wrong. They hadn't been our guards in the night. What time was it? How long had we been out? Had we cycled back through our guard shifts? Shit, again.

"It's all right, guys," I said.

"The hell it is," Rowe said.

"We can't let them in, Blake," Shadwell said, "not without clearing it with someone."

I looked farther down the hall, and there they were. Jamil and Shang-Da stood in front of whoever was behind; they were not small men and seemed to fill the hallway. Shang-Da was well over six feet, the tallest Chinese man I'd ever met. His hair was cut short, and he wore a long black trench coat. I knew it wasn't because of the summer heat. There would be dangerous toys under the coat. Jamil was almost five inches shorter, which put him at about six feet. He looked small, but then everyone looked small beside Shang-Da. Jamil's hair was in cornrows to his waist with tiny white beads showing. He wore a white suit that made his skin look even darker than it was. The suit was a generous cut, not the formfitting style he preferred. Some suits he had were for show, but this was a business suit of someone who wore weapons and didn't want them spotted. It was a tailoring challenge, I knew that myself.

They were Richard's bodyguards, his Sköll and Hatí, respectively. The names are the wolves in Norse mythology that chase the sun and moon. When they catch them, it will be the end of the world. In werewolf society they are the guards who keep the Ulfric, wolf king, safe.

I looked at them from Rowe and Shadwell's perspective. Even if you couldn't feel the otherworldly energy rolling off them, no self-respecting guard would let them inside any room. They just needed signs that said *bad ass*. No, strike that, they didn't need signs. It was too obvious to need anything else but them standing there.

"I don't know how to explain this to you, Shadwell, Rowe, but they are the bodyguards of my friend. They won't move out of the way as long as you have guns out. I appreciate the guns not being pointed at anyone, but they're just doing their job."

"We're trying to do ours, too," Shadwell said. He risked a tiny glance my way, then put all his attention back to the men in the hallway. "But you do not make it easy to guard you, Ms. Blake."

I didn't correct him to add the *Marshal*. I wasn't feeling very marshally right now. I was sore, and tired, and scared, and I wanted badly to talk to the wolves in the hall.

I made my own gun more visible against the door frame, simply by moving my hand up. "Oh, I don't know, Shadwell, I think I do a pretty good job of protecting myself."

My voice sounded so confident. Good for me; inside I was screaming. I could feel Richard just a few yards away. He had to be here for a very good reason, and the only reason I could think of was to help me, or tell me something, like why I couldn't feel Jean-Claude metaphysically. I wanted some answers, I needed some help, but me hysterical wouldn't get the guards to move. Okay, maybe it would, but if I lost it that badly, it wouldn't be pretend. I didn't want to be that weak in front of the werewolves. Shang-Da didn't really like me much. He thought I was bad for their Ulfric. There were nights I agreed with him.

"Don't make me come out there, Shadwell."

"That a threat?" he asked.

"No, more a plea, I can't find a robe. I'd rather not flash the hallway."

It was Rowe who gave me a longer glance than he should have, with what was standing in the hallway. All he could see was an arm to the shoulder, but there's something about telling some men that you're naked. It makes them a little distracted.

"Eyes front," Shadwell said.

Rowe did what he was told.

"I can't explain this to you, Shadwell, but I need them inside with me."

"Why?" he asked, without turning his gaze from the men in the hall.

What could I say that would make sense, and not out Richard further than he already was? Nothing came to mind.

Crispin came up behind me. He whispered, "Why do you need them when you have me?"

I gave him a look that has made bad guys run for cover. He lowered his head, almost a bow. "Fine, fine, don't waste the full look on me."

"The stripper slept over," Rowe said, and his voice made it sound like he didn't approve.

"Who I sleep with is none of your business, Rowe."

"How many men you have in there?" he asked.

"None of your business," I said.

"It is if we're supposed to guard you."

"Then go, just go. I don't need you. I don't want you. Go."

The stripper in question walked a few steps away and came back with the suit coat of the other tiger. Why hadn't I thought of that? Too easy, too hard.

Crispin stood in the doorway, obviously nude. We moved back enough from the door so I wasn't in view while he held the coat for me. He helped me into it while I traded hands back and forth with the gun.

"We can't leave without orders," Shadwell said.

"Fuck your orders," I said. I was glad that the red tiger was tall and broad. It meant that his suit jacket covered me completely, almost to my knees. Crispin helped me button it. I looked like I was five and playing dress-up in my father's clothes, but I didn't care. I was covered, and that was all that counted.

I stepped out into the hallway, and realized that my gun was still in my left hand. I did practice left-handed. You never knew when you'd need both hands, or injure your right. But it wasn't comfortable. But as I moved into the hallway, my left hand felt just right on the gun. It even had an ambidextrous safety, not that it wasn't already off, but still, if you had to shoot left-handed the Browning wasn't a bad gun for it.

I thought calm, mundane thoughts as I moved toward

Shang-Da and Jamil. Rowe grabbed my arm and whirled me back toward him. I let him do it, let his own momentum turn me back toward him; I turned my shoulder into his body, and my foot swept him as I came. He ended up on the ground with my arm still gripped. I twisted my arm in his grip, helped by the bulky coat, and ended with a one-armed joint lock on his elbow. I put enough pressure on the arm that he made a pain sound for me. He still had a gun in his other hand. If this had been a real fight, I'd have had to shoot him a second or two before this.

He started to bring his gun up, but mine was already pointed at his face. "Move, and die," I said.

"You point that gun at her," Jamil said, "and you die before she does."

I didn't look away from Rowe on the ground. I trusted that Jamil had a gun out and pointed where it needed to go.

I stared down into Rowe's face, kept the periphery of his hand and its gun in my sight. "Open your hand, Rowe, just let go of the gun."

"Fuck you," he said.

"I don't think so." I smiled and could feel it was unpleasant. It was sort of the smile I used sometimes when I knew I was about to kill somebody, but at the same time it didn't feel like me, exactly.

Why had I upped the violence in the hallway? I hadn't needed to do this, but it was a little late to say *oops*. I stared down at Rowe. His pulse was thick in the side of his throat. He could control his face, but the pulse and beat of his body gave him away. He was scared. Should he have been? Would I really shoot him? There was a small piece of myself that said, quietly, *If we have to, sure.*

I took a deep breath, and let it out slow. "You shouldn't

have grabbed me, Rowe. Maybe I overreacted, but you shouldn't grab a woman like that unless you know how she'll take it."

"Don't go all soft on us, Anita." This from Shang-Da.

"They helped me last night, Shang-Da. My Hatí was not there to protect me, but these two men were."

"You smell of fresh wounds. They did not do a very good job."

"The shift had changed to other men. These two did their best."

"Then why are you about to shoot one of them?" It was Richard's voice. That calm, matter-of-fact, hail-fellow-well-met voice. My chest actually felt like it squeezed tight at the sound of his voice. God, would I ever stop reacting to him like this? Honest answer: no. Answer I wanted to hear: maybe.

"He touched me, and I didn't want him to." My voice sounded rough around the edges as if I couldn't get enough air.

I felt him coming closer. Heard Shang-Da and Jamil protest. "They have guns; we can't let you go forward."

Richard said, "Shadwell, right?"

"Yes," Shadwell said.

"Put up your gun, and I'll come help."

"Help who?" Shadwell asked.

"Everyone." And there again in his voice was that confidence that he would do what he said. He would try to make it better. At his best, Richard really meant that. Problem was that sometimes there was no way to help everyone. He wasn't so good in situations where there were no good choices. He tended to freeze, or react badly. Of course, I was at my best when the choices all went south. We could have been a good team, if we hadn't hated each other. Okay, honestly, we didn't exactly hate each other.

I didn't really think that Shadwell would put up his gun, but he did. He even said, "Drop your gun, Rowe."

"Hell, no."

"You grabbed her first, Rowe. Maybe she overreacted, but you did touch her."

"No way, I am not dropping my gun."

"Just open your hand, and slide away from it," Shadwell said.

"They've mind-fucked you," Rowe said.

"She could shoot you before you even brought your weapon up."

"I'm her bodyguard, for God's sake, I wouldn't hurt her."

"Then drop the gun," I said, softly.

He gave me a look that was part hate and part confusion. "How the hell did we get here?" he said.

"You touched me."

"A lot of guys touched you last night, according to the last shift."

And there, there it was, the sad fact that once a woman lets more than one man touch her, some men think less of her. More than that, they think they should get a shot, too. A woman who will sleep with more than one man will do anything, right? Wrong, but he'd touched me out of anger, and frustration, and a confusion that had less to do with his job and more to do with him not understanding me.

It seemed a stupid reason to get shot, but I'd seen stupider. "You didn't touch me to keep me safe, Rowe. You touched me because there was a naked stripper in my room, and I was naked, and he helped me put on yet another man's coat to come out into the hallway, to meet even more men. You touched me in anger, and I reacted to that anger. Don't ever touch me in anger again, or we'll finish this talk—" I dropped his arm and fell on him at the same time, pinning his upper arms under my hands, with the gun still in one. He probably could have wriggled away, but his eyes were wide and startled. I had his gun arm pinned. I leaned over his face, and spoke low and soft; with each word I moved my face lower, until with the last few syllables I was just above his mouth. "And-you-will-not-like-the-end-of-the-conversation."

Richard's voice behind me said, "Anita, don't."

I moved back enough to see Rowe's eyes. He was afraid, I could taste that on the air above his skin, but underneath that, he wanted me to kiss him. He wanted me to finish what I'd started. He'd have let me do it, at least a kiss. That made me stop. That Rowe, with a gun still in one hand, would have let me press him to the floor and kiss the hell out of him, and not have fought back.

Something had gone horribly wrong with the *ardeur*. I backed off from Rowe and stood up, carefully. He'd let his gun fall from his hand. He stared up at me more like a child caught in the dark. He whispered, "Please."

I shook my head, and said the only thing I could think of. "I'm sorry." I went for the door to our room. The werewolves followed me, and this time neither Shadwell nor Rowe tried to stop them.

44

ONCE THE DOOR shut behind us, I wanted to run to Richard and be held. I wanted to demand to know what was wrong with Jean-Claude. But we had a stranger in the room. A stranger whom I really couldn't afford to kick out, not until I knew what the weretiger inside me was going to do. That much I remembered from last night.

I looked at Richard. He was wearing a baseball cap and sunglasses. His hair was piled up under the hat so he looked like he had short hair. He was wearing a bulky jacket. He had come, but he was still hiding. His day job was as a junior high science teacher. Parents don't like the monsters around their children. Too many fairy tales about the big bad wolf, maybe. So he hid to keep the job he loved, but it was like Clark Kent trying not to be Superman. In real life it's harder to pull off.

"This is Crispin," I said. "He's one of the Las Vegas tigers."

"What are you doing in town, Crispin?" Richard said, and his voice wasn't quite as friendly as it had been in the hallway.

"I was flown in for a bachelorette party upstairs. Then I felt the little queen call, and I had to answer."

Richard lowered his glasses enough so I could see the dark, perfect brown of his eyes. The look in them was not friendly either. "He's already calling you pet names."

"Ulfric," Jamil said, "business, please."

Richard sighed, deep enough that it made his broad shoulders rise and fall. He took off the jacket, revealing a plain white T-shirt. It set off his summer tan nicely.

"You're right, Jamil. Business first." He looked at the weretiger. "We need to talk in private and there is no place in this room far enough away that you won't hear us."

"I'm not sure it's safe for him to leave, Richard. The weretiger went very, very strange last night. I don't know what would have happened if Crispin hadn't been nearby."

"Who's this?" Shang-Da asked. He was looking down at the now-naked man on the floor at the foot of the bed. Apparently, my stranger had shifted back. He was still unconscious, but he wasn't furry anymore.

"He's another weretiger."

"Why did you need two?" Richard asked.

"Crispin is a white tiger, but this one is red and black. I remember enough to know that it was like the tiger inside me needed a variety. One tiger didn't fix what was wrong."

We couldn't talk in front of Crispin because he belonged to Max of Las Vegas. We couldn't afford for another Master of the City to find out that something was wrong with our power structure. But I was afraid to have Crispin leave, too.

I finally said, "Okay, we can't talk in front of Crispin freely, but tell me this, is Jean-Claude all right?" I had to know at least that.

"He's fine," Richard said, "honest, he's fine."

I must have looked like I didn't believe him, because he repeated it. A tightness in my stomach loosened, and I felt tears press at the back of my eyes. God, why was I about to cry?

There was a sound from the bed. We all turned to it. Jason moved just his head enough to see us all. "God, what happened?" His voice sounded choked, and thick with either old screams or long disuse. It occurred to me to ask what time it was.

"There's a better question," Richard said, softly.

"What's that supposed to mean?" I asked.

"What day is it?" His voice was gentle.

I stared at him. "No, no way."

"It's not the next morning, Anita. It's the day after."

"Jesus," Crispin said, "my boss is going to be pissed."

"Jean-Claude has been in contact with Max in Vegas."

I started to go to the bed and sit down, but there was a naked stranger by the bed. "Shit, Richard, what happened? What the hell happened?"

"What we've told Max is that you seem to carry a variety of beasts inside you. That you're a panwere. But being Jean-Claude's human servant prevents the beasts from manifesting completely."

I almost said out loud, *Is that really the truth?* but I let it go. Richard had very carefully said, *This is what we're telling Max*, the Master of the City of Las Vegas. The ultimate master of the weretiger I'd borrowed for two days.

"A panwere," Crispin said, "that's like not possible. I mean it's legend, but . . ."

"I've seen it for real," I said, softly. "He was one of the most frightening . . . he was evil, and I don't use the E-word lightly."

Jason's voice, still thick with sleep, or whatever, said, "*Little queen* isn't a pet name, Ulfric. It's what the tigers call dominant females that could be powerful enough to break off and form their own group, if the main queen allows it."

I nodded. "I remember part of that conversation before everything went dark."

"We need to talk, Anita, and we can't talk freely in front of him." Richard pointed at Crispin.

"I don't know if I have a room to go to," Crispin said. He frowned. "Why didn't Lucian come and find me?"

"Lucian is the vampire who came to strip with him at the party," I explained.

"Truthfully, I half-expected to find him here with you," Richard said.

I gave him the look the comment deserved. "Thanks, Richard, you always know just what to say."

He sighed. "Yeah, to piss you off."

I nodded. "Don't knock it, Richard, you have a real gift for it."

"Wouldn't it be good to know who this one belongs to?" Jamil said. He was standing over the last unconscious man.

"Check his wallet," Crispin said, "it's got to be on the floor somewhere."

It was a good idea. It made me think better of him. I don't know about Richard. It would take a lot more than one good suggestion for him to like a strange man who had had sex with me for two days in a hotel room. Then I had a thought, a really bad thought.

I went for the bathroom and my travel kit. The one that had things in it like toothbrushes, razors, birth-control pills. I knew what I'd find. Knew it. But I had to look, had to make sure.

I put the gun on the back of the toilet while I got out the little round of pills. There was an extra pill. Well, fuck.

Richard was in the doorway. "What's wrong?"

I just held up the pills. "Guess."

He looked stricken, like someone had hit him in the gut. "Mother of God."

I nodded. "I had sex with three men for two days and I've missed a pill."

"You didn't use condoms?" he asked.

My body chose that minute to remind me that what goes in, comes out. I shook my head. "We were all metaphysically mind-fucked, so no, we didn't take precautions. I need some privacy."

"Anita . . ."

"I need to clean up, Richard, okay?" I fought not to cry, or scream at him. I wasn't mad at him. I was too confused to be angry with anyone.

"This isn't your fault," he said.

"The *ardeur* went crazy, why?" I asked.

He stepped in, and whispered, "It had help going wrong."

I stared up at him. "What are you talking about?"

"We need privacy to talk."

"Shut the door, I'll turn on the shower. I need some answers, Richard. Hell, I need a morning-after pill."

"Doesn't that tread a little too close to abortion?" he said.

"Could you watch me be pregnant with some stranger's baby? Could you help me raise a stranger's baby?"

He opened his mouth, shut it. "I don't . . . no."

"No," I said. I shook my head. "Micah and Nathaniel were willing to help me when we thought I was pregnant from someone we knew, one of my lovers, our friends. But this is a stranger. God, Richard, God!"

He came to me then, wrapped his arms around me. I stayed stiff in his arms for a moment, and then I collapsed into his body. I clung to him. I let his strength and his nearness hold me. I let him hold me while I wept and screamed and wailed. I lost it completely, and Richard held me while I did it.

45

I CRIED UNTIL my knees went weak, and then Richard's arms tightened around me and held me. He held me standing, pressed against his body, when my own body would have fallen to the floor. When the crying began to quiet and he could feel that I was standing again, he loosened his hold on me enough to bend back and see my face.

"We'll get through this," he said.

I looked up at him. His hair was trailing down from the edge of the hat. Shoulder-length waves of brown with that hint of gold in the lights trailed around his face and the long firm line of his neck. I wanted to see all that hair loose around those perfect cheekbones. I went on tiptoe, found it hurt a little, but did it anyway. I lifted the hat off, and watched a little more hair spill down, but not all.

He turned his head so I could see the really bad bun that someone had done for him. I started to reach for it, to free his hair, but he gripped my wrists and set me back flat-footed in front of him. "Leave it."

"Why?" I asked.

He gave me a gentle smile. "Because once you start playing with my hair you tend to get distracted. We can't afford that right now."

I nodded, agreeing with him. "I'm too sore to get too distracted for a while. I wondered why I felt so awful, but two days of it, that explains it."

He kissed my knuckles on both hands, then let go of them. "Your face looks so lost."

I nodded again. "I feel lost." I looked up at him. "What happened to me, Richard? Why can't I sense Jean-Claude?"

He seemed to think about it, then said, "Turn on the water. The sound will help drown things out from the tiger."

I went to the shower without another word. I needed to get clean anyway. I could smell the men on my skin, whiffs of it as I moved. It wasn't a bad smell, really, but it was the smell of strangers. I had woken up with the perfume of someone's skin against mine before, but never a scent I did not know. I knelt, slowly, careful of all that hurt, and turned on the water.

Richard started talking, "Do you remember Marmee Noir?"

I tried to look over my shoulder, but found that the big claw marks on my back hurt too much to do that, so I turned more of me to look up at him. "The Mother of All Darkness is kind of hard to forget."

He looked relieved. "Good, Jean-Claude wasn't sure how much of your memory she'd wiped."

I stared at him. "What are you talking about, Richard? Marmee Noir didn't wipe my memory. I remember every time I've seen her, even in dream."

I did not like the look he gave me; it was too soft, too gentle, too . . . too you-poor-baby. "No, you don't."

"Stop hinting and just tell me, Richard."

"She rolled you two days ago. She's the reason the *ardeur* went crazy."

I tried to think back. What was the last thing I remembered clearly? But it was like the harder I thought at it, the more my mind kept sliding away, as if the surface of the thoughts were slippery and I couldn't hold on. I shook my head. "I'm a necromancer; vampires can't just mind-fuck me. Especially not from thousands of miles away. She's in freaking Europe. She couldn't have rolled me this completely from there."

He shrugged those wide shoulders. "Then why can't you remember what happened? What caused the *ardeur* to rise out of control worse than it's ever been before?"

"I don't know, but . . ." I swallowed hard enough that it sort of hurt. The water was too hot now, steam rising from it. I added more cold and tried to think about what he'd said.

"The tiger inside me went crazy first. It did things that none of my other beasts have ever done."

"Like what?" he asked.

I told him the quickest version I could think of. When I was done, he looked way too grim for comfort. "What is it, Richard? Why that look? What the hell is wrong with me?"

"We're not a hundred percent certain, but you put out a call to all the weretigers in this country. Maximillian, the Master of Vegas, called Jean-Claude with all sorts of threats. Said you'd stolen or were trying to steal away one of his weretigers. He didn't mind you sleeping with him, but you weren't allowed to call him as a mate."

"What does this 'call' mean? Crispin talked about it, too. Like it should be in capital letters or something."

"Christine was the only weretiger we had to talk to, but she's not a natural-born. She survived an attack, so she's not an expert, but the 'call' is a way for the dominant tigresses to get lovers, and eventually a mate. Only the very dominant can do it, and if Max's fit was accurate, your call blanketed the country, or damn near. Max thought it was just his clan because you had his tiger, but when his wife contacted the other clans, just to see . . . they were all hit by this 'call'."

"What does that mean, *hit*?" I asked. The water was the right temperature now. I badly wanted to get clean, but I wanted the information, too.

"Apparently, the unattached males all felt your call. Only the strongest dominant queens were able to keep their males from getting on the nearest plane, train, or bus to answer that call."

I stared at him. "What?"

He spread his hands and knelt beside me. "It wasn't you, Anita. You're good, but you're not this good."

"You're saying that Marmee Noir used me to call the tigers here."

"Yes."

"Why? What does she gain from it?"

"First, Jean-Claude wants neither you nor Jason to tell anyone that it was Marmee Noir that did this. He's afraid that if the other vampires know she can use you like this, they may kill you to keep her from gaining more power."

I understood the reasoning. If it hadn't been me that would have to die, I couldn't even argue with it. "Understood, but what does she gain from the tigers coming to me?"

"Jean-Claude isn't certain, but Elinore thinks that the

Mother is gathering her forces. The vampire council has finally found something that can unite them. They're terrified of what will happen if she wakes from her 'sleep' completely. They are very close to voting to make sure she never wakes."

I whispered, "You mean the council is going to kill Marmee Noir?"

"The last intelligence Jean-Claude got is that there is a vote before the council."

"Shit, Richard, shit, I mean, the—" I almost said *the Harlequin* out loud. I stopped myself because to say their name aloud was to risk death. They'd hunt you down and kill you just for saying their name. The only exception to that rule was if they contacted you first. Then, since they were the spies, assassins, jury, and executioner of the vampire world, well, you were in deep shit.

We'd had a visit just in December. Though they'd been sent to police Malcolm and his vampire church. They'd broken their own rules to give us a very solid scare. We'd lost good men in the fight. Hell, we'd nearly lost Jean-Claude, Richard, and me. It had been a very, very near thing.

Once the Harlequin had been Marmee Noir's right hand, but the ones we'd talked to seemed as frightened of her as the rest of the vampires. They'd given me something to keep her away. What was it?

I looked at Richard, searched his face. "They gave me something to keep her from manifesting around me. I know they gave me something, but I can't remember what it was." The first cold trickle of fear wormed its way through my veins. Most of the time with memory magic, the more you talked about it, the more you remembered. Not always, but for me, yes. Now this bit of knowledge was gone. She'd wiped it away. Wiped it away without ever being near me.

"It was a charm." He made a circle with his thumb and finger. "About this big."

"Did it have a many-headed animal on it?"

"Yes," and he smiled. "See, you do remember."

I shook my head. "No, I don't, but I saw the mark on Crispin's arm where it branded him. He said I jerked off my own cross and threw it away. He also said I did the same to my charm. I didn't remember the charm. I didn't remember it when I saw the shape of it burned into his arm. I still don't, Richard. I just remember the shape in his arm, that's it."

He looked way too serious again. "You need to get in the shower, but there's more news you can't share with the weretigers."

"Just tell me."

"Marmee Noir damaged your connection to Jean-Claude."

"Damaged it how?"

"We're not sure, but she cut his ability to sense you. Cut it so hard that he thought you were dead, but he wasn't hurt, and I wasn't hurt. That was the only way we knew that it wasn't injury or death. It's like she just put a wall between you and him."

I swallowed hard again. "Did she mark me? Did she give me her vampire marks in place of his?"

"She would have to drink your blood, and you hers, to do all four marks."

"It's the Mother of All Vampires, Richard. She was the first vampire. She can do all sorts of things that the rest can't." I hugged myself tight, and didn't know what to do.

"We don't think she did that. We think that even she needs to exchange real blood with you for the third and fourth marks."

"But not for the first two," I said, and stared up at him.

His eyes were so sad. "No, not for the first two."

"So you're saying that she has given me her version of the first two marks."

"Maybe."

"Maybe? Doesn't Jean-Claude know?"

"She's been asleep for a thousand years, Anita. He wasn't alive the last time she was mobile. We can't talk to most of the vampires who remember her awake without giving away what's happening. We can't risk them knowing."

"You risked a lot coming here, Richard. You could get outed with this much media."

"It had to be an animal she can't control. For whatever reason, she only does felines. Wolf is the only animal you have inside you that isn't a cat." He said the next in a rush. "Jean-Claude thinks it might be a good idea if you carried some other noncat lycanthropy strains. He thinks that might make it harder for her to control you."

"He thinks I should let some other shapeshifters cut me up?"

"If it would keep her out of your head and body, would it be so bad?"

I thought about that, then had to shake my head. "No, no, it's not worse than her."

"Jean-Claude is talking to the wererats and werehyenas about the possibility."

"I'd rather not get cut up again until I heal."

"We need you safe from her, Anita."

He was right. He was so right. "Okay, I'll think about it, but right now find the charm, and I need a new chain for my cross."

He reached behind his neck and lifted out a gold chain. He lifted a small gold cross out of his shirt. I'd bought it for him for one of our first Christmases as a couple. The cross was a little oddly shaped, from where it had once melted into my hand. Marmee Noir had been to blame for that, too. I would bear the scar in the palm of my hand for the rest of my life.

"Lift your hair," he said, softly. I did, but had to wince; something hurt across my shoulders. He fastened it around my neck.

He touched it where it lay against the bare triangle of my skin in the borrowed suit jacket. "There, you're safe."

I looked at him. "You might want to find the charm, too."

"I'll do that."

He helped me, carefully, to my feet. "We want to fly you home, but the other tiger queens can't seem to agree whether your fleeing and not being here when the tigers arrive is a greater insult to them. You made the call; you need to be where they can find you."

"Find me, what does that mean?"

"It means what it means, Anita."

I closed my eyes and took a deep breath, but that was a mistake because even standing this close to Richard I couldn't smell his skin. All I could smell was strangers, and mixed in with that was Jason. I knew the scent of his skin, but it wasn't enough. I smelled tigers.

I licked dry lips, eyes still closed. "Find the charm, Richard, please. I need to get clean now."

He kissed my hand again, and let me go. I opened my eyes to him walking to the door, then out. Something about watching him leave made the tears start again, but at least they were quieter.

46

I'D FORGOTTEN HOW much it hurt to have a shower with fresh claw marks. Or maybe I'd just never had this many of them all at the same time. I'd gotten cut up when someone was trying to kill me, but I'd never had this many shallow ones done in the heat of the moment. They weren't deep enough to kill or meant to maim, but they fucking hurt when the water hit them. I tried to see in the mirror what my back looked like, but it kept fogging up. What I could see was an impressive amount of damage, even for me. My back almost looked like someone had taken a whip to it. I had more marks on my arms, and a puncture wound on my ass. A memory came with that one. Crispin inside me in tiger form, his hands lifting my ass off the bed for a deeper angle. His claws sliding into my flesh at the moment of his release, and mine.

The memory jerked things low in my body, and made me stumble against the wall. God, what was wrong with me? The only one who could usually make sexual memories this potent was Asher. One of his gifts was that he could make you have total recall of orgasm with him. Think too hard and it was dangerous to drive. But it wasn't supposed to work that way with anyone else.

There were more marks on my hips, the inside of my thighs. It was like I ignored them the best I could until the water hit them. Then they hurt and I couldn't pretend anymore. I was marked up enough that I could have gone into any hospital or police station in the country and they would have believed rape.

Trouble was that rape like this by lycanthropes was a potential killing offense. I didn't want anyone dead; I just wanted a morning-after pill as quick as I could get one. I'd already taken the pill I missed. It was what they recommended if you missed one. If I wasn't pregnant, then I was safe again, at least from babies.

I knew the shampoo running down my body was going to hurt worse, and don't even talk about soap, but I had to get the smell of them off my skin. I had to not smell like strange men and sex. Even if it hurt, I needed it off me.

I ended up sitting in the bottom of the tub with the shower still running. I was clean, or as clean as I was going to get. I knew that my skin smelled like soap and me again, but I kept thinking I smelled them on my skin. I was pretty sure it was imaginary, but I still ended up sitting in the water, waiting to feel clean and safe and knowing I wasn't going to. I didn't blame the men, exactly; I blamed the Mother of All Darkness. She'd raped us all. It was even a killable offense in this country to use vampire mind powers to force sex. Magical rape could get a human witch or wizard in jail, and potentially on death row.

There was a soft knock on the door. I didn't say anything.

The knock came again, with a voice. “Anita, it’s Jason, are you all right?”

I said the only thing I could think to say. “No.”

“Can I come in?”

I thought about that, too. I thought about Jason. He was my friend. He hadn’t meant to hurt me. He hadn’t meant to maybe get me pregnant. I started to cry again, softly; he probably wouldn’t even be able to tell through the water from the shower.

“It’s okay, Anita, I understand you don’t want to see me right now.”

“No,” I said, “no, it’s okay. Come in.”

I could almost feel him hesitate on the other side of the door, and then I heard the door click open. I couldn’t see it through the shower’s frosted door. I heard him walk, and then the door moved, but not to open. He must have sat down on the floor beside the shower, his body bumping part of the door.

“Hey, Anita,” he said.

“Hey,” I said, back.

“Is it okay if I open the door a little?”

I thought about that, too. Finally, I said, “Yes.”

He opened the back edge of the door, away from the water. I moved my head so I could see him. I was hugging my knees to my chest, my cheek resting on my knees. He’d put on one of the robes. I looked into his blue eyes; his silky yellow hair stood out around his head in an odd way. I’d seen his version of bedhead, and his hair was too straight to stand up like that.

“What’s wrong with your hair?” I asked.

He almost smiled, then sort of grimaced, then said, “There was something on my pillow, and then I ran my hand through my hair.”

"Something *what* on your pillow?"

He gave me a long look.

"Oh," I said, and looked away again. I no longer wanted to meet his eyes. "Was it yours?" I asked.

"I don't know. I don't think so."

I huddled around myself in the hot water. If we'd been home I'd have used up all the hot water by now, but the hotel had more.

"You need to clean up," I said.

"Yeah, but it can wait."

"Did the other man wake up yet?"

"Yes," he said.

"Who is he?"

"He's a reporter."

"Shit."

"Don't worry, he's deep in the closet and doesn't want to be outed. This is one story he can't afford to report."

"Name? His, I mean."

"Alex Pinn."

"Short for Alexander?"

Jason made a movement as if he wanted to ask something, but just said, "According to his driver's license, yeah."

"You wondered why I cared what the name was short for, didn't you?"

"Yeah."

"Just seems like I should at least know a man's full name if I just spent the last two days fucking his brains out."

"Anita . . ."

"Don't try to make me feel better about it, Jason."

"That's why I came in here."

I turned so I could see him again. "I missed a pill while we were trapped in here. *The* pill."

He did a long blink, but his face remained neutral. His reaction told me it wasn't a surprise. "We couldn't help overhearing some of what you said to Richard before the water turned on. You were sort of yelling."

"So the tigers know, too."

He nodded.

I closed my eyes. "How did they take it?"

"Crispin was thrilled."

That made me open my eyes. "What?"

"Apparently, it's the duty of every good little weretiger to make more little weretigers. Every woman is expected to have at least one child, and two is preferable."

"So he's happy about this."

"He says it would bring great honor to his clan if you were his wife and bore a white tiger child."

I sat up a little. "Did you say *wife*?"

"Yep," Jason said.

I frowned at him. "Not that I don't appreciate the sentiment, but Crispin didn't strike me as the type to marry a girl just because he knocked her up."

"If you're with child, he's honor-bound to marry you and bring you and the child into his clan."

I stared at him. "Seriously?"

"Seriously," Jason said.

"Fuck," I said.

"Yeah, that's about what Richard said, though he used lots more words."

"What did this Alex Pinn say?"

"Apparently, he's spent most of his adult life trying to avoid being a member of the red tiger clan. He broke with them years ago, but if he got you pregnant he's willing to give you the chance to be taken back to his clan and introduced to them. He says if the child is truly his, it will need the other weretigers around it as it grows to make sure it gets all the training it needs."

"Training?"

"You know how none of the other wereanimals can carry a baby to full term because of the violence of the change?"

"Yeah."

"Apparently, the tigers do it routinely. They've just never shared that bit of knowledge with the rest of us. We all assumed they were keeping their women free of the lycanthropy until after they bred a couple of times, then bringing them into full weretiger. But that's not it. Apparently, they do what Crispin did for you. They put a male, or several males, with a female so she won't shift until the baby is born."

"But the baby will still be human, right?"

"If it's one of their children it will show signs of their clan at birth. Eye color, hair color that matches their tiger shape. They don't usually shift until puberty, but there have been cases where they shifted as early as nine. That's why Alex feels that the baby would need the clan for the first few years. Also, the baby would be with other children just like he, or she, is."

"If it's so great, then why did he leave his clan?"

"It's a little, no, a lot restrictive. It's almost like a religious cult. They homeschool the kids. They marry within the clan. It's only been in the last few years that they've been allowed to marry outsiders to bring in fresh blood. Modern genetics has let them realize that a pure clan is a sickly clan."

"Jesus, Jason."

He nodded. "I know." He started to say more, then stopped. He looked away from me.

"What, what is it?"

"There is a way to avoid the whole tiger clan mess."

"Yeah, a morning-after pill."

He gave a quick flash of smile. "Yeah, Richard mentioned you were planning that. The reporter, Pinn, is fine with that. It's your body. But Crispin says no. He hasn't bred before, so if it's his child, then according to clan rules you can't get rid of it."

"What do you mean, *can't*?"

"Apparently, the white tiger clan, and Max the Master of the City of Las Vegas, would take a very dim view of you destroying a potential weretiger of their bloodline."

"They don't have a choice. It's *my* choice."

"Yes, it is, but Max is pretty freaked, Anita. He made some vague talk about going to war with Jean-Claude."

"It's just talk, Jason. The vampire council declared that no Master of the City could battle another because it might fuck up the whole vampires-being-legal thing. Besides, you only fight about territories that border your own. It's about expanding so your lands touch. Vegas is too far away from St. Louis."

"Normally, you'd be right, but apparently, Max isn't doing the challenge by vampire law. He's called up some obscure weretiger law. Apparently, they think they're within their rights to block you from doing anything to a potential baby, and you need to be with the clan during the pregnancy so you don't lose the baby."

I moved back out of the water so I could see his face more clearly. "This isn't about weretigers, is it?"

"My opinion?" Jason asked.

"Please."

"I think Max knows that Jean-Claude hasn't given you the fourth mark. Which means, Anita, that if he's powerful enough to break the marks that Jean-Claude has on you, and he gets to the fourth mark first, he thinks he can keep you as his human servant. You're the first true necromancer in centuries. Any vampire who can truly control you will be unstoppable." Jason shrugged. "That's my theory."

"How did he know I don't have the fourth mark?"

"There are enough people who know, Anita. It's hard to keep a secret once enough people know."

He was right. Damn it, but he was. "Shit, Jason, would Max really start a war with Jean-Claude over this?"

"I think he might."

"Just because I want to make sure I'm not pregnant."

"Apparently so. Frankly, I think it's an excuse to make a play for your power, but I could be wrong. He's married to the queen tiger of Vegas. She might be pressing him. She might truly be more interested in the child than in you."

"Don't call it a child. I may not be pregnant at all."

"Sorry," he said.

I couldn't think of it as a child, because if I did, I'd start second-guessing myself. I couldn't afford to hesitate right now. I needed a doctor and a prescription today.

"There may be a way around the tigers," Jason said.

I looked at him. He looked away again. "What could be so bad that you keep looking away?"

"I'm afraid you'll be mad at me."

I sighed. "It's too late to be mad, Jason. If there's a way to avoid a war between St. Louis and Vegas, just tell me. I am like all ears."

"If there is a baby, it could just as easily be mine. That would make it human, or to the tigers, *lukoi*. They'd have no interest in the child of a werewolf."

I was back to thinking again. If Jason hadn't told me all the weird and bad news about the weretigers I might have been mad, or at least upset.

"You told me all the shit about the weretigers first so this would seem like better news."

"Yes," Jason said, still not looking at me.

"If we can convince the tigers it's your problem and mine, then can I get a morning-after pill?"

"Your body, your choice."

"How do we convince them it's mostly yours?"

"We lie."

"You can't lie to wereanimals; they smell a lie."

"You're so upset today that you smell like shock and fear already. Even your heart rate is up and down. They won't be able to read you right now."

"What's the lie?"

"That we had an accident with a condom before we left. Hell, Anita, we could bring in the fact that you had sex with Nathaniel just before we came here. He's a wereleopard; they wouldn't want a leopard any more than a wolf."

I thought about it. "Okay, wait, can you lie well enough to fool two wereanimals?"

"Five," he said.

"What?"

"We can't bring Richard, Jamil, and Shang-Da in here to tell them the plan. We have to lie to everyone in the room about this, or it won't work."

"Richard will . . . be . . ." I couldn't even finish the thought.

"Pissed," Jason offered.

"He'll be pissed I didn't tell him we had an accident with the condom."

"Yes, but if it gets the tigers off our backs then he'll forgive us when we have a chance to explain. But Richard and Shang-Da don't lie well enough for this."

"Jamil does?" I asked.

"Jamil lies like butter wouldn't melt in his mouth; he can even control his pulse."

"Nifty," I said.

Jason nodded.

"Can you control all that, too?" I asked.

"Nope."

"Then it won't work," I said.

"Anita, I got mind-fucked too. I'm a little shocky myself. But more than that, I am worried that it's mine. I mean, how do I tell my best friend in the world that I took the love of his life off for a weekend and got her knocked up? I mean, Micah will be pissed, but it's Nathaniel I can't face. Trust me, Anita, I've got enough emotion about this to hide any lie in all the truth."

I reached out and touched his shoulder. He leaned his face against my hand. "I should have protected you better. I'm so sorry, Anita."

"You couldn't have protected me against this, Jason."

He looked at me, his eyes haunted. "We go out there and lie our asses off, Anita. We get you to a pharmacy and we undo what we can. I can't undo it all, but we can do this much."

I nodded.

He took my hand in his and it wasn't scary or bad. He was my friend, and we both needed the touch of someone's hand.

47

I COVERED MYSELF in towels and Jason and I went out there and lied. He was right, it was easy. I was still damn near in shock. Even I couldn't tell what I was feeling from moment to moment.

In a way it was the first time I'd ever met the red tiger. I wondered if he felt the same way about me, or if he had more memories of the last two days than I did. Part of me wanted to ask, and part of me never wanted to know.

Knowing how tall everyone else was, I could estimate his height at around five-ten. His hair was the deep red of his tiger fur. It looked like a good dye job, if you were into shades of red that didn't occur in human hair. I think he understood that, because the cut was short and designed, I think, to look spiky on top. If your hair doesn't conform, you might as well get a haircut that doesn't conform either.

He'd found the other white robe. I think his clothes were

part of the mess on the floor, well, except for the jacket I'd borrowed.

His eyes were the deep, rich golden yellow with an edge of deep red-orange that I remembered from my . . . dream. But it hadn't been a dream. It was a memory. A memory that Marmee Noir had fucked with. If I hadn't had Richard to tell me, and too much evidence to the contrary, would I have been like any other human? Would I have simply thought it was a dream? If I had woken up with the weretigers not in the room with us, would I have just thought it was a funky nightmare and the claw marks were Jason's? Maybe, no, yes. That thought scared me a lot, because if she could do this, what else could she do to me?

"Anita," Jamil said, "Anita, did you hear that?"

I blinked and looked up into the solid brown of his eyes. "No, I'm sorry, but no. Can you repeat it?"

"She's in shock." This from the man in the robe. This from . . . Alex.

I studied his face, tried to "see" him, but it was as if I was only getting pieces of what I was seeing. What I saw was crystal-edged clear, but what I wasn't seeing was fuzzed and indistinct. His eyes seemed to distract me from the rest of his face. "You had contacts, brown contacts," I said, and even my voice sounded disconnected, flat.

He nodded. "You made me take them out."

"I wouldn't let you touch me until I saw your tiger eyes," I said, voice soft. "Why?"

Crispin answered, "Your tiger acts like a true-blood queen. Most of the time they won't mate with anyone who doesn't have the eyes."

"Why not?" I turned to him, and found that he was still nude. Unself-consciously so. Strangely, I had no trouble keeping eye contact. In fact, I seemed unduly fascinated with the pale blue jewel color of his eyes.

"The eyes mark us both as natural-born, and they prove our bloodline is closer to pure," Crispin said.

"I don't know what that means," I said, in that strange, unemotional voice.

"The clans have started to try to intermarry with other bloodlines in the last few years," the other tiger said.

"Why?" I asked, but again my voice made it sound as if I didn't really care about the answer.

"Our queens are having trouble getting pregnant, and the rate of birth defects was going up," Alex said.

"My queen has forbidden our clan to talk about it," Crispin said.

"I'm so high on my queen's shit list, it doesn't matter for me. Let me be very clear, Anita." He smiled and shook his head, and only then could I really notice that he was handsome. It was the smile, the turn of the head, a flash of personality that helped me see his whole face and not just the eyes. "I feel like we need to be introduced before I use your first name. Seems weird when you may be . . ." He stopped in midsentence, suddenly looking uncomfortable.

I finished for him. "Weird when I may be pregnant with your child." Just saying it out loud made me feel colder.

He nodded, and he looked very unhappy. "I don't know exactly what happened here, but I am sorry about my part of it. I thought when the call went out that my clan had found me and found a queen strong enough that I couldn't not come to her. I thought they were going to try to trap me into a pregnancy so I'd be forced back into the clan. But you look less happy about this than I am; you didn't want this either."

"No," I said, voice almost too low to be out loud.

He held out his hand to me. "I'm Alex Pinn, and I don't even know what else to say."

I almost smiled, which I guess was a good thing. "I'm Anita Blake." We shook hands, like civilized people.

His hand was large enough that he had to work to shake mine, but he did it. He didn't make it awkward just because my hand was small in his. I liked that.

"I can't do this." It was Richard. Of course, it was Richard.

I let go of Alex's hand and turned to find him leaning against the far wall. I'd avoided looking at him while Jason and I lied. One, it was a lie. Two, I did not want to see his face while he thought it was the truth. His face didn't disappoint me.

He'd undone his hair and put it back in a tight ponytail that left that painfully handsome face naked for the eye. All the men in his family had the kind of cheekbones and jaw that other men went to plastic surgeons for, perfect bone structure. If you were into that utterly masculine handsome look.

He leaned against the wall, his hands pressed behind him. He was flexing his hands behind his back, because I could see it in the muscles of his shoulders and the glimpse of upper arm. Flexing his hands over and over, which he did sometimes when he was angry. Angry, and fighting himself not to be.

Something about the lack of lamps in the hotel room had put his eyes in shadow so they looked even darker than the brown I knew they were. The shadows took the gold from his hair and made it seem simply chestnut brown.

Shang-Da was standing beside him. He was the only person in the room taller than Richard. Shang-Da glanced at Richard, then back to the room. There was a moment when Shang-Da's eyes met mine. Was it just shock, or had he, for a split second, felt sorry for me? Surely not.

Richard repeated, "I can't do this."

"Can't do what, Ulfric?" Jamil asked.

"I can't watch her take another man to her bed. I can't do it." His voice was calm, no anger, not even any of that otherworldly energy coming off him. Only the tensing and untensing of his muscles in his upper body showed the emotional turmoil under all that calm.

"I'm not planning to do anything with either of them again," I said, and there was the tiniest hint of some emotion in my voice.

"You never plan it, Anita. I know that. It's weirdly never your fault. If you just cheated on me and couldn't keep it in your pants, I think I could deal with it, or walk away, but you, honestly, don't do it on purpose." He pushed himself away from the wall. Shang-Da took up his post just behind him.

"What do you want me to say, Richard?" There, a little more emotion. I knew the emotion now: anger. I should have fought it. Anger is bad when you carry beasts inside you. But I didn't fight it, I welcomed it. I fed it sweet words and coaxed it hotter. Anger was so much better than the other emotions running through me—emotions so awful I didn't want to look at them, let alone feel them.

"I want to see you recoil from his touch, but you didn't."

"He was mind-fucked, too, Richard, you know that."

He nodded. His big hands were in plain sight now, flexing and unflexing. You could see the muscles work all the way from his hands to his upper chest now. "I know. I can't even hate him. I want to, but you're right. He didn't mean to . . . have sex with you for two days. He didn't mean to make you forget to take your pill. He seems as horrified as the rest of us." He took another step into the room, and the first warm prickle of energy tiptoed through the room.

"Don't you understand, Anita? You steal my self-righteousness away. You make me have to swallow so much, because if I react like a guy, I'm a bastard. But I am not saint enough for this. I'm just not. I'm sorry, but I'm not." His energy swirled out through the room like being too close to an oven.

Something stirred inside me, in that dark place. No, not this soon, not again. I closed my eyes, took a deep breath. I let it out slow, counting as I went.

Jamil's voice came. "Ulfric, please, you'll bring her beast again."

"I'll bring her wolf, you mean. I can't bring all her beasts, just like I can't be all she needs anywhere else in her life." For a moment the pain on his face was so raw, it hurt my heart to see it. Then he mastered himself, but the effort was visible. That made me feel bad, too.

"Richard, I—"

He waved a hand at me. "Don't, Anita, don't even try. It's not good, or bad, it's just the truth." He looked at me then, gave me the full force of those perfectly brown eyes. Only they showed the pain that had a moment ago decorated his entire face. Only his eyes showed how much he hurt. How much I had hurt him. I never meant to cut him up like that, just as he never meant to hurt me. We just seemed to keep doing it, by accident.

"I came here to check on you. I've done that. Our master sent me on one more task." He held out his hand to me. "But we need privacy for it."

I hesitated, staring at that offered hand. "If it has anything to do with sex, Richard . . ."

He let his hand fall away. "You're rejecting me?" His power slapped against my skin like the opening of an oven door, set far too high to do anything but burn.

"I'm sore, Richard. I hurt. Anyone would be getting a turn-down for a little while."

"You like it rough," he said.

And just like that, my pity was gone. The tenderness wiped away with that one oversharing comment in front of strangers. Yes, I'd had sex with them, but not while any of us were in our right minds. They were still strangers to me and my body.

"And there you go, Richard, there you go."

"What?" he said.

"You don't get it. None of us remember what happened except in snatches. What I like and what I don't is still something they don't know, unless you want to continue to overshare."

He took a deep breath in, then let it out slow. His shoulders hunched as if he'd taken a blow, and then he straightened up, shoulders back.

"I'm sorry, you're right. But you can't blame me for thinking that these two are just like the other lovers in your bed. That they know you in every way."

"Most of the lovers in my bed don't 'know me' in every way, Richard. We have sex; that's not a relationship."

He shook his head. "I need to do what Jean-Claude wanted me to do, and then I can go back to St. Louis."

"You're leaving," Jason said.

"I can't be here with this much media. You both know that."

I nodded. "I thought the same thing when you showed up."

"What did Jean-Claude want you to do?" Jason asked.

Richard pointed a finger at him. "No, I don't need to hear from you right now. You are one of my lesser wolves, and you may have gotten my lupa pregnant. That's a killing offense in most packs."

"We had no choice, Richard," I said.

He shook his head, sending the ponytail sweeping over his shoulders. "I don't mean what happened here. I mean in St. Louis. I mean making love because you wanted to, not because you fed the *ardeur*." He glared at us both, anger enough to burn in his eyes. "Don't try to tell me that you take Jason to your bed only because he's food. I bought that at first, Anita, but it happens too often."

"You sound like you've been listening to Perdy," I said.

"Perdita and I have had a few talks. She thought a little tit-for-tat might be interesting."

"What does that mean?" I asked.

"It means," Jason said, "that Perdy offered to have sex with him so they could have their revenge on us for cheating with each other." Jason's voice was empty when he said it, as if it hurt too much to share it even by tone of voice.

"I hadn't had sex with Jason in months, Richard, not even for food. I took him off the roster when I realized it made Perdy so uncomfortable."

He gave a harsh laugh, and again there was that slap of power, worse this time, like biting insects along my skin. He swallowed the power back, then said, "Uncomfortable? You broke her heart, the two of you."

Jason and I exchanged a look. He shrugged. Oh good, he didn't know what to say either. "Why would I lie to you about how often I've been sleeping with Jason, Richard? I have no reason to lie to you. We aren't monogamous."

"Thank you so much for reminding me of that." His voice was harsh when he said it.

"You're no more monogamous than I am, Richard. Don't try to pretend you are."

"I would be, if you would only . . ."

Shang-Da went down on one knee in front of Richard,

sweeping his long black coat out, so that you got glimpses of some of the armament underneath. He held one big hand up toward Richard. Most of the animal groups had a version of this. It was a request for attention, and a show of subservience.

Richard looked down at him. "What is it, Shang-Da?"

"Perhaps now is not the time to air our personal matters in front of strangers from other animal groups and vampire kisses." His voice was as empty as he could make it, but there was an edge of anger to it. That anger carried a thread of warmth that he couldn't quite swallow.

Jamil had moved closer to both of them, but it was clear he wasn't sure what to do, or how our Ulfric would take the interruption. The very uncertainty of Jamil in that moment let me know that I needed to pay more attention to my duties as lupa. They were afraid of Richard. That had never happened before. I'd urged him to be a stronger king, but seeing it now, like this, made me regret. So much about Richard made me regret.

The phone rang. I jumped. God, who could it be?

Jason said, "It might be the hospital about my dad." He looked at Richard, as if for permission.

Richard nodded. It made me feel a little bit hopeful. He was still Richard, somewhere in there.

Jason picked up the phone and said hello, then, "Just a minute, I'll see if she's available." He held the phone against his chest. "It's Peterson. He says he'll answer your questions now. Do you know what he means?"

"Yeah." I went for the phone.

"Who's Peterson?" Richard asked.

"The head security guy for the Summerlands," I said.

"And you're going to take his call, now?"

"I need to know how much danger we're all in. This call may tell us that."

"And that's more important than this?" Richard asked. His otherworldly energy grew a little hotter.

I kept walking for the phone; farther away from his power was better right now. I remembered another reason he and I had broken up. He never could understand that emotion, no matter how strong, shouldn't make you forget the bad guys. "Just because the metaphysics has hit the fan, Richard, doesn't make the other problems go away."

"How can you do that, Anita?"

"Do what?" I was at Jason's side now. All I had to do was reach out and take the phone, but I was afraid of what Richard would do.

"Concentrate on business, on bad guys, when you may be pregnant with someone else's child?"

"And why can't you concentrate on business in the middle of the crisis, Richard?"

His handsome face went angry, sullen. "Because I'm not a coldhearted bitch."

That was it. I held out my hand to Jason. He gave me the phone, but his eyes stayed wary and focused on someone behind me. I was betting on who. As for me, I didn't want to see Richard right now.

"Blake here."

"This could lose me my job," Peterson said.

"Then why tell me?"

"Because Schuyler seems like a better person than Keith. I don't want him dying for that little bastard."

"Talk to me, Peterson."

"Keith is hiding, even from us and his family. Last we heard he eloped to Vegas and married a vampire."

"Shit," I said.

"Yeah, but it's not legal. He can still marry his fiancée, and his family is determined he go through with it, if we can find him."

"So far, it's a scandal but it won't endanger Jason."

"Ask me why it's not legal."

"Okay, why isn't it legal?"

"The vampire bride is already married. She's married to a Master of the City."

I was quiet for a second, then said, "Seriously?"

"Deadly serious," he said.

"No master would take that kind of insult."

Jason looked at me, eyes a little wide; maybe it was my "master" comment, but truthfully he probably was picking up at least some of the other end of the conversation. He was standing that close, and his preternatural hearing was that good.

"The Master of the City in question has put a bounty out on Keith. He wants his wife alive and Keith dead. He's sent people to do the job; we just don't know who they are. Until you and Schuyler surfaced they were looking elsewhere for Keith, but if they think he's trying to hide in plain sight . . ." He let it trail off.

"They'll come for us," I said.

"Maybe."

"Is Keith this stupid?"

"Yes, but she pressured him. It's not an excuse, but she seemed to know him. Not him, but she seemed to know his great-great-whatever-grandfather, Jedediah. Something about him being the love of her life."

"Didn't Jedediah die by vampire attack, something about him either trying to convert the vampires to his faith or seducing the wrong vampire lady?"

"Those are the two versions," Peterson said.

"Are you saying that Keith has gotten himself mixed up with the same vampires that killed Jedediah Summerland?"

"Maybe."

"Well, shit."

"*Shit* about covers it," he said.

"What Master of the City is it, Peterson?"

"No, I won't tell you that."

"I might be able to take care of both our problems."

"No, we can't let this go public, Blake. It will sink the governor's chances of the nomination. We have to find Keith, and get the wife back to her husband as quietly as possible."

"You don't understand vampires; I do. The master won't back down. There's no quietly fixing this, Peterson. If his hired people don't do the job, then he will. Your little bastard is a dead man."

"No, Blake, my little bastard is too high-profile for the master to come after him personally."

"He might not be thinking that clearly, Peterson."

"I've told you all I can. If something happens, now you know."

"I really do appreciate it, but let me help you. Tell me the name, or the city. I can do things you can't."

"Someone's coming, I've got to go. Be careful, Blake." He hung up.

I turned to look at Jason. His face was a little pale, as if he'd heard just enough to understand how deep a hole Keith Summerland had dug for himself.

"Did you catch all that?"

"Enough."

Alex Pinn said, "Keith Summerland is involved with vampires. Oh, man, this is too sweet."

I'd sort of forgotten about Alex's job. "I was told you were too deep in cover to risk a story about this."

"About wereanimals, yeah, but not vampires. I'm not one of those."

"You cannot use this, Alex. Peterson risked his job warning me."

"What are you talking about?" Richard asked.

I wanted to share with Richard, but one look at Alex's eager face and I knew that I'd already overshared. I owed Peterson more than that. "I can't say right now, Richard; later."

"More secrets! More lies!" And just like that, Richard's power filled the room. My skin ran with heat, as if I'd been thrown into a hot bath. It didn't hurt, but it was hard to get a full breath. So hot, so thick, so powerful; Richard's power filled the room.

It called to all the wolves in the room. They could not help but answer their Ulfric's power with a little of their own. Jason was closest to me, so his power flowed along my skin first. It was like someone had turned on a second tap of hot water, to make warm water hotter. We didn't need hotter. We needed to cool down. The question was how to do that.

Shang-Da's power and Jamil's hit me almost at once, and I was suddenly drowning in the scent of wolf. That sweet musk and I could feel it, my wolf, inside me. Not see her, but feel her like the brush of fur against parts of me that nothing should have touched but a blade.

The sensation was so uncomfortable, so eerie, that I shivered. Richard mistook the shiver, because he said, "You can protest all you want, Anita, but you enjoy the power. There are things that the wolves can do for you that the vampires cannot. You just keep fighting it."

The wolf inside me moved through my stomach, like a hand in places it should never go. Nausea rolled over me. I had to swallow hard.

"She didn't shiver from pleasure, Richard," Jason said.

"Now you know her better than I do, little wolf?"

His power seemed to fill the room so there was no air left to breathe. My wolf didn't come running up that long tunnel inside me. No, the wolf was too close for that. I felt it move inside me, brush fur and claws against the inside of my body.

"Richard, please, something's wrong. Help me."

It was Crispin who came to me. Crispin who walked through the rising power. Still nude, still a stranger, but it was he who came to me.

"Don't touch her," Richard growled.

Shang-Da, still on his knees said, "Ulfric, please, you will bring her beast, and we will have yet one more problem to deal with." He looked up at Richard. I'd never seen Shang-Da look so imploring.

Jamil came to the other side and went onto one knee, as well. "Please, Ulfric, your power is choking us all. You will bring all our wolves."

Crispin stood in front of me now. He had stopped short of touching me, as Richard had asked. That got him an extra point. He was not making anything worse. In fact, looking up into his blue eyes, his tiger eyes, helped still that sense of fur gliding on the wrong inside-out of my skin.

Jason was closest to us, but I think he could sense my wolf so terribly close under the skin. He knew better than to add his touch to Richard's power. Jason walked toward the other werewolves. He stayed out of Richard's immediate reach, but he went down, not on one knee, but on all fours. He bowed his head and crawled toward the bigger man.

I'd seen the gesture before, from Jason and other wolves. It was his attempt to apologize to Richard for any offense. Only Richard stood there filling the room with his warm, crawling power, and made it too far. Why was it always Richard, lately, who pushed things worse? Or me? Never forget me. I could screw things up too, but not tonight. I was too scared to fuck it up on purpose tonight.

"Richard," I said, "did you find the charm?"

He turned and it was as if his power were some huge beast, as if his power turned with him and stared at me out of his wolf amber eyes. I don't know if it was the look, or the power, but it made that brush of fur whirl inside me. I stumbled, and only Crispin's hand kept me from falling.

The moment he touched me, the wolf receded. I could breathe through Richard's power. I clung to Crispin's hand with both of my own, and it was like the world was a little more steady. I waited for the white tiger to rise inside me, but it didn't. I just felt better.

Richard's power lashed out, coming with his voice, like something thick and touchable that slammed into me. "I said, don't touch her!"

Crispin staggered with me, as if whatever Richard had done was solid to him, too. But the weretiger kept us on our feet and drew me in against his body, shielding me from Richard. It was gallant, but if anything was guaranteed to make Richard more pissed, that was it.

He came for us, came for us in a blur of speed, and rage, and power, and I was still standing in a towel with only a gun in my hand, and a strange weretiger on my arm. If I wasn't willing to shoot Richard, I was about to run out of options.

48

CRISPIN SHOVED ME behind him and braced for impact. Alex Pinn, the other weretiger, was just suddenly beside Crispin. I didn't have time to decide whether that was good or bad. All I had time to do was decide that I wouldn't use the gun.

Then the blur of speed that was Richard met the wall that was Shang-Da and Jamil. They had used their own impossible speed to be there before him. The impact of their bodies hitting made enough force of wind and physical energy that it pushed against us like some kind of small explosion.

Shang-Da was yelling, "Ulfric, remember yourself!"

Jamil was simply trying to hold Richard down without hurting him, or being hurt. Richard was a serious weight lifter and had a black belt in karate. Holding him without being willing to hurt him wasn't going to work for long. Either they were going to have to hurt him, or he would most certainly hurt them.

Shang-Da tried again. "Ulfric, please!"

Richard's anger fed his beast, fed his power. I couldn't breathe; I was being baked alive with his power. His wolf pouring into me, into my beast. Such rage. I knew the taste of this anger. I knew it like a well-worn shoe, or a favorite sweater. The one that fits just right and makes you feel warm and safe. That was how my anger had made me feel for years. It was the only emotion I had allowed myself. It had taken the place of sorrow, pleasure, and love. My anger had been nearly everything to me once. I thought my therapy had helped me deal with some of that bottomless rage, but now standing there I realized that maybe it hadn't been therapy. It had been vampire marks. I hadn't just shared my anger with Richard through Jean-Claude's marks; I had given it to him. A big portion of my rage had simply transferred to my reasonable, calm Richard.

I stared down at the fight on the floor. I stared down at two grown werewolves barely containing the struggling, snarling, yellow-eyed man, and I thought, *This is my fault*. I'd known that what Richard got through me, through the marks, had been my anger, but I hadn't understood until just now what that meant. I'd had years of practice before I grew up with that rage. Poor Richard had had it dumped into his lap with no practice. I knew the burden he carried. I knew exactly how he felt. Fuck.

I wanted to help him. I wanted to end this without bloodshed. I wanted a lot of things. Then everything got worse, because the *ardeur* stirred within me. Fuck, and double fuck.

I pushed away from Crispin. He let me, but was clearly puzzled. But not touching him made Richard's power worse, harder to refuse. It felt like the wolf was trying to crawl up my throat, out my throat. I fell to my knees, the towel from my head falling away. My hair was cold and heavy around my shoulders, but the power was so hot I needed that cold. It was a good shock. A reminder that I wasn't truly wolf. I wasn't truly lupa. I was . . . a necromancer. But that wouldn't help me now. What was I? What was I? I was . . . a vampire. I just didn't feed on blood.

I'd gone two days without solid food; that made all hungers harder to control. Kneeling there with Richard's rage, my rage, and his power, throbbing around me, pushing at me, pulling at the furred thing that seemed stuck in my throat . . . I needed to feed, but I didn't feel sex. All I could feel was rage, anger. So familiar, so safe.

I knew anger, I liked it; it did make me feel safe, safer than sex. Jean-Claude had taught me how to feed the *ardeur* from a distance at his clubs. I could do it now, though it wasn't always easy, or didn't always work, but I knew how to feed on emotion. Feed on the emotion of lust, on love, and recently I'd learned that friendship is love done soft and pure. It wasn't a conscious decision. One minute I was kneeling choking on fur and power, feeling the *ardeur* trying to rise faster than the wolf inside me. The next moment, the *ardeur* was upon me. My own power chased back the feel of fur in my throat. I could breathe again. I was me again, sort of.

But the rage was still there, beating against my skin, like some old familiar friend. I opened to it. I drank it down, let it soak into my skin. I stood and let the last towel fall away. I stood nude and drank the wrath in through every pore of my body, every inch of me coated with hate. Because he did hate it. Richard hated the anger. He didn't understand it. He didn't understand it, because it wasn't his. It was mine.

I took it back. I sipped it, rolled it on my tongue, enjoyed the bouquet of it, the sweet, ashy taste of it. Oh, yes, this was a vintage of wine that I had kept in the dark, at just the right temperature for a lifetime.

I drew it out of Richard like some kind of sickness, or possession. I drew it out, and felt him grow calm, under the weight of the other men. And at the end of that calmness, I felt the wall between Jean-Claude and me shatter. The anger had been mine, but the vampire marks that had given it to Richard had been Jean-Claude's. I was trying to take away some of that mark, not on purpose, but in trying to remove what was not mine, I found my love again.

Jean-Claude looked up at me with those dark, dark blue eyes, as if the twilight sky could look back at you. He whispered, "*Ma petite.*" And with those simple words the marks between him and me were just there again. I could feel him again. I was his again. His and not hers. Though we both felt that she had left her own mark. We would deal with that another night. For that moment, there was nothing but Jean-Claude's smile, and his voice, and the sense of coming home again.

49

JEAN-CLAUDE DIDN'T SO much whisper, as I just knew, that he was going to have to shield from my feeding. He could not drink anger as he could lust or love. Anger was not his food. It was mine.

I stood there with my hair still cold against my shoulders, so not much time had passed, but it was one of those moments when minutes turned to hours. I drank back in my anger, but it didn't stay. It didn't go into that dark pit inside me, where my grief and rage fought and mingled. I ate the anger as I could eat lust and love and heart's desire. I swallowed the anger like food. But whereas lust confused me, and could get out of control and spread through me and to those near, anger . . . I was master of that. Anger I could control.

I stood there with my skin tingling with the energy of it. My body thrumming with the feeding. I wasn't just full, I was well fed. If it had been the normal *ardeur*, I'd have been forced to turn that energy into sex, but this wasn't the *ardeur*.

This was something else. This was mine. Mine in the way that the gun in my hand was mine. Mine, not Richard's, not Jean-Claude's. I had a food that my master couldn't even digest. It filled me with a fierce happiness. A happiness so sharp that it was almost anger. I was glad, so very glad, that finally I had some power, something that wasn't theirs. Jean-Claude's power was lust and love, but mine was rage. I was okay with that.

Richard's voice came, clear and oddly calm. "I'm all right, let me up."

I saw Shang-Da and Jamil exchange a look together, and then almost in unison they moved back and let Richard sit up. Jason crawled forward, abasing himself beside him. Richard touched his shoulder, but he looked at me. I expected to see the anger in his face, the resentment, but for the first time in a very long time, Richard looked up at me. His face, his eyes, held the Richard I'd fallen in love with, the one who had been too squeamish to kill the old Ulfric and take control of the pack. There was gentleness in his face that hadn't been there in so long that I'd almost convinced myself it had never been.

"It's okay, Jason," he said, "it's okay." He stood up, leaving his wolves on the floor to peer up at him, wariness plain on their faces.

Alex held a hand up, not exactly moving in his way, but not out of his way either. "You're calm now, Ulfric, but what we just saw wasn't calm."

Crispin moved closer to me, but I motioned him back. Richard was being reasonable; I didn't want another man to touch me right now, especially the only man in the room who was as naked as I was. Crispin took the hint and stayed where he was; he really did take directions well, that was nice.

Richard's white T-shirt was so badly ripped it looked like something one of the dancers at Guilty Pleasures would have worn partway through their act. His hair had slipped free of the ponytail, so he came to me with all that thick hair in a tangle around his face. He looked, as he could look, like some walking wet dream, but the smile on his face was gentle and had less to do with sex and more to do with softer emotions.

He touched my face, staring down into my eyes with that gentle smile and his brown eyes full of something more tender than I'd seen in months from him.

"Thank you," he said.

I touched his hand where it lay against my face. "It was my anger. I just took it back."

He let his hand cup the side of my face, and I let myself rest against the warmth of his hand. "I thought it was mine to keep."

"It may leak over again," I said, softly.

He leaned down, and I knew he meant to kiss me. I wanted that kiss, and didn't want it, all at the same time. I'd cut him out of my heart, this new angry, hurtful Richard, but the look in his face now, that was the old Richard. Richard before he'd been forced to make so many hard choices. Richard before he had become permanently angry with me.

He kissed me, his lips soft and full. It was a good kiss, but chaste by our standards of late. I realized as he drew back, eyes searching my face, that lately when we were together it had become nothing but sex. Harsh, fun, but harsh. He had come to me rough, because he knew I could take it, and like it, but even the sex had been more about anger than love. Makeup sex can be good, but not if it's all you do.

"I feel more myself than I've felt in months, Anita. A lifetime of therapy couldn't have done what you just did."

"If I'd known I could have taken it back, I would have, Richard."

"I know," he said. He took my hand in his as he turned back to the waiting wolves. I couldn't remember the last time he'd simply held my hand. He'd even stopped doing it in church, so that the only touch we gave each other was in private and all about sex. I'd actually begun to think I needed to go back to my old church, so that he and his family could keep theirs. If we broke up for good, it would be easier for me to change churches than the whole Zeeman clan. But this one moment of holding hands made me wonder what else had changed beside him feeling more himself.

I forced the thought away. I'd given up on Richard and me having the white picket fence a long time ago. He was just the one man who made me wistful about not having it. Holding his hand in that moment made me wonder yet again if I had missed the boat. Had he been the one man who might have made it all work?

The moment I thought it, I knew it wasn't my emotion, or my thought. Richard wasn't the only man in my life who made me wonder if he could have been the only one, if the *ardeur* weren't there. But holding his hand, sensing all that emotion, I did regret. The regret was mine.

"We need to find the charm," Richard said.

The three werewolves looked at him, as if they didn't trust this new Richard either. "Ulfric, are you well?" Shang-Da asked.

"Better than I've been in a long time," he said. His thumb began to rub across my hand.

"The charm isn't on the floor with the clothes," Jamil said. He looked past Richard to me. "Though we did find two of Anita's knives. One of them had blood on it."

Crispin spoke from behind us. "Mine."

Richard turned to look at the weretiger, my hand still in his. "Why did Anita cut you?"

"She didn't," Crispin said. He was looking at us, but his gaze wasn't on either of our faces, or my body. He was looking at our clasped hands.

"I did," Jason said.

Richard turned back to Jason, moving me minutely with him. "Why?"

"Can I plead the fifth on this one, Richard? You're not mad at me anymore; I'd like to keep it that way."

"And you think just answering the question will make me angry with you all over again?"

Jason nodded. "It might."

Richard turned to me. "What do you think?"

I squeezed his hand and said "Let's just say we all made friends eventually."

He frowned. "Did the tiger attack you?"

"He attacked Jason," I said, "and I took offense."

Richard stared down at me, searching my face. "Yet you ended up in bed with him."

I frowned at him and tried to take my hand back, but he held on, and I let him hold on rather than struggle. "Let it go, Richard, please."

Crispin said, "She wants you to let go of her hand, Ulfric."

"It's okay, Crispin," I said.

He shook his head. "You're a queen. Queens don't have to be touched if they don't want to be."

Richard drew me in against his body, never letting go of my hand. I put a hand on his chest, to keep us from cuddling as close as we could. "I do not need to be fought over, by either of you."

"According to our culture, you do," Alex said.

"What are you talking about?"

"I know that the little wolf shares well," Crispin said, "and so does the red tiger, but your Ulfric smells of monogamy and ownership."

"Crispin," Alex said, "you can't hold them to tiger law, if they don't know the rules."

"Explain the rules to us," Richard said. He tried to draw me in against his body again. I kept one hand on his chest to keep us a little apart, because I had another flash of certainty. I just needed to get everyone else out of the room. I needed only Richard. We didn't need anyone but each other. What had I been thinking with all the others?

I gazed up at Richard, and he looked down at me. The moment I stared into the perfect brown of his eyes, all I could think of was getting closer to him.

The arm I'd been using to keep us apart slid around his waist. He bent down toward me, and all I could think of was how much I wanted him to kiss me.

His skin was so warm where it touched my body; warm and smooth and simply . . . perfect. It was as if our bodies were meant to be together, always.

I rose up on tiptoe with my nakedness against the front of his clothes and shredded shirt. I rose up to help our lips meet, as Richard bent down. So tall, so far to reach, for the touch of his mouth, but oh so worth it.

The kiss grew from something chaste to a feeding at each other's mouths. Richard picked me up, and I wrapped my legs around his waist, pressing my most intimate parts against the front of his jeans. The pain was instant, and too raw to ignore. It cleared my head better than any cold shower.

I broke the kiss and tried to climb down from his arms, but he held me against him. "It hurts," I said.

He drew his face away enough to look puzzled, and then he let me down. He tried to make me slide down his body, but I stopped the movement in midmove, because the thought of rubbing myself down the front of something as rough as jeans made me cringe. No matter how nice the package inside the jeans might be.

He let me down onto the floor but kept his arms around me. I was back to putting my hands against his chest to try for some distance. I wasn't sure what had just happened, but it was wrong. It wasn't my thoughts.

"Anita, look at me," he said.

I tried not to, but it was almost as if I couldn't stop myself. The moment I held his gaze, the thought returned. I wanted to touch him, and be touched. I wanted . . .

Arms around my waist from behind, and I was jerked backward out of Richard's arms. I was also off the ground, held against someone else's nude body. I knew it was Crispin before I saw that flash of white hair out of the corner of my eye.

Alex moved between us and Richard. "Easy, Ulfric, but using magic is an unfair advantage."

Shang-Da and Jamil were on either side of Richard, but seemed unsure whether to help him against the tigers or grab him so it didn't get out of hand.

"I don't know what you mean by magic, but if he doesn't put Anita down, I'm going to use something a lot more solid on him than hocus-pocus."

For me, I felt better in Crispin's arms, clearer-headed. I patted Crispin's arm. "It's okay, you can put me down."

"He was trying to bespell you, the way you can do to others."

"I know."

Richard said, "I can't bespell anyone. I'm not a vampire."

I patted Crispin's arm again, and he lowered me to the ground, though he kept his arms around me, loose, but with a tension to them that let me know if I moved toward Richard again, he'd stop me. On one hand, he had no right to do that; on the other, I'd needed the help. What the hell was going on with Richard and me?

"You bespelled me like a vampire, Richard. When you touched me, it was harder to think, and when I looked up into your eyes it was impossible. It was like the whole world was nothing except need for you."

"That's how it's supposed to be when you're in love," he said.

I shook my head. "Pretty to think so, Richard, but this wasn't being in love. This was obsession. The pain helped clear my head, just like it does when a vampire tries to roll me. And all vampire powers are magnified by touch. You know that."

"But I'm not a vampire," he said.

"Me either, but I can roll people as if I am, sometimes."

Richard frowned at me, his handsome face closing down into those petulant lines. Why was it that pretty people did petulant better than the rest of us?

"I felt it, too," Jason said. "It was focused on Anita, but I've been rolled too many times not to know it when I smell it."

"You are all crazy," he said, but he looked less petulant, and more thoughtful. There was a good mind inside the pretty packaging. It was one of the things that had made me love him.

"You don't carry my anger anymore, Richard, but you're still part of the triumvirate with Jean-Claude and me. Maybe when you lost the anger, you gained something else."

He opened his mouth, closed it, then said, "Is that possible?"

"Let's call Jean-Claude and ask," Jason said.

Richard frowned at him. "Why don't you shower while we call?"

Jason fought to keep his face neutral. "Want me out of the way?"

"No, but if you don't want me pissed again, I need you not to smell like you rolled in Anita's body." He looked past me to Crispin. "You, too, Whitey."

"My name is Crispin."

"Whatever, but if you and Red here could go someplace else and clean up, that would help."

"I don't know if the room we booked is even still ours," Crispin said.

"I have a room that I booked for the week," Alex said. He looked at me, then at Jason beyond. "It is one of the social events of the year, plus politics, and a hint of scandal. I came down here for a story, though that seems like ages ago." He looked thoughtful, shook his head, and then looked back at Crispin. "Can he borrow the extra robe?"

Jason started untying the sash without being asked twice. He handed the robe to Alex. "I'll go shower." He just turned and went for the bathroom.

Alex handed the robe to Crispin. He didn't take it. He actually clasped me a little closer to him. "If we are not here to help her escape his powers, then he will have her and chase us out."

"Your word, Ulfric, that you won't touch her while we're gone."

"You have no right to ask that," Richard said.

"No, but something is going on here, something different. You gain powers if you are a vampire's animal to call, but you don't gain the powers that you and Anita are gaining. That's not part of the deal. Yet I saw you bespell her. I felt her roll me like a cheap date. Roll me partway like a weretigress, and part like a vampire. Again, very weird."

He gazed at the floor as if the answer lay somewhere on the carpet. "I need to give my paper something, or they are going to bitch about the hotel bill. They only footed it because the Summerlands are staying here. Their personal home is a museum now to the history of the family and the town's founding."

"They're that big a deal?" I said.

He smiled at me. "You truly don't pay attention to the media, do you?"

"Not really." I moved away from Crispin, took the robe from Alex, and handed it to him.

"You really want me to leave?" Crispin sounded hurt. The tone of voice, something about his expression made me put him on the far side of twenty-five. I'd thought he was older.

"I need some space, Crispin."

"How old are you?" Richard asked.

Crispin looked at him, then back to me as if to ask, did he have to answer him? I nodded, and he answered, just like that. Obedient, almost disturbingly so.

"Twenty-one."

"You do like them young, Anita."

"Nathaniel is the same age."

"I think that's my point," Richard said. "At least I'm dating people closer to my own age."

I turned and gave him an unfriendly look. "If we're going to fight, you can leave, too."

A look passed over his face. He had to try twice before he spoke, and the first two times didn't sound anything like what he finally said. "You aren't safe alone."

"I'm beginning to not feel very safe with any of you in the room."

"What does that mean?"

"It means that the vampire marks have gone all weird again, and I don't know why. It means I'm tired. It means I hurt. It means that I need to find the charm. It has to be somewhere in the room. It means I need to get dressed." I spotted the Browning on the carpet where I'd apparently dropped it when Richard had rolled me with his touch and gaze. I picked it up. "I dropped my gun, Richard, and didn't remember doing it. I forgot everything but you. Love doesn't make me forget that I'm armed, but vampire gaze can."

"He tried to trick you," Crispin said.

"Go," I said, "go to Alex's room, clean up."

"Can we come back here when we're done?" Crispin asked.

"I don't know, call me first."

"I'm going back to work once I put in my spare brown contacts," Alex said.

"You do that."

"Why do you sound angry?" Alex asked.

"Everything makes her angry," Richard answered, before I could say anything.

I suddenly wanted to be alone. I wanted them all gone. Fuck them all, or rather, not fuck them all. Jesus, but I needed to catch my breath, and I wasn't sure I could do that with a crowd around me.

"You two, out." I actually gave Alex a little push toward the door. "You"—I pointed at Richard—"behave, or you are so out of here."

"You aren't safe alone," he repeated.

"Maybe not, or maybe it's time I found out if I'm safe alone. We've been surrounding me with wereanimals for months and it hasn't helped. Maybe I need fewer of you around me."

"May I borrow a pair of sunglasses, before I go?" Alex asked.

"Sunglasses won't make the robe look any better, babe," Jamil said.

"It's to hide the eyes," Alex said.

"You must like being in your tiger form," Richard said.

"I was born with these eyes, just like Crispin was born with his. One of the signs that our blood was thinning out genetically is that fewer and fewer children are born with tiger eyes."

"The eyes mark us as pure bloodline of our clans," Crispin said.

"Your blue eyes look human enough," I said.

"If you don't know what you're looking at, yeah." He had the robe on now, though he hadn't tied it in place, so his body was framed by the white cloth. It was whiter than his skin, but not whiter than his hair.

"Out," Richard said, adding, "please," with a glance at my face. It wasn't a happy look.

"It's not your room, Richard."

"No, it's yours and Jason's." He didn't have that taste of rage that comments like that usually came with, but he still wasn't happy. I guess I couldn't blame him, and that, right there, was part of the problem. Part of me still agreed with Richard. You were supposed to grow up, find that special someone, marry them, and live happily ever after, till death do you part. Once, I'd believed that down to my toes. Now, I knew it wasn't going to happen for me. I didn't miss the wedding. Those always seemed like an expensive pain in the ass, but the concept of one single person being the be-all, end-all for you . . . that I missed.

"Do you really want us to go?" Crispin asked, and there was that wistful note in his voice that most of us grow out of by the time we get to be twenty-one.

I smiled, because that tone of voice made you either smile or want to kick someone's ass. "Go with Alex. Clean up. Get some clothes. Call the room, and we'll see how I'm feeling, okay?"

His face crumbled a little around the edges. Again, it was a younger gesture. I had a bad idea. "Are you absolutely sure you're twenty-one?"

"I would never lie to you, Anita. If you really are my queen, then I won't ever be able to lie to you."

Alex took Crispin's arm and started them toward the door. "We need to go."

Jamil held out a pair of sunglasses. Alex looked almost startled, then took them. "Thank you."

"They aren't cheap, so I want them back in one piece."

Alex actually looked at the side of the glasses. "Dolce and Gabbana, these must have set you back a few hundred. I'll treat them like the luxury item they are, thanks again."

Jamil said, "We have some people in our pack who can't go back to full human form. It's a pain in the ass."

"You don't need to chat, Jamil," Richard said.

Alex gave a little bow in his direction. "Good night for now, Ulfric. I am truly sorry if I distressed you."

"Anita," Crispin said, "please don't send me away. Please let me stay with you, please."

I knew that tone of voice. Shit.

"You've rolled him completely, the way you did Requiem," Richard said. I looked into his face expecting to see anger, but there was only something close to sorrow. Resignation, maybe.

"Not a topic for company," I said.

Alex stopped them just short of the door, with the taller man, Crispin, staring back at me like a child being dragged away from the fair too soon. *God, please, not another one.*

"This may not be vampire powers. Her call was that of a powerful tigress, a queen. Young males who have never mated before are more susceptible to the call of a queen. They are addicted to her until she chooses among them. When she chooses one over the others, then it's like the pheromones, hormones, whatever, go back to normal levels and the ones she didn't pick are free of her influence."

"I've never heard of this," I said.

"The only tigers I've met have been survivors of attacks, and it doesn't work for them like that," Richard said.

Jamil and Shang-Da agreed.

"But they aren't born tigers. In fact, most queens will kill a weretiger who deliberately brings over a full human against their will. It's considered a great gift to be invited to join a clan when you aren't born to it."

"Thanks, but no thanks," I said.

"If you truly sent out a call this powerful by accident, Anita, it will happen again. It's not a conscious thing always. It happens when you come into your power. Sometimes at puberty, but most of the time somewhere in your twenties. You look about the right age for it."

"I'm older than I look," I said.

"Not by much," he said.

Crispin tugged a little against Alex's arm. Not like he meant it, but more like he didn't realize he was doing it.

"I'm almost thirty," I said.

"You do look younger. I'd have pegged you for under twenty-five."

I shrugged. "Good genetics."

"If you say so," but he didn't sound like he believed it.

Frankly, with marks of at least two vampires on me, who was I to say that I wasn't aging a little slower than normal. Not to mention that wereanimals aged slower than human-normal, too. I guess he was allowed his skepticism.

"Please, Anita," Crispin said, tugging a little harder against the other man's hand on his arm.

I'd seen that look in enough faces to understand it. Alex could say it was tiger magic, but it looked like what I'd accidentally done to a few of the vampires and wereanimals in St. Louis. It was Belle Morte's power to be able to roll someone with lust, love, heart's desire. I had the ability to own someone. Trouble was I wasn't much into ownership. If I wanted to own something that would give me undying loyalty, I'd buy a dog.

I looked into those blue tiger eyes, and Richard was right, it was the look that Requiem had given me once. We'd freed him, because he was a master vampire, and had enough power, with help, to free himself. The help had been telling him that I'd never touch him again unless he freed himself. Reverse psychology, but it worked. Sort of. Requiem still liked me a lot better than I wanted him to like me.

"Go with Alex, Crispin. When you're both cleaned up, call first, but I won't just cast you out. Okay?"

The look of relief in his face made me a little sick to my stomach. I hadn't done this on purpose. Shit.

"Why aren't you as affected as he is?" Richard asked.

Alex answered, "I told you, it hits the young men harder. Ones who haven't been mated before. I'm older than I look, too."

"I'd say thirty, maybe a little over," Richard said.

"You're off by a decade and some change."

"Do all the weretigers wear this well?" I asked.

"Those of us of pure blood, yes." He put his sunglasses on, then reached for the doorknob with a firm grip on Crispin's arm.

"So you shouldn't have been forced to answer my call," I said.

He looked back at me, his eyes lost behind the black lenses. "No, I shouldn't have. Only the head of a clan can call all the unmated males regardless of age or experience. If you were a real weretiger from just one clan, it would be seen as a direct challenge to the clan leader's authority, and she'd have to kill you."

"But because I called to all the clans, they don't know what to do with me," I said.

"I'd bet that, but then I've spent the last two days with you, here. I'll try to call my family and see what my queen is planning to do. Just like you want privacy to talk with the wolves, I want it to talk to the tigers. So we'll clean up. I'll make some calls. We'll call you, and we'll go from there. Hopefully, I'll drop Crispin off here, then go to work."

"Why *hopefully*?" I asked.

"I may not be looking at you with big doe eyes, but trust me, girl, I do feel it. You've rolled me, make no mistake about that, but I am Li Da of the Red clan, son of Queen Cho Chun. If I'd been female I would have been groomed to lead after her. But even being just a man, my bloodline means something. It gives me certain protections from the powerful bitches. My mother has conspired for years to get me close enough to one of the clan queens to be called to breed. She'll be thrilled that you managed to get through all my shields. Baby or no baby, she'll invite you to join our clan, because once you've broken a male tiger to your call this roughly, I can't really say no. Not if you force it." His voice was so bitter that it almost hurt to hear it.

I don't know what I would have said to all that, but Shang-Da saved me from having to say anything. "You don't look Chinese or Korean."

"We never did. It's one of the reasons they were able to kill us off. We couldn't blend in. Those of us who escaped to other countries were forced to intermarry with the humans we found. There haven't been pure Chinese bloodlines since the time of Emperor Qin Shi Huang."

"The emperor who unified China and burned all books that he didn't agree with," Shang-Da said.

"Yeah, that one," Alex said.

"That's more than two thousand years ago."

"Clan tigers talk about going home the way that Jews talk about the Holy Land. We are in exile, and as long as the communists rule we always will be. A few of us went back when the emperors were overthrown, but the communists saw us as western spies. They killed us along with their rebels."

"My family has never spoken of this," Shang-Da said.

"The emperor destroyed any writings about us."

"The fox people still live in the homeland. Hidden, but they are there."

"Are the dragons still there?"

"No," Shang-Da said, "the last of them fled when the communists took over. Communists may not believe in God or magic, but they hired wizards to clear the land of rebels. Rebels were anything nonhuman."

I knew that dragons in China weren't just animals like they were in most of the rest of the world. In China they'd been shapeshifters; people. I didn't say it out loud, though. If I kept my mouth shut they might just keep talking. Sometimes if people forget you're there, you learn more. Silence can be a greater asset than any question.

"So we are all in exile."

"There are still fox people there, but they hide in plain sight."

"They can look like everyone else," Alex said.

"Yes," Shang-Da said.

Crispin was looking from one to the other of us. He almost looked like the history lesson was as new to him as it was to me. Interesting.

"Las Vegas is our home. We don't talk about going anywhere else," Crispin said.

Alex looked at me, then back to Crispin. "We need to go and clean up. Let's try to avoid any of my fellow reporters. I really don't want to have to explain why I'm coming out of this room in a robe, with another man in a robe."

"Homophobic?" I said.

He shook his head. "Being considered bisexual would be fine, but Crispin is a known weretiger. Your boyfriend in the shower is a known werewolf. It's not my sexual preference I'm trying to hide."

"I've got another friend who's a reporter who basically said the same thing."

He leaned in toward the door and drew in a long breath of air. "I smell the guards, but no one else. We'll go and take the stairs."

Alex opened the door. Crispin moved as if to come farther into the room again. Alex took hold of his arm and pulled him toward the partially open door.

Crispin pulled against the other man's arm. He looked at me. His face was raw with need, and something else. Was it fear that I saw in those blue eyes?

"Come on, Crispin, we need to clean up. I think I may even have some clothes that will fit you."

Crispin stayed at the door, staring at me. I knew what the look was now. Pain, fear, and longing, all on his face, so raw that it hurt to see it.

"You've rolled him," Richard said.

"Not on purpose."

"No, but unlike some of the others you've accidentally rolled, this one is . . ." He shook his head. "Young."

I knew what he meant. It wasn't the actual age. Twenty-one was plenty grown-up. Requiem had been several hundred years old when I accidentally bespelled him. That gives a man a lot of character to draw on, to help him break free. As Alex Pinn had said, it hits you harder when you've never been called before.

I sighed and went to him. He smiled at me in a way that you never want a stranger to smile. Too warm, too damn happy. It frightened me. I'd made Requiem break free of my powers, but he was a master vampire. He had his own power. Crispin was a weretiger, but there was no feel of power to him. I wasn't certain he had enough of him inside yet to break free of me, and without his willing help, I didn't know how to free him of what I and Marmee Noir had done. Shit.

Crispin touched my arm when I was close enough. I didn't try to stop him. But the moment he touched me, I thought, why did I want him to leave? It was silly. He could stay, of course he needed to stay. He was my tiger, my white knight, my . . .

I jerked back from him. I ignored the hurt look on his face. "Go with Alex. Clean up, get some clothes. Or see if your vampire friend—Lucian, right?—is still here."

Crispin nodded.

"See if he's still in the hotel. Your own luggage might be here somewhere. Your own clothes. Go, do what I ask."

"Can I have a good-bye kiss?"

Richard and I said, "No," at the same time.

I glared at Richard, but said, "Alex, get him out of here."

I kept my face turned away as the tigers left. I went across the room to the luggage. I needed clothes.

"What happened when you touched him just now?" Richard asked.

"I didn't want him to leave. It was like a lighter version of what you did to me when you were projecting your emotions all over me. I thought it was just you, but if Crispin did it, even a paler version, maybe it's something that Marmee Noir did to me."

"What?" he asked.

"I don't know." I laid the Browning beside the suitcase, and started pulling clothes out.

"You need to know what she did to you." This from Shang-Da.

I was surprised that he cared enough to comment. "I need to call Jean-Claude."

"Can't you just open the marks?" Richard said.

"Yeah, but when I fed off your anger, he shielded. He wasn't sure how to digest anger. I think the phone will be safer."

"You're afraid whatever is happening will leak onto Jean-Claude," Richard said.

"Yes." I had enough clothes to make me happy. Now I just needed to change. If it had just been Richard, I might have simply gotten dressed, but I didn't want to dress in front of Jamil and Shang-Da. I know it sounds weird. I mean I was naked in front of them, and they were cool about it. So why was getting dressed more intimate? I don't know, it just was. I don't like men who are not my boyfriends watching me put on clothes. There's always a moment when they let you know with their eyes that they are watching, and not in a completely neutral manner. Or maybe not, maybe it's just my hang-up, but regardless, I wanted privacy.

"Why go into the bathroom to dress?" Richard said.

"Either I go into the bathroom, or Jamil and Shang-Da go into the hallway."

"You're already naked, Anita," Jamil said, "we can't see more."

I shrugged. "Humor me."

The men all exchanged glances, and then Jamil said, "Do you want us in the hallway, or her in the bathroom?"

"I don't want her alone with Jason in the shower."

I might have protested that, but we all have our weakness. Seeing an attractive man all wet was one of mine.

Jamil went for the door, and Shang-Da trailed him. No one argued. The door shut behind them, and we were suddenly alone. The silence was thicker than it should have been.

I glanced at him, and there was that look in his eyes. That look that was very Richard. He was such a Boy Scout most of the time, such a good son, a good boy, a good teacher, a good man. Then, sometimes when we were alone, he'd look at me with those dark eyes. That one look that said underneath all the goodness was someone who liked to be bad. Someone who understood the darkness in me, as well as the light. If he hadn't hated the darkness in his own soul so terribly much, I could have loved him forever. But you can't love someone who hates himself so much, and hates you for loving the parts of himself that he hates the most. It's too complicated a dance to ever win.

I ignored that dark look, and tried my best to pretend he wasn't there. I actually turned my back on him to dress.

It worked for a while, and then I felt him behind me, close behind me.

I turned in time to keep his outstretched hand from touching me. I had jeans on, and a bra, but the shirt was still on the bed with my gun.

"Anita," he said.

"Richard, don't."

"Don't what?" he asked.

I closed my eyes so I couldn't see him. That always made it a little easier to turn away. "When you touched me earlier, it was like magic. If it hadn't hurt, or Crispin hadn't pulled me away, I would have let you do anything. It's not real. It's some metaphysical problem."

"How can you say that?" he said, and his voice was closer. He moved so close that I could feel the heat of his body against my bare skin. It wasn't his otherworldly energy I was sensing. It was just him.

I stepped back, eyes still closed, and nearly knocked the bedside lamp over. We both grabbed for it, and it put his body next to mine. His hand over mine around the lamp. We had one of those frozen, awkward moments.

I looked up at him, and he was so close, too close. He bent in to close that distance and kiss me. I threw myself backward onto the floor, knocking the trash can over, as I crab-walked back until my back hit the bathroom door hard.

"Richard, please, please, don't you feel that something's wrong? We're always attracted to each other, but not like this."

"I think if I touch you now, that you'll just say yes."

"Exactly," I said.

"I want you to say yes."

"Yes to what, Richard?"

"Everything," he said.

"So now that you have enough metaphysical abilities to roll me, you'll just do it. You'll roll over my free will and just make me into your little pet?"

He frowned. "It's not like that, Anita. I'm not making you feel things you don't feel. The emotions are real."

"Maybe, but they aren't the only emotions I'm feeling. You're trying to take away my choices, Richard."

He knelt in front of me. My heart thudded against my chest, and I pressed myself tighter against the bathroom door. He reached out toward me, and I said the only thing I could think of to stop him. "Aren't you trying to do the very thing that you keep accusing Jean-Claude of doing?"

His hand hesitated so close to my face that I could feel the heat from his skin. It wasn't just the warmth of his body this time. His power was there like something alive and almost separate from him, pulsing above his skin. Playing along my cheek like something smooth and warm and . . . I waited for it to raise my wolf, but it didn't. It was as if it wasn't that kind of power. It felt softer than his usual electric rush. It felt more like . . . Jean-Claude.

I opened my eyes, looked up at him, and found what I'd feared. His eyes were solid brown, glowing with the light of his own power. It was what his eyes would have looked like if he'd been a vampire. The way my own eyes looked from time to time.

"Your eyes," I whispered.

His hand touched my face, and the touch was too much. One breath, I was trying to fight; the next, I fell into the brown fire of his eyes. There was nothing but the need to touch him. Nothing but the feel of his mouth on mine, his hands on my body, my hands on his, and the absolute rightness of it all.

His hand went between my legs and grabbed me through

my jeans. Normally, it would have been exciting, but tonight, it hurt. The pain was immediate. It helped me swim back up to the top of my mind. I could think again, rather than just feel.

"Richard, stop," I said, and it was almost a yell.

He touched my face. "You don't want me to stop."

I stared at the floor, as if the stained, clothes-strewn carpet were all-important. "I *do* want you to stop."

"Look at me, Anita."

I shook my head and started to move away from him, still on my knees. He grabbed my arm. The feel of his bare skin on mine almost undid me, but whatever was happening was a type of vampire power and I'd spent years fighting that. I breathed through the almost crazed desire to have more of his skin touch mine. It was like a mixture of the *ardeur* and vampire gaze. Shit.

"Let go, Richard, now." My voice was breathy, but clear. Point for me.

"I can feel how much you want me to touch you," he said, and his own voice was tight with power, or desire, or both.

I felt his body, not just through his hand, but all of it. It was as if I could feel every inch of him, so warm, so alive, so . . . yummy. I did want to touch him. I wanted to strip off and roll around on top of him. Again, it felt like the *ardeur*, but different. But this time I was on the wrong end of it. It was as if Richard were the one projecting the *ardeur* at me, not the other way around. Jean-Claude held the *ardeur*, but he'd always behaved himself. In this moment with Richard, I knew just how much Jean-Claude had behaved himself.

I thought, "Jean-Claude, help me."

The bathroom door opened behind us. Jason stood in the doorway with a towel wrapped around his waist.

"Go away," Richard said.

"Help me," I said.

I had a moment to feel sorry for Jason. He was so screwed. If he helped me, his Ulfric would be pissed. If he didn't help me, I'd be pissed, and so would Jean-Claude. I had a moment to appreciate his dilemma, caught between the werewolf and the vampire. But even appreciating his problem, I couldn't care as much about his problem as my own. Richard had finally inherited the *ardeur*, and he was using it on me.

50

JASON SPOKE SLOWLY, carefully, in that voice you use for people on ledges, when they're far, far above the ground. "Richard, Anita, what's happening?"

"Leave us alone, Jason," Richard said. He tried to pull me in closer to his body.

I braced with my other arm and my knees, the way I did sometimes in judo. Not when you think you can win the fight, but when you've simply decided that you'll make them hurt you before they win. I wasn't strong enough to keep Richard from drawing me into his body, if that's what he wanted, but I was strong enough to make him hurt me to do it. It was the best I could do. The Browning was on the bed, and truthfully, I wouldn't shoot Richard. He knew it, and I knew it. Oh, there had been moments when I might have, and a knife I might have used, but not a gun. I wouldn't have risked killing him. Once you give up the idea of killing someone bigger and stronger than you are, you are, to an extent, at their mercy. You better hope that they're merciful.

I would have looked at Richard's face to try to see if there was any mercy there, but I was afraid to meet his eyes again. It was hard enough to fight his power with just his hand on my arm. I couldn't afford to fall into his eyes again. I wasn't sure I would be able to crawl back out. There was something different to his version of the *ardeur*. For lack of a better word, there was more life to it. My strongest powers lay with the dead, not the living. Richard was so very much alive.

"It's the *ardeur*," Jason said, "but it doesn't make me want to touch you, Anita."

"Go back into the bathroom, Jason," Richard said; there was a faint edge of growl to his voice now.

Jason gripped the doorjamb tight enough that his fingers mottled. "It's so strong, I can't breathe past it, but it's all directed at you, Anita. I can feel it, like a thought in the air. He wants you to want him, and only him. God, it's so strong."

I said, "Help me."

Richard said, "Get out."

"Richard, Ulfric, you're doing the very same thing you accused Jean-Claude of doing," Jason said.

Richard's head jerked up, and he looked at Jason. Jason looked away from that gaze. "Your eyes are glowing as if you were a vampire, Richard. I know not to look a vampire in the eyes when they look like that." Jason let the fear sound in his voice. It sounded real, and it was one of the first times I'd realized that he was afraid of the vampires.

I kept my arm braced on the floor as Richard tried to draw me to him. But it wasn't the strength in his hand that was hard to resist. It was the warm, crushing embrace of his power. It was like something alive, warm, and wanting. Something that pulled at me, as surely as his hand. It wasn't just about lust, but the promise that if I would just let go, he would wrap me in the warm safety of his love, and there would be no more pain, no more uncertainty. But I'd felt something like this before. Auggie, Master of Chicago, could make you love him. But even Auggie had never made it feel like this. This felt real. But of course, it was real, or had been. Auggie had been a stranger, the logic in my head had known it was a trick, but what Richard offered felt real, because once it almost had been. Once, the belief that his love would heal all the old wounds, and finally make me feel safe, had been true. True, and a lie. Love is real, and false, even true love. Because love alone cannot keep you safe, if there is still a trembling fear inside you. Still a knowledge of what it was like to love and believe and have it all taken away. It wasn't my fiancé in college that haunted me. It was, as always, my mother's death. If that truth couldn't hold, then what chance did any man have?

It was that thought that helped me push against the warmth of Richard's power. It was that thought that helped me swim against the current of his love. Just as his hands had been too rough and caused me pain, this loss was the biggest pain I had. It was the gaping black hole inside of me that had filled up with rage so long ago. It was the place that my anger came from, and went back to, like the tides of some bloody ocean. Pain always helped you push back vampire powers.

I let myself feel that loss, that I spent most of my time not thinking about. I let the rage and loss fill me, and there was no lust, no desire, no love, that could win against such sorrow.

People talk of sorrow as if it is soft, a thing of water and tears. But true sorrow is not soft. True sorrow is a thing of fire, and rock. It burns your heart, crushes your soul under the weight of mountains. It destroys, and even if you keep breathing, keep going, you die. The person you were moments ago dies, dies in the sound of screaming metal and the impact of one bad driver. Gone. Everything solid, everything real, is gone. It doesn't come back. The world is forever fractured, so that you walk on the crust of an earth where you can always feel the heat under you, the press of lava, that is so hot it can burn flesh, melt bone, and the very air is poisonous. To survive, you swallow the heat. To keep from falling through and dying for real, you swallow all that hate. You push it down inside you, into that fresh grave that is all that is left of what you thought the world would be.

I was not foolish enough to look into his eyes, but my voice was solid, and sure of itself, as I said, "Let go of me, Richard. You can't make me feel safe. You can't fix what's wrong with me."

"I love you," he said, and his voice was full of everything those words meant for him.

"You love me so much that you would use vampire wiles to force me into your arms."

He stopped trying to pull me to him and came to me. He closed that small distance and wrapped his arms around me. Minutes before, held in his arms like this, I would have done anything he wanted. But it was too late. He held my body, but my heart was cold. It was the way I had lived for years. Cold and hot, sorrow and rage; it had been the world to me until Jean-Claude found a way inside the walls I'd built.

I understood in that moment why it had been Jean-Claude and not Richard who had broken down those walls. Jean-Claude had had his own sorrow and rage when I met him. He had known what it was to have everything he wanted, real love, real security, and to lose it all. Richard hadn't understood. He had believed in the goodness of the universe.

I hadn't believed in that since I was eight. Jean-Claude hadn't believed in words like *goodness* for centuries.

Sometimes it's not the light in a person that you fall in love with, but the dark. Sometimes it's not the optimist you need, but another pessimist to walk beside you and know, absolutely know, that the sound in the dark is a monster, and it really is as bad as you think.

Did that sound hopeless? It didn't feel hopeless. It felt reassuring. It felt—real.

Richard held my chin in his hand. It began as a gentle gesture, but when I didn't meet his eyes, his hand squeezed. He tried to force me to look into his eyes. I couldn't stop him, but I could make him hurt me to do it. The pain helped me distance myself from him. He held me so close that it was like being wrapped in a warm blanket of energy, but what he meant to be comforting felt as if I were too hot. It was a choking, close heat, as if the air were too thick to breathe.

His hand on my jaw was painful, just this side of breaking bones. I kept my eyes closed, but even through closed lids I could feel the press of his gaze.

"Look at me!"

"No," I said.

Jason said, "This is the first time you've felt the *ardeur* yourself, Richard. You're power-drunk."

"Anita, look at me!"

"No!"

He kissed me then, and it didn't matter that I didn't look at him. For the *ardeur*, a kiss was as good as a glance. Maybe better.

He kissed me, and all the lies flowed over my anger, cooled the rage, and filled me with a sweet certainty that nothing could ever hurt me while I was in Richard's arms.

51

ONE MINUTE, I was safe; the fear, the anger, all of it fell away. It was as if Richard's arms, his mouth, his body were food, drink, air, and every good thing all rolled into one person.

The next minute, I was drowning. The kiss that had been like air, sweet and pure, was suffocating me. The arms that had felt so safe were a trap from which I had to break free.

I went from melting into his body to fighting with everything I had to get away.

Richard fought to keep kissing me, holding me. But there were other hands on my shoulders, helping me fight. Not by fighting Richard, but helping my mind, me, fight. Richard's hand went to my hair and tried to keep my face pressed to the kiss, but another hand was there, another arm, helping pull me away, another body pulling me backward.

Jason's fear washed over me with his touch. Fear of what Richard was doing. Not just fear of Richard's new vampire powers, but fear of how I felt in his kiss. Fear of the drowning, perfect obsession of love.

Jason felt my emotions, felt what Richard made me feel, and I felt Jason's terror of what he said he wanted. Terror of being consumed by one person. Fear of belonging to just one person. Jason said that his heart's desire was this, but he lied to himself. In one suffocating, drowning, hand-filled moment he and I both knew he did not want it. The thought of only one person forever made his blood run cold.

I was caught between the two of them. Two men strong enough to rip me apart, literally. It was like being a baseball bat in that childhood ritual where you try to be the hand on top of the wood. Except this bat was helping break free of one set of hands. I pushed at Richard, fought his grip, until more of me was cradled in Jason's arms, and only one hand was left digging into my upper arm.

Jason and I were on the floor, with his back against the side of the bathroom doorjamb. He held me as close as he could, even his legs wrapped around my waist from behind. I could feel his heart thudding against my back, taste his fear like something metal on my tongue. I didn't have to be able to see his face over my shoulder to know his blue eyes were wide, his lips parted, and his skin pale.

Richard was on his knees, staring down at us. His eyes had bled back to his normal brown. "I can feel how afraid you both are of me."

"You tried to mind-fuck me, Richard. You tried to take my choices away."

"I want you to want only me, Anita. I want it so badly that it drives me mad sometimes. I hate the thought of you with other men."

I wisely kept my mouth shut, because I knew that he

enjoyed watching me with Jean-Claude, sometimes. He liked sharing with Jean-Claude, sometimes. But, as with much of Richard's inner life, he didn't want to accept it. If I'd asked him, he shared me with Jean-Claude because he had no choice. He did it rarely, because he didn't like it. Right? Not necessarily. I thought he did it so rarely because he was afraid that he did like it.

"You're hurting my arm, Richard."

He looked at where his fingers had made imprints in my skin, as if he didn't remember he was doing it. He let go, and sat back on his heels, still kneeling. He looked puzzled.

"I didn't mean to hurt you," he said.

"I know," I said.

Jason just kept holding me, while his pulse started to slow.

"If Jason hadn't interfered, you would have done anything I wanted. But I believed it, too, Anita. I believed in that happily-ever-after moment again. I thought marriage and kids and . . ."

"I felt you think it," I said.

"But you thought it, too." He looked at my face, and he was so sincere, so full of his truth.

"You made me think it, but it was your thought, not mine. I won't apologize for that anymore, Richard. You got your first taste of your own version of the *ardeur* and you would have used it every bit as ruthlessly as you've ever accused any vampire."

"That's not fair," he said.

"I felt what you were doing to her, Richard. You took away her free will, and filled her up with this false happiness," Jason said.

"It's not false."

"It's not her version of happiness, Richard, it's yours."

"You have no business interfering between your Ulfric and his lupa."

"Maybe not, but I couldn't stand there and feel what you were doing to her. Anita asked me to help her, and I had to do it."

I touched his arms where they were still wrapped around me. "What do you mean, *had to*, Jason?"

"You're my friend, and the main squeeze of my best friend. I couldn't let him rape you like that."

"That is not what I was doing," Richard said.

"By definition of the law, using magic or psychic ability that takes away someone's choice is rape." Jason said it, but I'd thought it.

I felt Jason go quiet around me, and I think I did the same thing in his arms. "Did you just say out loud what I was thinking?" I asked.

"Did I?"

"I think you did," Richard said. He leaned in toward us, sniffing the air. I still found it a little unsettling when my lycanthrope friends did very animal things in human form.

Jason drew us back, as if his back could push through the wall and gain us distance. "What are you trying to smell?" he asked.

Richard was on all fours now, sort of looming over us, with his hair falling in thick waves around his face, so I really couldn't see his expression. I think Jason could. "Jean-Claude could have broken her free of me. Maybe even Micah or Nathaniel, because they have their metaphysical tie to her. Damian could have shared his coldness, his control, and drowned me out. He is her vampire servant." Richard leaned past me, nearly pressing his chest against my face, so he could sniff Jason's face over my shoulder. "But you're just food.

You're Jean-Claude's *pomme de sang*, but you're nothing special to Anita."

It was a little hard to speak firmly while being wrapped arm and leg by one man, and nearly kissing the chest of another, but I did my best. "He's my friend."

I heard Richard take in a huge, noisy breath. He jerked back, as if something had hurt. "He's more than that now," he whispered.

"What are you talking about?" I asked.

"Can't you feel it, Anita? He's your wolf to call."

Jason tensed against me, and I said, "What?"

"Before, he smelled of pack; now he also smells of you. The same way that Nathaniel does, or Micah."

"I live with them; of course, we start to have a family smell."

Richard shook his head. "No, Anita, never try to argue sense of smell with a werewolf. It's as if a little piece of you rides around in their skin. Micah always smelled that way, but Nathaniel . . . his scent changed. Damian's scent changed. Now, Jason smells like he has your touch like a perfume against his skin."

"I'm holding her, Richard, that's what you're smelling," Jason said.

Richard shook his head again. "No, Jason, I know the difference between proximity smells and changed smells."

"I couldn't have made him my wolf to call, Richard. I'd remember doing it."

"You don't remember most of the last two days, Anita."

I thought about it, tried to argue it wasn't so, but a hard, cold lump started forming in my stomach. The moment my stomach started reacting, I knew the truth. I tried to push past the fear and use my own abilities to test the theory, but I was too panicked. Had I bound Jason to me like that and didn't even remember doing it? And if I'd done that without remembering, what else had I done? What else had all of us done? Shit, shit, shit.

"I remember it was dark," Jason said, "and you called me. I remember trotting through these tall trees that I'd never seen. I thought it was a dream."

"That's what I see inside my head now, since Marmee Noir fucked me over. Tall trees and shadows and darkness."

"You called me, not *this* me, but my wolf. You called me."

I hugged his arms. "I'm sorry, Jason, I'm so sorry. I did to you what you just saved me from."

"Being able to call him as your wolf is probably what broke you free of Marmee," Richard said.

I looked up at him. "What do you mean?"

"She controls cats, including tigers, but not wolves. Why didn't she just keep you, if she'd mind-rolled you that completely, Anita? Maybe because when you called a wolf to you, she couldn't fight you both."

"She's the night made flesh, Richard; trust me, Jason and I aren't powerful enough together to kick her out of anything."

"Thanks a lot," Jason said.

I patted his arm. "You know what I mean," I said.

"The connection between a vampire and their animal to call is more than just the strength of the two. It doesn't just double your power, it makes both of them more than just the sum of their parts, Anita. It's like . . ." He seemed to grope for the right word, and finally settled for, "Trust me, Anita, both the vampire and the wereanimal gain a lot more than just combined powers."

"Is that how it is with you and Jean-Claude?" I asked.

He nodded.

"So if Anita hadn't bound me to her, then we might still be trapped by the Mother of All Darkness?" Jason asked.

"One of the reasons Jean-Claude sent me was to use wolf to break Anita free, but you'd already done it."

"But I'm compelled to touch Micah and Nathaniel, and you. Jason and I like each other, but it hasn't changed since we woke up." I turned in Jason's grip and tried to see his face as I asked, "Has it changed for you?"

"No," he said. "I might have been disappointed before I felt Richard's version of the *ardeur*. Now I'm just grateful."

"You have a lot more control over your powers now, Anita. A lot more than when the *ardeur* first rose, or when you marked Damian and Nathaniel. I mean, we didn't even know you could do that, then."

I nodded. It made sense, sort of. "So I can make people my beast to call, without being compelled to move in with them?"

"I think so."

That actually made me feel better. Good that something did.

He stood up. "I'm going to get Jamil and Shang-Da, and fly back to St. Louis."

"Anita needs you here," Jason said, "it's why Jean-Claude sent you."

"She has a wolf that she's metaphysically tied to in you." He held up a hand. "I'm not jealous; okay, I am, but not like your face says, Anita. The *ardeur* has risen for me for the first time. I need to get home to Jean-Claude before it happens again. We're just lucky that my version is narrowly focused."

"You mean just on Anita," Jason said.

Richard frowned at him.

I patted Jason's leg, trying to tell him not to help too much. "It may not be that narrow a focus, Richard. I'd be careful around any woman you've had serious thoughts about. Not just sex, but marriage."

"I'm not—"

"Please, Richard, you want to be married. It's been my experience that when someone wants to be married that badly, they find someone."

"I want it to be you," he said.

I sighed. "I know, but that's not what I want."

"Are you really serious that you'll never marry?"

I looked up at him. "If you mean monogamy and till death do you part, then no."

"Someone will come along, Anita. He'll sweep you off your feet, and you'll want what I want, just not with me."

"I think Anita is like me, Richard," Jason said. "I think she likes to keep her options open."

Richard shook his head. "I've got to get out of here."

"Richard," I said.

"No, Anita, if Jason hadn't interfered I would have done exactly what you accused me of. Hell, if we'd been in Vegas, I could have talked you into marriage. I can still taste how compliant you were. I've never felt you so willing, so . . . weak." He shook his head, and took a step back from us. "I don't trust myself not to try again. That's the truth, and I need to get farther away from you until it's not the truth."

I'd have liked to argue, but couldn't. He went to the door, then paused with his hand on the knob. "I love you, Anita."

In that moment, still wrapped in Jason's body, I said the only truth I was sure of. "I know."

He nodded, opened the door, and went out. Jamil and Shang-Da would do what their Ulfric told them to do. It was back to being just us again, but now it was just us and the most powerful vampire on the planet hunting me. Somehow I wanted more help.

Again, it was as if Jason read my mind. "We need more help."

I cuddled in against his body, and he hugged me with arms and legs, and for once it wasn't sexual in the least; it was more like two scared kids huddling in the dark when they knew the monster under the bed wasn't just real, but was holding a grudge.

52

WE SAT THERE for a few minutes after the door closed. Jason was still wrapped around me, and I leaned back against him. He leaned his head against the side of my face. It was as if both of us let out a long breath we'd been holding. I should have felt worse that Richard had left, but after that momentary fear, I felt better—calmer, at least.

"Why do I feel calmer?" I said.

"Because I'm not afraid of getting my ass kicked by my Ulfric for being another wolf who's metaphysically tied to his lupa. He could have taken it like you were cheating on him with me. He outweighs me by more than fifty pounds, Anita. Most of that's muscle."

I snuggled against him, stroking his bare legs where they were still wrapped around my waist. "Yeah, neither of us would win if it came to a fair fight with Richard."

I felt him smile just by the movement of his lips against my temple. "You think like a guy, Anita. Richard would never fight you the way he would fight me. Enjoy that part of being a girl."

I ran my hands over the surprising smoothness of his legs, and realized that there were tiny, fine hairs on his legs. So blond, so delicate, that you couldn't really see them unless you touched them. I played my hands along those fine hairs, a gentle back-and-forth. I'd found that touching helped me think lately. Micah said it was the beast in me. Maybe, or maybe I would have always been like this if I'd let myself. It was a chicken/egg kind of question. I let it go, and just enjoyed that it helped me be calm.

"I've spent most of my career having to fight bad guys who didn't give a shit that I was a girl, Jason. It changes how you look at things."

"If you say so, but if Richard hurts you physically, it's by accident. If he hurts me, it's on purpose."

"A lot of his anger was from me, literally. I think he'll be a lot more reasonable now."

Jason nuzzled his face against my hair. "If that was your anger, then I'm with Richard, you have amazing self-control."

I laughed, an abrupt, not exactly happy sound. "I know people who would argue I have no self-control at all."

"They're just jealous," he whispered.

Hadn't I thought something like that earlier? I did not want or need another man tied to me metaphysically. I just seemed to keep collecting them. I didn't mean to.

"Let's get dressed," he said, kissing the side of my face and beginning to untangle himself from me.

I laughed, and this time it was real. "You suggesting we get dressed? Usually, having someone be my animal to call makes the physical stuff more compelling, not less." I turned in time to catch his grin, as he stood fastening the towel more securely around his waist.

"I promised my dad that we'd see him yesterday. I don't know what excuse I can give him, but I want to see him."

"You seem . . ." I didn't know what word to use.

"I feel"—and he seemed to search for a word, too—"more solid." He grinned down at me. "You are one of the most certain people I know; maybe that's what I'm getting from you. Oh, God, me with actual ambition and goals. Too weird."

"You have goals," I said, kneeling.

He shook his head. "No, Anita, I float. I went to college because you're supposed to. Once my folks wouldn't let me major in drama, college didn't really matter to me. Then I met Raina, and she showed me the kinkiest sex I'd ever imagined, and she made me a werewolf. I said yes, because she was beautiful and insatiable. Not because I wanted to be a werewolf. I worked at Guilty Pleasures because it pissed my family off and helped me have some money of my own. I didn't say as a little boy, 'I want to grow up to be an exotic dancer.'" His face fell into serious lines, so rare for Jason. "I let Jean-Claude feed on me the first time because Raina gave me to him. Giving him donors from the pack was part of the bargain between Jean-Claude and the wolves."

That I had known, because it was how Richard ended up with Jean-Claude, though he had refused him blood. You can give a vampire a werewolf, but you can't make the werewolf cooperative. "I knew that part," I said.

"I think part of the appeal to being Jean-Claude's *pomme de sang* was that it would bother my dad so much." He smiled, quick and so him. "Besides, Jean-Claude is sooo hot."

I frowned at him. "You are not as bisexual as you pretend to be."

He grinned at me. "And how do you know?"

I frowned harder. "I think Jean-Claude is an exception to your rule, just like Belle Morte is . . ." And then I stopped. I hadn't meant to say that.

Jason gave me a look. "Are you telling me that you did Belle Morte?"

I started concentrating on picking up the trash that we'd knocked onto the floor when the trash can fell over. "It was a vision. She shared enough energy with me to keep Jean-Claude and Richard from dying when the"—and I had to stop myself from saying *Harlequin*, and finished with—"the scary guys with no name came to town."

Jason knelt with me and helped me pick things up and drop them in the small container. The bedside trash cans are always too small in hotels.

"But, that you mentioned it out loud means something."

I shook my head. "I know that Jean-Claude loves her still. I know that to once love Belle Morte is to always love her. It's like an addiction; you can stop taking your drug of choice, but you'll always crave it."

"Do you crave her now?"

I shook my head. "No, but, I know if I ever saw her in person and she wanted me, I wouldn't be able to say no. She's not . . . she's Belle Morte." I shrugged. How do you explain someone who simply is sex? Sex and power were merged for her, and thanks to Jean-Claude's memories I was sort of pre-addicted. I wasn't even embarrassed about it, which wasn't like me. I got embarrassed about every damn thing.

I put the trash can back in its place with all the little bits of debris back inside it. Jason said, "You've missed something."

I looked at the floor. "No," I said.

He pointed at a spot on the carpet. "Right there."

"There's nothing there, Jason."

He picked up something from the floor. The moment he held it, I could see it, but up to that moment I had not. He held his hand out with the charm on his palm. "Can you see it now?"

I nodded, trying to swallow past the sudden choking of my pulse. I knew Marmee Noir had mind-fucked me, but it should have passed by now. This proved it hadn't passed. How royally screwed was I? But the fact that she didn't want me to see the charm meant she feared it. That was a good thing to know.

I held out my hand and Jason gave me the charm. The moment it touched my skin, it was as if the world shifted, or at least the inside of my head did. A moment of nausea, dizziness, and I wrapped my hand tight around the charm. God help me, what was she trying to do to me?

Again, Jason echoed me, almost. "What does she want from you, Anita?"

"She wants me as her human servant, I think."

"Maybe," he said, "but I think it's more than that."

"What could I do for her, Jason? She's the most powerful vampire on the planet."

"You're the first real necromancer in the last several hundred years, Anita. Whoever has you as their human servant gains a lot of power."

"You haven't felt her yet, Jason. She is scary powerful. She doesn't need more."

"All vampires need more power, Anita, even I know that. They're always afraid that someone else with more will come into their territory and take it all away from them."

"The vampire council has declared it illegal for masters to fight in this country until the whole legal thing is more secure."

"Then she's breaking her own laws."

I nodded. He was right. The vampire who had given them their laws was breaking them. Why? Then I made a mistake. I thought, "What do you want from me?"

I smelled jasmine.

Jason grabbed my arm. "I smell perfume."

The moment he touched me the scent of jasmine faded, like perfume when you come into a room, and the woman who wore it has just left. Some women are like that; just their scent can make you walk from room to room until you put a face and body with that perfume. I shook my head, and tried to shake the thought with it. That didn't sound like my thought.

I looked at Jason, with his hand still on my arm. "Who wore perfume that you liked so much that you followed her from room to room?"

"I don't know what you're talking about," he said, and then a look came over his face. He seemed to be staring at something in the room, but his eyes said he was seeing a memory. That look of staring at far, far away things filled his blue gaze.

"There was a woman when I was in high school. She was the first crush I had who wore expensive perfume. It lingered on the air, delicate, just a hint, so you could follow her through the school."

I touched his arm. "I thought just now about that very thing. About how a woman's perfume could lead you from room to room. It had to be some crush for me to get that image so clearly from you."

He looked at me then, rather than the memory in his head. "You know that night that my sister Bobbi swears she saw me having sex with a man?"

"I remember the argument."

"I was with that crush. She was married, and my teacher. I promised her I'd never tell, and I never have."

"How old were you?"

He smiled, somewhere between his grin and something wistful. "Legal, but barely. She waited until I was legal."

I didn't know what to say to that. When I was in high school it would never have occurred to me to approach a teacher. They simply did not exist for me as sexual objects. The taboo was too great. I was in college before I found a teacher who made me, even fleetingly, think of crossing that line.

"So you can prove it wasn't you that your sister saw, but not without ruining the life and reputation of this woman."

He nodded.

Ironic, I thought.

"Ironic is one word for it," he said.

I stared at him. "You do know that I didn't say *ironic* out loud, right?"

Jason looked startled. "I heard it."

"I only thought it, Jason."

We looked at each other. "Do I apologize?" he asked.

I shook my head. "No, let's just finish getting dressed and see if the hospital will let us see your dad."

He stood, and we both kept holding on to each other's arms as we stood, so it was anyone's guess who helped who stand.

"I guess it is past visiting hours, but Anita, we need to go home. We need St. Louis, and Jean-Claude, while we do this new metaphysical stuff, but I can't go until we see my dad again."

"Agreed." I let go of him, and we stepped apart. I stood still, I think waiting to see if I smelled jasmine again.

"Okay?" he asked.

I nodded and reached up to the gold chain around my neck. I slid the charm onto the chain so that the cross and the charm both touched my skin. There, that was better. It was like I could breathe a little easier. I reached for the T-shirt I'd put on the bed and slipped it on. I was in the process of putting it on when there was a knock at the door.

We looked at each other. He shrugged. I picked my gun up off the bed and walked to the door. I looked through the peephole and found yet another pair of the suited guards with the addition of two of the hotel security guys in their blazers.

"Security," I said, and looked back at Jason.

A man's voice called, "Mr. Schuyler, there's been a problem."

I opened the door. The suited guard was Rowe. "What's up, Rowe?" I asked.

He looked way too serious for comfort. "The room has been compromised. We need to move you."

"Compromised how?"

"The vampires who are looking for Keith Summerland have been given this room number. We need to make sure neither of you is here when the vampires arrive."

I wanted to argue, but there was something about how serious he was, and how serious all the security had been, that made me decide to argue later. There was always time to argue later.

Jason went for the suitcases. "Let them in, I'll change in the bathroom."

I stepped back to let Rowe and the rest into the room. "Where's Shadwell?"

"He's on a break." The two hotel guards stayed in the open doorway. I looked at them. They looked human. They had fed on someone to give color to the pale cheeks, but one look and I knew what they were. I started to raise my gun and yell, "Vampires!" Then one of them threw something into the room. Threw it so fast that the movement was seen, but not registered in my head, before the flash-bang grenade went off and the world went away. Oh, I was conscious, but I was also blind, and so disoriented that the next thing I felt was pain. I reached for what hurt and found a dart. A tranquilizer dart from the feel of it. I tried to bring my gun up to where they'd been. I tried to see them, but with the combination of the grenade and the drug, the world was full of swirls of color, and shapes that didn't hold still. I heard Rowe yelling. I fell to my knees. Someone took my gun and I couldn't stop them. I couldn't make my body move. I fell to the carpet and the mess of clothes and drying body fluids, and then the world went away, as if someone had turned off the lights. One moment I knew I was on the carpet in our room; the next, nothing.

53

THERE WAS A voice in the darkness. I thought at first I was hearing the bad guys, and then I understood the voice, and knew that it was much worse than bad guys. "Necromancer," the voice whispered.

Fear stabbed through me in the dark, fear like fine champagne. I had a moment of being able to feel my body. A flash of knowing I was lying on a floor, and then I was back in the dark.

"Necromancer."

Fear, and I was thrown into my body again. A moment of lights, and sensation, then darkness.

"Necromancer."

I think I opened my eyes, but it could have been a dream. The darkness kept eating the world.

"Necromancer, if you stay in the dark, you will die."

The room was white, and I knew my hands were tied behind my back. Then the drugs sucked me into the dark again.

"Necromancer!" She reached for me. It was a woman's hand, small, delicate, and it was the paw of some great beast with claws, and fur, and . . . The claws struck; pain ripped through the darkness and made it run with blood. I woke, gasping for air, pulse, heart, everything racing.

My chest hurt. I looked down and found the front of my T-shirt cut. Blood drops spattered the white tiles I was lying on. I worked to get a better look at the front of me, and finally realized the front of my shirt had been shredded by huge claws.

I remembered her reaching for me in the dark, and I knew she had done this. Somehow Marmee Noir had done this. Mother of God. The last of the drugs washed away on a flood of pure terror.

I fought not to panic. The fear had helped me wake up, helped get the drugs out of my head and body; now I had to make sure the fear itself didn't cripple me.

Other than the claw marks, was I hurt? I had a headache, but that could have been the flash-bang as well as the drugs. What kind of vampires used modern grenades and drugs on their victims? The adrenaline was doing its job. I seemed to be thinking faster, everything crystal edged. Had Marmee Noir scared me on purpose to wake me up and get me going? I pushed the thought away for later. Stay alive, and worry about the rest later.

I was lying on cool tile. Not horrible. But my hands were tied behind my back, which was horrible. Nothing good ever happens when the bad guys tie you up. I might have panicked about it, but one, it does no good to panic, and two, Marmee Noir wasn't in this white room. It was good. Where was I?

The tiles I was on were a nondescript color somewhere between off-white and beige. I tried to see things without moving much. I had no way of knowing if they had a way to see me. I did not want them to realize I was awake, not yet. The more time I had to think before they came back, the better. People do not tie you up and leave you on cold floors if they plan on doing nice things to you. No, bad things were coming. Which made me wonder, where was Jason?

The urge to roll over and see if he was in another part of this room was so strong that I tensed up, and now my pulse was higher. Shit. My hands clenched before I could stop them. So much for pretending to be asleep.

Then, distant, like there were doors and rooms between us, I heard a man's voice, yelling, "Where's Lorna?" I didn't know the voice. Then came a voice I did know. Jason was yelling, screaming actually, "I don't know!" Then he was just screaming.

That did it. Fuck caution. I sat up and discovered that my body still ached some from the abuse I'd given it in the hotel room. But it didn't hurt that much; I was healing, and if I didn't get us out of here, things would hurt a hell of a lot more.

I was in a small bathroom with a stool and tub/shower combo behind me. There was a sink with cabinet and mirror to one side. I looked up near the ceiling for cameras. If they had cameras on me, I was sunk. I was no expert on surveillance, but I couldn't see anything that looked like a camera. Most people didn't put shit like that in bathrooms. If you were a good guy, it was illegal and an invasion of privacy. You could go to jail for it in a lot of states. Of course, these guys were already looking at kidnapping and assault. I wasn't sure they'd sweat a little sexual perversion charge.

Jason screamed again. I crawled on my knees to the cabinet. It had to be a private residence; they wouldn't have let Jason scream like that in a hotel. Which meant that underneath the sink should be some very dangerous and potentially useful things. *Please, don't let them be the kind of people who put everything under the kitchen sink. Or worse yet, don't let them have thought to remove all the fun stuff.*

I prayed as I turned around and opened the doors with my bound hands. When I had the one door opened, I turned around to see what I had to work with.

There were two bottles that were caustic and had warnings about not getting them in your eyes, and poison if swallowed. The poison part wasn't helpful with vampires, but the eye damage was. It wouldn't damage them the way it would damage a human, but it would hurt, and maybe give me a few seconds to do something more permanent to them. I'd had success with throwing shit in a vampire's eyes before. If I could get my hands undone, that was. If I couldn't manage that, then it didn't matter how many goodies were under the sink; I was screwed.

Jason screamed again, just one long ragged sound. It pushed my pulse into my throat and made my body jerk. The jerk made me think about what held my wrists. It was a flex-cuff. That's basically a great big twist tie, sort of. There was a drawer to the side of the sink.

I stood and turned my back to the drawer so I could open it. *Please, let there be a nail file or something in here. Please.*

When I turned and looked, it was even better. There was a pair of small manicuring scissors. Someone up there liked me. It's harder than it sounds to use tiny scissors behind your own back to cut through a pair of flex-cuffs. It's doable, and it beats the hell out of trying to saw through them with a metal file, but it's still a lesson in frustration. Of course, the frustration could have been because Jason kept screaming. He'd scream,

I'd jump, and I'd have to readjust the scissors. I finally had to close my eyes, so that I could concentrate on just the scissors on the plastic, and I forced myself to stop jumping every time Jason made a bad noise. What the hell were they doing to him? I forced myself to not follow that line of thought. My imagination was way too vivid to be helpful. I'd get my hands free, and then we'd save Jason. Simple, easy, sure.

The scissors bit through the last piece of the cuffs, and my hands were free. I'd been concentrating so hard on it that for a second I didn't move. I let out the breath I'd been holding and opened my eyes. Then I very carefully let my hands come forward. Sometimes when you're cutting through things behind your back, when you free yourself, you lose concentration for a moment and cut yourself after you're free. Yeah, they were just little scissors, but I'd done it before with knives.

I stood there for a second, free at last, and then Jason screamed again. I knelt by the chemicals under the sink. I had rubbing alcohol, toilet bowl cleaner, tile scrubber, and a refill for the liquid soap dispenser beside the faucet. I heard footsteps in what I assumed was a hallway. Someone was coming this way. Jason screamed again from a distance, so it wasn't him, which meant no one coming through the door was my friend.

I'd have liked to have time to plan, but time was over for planning. It was time to act. I grabbed the alcohol, uncapped it. Hands touched the door and used a key to unlock it. I raised the bottle back. If I missed the eyes, I'd just irritate him. The door opened. I saw a face, and I tossed the alcohol into it.

He yelled, "What the hell!" and then he just yelled. I hadn't missed. His hands were clutching his face. I stepped back enough to get room, and being small helped me get enough force to put my foot into the side of his knee and destroy the joint. Everyone has joints, even vampires.

He screamed. I heard a second male voice down the hall say, "Troy, what the hell are you doing down there?"

Troy was on the floor. I could see his gun at his waist and his extra magazine. I took both. I heard someone coming down the hallway. I had a second to choose who to shoot first. Troy was hurt, the other guy wasn't.

I rolled my shoulder around the doorjamb with the gun in my hand and ready. I used the edge of the door to help steady me one-handed, because the magazine was in my other hand. The vampire was spattered with blood. It wasn't his. He looked surprised to see me.

He actually let me shoot him in the chest three times, while he stared at me. It was like shooting humans. His knees hit the ground and I put another round in his head. Either I was getting better or he'd never been that good. Being a vampire can only make you so much better; if you suck to begin with, you'll still suck once you're undead.

I heard Troy moving behind me, and I threw myself into the hallway, shooting into him as I put the far wall against my back. I put two in the center of him as he crouched in the doorway. Blood started out of his mouth, and I walked closer so the two I put just above his eyes would blow the back of his brains out his skull. At that range, it did exactly that. Once you see that much brain on the outside spattered around, a newly dead vampire is truly dead. Just seeing brains through the skull doesn't count. If the brain is still attached and whole you can still get vampires that rise up and try to kill you again. Also, be careful about destroying the higher brain and leaving the lower. You can end up with revenants then, and they are a bitch. Eating machines, like zombies, but not.

I had to change magazines to shoot a bullet into the base of his skull. Like I said, the brain needs to be well and truly scrambled or the damn things can still get up. I didn't want anything alive left behind me. Normally, I'd have made sure the heart was destroyed, too, but I wanted to save ammo in case I needed it for other bad guys. It was a gamble, but they were the newly dead, so I was pretty secure with the choice.

I went to the guy in the hallway, and found a nice-sized hole in his chest. I'd hit the heart, so that was good. I put the muzzle to the base of his skull and fired off one more round. That took care of the lower brain and the spine. If I found a big enough blade, or more ammo, I'd come back and make absolutely sure they wouldn't walk again, but for now, I wanted to get to Jason.

I found a second gun on this one's belt. There was even a spare magazine. They used the same kind of gun. Great, I had more ammo.

I wanted to run to where I thought Jason was, but I forced myself to check the place first. There was a door at the end of the hallway that looked like it led out. There were two more doors on either side of the hallway just short of that door. Maybe I should have checked all the rooms first, made sure we were alone, but I didn't know how badly hurt Jason was. If he bled to death while I was playing supercop, it wouldn't matter that I'd been thorough.

I knew whose blood the vampire in the hallway had been covered in. Did I feel bad about killing them? No. I walked down the hallway, keeping near one wall, gun ready in case there were more of them. I was searching for vampires with that part of me that likes the dead. Years ago I'd watched my mentor Manny Rodriguez be able to sense vampires in a house. He was always right. It had seemed like magic back then; now I sent my necromancy out through the house and couldn't sense any more of them. Unless they were really, really good, better than me, I'd killed the only two vamps in the house. The real danger now was human servants; I couldn't sense humans the way I could vamps.

The end of the hallway just had an opening into a larger room. What I could see looked like everyone's living room: couch, television, floor lamp. I came out of the opening with my back pressed against the wall. I knew the corner nearest me was clear, and I put that at my back while I used the gun to sweep the room.

There was something in the middle of the room, in front of the couch, not quite to the love seat against the other wall. Something that lay in a pool of blood that had changed the gray carpet to black. My mind would not see everything about what lay on the floor. My mind refused to see it, I think. I let my mind play its tricks, because I knew what I was trying not to see. It was Jason. It had to be Jason.

One of the hardest things I'd done in years was sweeping that room, and not rushing to Jason's side once I saw him. I forced myself to see every corner, including the corners at the ceiling. I'd seen vampires fly; hovering near the ceiling was nothing. I forced myself not to look at Jason until I was sure the room was clear. Only then did I let myself go forward. Only then did I let myself make the noise that had been caught in my throat. I didn't scream, honest. It was worse than a scream. It was that sound you make when the worst has happened and no word ever invented will say your pain. The Irish called it keening.

I knew it was Jason on the floor because of his size and the little bit of his hair that wasn't blood-soaked, but those were the only clues the vampires had left. The carpet squished under my knees as I dropped beside him. The room smelled like raw hamburger, and the carpet was a sea of blackness.

I think I went a little crazy for a few minutes. I dropped the extra magazine and the gun into the blood-soaked carpet so I could undo his hands. I fixated on undoing the bonds. If I could just get him free, it would be better. If I could just get him free. They'd used flex-cuffs and hinge cuffs through a metal loop that they'd drilled into the floor. I needed a knife and a key. I looked up and found knives lined up on the end table by the couch. Lined up on a towel, like some kind of macabre surgery. There was a wallet, a ring of keys, and a cell phone near the lamp, as if the vampire had emptied his pockets before starting the torture. It was so terribly organized. He'd done this before. I got a knife that was less bloody, and the keys. The flex-cuffs cut easily, but I couldn't find the right key. I had to force myself to slow down, to stop fumbling.

I got his hands free, finally. I crawled down to his feet, because they were bound the same way. It was only after I got him free that I even thought I was doing this in the wrong order. But I had to undo the chains, I had to. Jason hadn't moved, at all. He was free of the restraints, but he . . .

I reached for his neck. I prayed, "Please, God, let me find a pulse. Please, oh, please."

His skin was cool to the touch. Not good. I couldn't find a pulse. My pulse seemed to speed up like it would beat for both of us. I put my hand on his chest, and there, I could feel his heart. I didn't know if I couldn't find his neck pulse because I was bad at it, or if he'd lost that pulse. If the latter, then that was bad. I couldn't seem to think.

"Think, Anita, think, damn it!" I had to get the bleeding stopped, but there were so many wounds. How do you put pressure on someone's entire body? God.

I was remembering Cisco dying. He'd been a wererat and he'd bled to death with a team of doctors around him. But they'd tried to make him shift form. If you could get a lycanthrope to shift form, it healed them a little.

I put my hand back on his chest. His heart was faltering. *No, no.* I said, "Jason, Jason, fight, I'm here. Help me."

I wanted him to open his eyes, anything, but he just lay there, and his heart wasn't right. The rhythm was too slow. Shit.

I did the only thing I could think of, with his heart dying under my hand. I called my wolf. There was no running up the long corridor inside me, or trees; there was just an image in my head behind my eyes of the white and dark of her fur. I let that image fill me; in that moment if truly becoming a wolf would have saved him, I'd have done it. In that moment, I accepted what I was, and what was in me; there was no fighting now, only a desperate need. I shoved my wolf into him as I'd done with tiger and Crispin, as I'd done with so many others. I shoved my beast down my hand and into that slowing heart. I willed him to change, and knew that if it didn't work, nothing was going to. If he was too hurt to shift, then he was . . .

For the first time, there was no pain to giving my beast, because I wasn't fighting it. There was warmth and power, and a feeling of something pulled out of me, like an extra body part that I hadn't known I had, and suddenly it was there and I could feel it and use it, and it was gone again. It pushed into Jason, and I could feel it, going deep inside him. I could feel that part of me seeking a matching part of him. I found his beast, and what had been gentle and loving was suddenly explosive. I needed him to change now. The beasts seemed to sense my urgency, or maybe his wolf didn't want to die either.

Jason's body jerked under my hand. He gave a sound, a cry,

and fur flowed under my hand. His body shrank and reformed. Once, feeling Richard shift and change against my body had frightened me to death; now it was the most wonderful thing in the world. It had worked. I kept my hand on him while the power of it danced across my skin like the kiss of something electric and alive.

When it was done, a gray wolf lay on its side, panting. The heart under my hand now was thick and steady. He opened wolf eyes the color of new spring leaves. For a moment he saw me, and he gave me that look that no real wolf will ever give, and then the eyes fluttered shut, and the body under my hand began to flow and move again. His human body flowed up and around the wolf, and I was left with my hand on Jason's side.

I put a hand on the middle of his chest, and his heartbeat was there, thick and steady. His skin was still cool to the touch, but his heart felt better. I wiped my hand on my jeans, trying to get the blood and wet goo off of it. I put my hand back on his neck. I searched for his pulse, and found it this time.

His naked body was free of blood, so that it looked like he'd just been laid down in the middle of the carnage. Now the wounds that hadn't healed were clear on his skin. He was covered in knife cuts like evil red mouths; from shoulders nearly to ankles he was covered in wounds. They began to bleed again as I watched. I'd bought us some time, but this wasn't going to heal by magic; we needed doctors.

I picked up the gun from the floor and reached for the cell phone.

54

I DIALED 911. A woman's voice said, "Nine-one-one, what is the nature of your emergency?"

"Anita Blake, Federal Marshal." I gave my ID number, then said, "Female, five-foot-three, long black hair, T-shirt, jeans. Two down. Officer-involved shooting. Partner wounded." Technically, Jason wasn't my partner, but he was mine, and they'd come faster for a wounded cop than a civilian. I'd sort it out later, after we survived.

"Address."

"Shit, I don't know." I got up and looked out a window. There was nothing but trees. "They drugged us and we woke up here. I don't know where here is, can't you trace me by the phone?"

"Is there a landline?"

I looked around the room. "I don't see one."

"Try another room."

"I don't want to leave him alone."

"We need a location to send help, Marshal."

She was right, but I hated leaving him like that. I touched his hair, laid my cheek against his, and whispered, "Don't die on me." I walked back down the hallway past the bodies and tried the first door. It was a bedroom. No phone. The second door I tried was a kitchen, and there was a phone on the wall. "I see a phone, let me see if it's working." I had to put my gun down to pick up the second phone. "I've got a dial tone."

"Call us back on that line, and we'll be able to trace it to you."

"Okay." I clicked the cell phone shut, and dialed 911 again. It was a different woman's voice, and I told an even shorter version.

"We have your location, Marshal, help is on the way."

"How long?"

"You're pretty isolated. We'll try to get a chopper up, but there's no place close to you to land it."

"Okay. We'll wait."

"I can stay on the line with you if you want," she said.

"No, I need to try to stop the bleeding on my friend, and I need my hands for that. Thanks though." I hung up before she could say anything else. I clicked the safety on the gun and tucked it down the front of my belt. I'd bring Jason in here. I wasn't sure how to stop the bleeding from so many wounds, but I knew keeping him warm was better.

Help was coming. We just had to hold on until they got here.

I knelt beside him. His hair was strangely clean, except where the side of his face had been on the blood. He looked like Jason again, instead of so much meat. I swallowed past something that tasted like tears. I'd cry later when he was safe. No time now. I rolled him into my arms, and he felt like dead weight. The heart was going and the pulse was moving, but there is a difference in bodies. Even unconscious, a body doesn't roll like this. Just the way he felt in my arms scared the hell out of me. He rolled, and flopped, like he was already dead. His skin was too cold to the touch. I had to get the bleeding stopped. I had to.

It wasn't weight, but sheer awkwardness that made me put him in a fireman's carry across my shoulders. Blood trickled down my body from him. Shit. I tried to think of other things. I was glad that of all the men in my life, it was one my size. There probably wasn't twenty pounds' difference in our weight. I could carry him. Not forever, but down the hall. I carried him past the body of the vampire who had tortured him. My only regret in that moment was that I couldn't kill him again.

I laid Jason down on the bed. He lay so still, so horribly still. I folded the coverlet around him, hoping to keep him warmer, and then I went in search of a first-aid kit, something, anything. I'd have traded my skills at killing for a little more first-aid training right then.

I knew what was in the bathroom, so I checked the kitchen first. There were towels, but no way to bind them in place. Maybe I could cut up a sheet to use as strips?

I got all the small towels and washrags that the kitchen had and carried them back to the bedroom. The only thing that showed above the coverlet was Jason's hair, so yellow, so vibrant, but he hadn't moved. I wanted him to move, so badly.

I put the rags down on the unused side of the bed and searched for sheets. They were in the closet. I had to go back to the kitchen to fetch a clean, sharp knife to cut the sheet up. I was glad the vampire hadn't used all the knives in the kitchen, because I didn't want to touch the bloody ones in the living room. It felt somehow like they were cursed. Not for real, but unclean, maybe.

I cut the sheet into strips, and then I had to uncover him and start looking at the wounds. They had bled into the coverlet, but no wound seemed worse than the others. It was like any one cut would have been fairly minor, maybe a few stitches. It was the culmination of all of them together that had nearly bled him to death.

I picked a wound in his arm that seemed to be bleeding more than the rest, pressed a rag against it, and started trying to tie it in place. His arm was so limp that I had to trap his lower arm between my knees to get the knot tight enough to put pressure. But not too tight. I couldn't remember, could lycanthropes suffer from getting their circulation cut off? I mean, if you could grow back a limb, then would too tight a bandage hurt you? I treated him like he was human, because I didn't know. It had never come up.

It was when I was tying a wound on his thigh that I saw the first burn marks. Tiny, roundish burn marks on his thigh. More of them on the hip, and finally most of them on the groin. How had I missed these? They were smaller, less obvious than the bloody wounds, I guess. I knew I was in shock. I knew that. Shock softens things. It helps you see things in pieces sometimes; a little horror here, a little more when your mind thinks you can handle it. Shock, if you don't go too far, helps you cope. I knew what had caused him to scream now. Burns didn't heal on a lycanthrope like everything else. Burns had to heal human-slow.

I found more of the little burns all over the front of his body. The back of his body was untouched because he'd been tied on his back. To bind the wounds on his chest, I had to lift him, and he was still just dead weight. I should have seen the wounds beginning to heal by now. They looked the same. I knew in reason that he'd healed from the first moment I'd seen him. I knew that the shift to wolf form had helped him heal, because he wasn't bleeding as badly as that carpet . . . but he wasn't healing as fast as I was used to seeing lycanthropes heal. I didn't know if Jason was simply a slow healer, or if there had been that much damage, or if the vampires had done something to the wounds to make them worse.

When I'd bound all the wounds I could figure out how to bind, I lay down beside Jason, with me propped up on the pillows, and rolled him against my body. I held him against me, and I prayed, prayed with that energy that true tragedy gives you. The loudest prayers must be when you hold someone you love and feel him go cold.

I knew warmth was important to healing lycanthropes. Cold was bad, that much I knew. My body heat was all I could think of. I got the gun out of my belt and laid it on the pillow beside me. I'd done everything I could think of; now we waited for help to arrive. Waited and prayed.

Jason didn't feel like Jason in my arms. The washrags and sheet strips were rough and ruined the smooth feel of his body. My clothes were drying to my skin sticky with his blood. I should have taken them off before I lay down, so that Jason could be closer to my skin, but it had seemed to take so much effort to get him against me. I lay there, too tired, too shocky to move.

Why? Why had they tortured him? Why had they taken us? I remembered the man yelling, "Where's Lorna?" We didn't know anyone named Lorna, or I didn't. Who the hell was she? I was betting that this had nothing to do with Jason, and everything to do with the Summerlands. Had Jason taken another beating for Keith Summerland? Was it that simple, or was something else going on that I didn't know anything about? In that moment, holding Jason, feeling his blood drying my clothes to my skin, I was willing to believe there were lots of things I didn't know.

I heard the door open. The outside door, because I heard the screen hit. Whoever it was, hesitated in the hallway. They'd seen the body. If it was the rescue crew they'd have called out.

I picked up the gun. The safety was already off, a round already chambered. I'd done that before I laid the gun down beside me. If anyone came through that door before the EMTs, they would not be my friend.

I sighted at the doorway and let out my breath. I let my body go quiet, and the gun was the focus of all that quiet. If Jason had moved in that moment I'd probably have screamed.

A man's voice called from down the hallway. "I hear your heartbeats. I smell his blood. I see my men are dead, so I assume you have at least one of their guns. Mr. Summerland, I didn't think you had it in you to be this dangerous."

I didn't say anything. If I was quiet enough, he might come closer for a look. If he came close enough I'd shoot him.

"Mr. Summerland, why don't you answer me? If you would simply tell us where Lorna is, then we would let you go. We have no wish to harm the son of a governor."

He was lying.

"Mr. Summerland," he said again, "are you in there? Why don't you answer me?"

I could smell dawn on the air. Not here yet, but close. I wanted to know if this was a vampire, but if I used my necromancy to sense him, he'd know what I was. I think they had thought I was just another of Keith Summerland's women. It's why they had left me in the bathroom, with no guard. It's why this one was assuming that Keith Summerland had gotten away somehow and killed the two vampires. This guy was assuming that because I was a woman I wasn't dangerous. Was it time to let the last man standing know that he'd made a mistake?

"Mr. Summerland?" His voice sounded a little closer. Did I wait for him to maybe get close enough for a shot, or did I try to get some answers?

Dawn was so close. If he was a vampire he'd be running out of moonlight, literally. If he was human it didn't matter. I decided to try for information.

"Why would you think Lorna would be with him?"

"Oh, the girl." He sounded genuinely surprised.

"Yeah," I said, "the girl."

"Do you know where Lorna is?" he asked, and there was a hopeful lilt to his voice.

"After what you did to my boyfriend and me, I don't think I want to answer any of your questions."

"We were harsh, and I am sorry for that. Genuinely sorry."

"Liar," I said.

"What is your name?" he asked.

"You first," I said.

"They call me George."

"I want to know your name, not what they call you."

He laughed then, and he was good. It was a nice laugh, as if he weren't standing in a hallway staring at the dead bodies of men he'd hired to kidnap and torture us. Of course, maybe he was just a charming sociopath. In that case the laugh was real. When you have no empathy for anyone else, other people dead or hurt don't mean anything to you.

"Edmond, my name is Edmond. What is your name?"

I decided to try lying. "Katerine." It was my middle name.

"Now who's lying?" he said, and he made it sound playful.

Fine. "Anita, my name's Anita."

"Anita, now that is a lovely name."

"What happens if you don't find Lorna?" I asked.

He was quiet for a second or two, then said, "Her husband will not be pleased."

"So, you find her and you're going to force her to go back to him?"

"He is her husband and her master."

Master, that was an interesting choice of words. Was Lorna the wife of the Master of the City Peterson had told me about? "He your master, too, Edmond?"

"He trusted me with this errand."

"Yes, then," I said.

"You do not speak like one of Keith Summerland's bimbos."

"Is Lorna a bimbo?"

"I would never call my master's wife such a thing."

"Then why did she think she could leave her master and husband and go off with Keith? Doesn't sound very bright."

"He looks too much like her long-lost love. She does not see his faults, only his face, like a ghost of things lost and forgotten."

"She had the hots for Jedediah Summerland?"

"Who are you, girl?"

"Jedediah was killed by vampires; are you saying that Lorna saw Keith and decided to try to relive old times?"

"You are taking this all very in stride, girl. Anita, you said your name was?"

"I did."

"You smell of blood, and sorrow, but you are calm. What is your last name?"

Dawn pressed like a weight against the window and its

heavy drapes. He wasn't panicked enough for a vampire above ground. Human, then, but I was betting human servant. Not just a human that hung with the vamps, but a true servant like I was to Jean-Claude. He said he could smell blood and sorrow, and if he was a longtime servant he might have gained the ability.

"You answer my question, I'll answer yours."

"Yes, she's trying to relive her lost affair with Jedediah. He was misled by his own power, but he was a compelling man. The boy is nothing to compare to his ancestor, but the resemblance is almost enough to make one speak of reincarnation."

"Genetics, Edmond, nothing but genetics."

"I have answered your question, now you answer mine. What is your last name?"

"Blake," I said.

The quiet was strangely loud, as if I could feel him thinking furiously. "Anita Blake," he said, finally.

"Yes," I said.

"Anita Blake, human servant to Jean-Claude, Master of the City of St. Louis?"

"Among other things, yes."

"We did not know. I swear to you we did not know. We were told the room belonged to Keith, and Lorna was with him. We would never have harmed the human servant of another Master of the City."

"Yeah, vampire law frowns on that."

"I swear to you that I would never have sent these two to harm you. When I saw you, and realized you were not Lorna. I was told that these two were professional. I was misinformed. I mean, what sort of vampire mistakes a human for another vampire?"

"A bad one," I said.

"Why were you with Keith Summerland?"

"Did he tell you his name was Jason Schuyler?"

"Yes, but you only have to look at him to know he is one of the Summerland twins."

"They were always getting mistaken for each other in school," I said. I was calm; my voice had almost no inflection. Part shock and part certainty. I was going to kill Edmond, because killing him would most likely kill his master, and I wanted his master dead. Revenge, yes, but also, Edmond couldn't let me walk out of here. I'd tell Jean-Claude, and he knew I would. If Edmond was to hide his mistake from his master, he had to kill us.

"What are you saying?"

"Don't master vampires keep track of the names of the *pommes de sang* of other masters of the cities?"

"Not really, they are food."

"We're Belle Morte's bloodline; I guess we treat our food better. Jason really isn't Keith Summerland. He really is my boyfriend. He really is Jean-Claude's *pomme de sang*. Do you know what vampire protocol is about harming someone's *pomme de sang*, Edmond?"

"You can always get more food."

"Do-you-know-what-vampire-protocol-is-on-the-harming-of-another-master's-*pomme-de-sang*?" My voice wasn't neutral now. I was beginning to rediscover my anger. If Edmond really meant to flee and leave us alive, he'd have started to leave then, but he was closer to us when he spoke next.

"It is within the master's right to either demand a new *pomme de sang* from the offending master, or challenge the master to a duel."

"I don't think we'd like the kind of *pomme de sang* your master would choose, Edmond."

"Jean-Claude would challenge my master to a duel?"

"Something like that," I said.

"The *pomme de sang* is not dead. Let me call for help, get him to a hospital."

"I've already called," I said. "They should be here soon."

"You called for help?"

"Yes."

"When?"

"Before you came."

"I don't mean you any harm, Anita Blake."

"Then why aren't you running away, Edmond? I've told you the police are coming, but you're still standing there. Why don't you run?"

"What will you do if you trace my master back to his city?"

"What do you think I'll do?"

"You are not just Jean-Claude's human servant; you are also a vampire executioner. Would you try to get a warrant against my master?"

"I don't know who your master is, Edmond."

"Do not treat me as if I am stupid. There are not that many Masters of the City."

"How many are married to a Lorna, you mean? How many have human servants named Edmond? I guess it does have to be a short list," I said.

I heard him chamber a round into his gun. It's funny, but once you know the sound of a slide going back, you never mistake it for anything else. I aimed my gun at the doorway, raising my knee up a little to help steady me, because my other arm was still touching Jason.

I saw his gun come around the doorjamb. I think he expected me to wait to see more of him, but I'd used this gun, this ammo, and it was an old house. I shot through the wall, behind his hand. He made a satisfying sound, a pain sound, and then he shot into the room without seeing first. I fired two more shots that went wide before he staggered into the doorway. I had a glimpse of a tall, pale man, with short brown hair, and a nice tan suit, and a shirt that was blossoming red, before I shot him in the head. He tried to raise his gun as he fell, and actually squeezed off a shot that went into the foot of the bed. I crawled out of the covers and fired twice more into his body. I walked to him, the gun aimed at him, held two-handed. I kicked his gun away from his limp hand, and then I put two more bullets into his head, until bits of skull and brain exploded onto the floor.

My ears were still ringing when I heard shouting, distant, tinny. "Marshal Blake, Marshal Blake!"

I yelled, probably louder than I needed to, "In here. We're in here!" The cavalry had arrived.

55

HOURS LATER I was sitting in a chair back in the hospital in Asheville. Jason was in the bed, hooked up to machines and drips, but alive. The doctors said he was going to make it. He'd heal. I knew his body would heal, but I knew enough about violence to know that there were things that doctors couldn't see, and IV drips couldn't help. I sat in the chair, having moved it close enough so that I could hold his hand. The doctors said he was going to be all right; I believed them, but when I felt his hand squeeze mine, then I'd really believe it. Was that stupid? Maybe. But I was past caring. I sat in the chair and held his hand, and waited for him to wake up enough to hold my hand back.

I was wearing a borrowed pair of surgical scrubs, because they'd taken my clothes for evidence. I guess I was covered in blood. The techs had even combed pieces of brain and bone out of my hair, apparently. Blowback is a bitch.

They'd taken all the guns at the scene. Because I'd used the fact that I was a federal marshal to make the 911 call, actual federal marshals had come with the rest. They'd come to rescue me. They'd come even though I was one of the preternatural branch, and not all the marshals liked us very much. I couldn't blame the ones who were leery of us. For some of us it was more like giving a badge to a bunch of bounty hunters with license to kill. We were a real administrative headache for the marshals. But when I put out the SOS they came. People I didn't know, but who just shared the same badge. Maybe I was just feeling all sentimental because of Jason, but it meant something that they came.

But it also meant that I was on review for the shooting. I hadn't had a warrant of execution for these vampires, let alone for the human servant I'd killed. Heck, they had only my word for it that he was a human servant and not simply human. I had invoked the new Preternatural Endangerment Act. It allowed a vampire executioner to act using deadly force if civilian lives were in imminent danger. The act had come into being after a couple of civilians had died while my fellow preternatural marshals waited on warrants. I'd thought it was just asking for civil rights violations, but now I was hiding behind it. Hypocrisy at its best. For at least the next couple of weeks I would be badge-less and gun-less. I wouldn't be allowed to take on any warrants until they reviewed the shooting. They took my official duty piece. That was fine; it wasn't like I didn't have others. I even had carry permits for several of my guns, because I'd spent so many years being technically a civilian but needing to carry a gun. It was going to be helpful while they looked over the evidence.

It looked like it would be ruled a clean shot. They'd found drugs still in my system. They were just impressed that I was able to function with that level of animal tranquilizers in me.

I left out the bit about Marmee Noir waking me up. They did ask about the claw marks on my chest. I just said I woke up that way. Truth, as far as it went.

I'd asked for and been given a morning-after pill. They'd offered me a SART exam, Sexual Assault Response Team, and I had declined. When asked why I needed the pill, I replied I'd had sex before we were taken but not had a chance to take my pill for that day. Again, truth, as far as it went.

We had a uniformed officer on the door. I'd have liked to fetch some of my guns from the hotel safe, but wasn't sure how the other marshals would feel about me carrying when I was supposed to be under review. I felt naked without a weapon, but I'd flashed the badge and I had to abide by that. It also meant that the other bodyguards Jean-Claude would have sent to me couldn't come in either. None of them had badges, and some of them had records.

The door opened, and I tensed, my free hand going for a gun that wasn't there. Damn. But it wasn't a bad guy, it was a wheelchair being pushed by a nurse. In the wheelchair was Frank Schuyler, Jason's dad. He had tubes up his nose and an oxygen tank on the back of the chair, and two different IV drips, but he was here.

The nurse said, "I told you he won't wake up until morning, Mr. Schuyler."

"I had to see him," he said in that deep voice that Jason would never have, and then he looked at me with those cavernous dark eyes. It wasn't exactly a friendly look, more intense. Like so many people when they get whittled down by a disease, he was pared down to nerve endings, emotions, demands. It was there in his eyes, angry eyes—no, rage-filled. Angry at his body, maybe? Or angry in general. Whatever the cause, I was okay with it. If he thought he'd come in here and yell at me, or Jason, then he was wrong. Oh, he could yell, but I'd yell back. I was taking no more shit, and I was definitely making sure that Jason took no more, not from anybody.

Apparently the silence and the staring at each other had gone on long enough to make the nurse nervous. "Why don't I take you back to your room?"

"Push me closer to the bed, damn it. I didn't come all this way just to look at him."

The nurse looked at me, as if for permission, or apology.

"If you can behave yourself, you can come closer; if you came here to bitch or yell, you can go," I said.

He glared at me, and then his gaze shifted to my hand holding Jason's. "You really are Jason's girlfriend, aren't you?"

"Yes, I am."

"And the fact that I'm his father doesn't cut me any slack with you, does it?"

"Not today it doesn't."

"You'd really kick me out of the room. His dying father, out of his only son's room."

"If you get nasty, in a heartbeat."

"And who decides what's nasty?" he asked.

"Me."

"You," he said.

"Yes," I said, and squeezed Jason's hand a little tighter.

He looked back at the nurse. "Push me closer, and leave."

She looked at me again. I nodded. She pushed him closer, but not like she thought it was a good idea. I wasn't sure either, but I wasn't sure it was a bad idea either. I didn't move back, and my chair was moved up so I could hold Jason's hand. The wheelchair was close enough that our legs almost touched.

It was almost too close for comfort, too much interpersonal space crossed, but I stayed where I was, and he didn't tell the nurse to move him somewhere else.

He laid his hand on Jason's leg under the covers, then said, "Get out, I'll buzz you when I need you."

The nurse gave a look like she wasn't sure she should be doing it, but she left. He waited for the door to hush closed behind us before he spoke. "I'm sorry I didn't believe that you were his girlfriend."

"Me, too."

We sat there in our chairs, me holding Jason's hand, him with his big hand on his son's leg. The room was very quiet, only the whirrs and hush of the monitors on Jason, the faint drip of the various IVs, his and Jason's. It was the kind of quiet that stretches out and makes your hair itch, because you know you need to say something, but nothing comes to mind. This wasn't my father. This wasn't my mess, but somehow I was the one sitting inches away from a dying man while he looked at his injured son.

"You're not like most women," he said.

I actually jumped a little, just from him breaking the silence. "What do you mean?" I asked. There, that was a good question, make him talk again.

"Most women need to talk. They hate silences."

"Sometimes, yes, but I'm okay with quiet, especially when I don't know what to say."

"You don't know what to say to me?" he asked, giving me the full weight of those deep-set eyes.

"Not really," I said.

He smiled, and squeezed Jason's leg at the same time. "But you admit it, most people wouldn't."

I shrugged. "I'm not most people."

"I heard you killed three men to save Jason," he said, and this time he looked at Jason, not at me.

"Two vampires and one man, yes."

He looked back at me, when he asked, "Does it matter to you that two of them were vampires?"

"Vampires are harder to kill; it makes the story more impressive."

He almost smiled. "You are a strange woman."

"Would any other kind be able to keep up with your son?"

He looked at Jason then, and a look more tender than anything I'd expected to see filled that harsh face. "We've always been too different to get along. I blamed, well, you know what I blamed."

I had no idea what he blamed, but I kept it to myself. I had the sense that I might learn something if I kept quiet.

"Why did they do this to Jason?" he asked.

"He took another beating for Keith Summerland, just like in school."

"They did this because they thought Jason was Keith?"

"Yes."

"Why did they want to do this to the Summerland boy?"

"Apparently, Keith was messing with someone else's wife, and the husband took exception."

Something crossed Frank Schuyler's face, some pain that flitted through those dark, hooded eyes. "You know, don't you?"

"I know a lot of things," I said. "You'll have to be more specific."

He reached up to Jason's hand, which was still in mine. He hesitated, as if he might put that large hand over both our hands. That seemed disturbing, so I moved my hand. I left Jason's hand empty, and Frank Schuyler wrapped his big hand around Jason's. He held his hand as if they were any father and son. It was a shame that Jason wasn't awake to see it.

"Iris and I had separated. My fault, I've always had a temper. We dated while we were separated like most couples do, and when she got pregnant with Jason, we got back together. He was our reconciliation baby." He held Jason's smaller hand in his large one, and stared down at his son.

"A lot of people get back together that way," I said. I wasn't sure where the story was going, but I wanted to hear it.

"I thought I finally had a son of my own. I thought that he just looked like Iris, until I saw the Summerland twins. Then I knew, I knew she'd been with Summerland."

"Have you seen the kids in this town, Mr. Schuyler, most of Jason's friends look like they were chipped off the Summerland block."

He gave me an unfriendly look. "I asked Iris, and she didn't deny that she'd dated him. The Summerlands were separated at the same time we were. It was a rough year in the town, tempers short. We all got back together because we thought we were going to have children." He rubbed Jason's hand with his fingers.

I realized then that I'd been slow. Jason had hinted at it, and there had been other things, but so many of the girls in the wedding had looked just as much like Jason. His mother looked like the Summerlands, for God's sake.

"Jason said you were always mad at him, no matter what he did."

He nodded. "That's fair. It wasn't just that he looked like the twins. He didn't do sports. He danced. He was just so . . ."

"Not the son you wanted," I finished for him.

He gave me an unfriendly look again; this one had some real anger back in those dark eyes. "You have no right to say that."

Maybe it was because I was tired, or because I loved Jason and couldn't understand why his own father didn't love him, but I said what I was thinking, "I said it because it's true."

He glared at me, and I gave him empty cop eyes back. I was too tired to be angry. Finally, he looked away. "Maybe, all right, yes. Every man dreams of what his son will be like. I guess I wanted someone to carry on, and he seemed to be carrying on the Summerland values, not mine." He kept holding Jason's hand while he said it, though.

"Jason's values are just fine," I said.

"I've half-hated him all his life, blamed him for not being what I wanted him to be. When I heard he . . . I made them bring me down when he came into emergency. I saw him hurt." He held on to Jason's hand, tight. "I didn't think, *There's that Summerland bastard*. I thought, *There's my boy, dying*. I remembered his first Christmas, and how happy I was. It was before I knew. But when I saw him like that, I thought about him when he was little. I thought about him in the plays and musicals in school. I realized that I've missed a lifetime with my son. I missed it and he was right here."

I stared at him. It was a Hallmark moment. I didn't trust Hallmark moments; they were usually fake. I watched the first tear glitter down Frank Schuyler's face, and had to believe that he meant it. I guess sometimes miracles really do happen.

Then we got our second miracle. Jason said, "Dad," in a voice that sounded so weak, so un-Jasonlike, but his eyes were open, and he repeated it. "Dad."

Mr. Schuyler held his hand tight and said, "Jason, I'm here."

I got up to leave them alone. Men need privacy when they finally break down. Jason said, in that weak voice, "Anita."

I turned and looked at him. "I'll be back."

He managed a very weak smile, then said, "Love you."

I smiled. "Love you, too." I wasn't sure if the love was for his father's benefit, to prove his heterosexuality, or if it was simply true. We'd never be each other's one and only, but I think we might always be each other's now and then. I was okay with that, and so was Jason. What more did we need?

56

JASON HEALED ENOUGH to fly home. His father has had one of those amazing remissions that you get sometimes with cancer. The doctors don't explain it, they can't, but they're giving him a little longer to live. Not cured, no, but months instead of weeks, maybe. A little less pain to deal with. Jason's planning on flying back alone to visit them all in a week or so. My excuse for not going is work; besides, I think that Jason and his family can handle it on their own.

The Master of the City of Charleston, South Carolina, mysteriously died. His human servant was Edmond, and his legal wife is Lorna. She's free to marry Keith now, and if what I saw on the news is any indication, he's going to do it. The marriage to Lisa is off, and I think Lisa is well out of it. So are the governor's plans to run for president on a family conservative ticket. You can't have your son being an adulterer with a vampire's wife, and even worse marrying a vampire, and have it play well in the press.

Peterson told me that it was Chuck who used our room and us as a stalking horse for the vampires. Chuck's defense: he thought we'd win. I guess no one expects vampires to use flash-bang grenades and tranquilizer darts. I'm still hoping to hurt Chuck in some way. I just haven't figured out a justification for it that doesn't seem petty, or illegal. If he vanished now, I think the cops would come knocking on my door.

J. J. is planning on visiting St. Louis and spending a few days with her old friend Jason. He's the one man she's never really gotten out of her system, and she's the girl he might have married if she hadn't liked girls as much as he did. They're both still looking for Ms. Right. Maybe they'll look together for a while. It was Jason's fear of commitment that saved me from Richard's version of the *ardeur*. But he's pretty thrilled that J. J. is coming to visit. She's already made noises that she's cool with the vampire thing. Good to know.

I was cleared on the shooting. The two vampires actually had records as humans. They'd been bad guys when alive, and being dead had made them worse. The one guy really was a torturer. Someone you called in when you wanted information. He'd worked for some very bad people over the years. Apparently, in private, I'd done the world a favor. In public I was cleared, but we weren't allowed to be so cheerful about it. I sleep just fine about killing them. My sleep is a little disturbed about Jason. I've had a few dreams where I find him on the floor again, or I realize it's not Jason and it's one of the other men in my life. Jason's bunked over a couple of times; he's sleeping rough, too. But he sleeps better when someone's there to wake him from the nightmare, and cuddle him back to sleep, or as on a couple of mornings, get up with him and drink coffee in the kitchen. Nathaniel and I have been taking turns watching dawn come up through the trees with him.

Jason is my wolf to call, which raises the possibility that I'll be able to have an animal for each of my metaphysical beasts. Only the Master of Beasts, a vampire council member, has been able to do animals to call that are both canine and feline, oh, and he does rats, too. We'll see how I do.

Jean-Claude let it be known through the undead grapevine that Jason and I will be punished for our indiscretion, once he's healed. I already felt punished, and I hadn't even done anything wrong. But we are doing what Jason had suggested, confirming the rumors. We've started with Asher, because that's the easiest. Now it's a matter of asking which of the men are okay with it being confirmed. Have you tried asking a heterosexual man if he's okay that he and you acknowledge publicly that he's bisexual, and does men? Not an easy sell.

Asher would be more thrilled if the truth were really the truth. We've set up a date between the three of us—Jean-Claude, Asher, and me—to see if that boundary can really come down, or if my head will explode. We'll see.

I've agreed to be less of a pain in the ass in the outward vampire community so that it looks more like I'm being a good little human servant to Jean-Claude. Yeah, I know, how long can I behave myself? But I am trying. Jean-Claude says I get points for trying, since he knows it is opposite my personality. Gotta love a man who loves you in spite of, and sometimes because of, your little foibles.

Rowe is being charged with kidnapping and attempted murder. You don't have to wield the knife to be charged; just helping the killer get his victim is enough legally.

Why did he do it? Some money, but mostly I scared him in the hallway with the *ardeur*. He was convinced I was a vampire and the only way to save himself was to get rid of me.

Was he always a bad guy, or had the *ardeur* and I done

something to him? No way to tell, but I take some blame for Rowe.

Max is still pissed I rolled Crispin, but Jean-Claude made noises that once Max knew how much our Jason looked like the Summerland boy, he should have warned us. Because, of course, Max knew about Keith and Lorna's elopement. Max would never admit that he didn't know, so the two Masters of the City traded insults, but we have a truce. We also have plans for Crispin to visit St. Louis. Not sure how I feel about that, but I did roll him, and at twenty-one, and very mortal, he doesn't have the strength of will to break free of me. I owe him something, even if it was all accidental on my part.

The weretigers cut me some slack because of the whole kidnapping hospital thing. But they are coming to St. Louis. Apparently, Crispin and Alex Pinn have gained power from being with me—powers that are only legend among the tiger clans now. But it isn't me who did it. I know it was Marmee Noir. I don't know what she's up to, but she wants the tigers, and she's using me to get them. The call has gone out, and to the tigers I made the call, so I'm stuck with the results, but I know who really called them. She woke me up when I was drugged. She helped me save Jason, sort of. She also cut me from a great distance with the claw of a cat that hasn't walked the earth for a few thousand years. The marks are healing, but her being able to cut someone up from a distance is a power she hasn't had in a while. Maybe the tigers aren't the only ones gaining powers from dealing with me.

The vampire council is voting on whether to kill her before she wakes. If anyone were asking me, I'd say do it. But I think she knows what they're planning. I think the Mother of All Darkness is afraid. She's still weak, still trapped somehow in that false sleep. If they try to kill her, will it work? Can you kill the darkness itself? Can the night die? I don't know. The really scary thing is that I don't think the vampires know the answer either. Some are even afraid that if she does die, all vampires will die. That somehow she'll take them all to the grave with her.

All I know for certain is that I asked for and got extra charms. I sleep, bathe, everything but make love to vampires in a cross and that charm. So far, so good, but good has nothing to do with the Mother of All Darkness. No, bad is definitely more her style. She saved my life, and by accident, Jason's. I'd be more grateful if I weren't so certain that she only protects what she finds useful. She only protects that which she needs. Why does she need me? Is she really gaining power through me? The truly frightening part is that I think if I thought hard enough in the night, she might answer me. If you could ask the darkness anything, would you ask? If you did ask, would the darkness lie? Bet on it.

extras

www.orbitbooks.net

about the author

Laurell K. Hamilton is the bestselling author of the acclaimed Anita Blake, Vampire Hunter novels. She lives near St. Louis with her husband, her daughter, one pug and two part-pug dogs and an ever-fluctuating number of fish.

Find out more about Laurell K. Hamilton and other Orbit authors by registering for the free monthly newsletter at www.orbitbooks.net

if you enjoyed
BLOOD NOIR
look out for

DYING WORDS

by
Shaun Hutson

1

London, Monday the 15th, 12.32 p.m.

The car missed the bus by inches.

There was a high-pitched scream of rubber on tarmac as the Renault skidded past. The driver of the bus sounded his horn angrily, the sound adding to the cacophony already filling the air.

Detective Inspector David Birch gripped the wheel of the car more tightly and drove on, pressing his foot down harder on the accelerator. Ahead of him, his eyes fixed like laser sights upon it, the silver-grey Nissan he was pursuing also speeded up, scraping the side of a Mini as it pushed and barged through the traffic on Jamaica Road.

More horns blared as the two cars hurtled along the thoroughfare, Birch keeping the Renault as close to the fleeing Nissan as he could. There was perspiration on his face. His shirt was sticking to his back.

'Where the fuck is he going?' Birch muttered, aware that they were approaching another set of traffic lights.

The Nissan showed no signs of slowing down and shot through the junction with the lights on red.

Birch followed without hesitation.

Beside him in the passenger seat, Detective Sergeant Stephen Johnson glanced at his watch.

2

There was an unedifying jolt as the Renault momentarily mounted the pavement to avoid the damaged cars blocking the thoroughfare. Both policemen grunted as Birch swung it wildly back on to the road again.

Up ahead, the uniformed motorcyclist was less than twenty feet from the rear of the speeding Nissan.

'Just stay with him,' Birch muttered under his breath.

The bike was gaining by the second.

'Moving down Stamford Street,' Johnson said into the two-way. 'All units converge.'

More traffic lights.

The Nissan shot through the next set, narrowly avoiding a collision with a Mercedes. There were more blaring horns and the shriek of tyres, and as the Renault sped onwards after its prey Birch could smell the stink of burning rubber strong in his nostrils.

The police motorbike was now within ten feet of the Nissan. The rider suddenly accelerated, coming up on the inside of the vehicle.

Birch shook his head. 'Tell him to stay back,' he snapped.

Johnson had the two-way to his mouth when the Nissan suddenly swung violently to the left. It hit the motorbike and sent it veering out of control.

The two wheels mounted the pavement, and the rider managed to control the bike long enough to guide it back on to the road.

'No,' snarled Birch.

The Nissan lurched left once more, its driver wrenching the wheel violently, slamming into the bike with even greater force.

This time, the motorbike was shunted towards a line of parked cars. It struck the side of a Vauxhall. The impact sent the bike rider flying from his seat. He hit the bonnet of the Vauxhall, skidded across it and landed on the other side. The bike crashed on to its side and ricocheted back into the road, tyres still spinning.

Birch twisted the steering wheel to avoid the obstacle, his offside tyre clipping the bike.

There was a sound of shattering glass. Pieces of the bike's windscreen and portions of one Renault headlight skittered across the tarmac like crystal shrapnel.

Somewhere behind he heard screams but his eyes never left the road. Never left the Nissan that he was still pursuing.

Johnson turned slightly in his seat and saw the injured police motorcyclist lying motionless on the pavement, people running towards him, some to help, others to merely gaze in bewildered fascination at his body.

On the right, the gaunt edifice of the National Theatre appeared.

Up ahead, traffic on the roundabout was heading straight for them.

'He's going for Waterloo Bridge,' Birch said.

'All units,' Johnson repeated into the two-way. 'Suspect is crossing the river at Waterloo Bridge.'

Birch twisted the wheel left and right, intent only on not hitting anything. In front of him, the Nissan wove in and out of the heavy traffic, ignoring the blaring horns, somehow finding a path through. It finally swung left on to the bridge.

Birch followed, narrowly avoiding a taxi whose driver gestured angrily at him.

'Get out of the road,' the DI roared as he drove on, his teeth gritted as he saw people ahead crossing.

Ahead, the Nissan ploughed on.

It hit a woman and sent her careering backwards on to the pavement. She flopped down on to the flagstones cracking her head hard on the concrete.

'Close the far end of Waterloo Bridge,' Birch rasped.

The police helicopter, seeing the open space over the river, suddenly swooped down again, dropping to within a hundred feet of the fleeing Nissan.

'All units converge,' Johnson ordered. 'Strand and Aldwych.'

'Bastard's got nowhere to run now,' hissed Birch and pressed down harder on the accelerator.

3

The sunshine glinted on the dirty grey surface of the Thames as it snaked through London, but Birch cared nothing for the river beneath him as he sped over Waterloo Bridge. All that mattered to him was the Nissan and its occupant and he was closing on them with every second.

I've got you now, you bastard.

He guided the Renault round an Interflora van; nothing now between him and his prey but open road.

Look in the rear-view mirror, shithouse. Look and see. You're going nowhere, you murdering fuck.

The police helicopter wheeled away back up into sky and Birch nodded to himself.

'Hang on,' he said, through clenched teeth.

Johnson did as he was instructed, and the Renault shot forward as Birch stamped on the gas pedal.' The dark blue car slammed into the rear of the Nissan, the impact causing both cars to skid slightly.

Birch smiled thinly.

That's for the first of the five, you piece of shit. How long ago was it now? Eight months? That's how long we've been hunting you, isn't it? Eight long fucking months.

He hit the accelerator again and sent the Renault crashing into the back of the Nissan a second time. The impact was so savage that part of the Nissan's rear bumper came free. Portions of shattered tail-light spilled into the road.

That's for the twelve-year-old you raped and murdered.

The Nissan swerved. Birch rammed it again.

That's for the one who was fourteen. The one you strangled with electrical flex after you'd raped her. The one you hung from the highest diving board at Southwark Park swimming pool. Just to taunt us, eh?

'Suspect's vehicle is in Lancaster Place,' Johnson said into the two-way, glancing briefly at his superior's blazing expression. 'Why wasn't the road blocked?'

A fourth time, Birch sent the Renault slamming into the Nissan's rear end.

And that's for the latest one. For the little nine-year-old. The one you buggered as well. Raping her wasn't quite enough this time, was it? Nor was blinding her with a soldering iron while you did it.

The traffic lights at the end of the road were on amber. Someone tried to cross but the Nissan drove through anyway, narrowly missing them.

'Turning left into the Strand,' Johnson continued.

Birch saw uniformed men on the street. The wail of sirens filled the air as more police cars came hurtling from the direction of the Aldwych.

End of the line, cunt.

'We've got him,' the DI breathed, eyes blazing.

He momentarily eased the pressure on the accelerator, cursing to himself as he saw the Nissan heading directly for two police cars trying to block the road. It hit them with a thunderous crash, the impact enough to open a gap between them large enough for the Nissan to scrape through.

Uniformed men ran towards the stalled grey vehicle. Birch hit the brake and he and Johnson hauled themselves out of the Renault.

The driver of the Nissan, blood running from a cut just below his hairline, was already out and running towards Southampton Street.

Don't let him get away. Not now.

The DI saw him pull the long, sharp blade from inside his jacket as the first of the uniformed men came within reach of him.

'Watch it,' bellowed Birch.

The blade flashed. Wielded with a combination of effortless expertise and demonic force, it caught the constable across the right ear, sheared off part of the lobe and hacked into his neck deeply enough to sever a major artery. A fountain of blood erupted from the wound as the man fell to his knees shrieking helplessly, hands clutching at the yawning gash.

'Fuck,' snarled the DI and ran on, Johnson close beside him.

Some of the uniformed men were gathering around their fallen companion, others had already run to their cars. More were joining the two detectives in the chase.

'He's heading for Covent Garden,' Birch gasped as he and Johnson ran.

Ahead of them, the bloodied knife still clutched in his fist, their quarry sprinted away with surprising speed for a man in his early fifties.

'If we don't stop him we'll lose him in the crowd,' panted Birch.

4

Birch sucked in a deep breath, feeling it rasp in his throat as he ran, Johnson pounding along beside him. Both men had their eyes fixed on their target.

He was less than fifty yards ahead of them but, Birch thought, if he managed to disappear into the maze that was Covent Garden Market he could vanish as easily as a puff of smoke in a high wind.

So many people to hurt. So many places to hide.

Behind him, Birch could hear sirens. Uniformed men were now joining the pursuit, but the two detectives were still the closest to the suspect.

Up ahead there were screams. Shouts of fear and shock as members of the public caught sight of the knife held by the running man, who sometimes crashed into them in his haste to get away.

Birch and Johnson did their best to avoid collisions with the hapless bystanders but it proved impossible. The DI hit a group of teenagers and sent two crashing to the ground. Some of their companions laughed, while others shouted abuse at the two policemen.

The suspect dashed through one of the stone archways leading into the market itself and Birch lost sight of him.

'Steve,' he shouted, still running, gesturing to his companion. Johnson understood and veered off to his left, taking a route that would lead him to the far side of the market.

Birch blundered on through the same arch, almost colliding with two women carrying large blue shopping bags.

They looked in bewilderment at his sweat-stained face. The DI looked wildly to right and left.

No sign of the man he sought.

'Where are you, you bastard?' he whispered under his breath, walking now through the hordes of browsing shoppers gathered round the many stalls in the market, inspecting the wares on offer.

His quarry could be anywhere by now. He might even have run straight on, out through the other side of the market and up to Covent Garden Tube station. If the bastard had managed to get down on to the platforms and board a train, they hadn't got a hope in hell of finding him.

Birch walked up an aisle, checking the sea of faces that surrounded him, his heart thudding not from the exertion he'd just subjected it to but from nervousness. He swallowed hard and tried to control his breathing.

Come out, come out, wherever you are, you scumbag.

He passed a jewellery stall where two women were inspecting silver rings. Another vendor was selling framed photos of London. Potential buyers were perusing the selection. Birch reached the end of the aisle and peered out across the cobbled area beyond, scanning the faces there.

'We've lost him.'

He heard the voice close behind but didn't turn.

'I said—' Johnson began again but Birch raised a hand to silence him.

'He's here,' the DI said quietly. 'I know he is.'

'How can you be sure? He could have made it to the Tube station or be hiding in any one of these shops,' Johnson insisted.

Birch took a step away from his companion, still raking his gaze back and forth over the crowd.

'He could have cut back towards Bow Street. I'll get the other units to seal off Long Acre.' The DS reached into his jacket pocket for his mobile phone. He was about to say something into the mouthpiece when Birch slapped him hard on the arm and pointed towards a figure moving briskly away from the market, looking furtively around him.

'I told you the bastard was still here,' he said triumphantly.

He set off running, his feet pounding across the cobbles. Johnson joined him. They were less than thirty yards from the man when he spotted them.

'Stop,' roared Birch, but the suspect was already running.

5

Along King Street they raced. Those walking towards them paused to allow them past. Some tried to sidestep, wondering why these men in suits were running so fast and so purposefully. Others glanced at the figure they were pursuing: the older man in the leather jacket who occasionally looked over his shoulder at those who followed him.

For Detective Inspector David Birch, the world had narrowed to just the twenty yards that separated him from his quarry. Faces of onlookers were indistinct as he passed them. All he was aware of was the thudding of his heart, the rasping of his breath and the growing ache in his muscles. But he pushed those feelings to the back of his mind and concentrated on the only thing that mattered to him. Catching up with the man he was chasing.

Ahead of him, his quarry dashed down Garrick Street then across St Martin's Lane, slamming into a man coming the other way. The man jumped to his feet and turned to grab at his assailant, but he hesitated when he saw the knife swing into view.

There were more screams as the blade cut through the air, missing the man by inches.

Those in the path of the runners dodged to escape the onrushing men, in particular the one wielding the knife. The blood on it was starting to congeal now.

Birch tried to force more speed from his pounding legs, and Johnson kept pace with him, shoving people aside if he had to in his eagerness to reach the quarry.

Off to his right he heard more sirens, but the sound drifted meaninglessly on the air with the shouts and screams of those on the pavements. Cars sounded their horns as the men ran into the road.

Birch sucked in another deep breath, telling himself that his prey was slowing down a little. He almost tripped as he rounded a pile of rubbish bags stacked on the pavement outside a cafe.

Getting tired, you bastard?

The older man looked back, almost stopped running for precious seconds.

Birch, encouraged by this show of weakness, found extra strength and ran on even faster.

There was now less than fifteen yards between himself and the suspect.

'Stop there,' he bellowed.

The man swayed uncertainly for a moment.

'Sanderson,' the DI roared.

Malcolm Sanderson wiped sweat from his face and spun round once more, determined to escape. Just ahead of him, he saw the means.

'He's going into the Tube,' Birch said, shooting out a hand and practically dragging Johnson along with him. Sanderson had already disappeared into the entrance.

Birch and Johnson rushed after him, buffeting their way past people climbing up from the subterranean depths of Leicester Square station.

The policemen took the stairs two at a time, hurtling down the steps with little regard for their own safety.

'There,' Birch snapped, seeing Sanderson struggling over the automatic barriers.

A uniformed London Transport official was shouting

angrily at Sanderson, trying to stop him from scrambling over.

'Get away from him,' Birch shouted as the older man landed on the far side and ran towards the escalators.

The uniformed man watched in bemusement as Birch also clambered over the barrier. 'What the hell are you doing?' he shouted, but the two policemen ran on.

Sanderson was already on his way down the moving stairway, knocking people out of his way where he had to, almost falling. Birch and Johnson followed, feet pounding on the metal slats. Those watching from the rising escalator looked on incredulously. Someone laughed. There was even a cheer.

Sanderson reached the bottom and tripped.

He rolled over, got to his feet with surprising agility and ducked into the archway that led through to the Northern Line.

Birch jumped the last three steps and landed heavily, also rolling over before scrambling to his feet to continue his pursuit.

Johnson was right behind him. But the DS misjudged the jump from the escalator and landed heavily on his left ankle. He cursed and felt red hot pain shoot through the joint and up his leg. However, he dragged himself back to his feet, trying to ignore the increasing pain, forcing himself on in spite of his injury.

They pounded down the short walkway and then the stairs that led to the platforms.

Birch recognised an all too familiar sound.

A train was pulling in.

'If he gets on that we've lost him,' he panted, skidding out on to one of the platforms.

He scanned the faces of the passengers waiting there.

No sign of Sanderson.

'Other platform,' Johnson gasped and spun round.

Southbound, a train was preparing to pull out. Johnson, wincing against the pain from his ankle, ran down the length of the six hundred ton transport, peering through windows, looking for their suspect and hoping to Christ that he didn't see him. If he did, that meant he was seconds from escaping.

He suddenly turned and hurtled back as fast as he could towards the driver's cab.

Stop him pulling out. Stop the fucking train.

From behind him there was a scream. Shrill. Terrified.

He stopped and headed back to the northbound side, where he saw Birch advancing slowly towards the far end of the platform.

Another scream echoed through the underground cavern, reverberating off the walls and curved ceiling.

The thunder of the approaching train was growing louder but Birch seemed oblivious of it. His attention was fixed on something else. For a moment, Johnson almost forgot the pain from his ankle.

'Oh, Christ,' he murmured.

6

The woman Sanderson held captive was in her early thirties.

Smartly dressed. Pretty. She'd been carrying a briefcase but had dropped it when he'd grabbed her. It lay at her feet, some papers spilling from it. Something to do with her work, Birch thought as he advanced on her and the man who held a knife to her throat. All kinds of thoughts tumbled through his head as he walked to within a few feet of the woman.

Where was she going? Where had she come from? Was she married? Did she have kids? It was as if any of those thoughts were preferable to the one that stuck most stubbornly in his mind. The one that told him she was going to be dead in a minute or two.

'Stay back,' Sanderson hissed, pressing the bloodied blade more urgently against the woman's neck. 'Or I'll cut her throat.'

'I don't doubt it,' Birch said evenly, looking past the terrified woman's face.

Johnson moved up alongside his companion, his breath still coming in gasps. By now it felt as if someone had stuck an air pump into his ankle and inflated it. The joint was throbbing fiercely.

'I'm going to get on that train,' Sanderson said, nodding in the direction of the carriage now rolling to a halt alongside him. 'And you're not going to stop me. If you try, I'll kill her.'

'Then kill her now,' Birch rasped. 'Because there's no fucking way you're getting off this platform except in cuffs. Got that?'

A look of uncertainty flickered momentarily across Sanderson's face, then he seemed to shake off the threat, pressing the knife more firmly against the soft flesh of his captive's throat

'Don't open the doors,' Birch roared towards the tunnel mouth, his eyes never leaving Sanderson. 'Driver. Can you hear me?'

'I'll kill her,' the older man insisted. 'Don't play games with me.' He tugged harder on the woman's hair, dragging her head sharply backwards to expose her neck even more.

'Driver,' Birch shouted again. 'Can you hear me? I'm a policeman. Use your radio. Check with your controller if you don't believe me. He'll tell you what's going on.'

There was a moment of interminable silence, punctuated only by the terrified woman's sobs.

'I can hear you,' a voice from just inside the tunnel called.

'Don't open the doors. Don't let anyone on or off. Take the train out of the station now,' Birch commanded. 'Do it.'

'Do you want her death on your conscience?' Sanderson said quietly. 'Because it'll be your fault when she dies.'

'I'll live with it,' Birch said flatly, his blazing gaze never leaving Sanderson's.

Johnson looked at his superior briefly, then turned to see uniformed officers spilling on to the platform at the far end.

'Keep them back,' Sanderson rasped, some of the bravado now missing from his tone. 'If one of them comes any nearer I'll kill this bitch.'

Johnson, leaning against the wall to take some pressure off his injured ankle, held up a hand to halt the advance of the uniformed men. 'Clear the platform,' he shouted. 'Get everyone out of here.'

'Driver,' Birch shouted. 'Take this train out of the station now. Move.'

There was a loud hydraulic hiss and the train began to pull slowly away. From inside the carriages, people stared out at the drama being enacted before them. At the far end of the platform, the uniformed men were hustling the last of the waiting passengers to the exit.

'You bastard,' snapped Sanderson.

Birch smiled almost imperceptibly. 'I can't see from here,' he said quietly. 'But I'm guessing that the policemen who've just arrived on this platform are from an ARU. That means they're carrying guns and it means they're very good shots.' He ignored the sweat that ran down his face in rivulets. His eyes never left Sanderson's. 'Now usually in a hostage situation if some mad bastard's got a gun to someone's head or a knife to somebody's throat, then the marksmen have to be careful that they've got a clear shot. Because if they shoot and the bullet hits the wrong area of the body they run the risk of some kind of muscular spasm when the bad guy dies. Then maybe his finger'll tighten on the trigger and blow the fucking hostage's brains out anyway. But down here, they haven't got that problem. They've got a clean shot at you. They'll put one through the base of your skull and sever your spinal cord, and it'll all happen so quick that knife will just drop to the ground.'

Sanderson swallowed hard.

'It's up to you. If I give them the signal they'll shoot now. Kill you and her. If you cut her throat they'll shoot you anyway. However you look at it, the only way you're going to walk off this platform is if you let her go.'

The woman was sobbing almost uncontrollably now.

'Let her go and you live,' the DI continued. 'Anything else, you're a dead man.'

Sanderson gripped the knife handle so tightly his knuckles turned white. He looked from Birch to Johnson then beyond to the uniformed men clogging the far end of the platform.

'Let her go and you live,' the DI repeated evenly.

Sanderson was breathing heavily. He tried to swallow but his mouth was chalk-dry.

'Just drop the knife,' Birch murmured.

The woman was crying softly, her body shaking.

'It's your decision,' said the DI, raising his hand.

'What are you doing?' Sanderson demanded.

'Giving them the signal,' the policeman told him. 'When I drop my hand, they start shooting.'

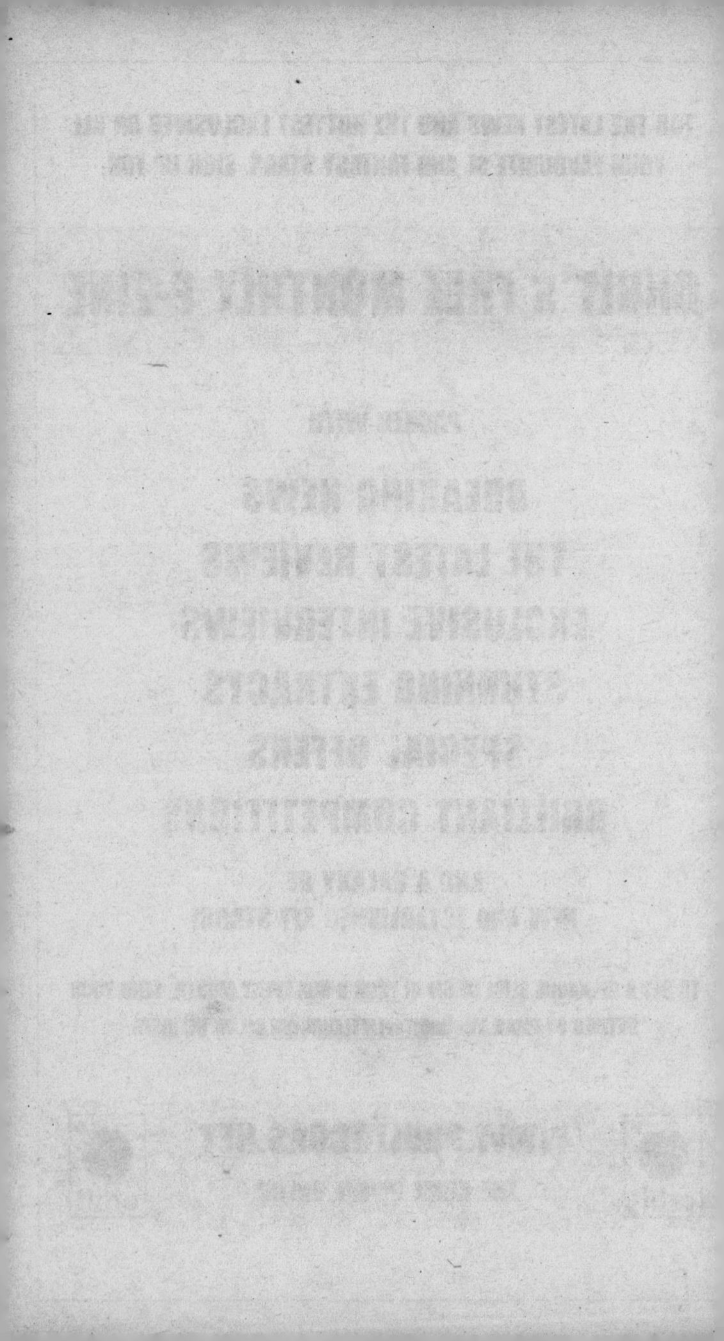